Love-Lines
Sheri Langer

Love-Lines

Red Adept Publishing, LLC

104 Bugenfield Court

Garner, NC 27529

http://RedAdeptPublishing.com/

Chapter One: Eat, Play, Love

"Okay, spill." Fordham Price was determined to get answers, and she wasn't about to relent without a struggle. She assumed a tone learned from watching episodes of *Law and Order* and cocked her head, sending her long dark-brown hair dangling down her back. "So?" She widened her eyes as she waited for Margo to supply her with a story that would make their lunch date less about business and more about fun.

"Fordham, darling, I have no idea what you're talking about." Margo Flax was probably ten years older than Fordham's forty-plus—nobody knew Margo's true age—and still a head turner. She was elegant and sophisticated—if a bit pretentious—and as stubborn as a poppy seed wedged between two teeth.

Their waitress, a toned, bronzed blonde, arrived with an enormous banana-split sundae she carried as if it were the Hope Diamond. She quickly set the dessert in front of Margo, looking nervous, as if fearful that she too might be on Margo's menu if she stuck around long enough.

Margo clapped her hands. "Wow! This looks amazing!"

"I think a dozen cows went into a coma just to make this happen," Fordham said.

Margo took a slow, calculated bite like a woman rehearsing a scene from *Fifty Shades of Grey*. "Mmm. It even smells exquisite. Oh, come on. Have a sniff." Margo tempted Fordham with a heaping spoonful as if coaxing an obstinate toddler.

"I can't." Fordham pushed the spoon away. "The last time I was near one of those was over a decade ago on a date at retro night at the drive-in with Marshall Jaro. John Travolta was in a white leisure suit, scaling the Verrazano Bridge, and every time Marshall went to kiss me, hot fudge would slide down my throat. Since then, whenever I hear the Bee Gees, I swear I gain ten pounds."

"You have an interesting history, Fordham, but you don't know what you're missing." Another bite of vanilla fudge ice cream disappeared between Margo's lips.

"Oh, yes, I do. An extra year on my treadmill. You are aware that you're Margo Flax and you're eating a banana split?"

In the three years they'd been friends and coworkers, Fordham had only seen Margo eat outside the food pyramid once. It was at an office party, and she was drunk. The hot mail guy had dangled a churro from his open fly.

"Of course I'm aware, darling. I'm celebrating."

"I assumed you were celebrating when you ate all the croutons in your salad. Not to mention the hamburger. What happened to, 'Water, no lemon' and 'Garnish is just a pretty word for calories'? Margo, this is just plain nuts."

"Mmm, no, not plain. Candied... candied walnuts, and they are beyond delicious." Margo licked her lips. "This is almost as good as sex."

"Considering that the last sex I had couldn't rival mung beans, I'll pass, thank you." Fordham squeezed a tired wedge of lime into her seltzer. "Margo, I'm worried about you. You seem happy, but your fondest sex tip is, 'Go with Cool Whip Lite, especially if you swallow—it's fewer carbs.' What exactly are you celebrating, anyway? Last night's orgasm?"

"Last night's... the one from the night before... the one after breakfast this morning. I'm celebrating love. It is so much better the fourth time around."

"Guess I'll have to take your word for it." Fordham's tone sounded more defeated than she had intended.

"The little girls' room is calling again." Margo stood and patted Fordham on the back. "Help yourself, if you dare." She smoothed her dress over what Fordham guesstimated was an additional five pounds on her tiny frame and strolled away with a confident swagger.

Celebrating love was a notion Fordham couldn't relate to. For one thing, her ex-husband had taught her everything about love she never needed or wanted to know. And judging by Margo's behavior, love involved having to shop in the plus-size department. When Elizabeth Taylor fell in love with John Warner, she gained the state of Virginia. And it ended anyway. It *always* ended.

Fordham checked the time. She'd asked Margo to lunch because she needed a favor, and so far, her request was the only ingredient not to make it into the sundae. Still, Fordham wanted to get out of there. Sure, she adored Margo, but the excessive cheeriness was daunting and getting on her nerves. Maybe Fordham could speed the process along with an urgent message that would allow her a polite, expedient exit. She checked her texts and emails. Nothing. She'd feel too guilty if she made something up. No, even though they met at work, she and Margo were friends first. She'd suck up her discomfort, and when the time was right, she'd ask for the favor.

Fordham grabbed a toasty breadstick calling her from the basket, studied it, and tossed it back in. She rarely went out for lunch, and when she did, Café Panache on Amsterdam and West Seventy-Ninth Street was not her kind of place. She preferred the diner around the corner from her office at Haskins Publishing in Chelsea. They served giant cups of coffee with long rock-candy stirrers and fat-free muffins that tasted as if her jeans would still fit when she was finished. The restaurant she sat in at the moment didn't have much of what she considered *panache*, despite its name. With its high-tech lighting and monochromatic furnishings, the place felt cold and impersonal, though commanding and pretentious, as if everybody was somebody and anybody who wasn't somebody could pretend they were and have others believe it. Fordham didn't think anyone noticed her in the mix.

In need of immediate gratification, she picked up the rejected breadstick and treated herself to a bite. *So this is what all the fuss is about.* She had to admit, she'd never tasted a carb that offered so much personality.

Only a few tables were filled, but given the late hour, that was understandable. Fordham was sorry she hadn't brought her tablet with her. She could have been watching the Nora Ephron marathon on Turner Classic Movies. She couldn't understand what was taking Margo so long. In a corner booth sat a woman in her seventies with big eyes, shiny red lips, and short grayish hair. She was with a distinguished-looking man of about the same age. He had the kind of hair that made balding thirty-year-old guys say, "Yeah, but I bet he has a small dick." The two were in their own world, talking and staring into each other's eyes. Each time the man would say something, the woman would giggle and touch his arm. The old guy motioned for the waiter, who promptly came over to their table with a bottle of champagne chilling in a silver bucket.

The waiter ceremoniously popped the cork, poured, and went to speak to another server. The old man gave a toast, and they both drank from their flutes. Afterward, he stood up, reached into his pocket, and effortlessly dropped onto one knee. Fordham couldn't see the diamond sparkling in what appeared to be a velvet box, but she could imagine it. Her heart beat a little faster when the woman squealed in delight while the man slid the ring onto her finger. The two began kissing as if they were in a high school cafeteria. The self-involved power lunchers didn't seem to notice the couple. Fordham turned away, a little embarrassed to witness such a personal moment.

Margo marched out of the ladies' room and, as if she could sniff the diamond, made a beeline for the newly engaged couple. Of course she did. Margo was in love and needed to share her excitement with people who could relate. They offered her a glass of champagne, but she refused and shot a nod in Fordham's direction. Hugs were exchanged as if they were all members of the same secret club.

Great. Just great. But Fordham refused to follow through with that thought. Jealousy was for losers. Still, Margo looked stunning, and it had nothing to do with the ocean-blue Donna Karan dress she'd bought at Neiman Marcus the week before—"Darling, they had the most wonderful little sale"—or her perfect auburn hair cut to the appropriate length to both gently convey and masterfully hide her age from every telling angle. Fordham had to surmise that love looked good on Margo. The woman's radiance even transcended her finishing powder.

She sat across from Fordham, smiling like a cat who had discovered an aviary in her backyard, then resumed taking enthusiastic bites of her dessert. Fordham returned to her garden salad tossed with a mound of sprouts and an adventurous handful of Chinese noodles.

"So, who's the lucky guy who is worth all the...?" Fordham used her finger to outline a circle around the ice cream.

"Oh, I'm the lucky one, but my mouth is zipped on this. At least for now."

"It's someone from the office!" Fordham shrieked. Maybe she'd finally gained some ground in solving the mystery.

"I didn't say that. I didn't say anything, and I'm not going to, either. No jinxing. So just drop the inquisition." She followed the order with a few more spoonfuls of hot fudge.

"Fine. I guess your secret will come out when you have to let your pants out. Did you know that menopausal women addicted to sugar invented the elasticized waistband?"

Margo speared a slice of banana, laid the fork down, and hugged Fordham's hand. "Fordham, you're too much."

"*I'm* too much? Ha." It took a moment, but Fordham realized that *she* was the rude one. Margo hadn't done anything except smile excessively. "I'm sorry. I'm being a bitch. It's just all the dating and all the starving because of all the dating."

"Sorry, sweetie. Just give it time. You and Gil have been split... what, a year?"

"Actually, over three, but I've stopped counting since my mother now does that for me."

Margo raised an eyebrow. "I have some idea what it's like to *be* a daughter, but what's it like to *have* a daughter?"

"Amazing. Whitty is a little bit of everything I always wanted to be. I think my mother sees that too." Fordham sighed. She still had trouble living up to her mother's expectations.

"I wish I had a mother like Dorie around. I would never have to worry about bad bras or the wrong eye shadow. You're so lucky."

"True. Every day with Dorie feels like a day on *What Not to Wear*."

"How is it going having Dorie living with you and Whitty?"

"It has its moments. Sometimes, I want to pull out every hair on my head. Other times, I want to pull out every hair on hers. But for the most part, she's been really great. She adores Whitty, and she helps keep the house safe from the clutches of *schmutz*, her pet name for anything that can't breathe but can be captured by a sponge."

Margo nodded. "But how is she doing? It must be so difficult for her to deal with all the changes."

"Other than an obsession with online Scrabble that keeps her up till all hours, I think she's managing. I know she misses my dad and her own space. I hear her crying sometimes. He was a great guy—one who couldn't say no to Atlantic City or Belmont or Fantasy Football... or to her. I guess he figured what she didn't know wouldn't hurt her."

Margo waved her spoon. "Famous last words. Sorry, but I've never known a liar who doesn't think of himself as some kind of hero."

"Lying was only a symptom. He was sick. We just didn't know it. But we certainly found out the hard way." Fordham poked at her arugula. "And with it all, we were close. At least, I thought we were. I still miss him, and it's been almost a year. Every time Sinatra comes on the radio, I know my dad is visiting me."

Margo sat back. "I'm so sorry, Fordham." She dabbed her lips with a napkin, missing a thin line of hot fudge. "So no men, no sex, no sweets, and no money. Even Mother Teresa traveled. How are you managing?"

"I'm fine. Really. Gil went to Istanbul to start some outsourcing service, and even though Whitty misses him, I sing 'Happy Happy Joy Joy' every day. She seems to be holding her own without him, anyway. And I'm paying my bills by doing something I love. It's funny. A few years ago, I didn't know what a public relations manager was, but Abe saw something in me and hired me anyway. Sometimes, I'm still not sure what I'm doing, but he's been great about giving me autonomy and letting me make the position my own. The man is a gem."

"Yes, he can be wonderful. Of course, I want to slam him for giving me this latest Flowers from the Heart book, *Love Online*. I know. It sounds sweeter than this"—Margo pointed to her almost-finished ice cream—"but it isn't."

"Why?" Fordham was genuinely puzzled. The Flowers from the Heart series was a Haskins original and the first endeavor to give the tiny publishing company any kind of attention among its mighty brethren. The concept was simple but brilliant: books that were like reality shows that people could read. The editor targeted a specific audience that shared a common interest or experience and solicited relevant personal stories, which she then organized into a collection and compiled into a book. Hell, even a ten-year-old like Whitty could probably edit one.

"It's a different concept from our usual format. It's far more extensive, and I'm so inundated with material I can't get a solid handle on how to fit it all together." Margo was so distraught she dropped her spoon. "I was told it was going to be like *Flowers from the Heart: The Bridesmaid Who Is Never the Bride*. I loved working on that. This sounded like it was going to be just as much fun, but it's become a huge headache. I have to comb through emails from people who either have no insight, no couth, no conscience, or no shrink. I had to scrap everything, and now I'm back to square one. I'm sorry I agreed to do it."

"Could you have refused?"

"I don't see how. Sunny Wallerstein might have done it, but now she's doing *The Birdwatcher* so I get *Love Online*. At least I have until next summer to get it done. It's going to take me almost that long just to choose submissions and edit."

Fordham's job involved being behind the scenes: talking to authors and agents, setting up photo shoots, and arranging promotions and tours. Although she'd recently amped up her time at the office, she realized it had been a mistake.

Margo went back to the sundae, scooping up the nuts with the help of a breadstick.

"Margo, I hate to ask, but..." Fordham paused as she watched the engaged couple leave the restaurant amid cheers from the staff.

"Fordham, what is it?"

"It's Whitty," Fordham said. "I think I've been working too much, and I'm afraid I haven't been giving her enough quality time."

"Ooh! Has she been complaining?"

"No, not at all, but that's not typically her style. So I was wondering, do you think you could handle some of the PR for this project?" Fordham motioned to the server to bring the check and continued.

"I mean, you have so many connections, and you're so good at knowing and getting whatever you want.

"That's true." Margo sucked on a maraschino cherry.

"And if possible, I'd like to keep this just between us."

"Like sisters?"

Since neither of them had siblings, *sisters* was fine if Margo needed to hear it to comply with Fordham's request.

"Sure," Fordham agreed. "Like sisters."

"Okay," Margo said, taking the final bite of banana.

"Thank you, Margo. You have actually made my weekend."

"Glad I could help." Margo jumped up suddenly. "Sorry, I have to run. I have an appointment downtown!"

"Oh, okay." Fordham reached into her bag and pulled out a credit card.

"No," Margo insisted. "This one's on me."

It wasn't worth arguing. Even though Fordham was doing okay with Gil's support checks augmenting her salary, Margo was from old money. As stipulated in her trust-fund agreement, the checks would keep coming as long as she had gainful employment. Regardless, Fordham would insist on paying next time.

"It's all going to work out," Margo said. "Just let yourself be happy."

Pretty Zen. Maybe Margo had been in touch with the guru she slept with when she was working on *Yoga Enthusiasts.* They'd broken up on the way to a tantric-sex workshop in Cairo, New York. *What a shame.* He had late '70s Dustin Hoffman hair and could make Margo laugh at herself.

Fordham's phone buzzed for an incoming call, and before she could answer it, Margo gave her a peck on each cheek and hurried toward the door. The guy calling was from tech support, letting her know they were still trying to retrieve her lost folders. As Fordham was talking to the whiny rep, she noticed a card fall from Margo's purse onto the restaurant floor.

After a few heated exchanges, she ended the call and went to retrieve the card. Margo was already gone. The colorful business card read, "Henna Hora Artistry. Mehndi design—appointment time 7:00 p.m."

Fordham couldn't imagine why Margo would be interested in getting any kind of tattoo, especially one as intricate as a mehndi design. She didn't even have the patience to sit through a Disney movie. There had to be some explanation. Chances were good that Margo was trying to curry favor with someone.

Chapter Two: Runaway Pride

Fordham scanned the library, relieved she wasn't seeing any familiar faces. She hadn't had a chance to shower before leaving the house, and her hair could have had her mistaken for the eponymous star of *Lassie Come Home*. It wasn't her fault. Her mother had gotten a frantic call from her cousin in Staten Island, who had no clue how to host a dinner party for her son's new Jamaican in-laws. Terrified of being the only jerk on the menu, she begged Dorie, a lauded culinary expert compared to anyone else in the family, to help her cook and entertain. Always the consummate savior, Dorie packed a bag and headed out at the crack of dawn, which was precisely when Whitty had pounced on Fordham with the news that she had to go to the local library's art exhibit for a homework assignment.

"Mom!" Whitty shouted. "Come here."

Fordham quickly ended her post. She could tweet about her new remedy for cat hair balls later. She walked past a few forgettable ink sketches toward Whitty, who was looking more mature every day. Fordham only wished her lovely ten-year-old daughter, with her long wavy hair and angelic face, didn't have to deal with the congenital hip malformation that kept her from being like the other girls.

Whitty jabbed her finger at a large painting in a wood frame. "Look at this!"

"What am I looking at?" Fordham asked, peering at the image of a vase filled with flowers.

Whitty sneered. "The flowers. Duh."

"Okay, they're flowers. What's the big deal?"

"They look like vaginas," Whitty said matter-of-factly.

Though happy that her daughter was outspoken and opinionated, Fordham was grateful no one else was in earshot. "No, they don't!"

"Yes, they do." Whitty was tracing the proof of her theory with her pointer finger inches away from the painting.

"Okay, okay, I get it," Fordham said, pushing her daughter's hand down. "But for the record, they're called calla lilies.

"Well, they look like purple vaginas to me. A whole bunch of them."

The calla lilies did look like vaginas, and the artist was clearly making that statement by entitling the work *Her Spring Climax*. Whitty's ability to process such sophisticated symbolism had to mean she was growing up, which meant that Fordham was getting closer to assisted living and dinner at five. "Art and life go hand in hand, so it's entirely possible for you to see that."

"You don't?" Whitty asked.

"Does it matter?"

Whitty shrugged. "Kind of."

"It shouldn't. Art is personal. Everybody sees things their own way. That's what makes it interesting."

"You think I'm weird."

"I think you're ten going on forty." Fordham patted Whitty's head. "Speaking of age, I think Aunt Margo is going through another midlife crisis."

"She already has a Ferrari. Did she finally pierce her belly button?"

"No, but you're close."

"Oh, yuck, did she pierce her—"

"No, and I won't ask how you even know about that."

"YouTube," Whitty said.

Fordham rolled her eyes and gave Whitty the business card Margo had dropped. "Did she say anything to you about this when she watched you last week?"

"Um, no. I just did her toenails while we watched *My 600-lb Life*."

"That sounds about right."

"What's a mehndi, anyway?" Whitty asked, handing the card back to Fordham.

"A henna tattoo. They're popular in Indian culture."

"She doesn't look Indian."

"Quite true. Maybe it's research for a new book." Fordham put the card back in her bag. "Anyway, are you hungry?"

"I'm a kid. I'm always hungry."

"Good, because I could really use some coffee and a carb."

Whitty sighed deeply.

"What's wrong?" Fordham asked.

"Nothing."

"You're a bad liar." Fordham cupped her daughter's chin in her hand and lifted her face. "I'm your mom. You can tell me anything." She silently hoped Whitty hadn't gotten her period yet.

"Okay, but you're not going to like it."

"I don't like okra, but every once in a while, I manage to eat it. Try me." Fordham's phone played the theme from the movie *9 to 5*, the ringtone for Abe. "Sorry, honey, it's work. Give me a minute."

Whitty scowled and went to dissect another painting. Fordham summoned her casual weekend voice to answer the phone, but all she got was static. After struggling to extract a few snippets from the conversation, she ended the call and tried calling Abe back. The call went straight to voicemail, then her phone ran out of juice. Abe didn't typically call on weekends unless he was stuck on a crossword puzzle or needed a movie recommendation. But he seemed preoccupied lately, and she sensed that this time, something was up. She'd try him again later.

She spotted Whitty analyzing a Cray-Pas reproduction of a Warhol classic.

"I don't get it. Who cares that much about soup?" Whitty asked.

"It was a pretty big deal back in its day."

"If you say so, but I'd rather draw a stack of crackers." Whitty reached into Fordham's bag and pulled out a stick of gum. "What did work want?"

"I'm not really sure. We had a bad connection, and all I got out of it was that he needed me to come in early on Monday."

"Like that's new."

"Hey, you know, I've been trying to be around more often, but work has gotten busier." Fordham put her arm around Whitty's shoulders. "Just so you know, I spoke with Margo, and she said she's going to help with that."

"Fine. Whatever."

"Do you have what you need so we can get out of here?" Fordham asked.

Whitty nodded.

"Good. Let's go to Cindy's and get some waffles."

THE HOSTESS, A SIX-foot-tall platinum blonde with red hoop earrings, led Fordham and Whitty to a booth near the front window of the small diner. Large pitchers of different syrups on each table suggested that the pancakes were a safe bet. The place wasn't as crowded as usual, and Fordham figured they might have time to go to a matinee if they could agree on what to see.

After they gave their drink order to the server, Fordham picked up a menu. "So, we got caught up in a bunch of other stuff, and you never told me what you were going to tell me."

"I was hoping you forgot."

The server, a young brunette, dropped off Fordham's coffee and a mug of hot chocolate for Whitty then hurried to the next table without a word.

Starting to feel uneasy, Fordham grabbed a couple of packets of real sugar and a container of half-and-half. She eyed her daughter as she stirred. "Just tell me."

Whitty slurped her hot chocolate. "I kind of found out something that I'm not sure I'm supposed to know." She dipped her spoon into the whipped cream and licked it clean.

"Are we going to play twenty questions, or are you going to tell me?"

"Twenty questions sounds like fun."

"Whitty!"

"Ari's mom is seeing Dad," Whitty blurted through clenched teeth.

Fordham spewed coffee onto the table. Once her coughing fit was over, she snatched some napkins from the dispenser and sopped up the mess. "Kara Gittelman? We were on the same PTA committee for community cleanup. And your father and I used to bowl with them on a couples' league." She began making little balls from pieces of shredded napkin. "I think they got divorced right before we did."

Fordham wasn't really surprised. Kara had always been a flirt. All those lingering high fives when Gil or Kara threw a strike suddenly made sense.

"You guys were friends?" Whitty asked.

"Not friends. We just knew each other and did some of the same things."

"I guess that's better."

Fordham had to agree. No matter how done she was with Gil, the image of him being intimate with a close friend was still too uncomfortable to consider.

"But how did you find out about it?" Fordham asked.

"Ari got in trouble for spitting on Kendra's new Nikes, so his mom had to come in. I was in the supply closet, putting stuff away. I heard Ari's mom tell my art teacher she was seeing Dad. So I stayed in the closet until they left."

"Excellent PI skills. What kind of *seeing*?"

"Um… I didn't ask. Did you want me to?"

"No. Of course not. I mean, because he's away. Far away. On business."

"Kara said they went out a few times before he left. She said she was going to visit him there because he was *that* good." Whitty stuck her face right up to her whipped cream and ate it without using a spoon. "Whatever that means. I don't think he's so good."

Fordham winced. As if she knew she was on a rescue mission, the server came to take their order. Whitty wanted the most decadent waffle dish on the menu. Fordham was no longer hungry.

"I'm not even sure Ari knows," Whitty continued after the server left. "But he's in my class, and I didn't want to say anything."

"I wouldn't be too worried. Knowing your father, it could be over and done already."

Gil Presser couldn't make a solid commitment to a menu item in a restaurant. Fordham couldn't imagine that a needy single mom could be part of his order for long.

"I don't know," Whitty said. "Maybe. But I'm not asking anyone."

"How do you feel about this?" Fordham took a sip of coffee. "I'm guessing it's pretty awkward."

"Yeah. And Ari is really gross. He wipes his nose on his sleeves, and sometimes he forgets to zip up after he goes to the bathroom."

"That is gross. Are you sure he isn't your father's son?"

"Not funny, Mom."

"I know," Fordham said. "I'm sorry. But seriously, how do you feel about this?"

"I feel like I hope Ari doesn't end up being my brother."

Fordham found her compact mirror and smoothed out a few unruly eyebrow hairs. Then she applied a quick swipe of Forget Me Not lip gloss.

Chapter Three: From Here to Maternity

Monday morning, Fordham stared at her cluttered desk. Her office was her domain, and she'd tried her best to create an inspiring atmosphere. She painted the walls a soothing sage green, bought a pair of oak bookcases that she filled with everything from vintage dictionaries to her favorite Golden Books, and hung an antique mirror that Grandma Sadie had given her when she moved into her first dorm room. Framed pictures of family and friends stood on top of her bookcases, reminding her to smile during the rough spots and be thankful that shoulder pads were no longer a fashion necessity.

But she still couldn't shake Whitty's news about Kara Gittelman and Gil. It was too close to home. People would talk, and that couldn't be anything but humiliating. She didn't like messes. For the first time in a long time, she wanted to be anywhere other than where she was.

Despite that, she was grateful for her job. She'd searched for months and had come up with nothing in her area. The job market was slow, and no one in the suburbs was keen on hiring a single mother who'd been out of the work force longer than she'd been in it. Even though she was getting some support from Gil, it wasn't enough, and it seemed unfair to make Whitty wait for her wallet to catch up with what all the other kids had.

Abe was a godsend who'd been willing to take a chance on her. At first, Fordham had been hesitant to respond to the ad on LinkedIn. She was unsure of what the job of "project manager of growing boutique publishing company" entailed, and she wondered how her antiquated skills would make her a reasonable applicant. But ultimately, the offer of autonomy and flexibility was too attractive to pass up. She flirted with the fear of rejection then answered the ad. She was called to interview the next day.

Abe was a somewhat tall, attractive man with warm, smiley eyes. Though pushing seventy—as he proudly let her know the moment she sat down—neither his face nor his body had gotten the memo. After a lot of the usual questions, he caught her off guard when he said, "I'd like to offer you the position."

"I'm a single mother," she blurted.

"Yes, I know." Abe picked up her resume. "According to this, you're also 'a people person' and 'highly organized.' You graduated magna cum laude from SUNY Binghamton with a double major in English and theater. But my favorite is 'I can have a big mouth when asked to use it, but I can use discretion otherwise.'" He laughed. "That works for me."

She adjusted the bracelet Whitty had given her for Mother's Day. "My daughter is still young, and I would prefer to work from home whenever possible."

"That shouldn't be a problem."

"Also, I'm not into public transportation. I want to drive into the city when I have to be here."

"I think you're crazy, but as long as you make your meetings on time, I don't care if you swim here."

Abe bit into a Danish, leaving some of the jam hovering over his top lip. It was a classic move of her father's. She couldn't help but think it made Abe look paternal.

"I enjoy driving," she said, wriggling in her seat. She wasn't going to tell her almost new boss that she considered herself a sane person with reasonable control issues. He didn't need to know that she was willing to pay for gas, tolls, and even parking just to have her car handy.

"Fair enough," Abe offered.

"You're very understanding."

"I know," he said. "So why are you trying to get me *not* to hire you?"

Fordham went into her bag for a few clean napkins she'd stashed away from her breakfast with Whitty. "Of course, I want you to hire me. I just..."

"Need a break? I know what that's like. Now you've got one. Take it easy. I'm a good judge of character. You're going to do great."

Fordham handed Abe a napkin and showed him where to wipe his mouth.

"Thank you," Abe said, blushing.

"Thank you, Mr. Goldmann. Thank you so much!"

"Oh, by the way, I take the PATH, but I have a prepaid parking spot at a garage down the block. It's convenient, and it's yours."

"So you're my Santa Claus?"

"No, I'm your boss. And it's Abe to you. Now get out of here and get yourself a good pair of sneakers. When you're in the city, you're going to need them."

He was right. She'd done more walking and driving in the three years since she'd taken the job than she had in her whole life before that. And Abe had become a good friend. He understood her quirks, forgave her idiosyncrasies, and still teased her about having a neurotic relationship with her car. She argued that she simply liked the freedom of coming and going as she pleased. She wasn't willing to be stuck at the mercy of a bus driver with a sinus headache or stranded because of a water-main break in the subway station. The clincher had come a few months before her interview, when Whitty got strep throat and a high fever on a day Fordham had taken the train into the city for a date. There was an accident on Fordham's line, and her bus wasn't running. Her mother took Whitty to the doctor and sat with her afterward. Fordham vowed she would never be in that situation again.

A low, steady buzz that sounded like a swarm of bees in heat broke into her thoughts, but she couldn't figure out what it was or where it was coming from. She went to the closet, and when her coat didn't yield results, she followed the sound to her pocketbook, which was hanging behind her coat. She dug deep into her bag and pulled out the offender: a tube of lipstick. At least, it appeared to be a tube of lipstick. But lipstick didn't buzz, and on closer inspection, she remembered it was the vibrator she'd gotten as a party favor at Margo's last birthday bash. She breathed a sigh of relief, appreciative that Whitty wasn't into makeup yet and that her mother, a solid autumn, would have never entertained the color. Why she'd kept a vibrator nestled in her cosmetic case was as baffling as how the thing had turned on by itself. If the ghost of her grandmother wasn't fiddling with the on-off switch to express her disapproval of Fordham's singledom, maybe the battery had been triggered by Fordham slamming the door and jarring the bag. Either way, it wasn't worth pondering on an empty stomach. She'd come in early, as Abe had asked, but despite having called several times, she hadn't been able to reach him. Maybe he'd overslept. That happened from time to time.

She smacked her lips. She could use some water. And maybe there was something to nibble on in the lounge. As she strode down the corridor, past the private offices around the perimeter and the large cluster of cubicles in the center, she noticed how bland her surroundings were. Like most offices, the décor of Haskins was heavy on metal, light on wood, and scant on color. Maybe neutrality was a way to make the company seem more colorful.

A quick peek out the window informed her that Cortazzo's was having a special on salads. *Lunch*, she decided as she waved to a few assistants chatting about a web series that followed people going hand fishing. Fordham's morning coffee had tasted like the bottom of a marsh, and anyone who tried could likely yank a putrid bass from the back of her tongue.

She got a bottle of water from the lounge, grabbed a packet of smoked almonds, and headed back to her office. Fordham tried to get back to work, but her mind kept shifting back to wanting the comfort of her bed, Netflix, and a takeout menu. She idly worked on a message for Zoe, the intern she'd insisted Abe hire.

Someone called out in the whiny tone of a wounded hound, "Fordham? Fordham?"

Focusing on the message she was writing, she did her best to ignore the cries. *Bingo says thank you for the adjustment and hopes he'll see you at Vincent's.* Gay, sassy, and a far cry from the John Smith he'd been named at birth, Bingo Smack was one of their best-selling authors.

She was trying to process the note when Abe burst into her office as if delivering the last call to get on the ark before the flood. "Fordham, didn't you hear me calling you?"

"Of course I heard you. North Korea heard you. What's going on?"

"What's going on? You wouldn't believe what's going on." He pushed over a pile of papers and parked himself on the corner of her desk. Anybody but Abe would have been given the evil eye for that, but he was more like a father than a boss, and that came with a lot of latitude.

"Try me. It's Monday. I'm approachable."

"We need to talk." Suddenly, Abe wasn't sounding very paternal.

"Why? Everything is great. I know you were a little upset about the Zoe thing, but I promised to straighten everything out with Bingo, and I did. I told him she's inexperienced but certainly enthusiastic. He knew she didn't mean to grab his balls during the photo shoot, and according to a note I just read, I think he kind of liked it anyway. Truthfully, in those pants, he really was hanging way too far to the left. She was trying to get him at his best angle. And that nose is probably about as long as his—"

"Breathe, Fordham. This isn't about Bingo Smack or Zoe. And for the record, I know you're doing a great job. This is about Margo Flax. She's pregnant."

Fordham chuckled. "Very funny. Really, what's going on?"

"I'm telling you the truth."

"Abe, what did you drink for breakfast? There is no way Margo is pregnant. I just had lunch with her Friday. We were chatting away. She said nothing. And she was eating—oh my God, was she eating! But it's impossible. The woman is at least fifty. I was at her last birthday party. They were handing out estrogen with the favors. Granted, she looks great for her age, but Botox can't perk up a uterus."

"She left." Abe turned to the top of the file cabinet and picked up a framed photo of the three of them at an office picnic.

"As in, she no longer needs to move her car for alternate-side-of-the-street parking? As in, 'Abe, here's my bathroom key?' Left, as in *moved*?"

"Oh yeah. She left the country!" Abe ran his hand over the picture and set it back as if it were a Fabergé egg.

"Just like that?" Fordham stood at the window, and even though the windows on their floor didn't open, she began breathing in deeply and slowly. She stared down at the cars going by as if they were the minutes of her life. She wasn't sure which upset her more—the fact that Margo was gone or the fact that Margo hadn't trusted her enough to tell her about the move.

"Why didn't she just get a Yorkie like normal childless Upper West Siders?" Fordham asked.

"Margo is one of a kind. I knew that the day I met her."

"Sorry. Responsible people don't just wake up one morning and say, 'Oh, it's nice and sunny today. I think I'll get pregnant by my flavor du jour, quit my job, and leave the country.'"

"You're right. No one except Margo." Abe let out a deep sigh.

His secretary, Myra—a short, stocky woman in her early sixties—bolted into Fordham's office. "Abe, Allen Clifford is on line one, and he insists on talking to you personally. What do you want me to tell him?" Her tone was as no-nonsense as her hairstyle.

"Oh, I'll take it." Abe got up. "Big possibilities there!" He met Fordham's eyes. "Stick around. We're not done yet."

Before following him, Myra flashed a sympathetic smile that gave Fordham every reason to worry about what else Abe had to say. She was doing a good job. Abe had acknowledged that. Margo was gone, but the woman was emotionally needy and flighty. *Thoughtless and egocentric. Self-serving and impulsive.* The real shock was that she hadn't planned her own surprise going-away party. Fordham winced. Maybe there had been a party, and Margo had chosen not to invite her.

She went to her file cabinet, picked up the photo, and was about to throw it against the wall when she decided to weigh her options. She could call Margo. Confront her. Tell her how hurt she was. Make her feel good and guilty. But that would be showing her hand, and she wasn't in the mood to be that vulnerable. It was easier to be angry.

There was the possibility that Abe had misunderstood the situation. Maybe Margo was just taking a little break, like the time she told everyone she was going to Vegas to marry her personal trainer but really went to Mexico to get a tummy tuck and have her breasts lifted. When Margo returned, she claimed that she and her new husband had agreed to a quickie divorce, but her cleavage told a different story. When Fordham confronted her, Margo admitted that it had been a sham but swore her to secrecy. Fordham found it amusing to have something so benign to use as collateral should she ever need it.

If Margo's office was still home to her eyelash curler and her Clinique 50 SPF sunscreen, the whole situation might be chalked up to a face-lift. Somehow, Fordham doubted that would be the case.

But the most infuriating part of all of this was that Margo had agreed to help her. At lunch, she seemed to understand that Fordham needed to spend more time with Whitty. The fact that she could so easily say one thing and do another was unforgivable.

Feeling a little adrenaline rush, Fordham got up and snuck quietly into Margo's office like one of Charlie's less experienced angels. Other than the aubergine-colored walls, a box of Kleenex, and the faint smell of Poison—Margo's signature scent—everything was gone, and nothing suggested that she had any intention of returning. Fordham felt a few tears well up in her eyes, but she wiped them away before they got out of hand. She was tossing away the tissue when Abe surprised her.

"So this is why I couldn't find you. What—did you think I was lying?" Abe tried to sound insulted.

"No, I just wanted to see... I wanted to see if she left anything I could use."

"Here." He picked up a jar of Oil of Olay from the top of a bookcase and tossed it to her.

Fordham caught the bottle and set it on the desk. "Wow, she must have been in a real hurry."

Abe pulled out a folded envelope from his pocket and handed it to Fordham. "I found this taped to her computer screen. You read it to me. My eyes are tired."

Fordham snatched the paper out of Abe's hand, ripped open the envelope, and whipped out the sheet of paper.

Hello, Gorgeous.

I'm assuming Abe or Fordham is reading this. If it's Myra, a few highlights framing your face will immediately brighten your complexion and add interest to your eyes.

Fordham, it turns out you were right. My secret is out, right along with my waistline. I'm pregnant! Please don't hate me for not sharing sooner. I've waited for this moment all my life, and I wanted to make sure everything was in place before I told anyone. I haven't been this ex-cited since I hired my first personal shopper. I'll fill you in on the details when I have the time.

My plane leaves in an hour, and I've only packed four bags. Can you imagine? And Fordham, I know you're upset with me, but stop wrin-kling your forehead, or you'll end up with premature lines. They say everything happens for a reason. I know you'll understand someday."

Fordham ripped up the note and threw the pieces into the waste-basket. "No, I will never understand, and I will never forgive her! And for the record, Margo Flax doesn't fall in love. She falls in bed. End of story."

"Okay, champ." Abe picked up the face cream. "Maybe, but this time, it sounds king-sized. She called as she was boarding the plane." He spun the top off the jar. "Does this stuff work?" he asked, ap-plying some under his eyes. "Anyway, she met the guy on a dating app. He's some Hindu descendant of royalty, and she says she's crazy about him."

Fordham felt like a bottle of cheap champagne—bitter and wait-ing to explode. She didn't know why she was so angry or why she couldn't just let it go. And Abe was taking the news way too well. At the very least, he could have confronted Margo and given her hell for abandoning everyone.

Abe waved his hand. "So here's what I'm thinking. You and Mar-go are friends—"

"*Were* friends," Fordham corrected.

"Okay, you and Margo *were* friends, and you'll be friends again when you get over this ridiculous, uncharacteristic bout of schoolgirl jealousy. And you two are about the same age—"

"I told you. She's fifty—at the very, very least!"

"Okay, you're a kid. The point is, I don't have anyone I trust enough to step into Margo's project. We're on a tight schedule, and I can't afford to have some wet-behind-the-ears freelancer waltz in and botch this up. I need you to do it."

"Me? So *I* can botch it? I'm a public relations manager, not an editor. Abe, I'm sorry, but there's no way. I'll go over her instructions if you want me to and give you my opinion, but—"

"There are no instructions. And there is no 'but' or 'I'm sorry.' This is your project now."

"That's not fair. Margo told me this project is a nightmare. Why should I be punished because she decided to go play instead of work?" She knew she was behaving like a kid ragging on her big sister. It was an act of desperation, but there seemed to be no alternative. A small part of her believed that if she stuck to her guns, Abe would cave and give the assignment to someone else. "Honestly, did she leave any kind of directions?"

"No directions, just some sketchy notes and a bunch of assorted papers. I can't tell what's what."

"So where does that leave me?"

"With a book to edit." Abe hit his hands against the desk.

"Out of what? I've never done this! I have no idea what you need, and if there are no notes, what am I supposed to work from? Do you have Miss Marple hiding out somewhere? Maybe she has a clue."

"You're a professional. You'll figure it out. Besides, I think you're so upset with Margo you'll try to outdo her."

"Margo isn't outdoable. She's just *out of here*, and I'm done talking about her."

Chapter Four: Lovers and Other Dangers

Fordham stared at her computer, wondering what she was going to do. The book was due in May, only a short eight months away. Her pregnancy had seemed far less daunting. A recorded voice was blabbing on about Margo's cell number no longer being in service, and of course, she hadn't left another number where she could be reached. She'd told Abe they'd be traveling on official royal business and it would be impossible to keep in touch, at least for a while.

Sifting through the papers Abe had given her, Fordham could tell there was nothing of value. *The nerve—the gall—to dump this in my lap.* She closed her eyes and tried to meditate... a warm tropical beach, a frozen daiquiri, the salty, pungent air... and then the shark showed up. She was standing, waiting for the waves to embrace her feet, when the great white jumped up to swallow her as if she were an amuse-bouche at a cocktail party. She opened her eyes. Clearing her mind was not possible.

She went down the hall and grabbed a cup of stale coffee. Everyone had already left the office except for a couple of janitors who couldn't finish while she was still there. She offered an apologetic nod, but none of this was her fault. Fortunately, her mother had taken Whitty for tacos and school-supply shopping. They'd be out for a while.

She went back to her office, played with the stress ball Evie had gotten her when she started the job, and sat back down at her desk. There had to be something constructive she could do before she left for the night. Evie, her best friend since elementary school, had said something about personal ads on Craigslist. Maybe she could ask for submissions that way without having to deal with the hassle of dating sites and the inevitable red tape that would come with them. Businesses were all about making money, but all she was after were stories. It was worth a shot. She went to the site and jotted down a quick post.

Haskins Publishing needs you for the next book in our Flowers from the Heart series, Love Online. *We're anxious to hear stories about your online dating experiences. Whether you found love, had fun, met your forever partner, or just learned something worth sharing, we're interested. Don't worry about length—we'll do the editing. All submissions should be sent to Haskinspublishing.org and will remain anonymous.*

IT WAS POURING WHEN Fordham finally left the office well past dusk. She hadn't remembered to bring an umbrella, and of course, this was the one day her usual parking lot was closed for repairs. She grabbed a garbage liner from the supply cabinet and caught the elevator. When she got to the lobby, she slapped the bag over her head and braved the storm to her car, which was parked on the street several blocks away. Never mind Manhattan's legendary traffic—she couldn't wait to drive home.

She had no problem working in the city but was happy to leave it at the end of the day. There were too many people, and everyone looked intense and constipated. They'd think nothing of bumping into someone to get wherever they were going, which was always more important than where anyone else needed to be. The air always felt as if it was straining to be present and smelled like something that had nothing to do with nature. It was impossible not to feel lonely. No matter what people said about minivans, diner food, and soccer moms, Fordham loved the suburbs and couldn't care less that she had to, as Margo put it, "drive across the map to find decent tiramisu." Margo could take her tiramisu and shove it right up her—

A chain of police cars went whizzing by, sirens screaming. She had to jump back onto the curb to avoid being run over—never mind that she had the light. Despite the plastic bag, she felt as if she'd been dropped in a dunk tank. All she could think about was getting home, changing into sweats, and crawling into bed in her nice cozy house.

When she got to the car, she kicked off her wet open-toed shoes, tossed the plastic bag into the back, and sank into the seat. She would have to start listening to the weather report before she left the house in the morning or run the risk of looking like something the cat dragged in by evening. She went to turn the ignition, but there were no keys. *Where did they go?* She'd just had them in her hand. Fordham searched the front, but all she came up with was a near-empty container of Tic Tacs in a flavor she hadn't bought in years. To avoid getting out of the car, she climbed over the console and combed the area. After retrieving a brush, a matchbook from a date at La Cucina that she preferred to forget, an old bank statement, and three used tissues, she finally found her keys hiding impudently under the mat in the back seat. *Weird.* Keys couldn't live independent lives, yet they showed up in unexpected places.

She couldn't imagine anything else going wrong until she turned the ignition. Nothing happened. She tried again with the same result. She could not control a few tears of pure frustration. There was no explanation for days like this other than that they taught her to relish the ones that only involved deadlines, traffic, the frizzies, and water retention. She popped the hood, threw on her wet shoes, grabbed a flashlight, and hoped for the best.

This was the first time in nearly three years that she'd been near anything that made a car function. The last time she'd looked at an engine had been at Evie's suggestion. Although Fordham hadn't been remotely interested in mechanics, Evie—the only friend who understood what she'd been through with Gil—insisted she find ways to broaden her scope.

"Divorce is a time for new discoveries about yourself and the world around you," Evie had said, reading from a self-help book Fordham bought after the divorce. "Buy a new shade of lipstick, try growing your own tomatoes, take a memoir-writing class, but above all else, don't allow yourself to get stuck in a rut, binge-watching every series with a fan page on Facebook and eating takeout when your ex has the kids."

Evie—and the book—had her pegged. "You're not emotionally prepared to meet your future husband," Evie insisted and read again from the self-help book: "Find a transitional activity to establish a new identity as a single person."

A single person. Fordham remembered saying it out loud and feeling stabbed. She was on her own. She didn't have a husband to worry about her transmission or braking system. She had to personally fear what would happen if she overheated or leaked some vital fluid. The next day, Fordham had gone online and bought a book and a tutorial to learn all she could about auto basics.

Meanwhile, the car still wouldn't turn over. Fordham went back under the hood and poked at a red wire. Her head felt heavy, and figuring it was due to all the water, she wrung out her hair.

"Hey," said a familiar voice. "Need some help?"

She looked up, not quite sure who he was. The man was medium height, with brown curls that stuck out from under a Mets cap. He certainly had a where-have-we-flirted-before manner about him. Her mood lightened when she finally placed him as Frankie Tancredi, the adorable manager of the Getty station near her old house.

Once she recognized him, she remembered how into her he'd been. He'd say, "I hope your husband knows how lucky he is to wake up next to a beauty like you every morning. Check your oil?" Then she'd blush, and he would clean her windshield till it sparkled.

"Hey! Yeah. Hell of a night to be out." Fordham said, wiping the corners of her eyes in case she was pooling mascara. "I can't get the car to start."

"No worries, beautiful. I just left my sister's. I was watching my nephew." He cleared his throat. "Hey, heard through the grapevine you got divorced. Not to worry. Frankie'll take care of you."

Fordham was glad it was dark and Frankie couldn't see her grimace. Three years after the divorce, she could only imagine the stories that her bored, shallow neighbors had circulated about the demise of her marriage.

He pulled out a pocket flashlight, went under the hood, and stroked each wire with such care and precision that Fordham wished she were one of them. "You just need a charge," Frankie said, shutting the hood. "I'm kinda cold. How about we get some coffee first?"

Fordham checked the time. Whitty would still be out with Dorie. She hadn't been out with a man since the summer, when an ex-coworker had set her up with his unattractive friend, some weirdo who took her picture the second she stepped out of her car. He said it was to commemorate their first meeting, but she got a *Silence of the Lambs* vibe and split before dinner. But this would be different since she already knew Frankie—sort of.

They went to the Starbucks around the corner and sat in a booth. It was moderately busy. She wondered if sitting at a table would be more appropriate. This wasn't a date. A date would involve some kind of plan and an hour or more in front of a mirror scrutinizing hair, shoes, and cellulite. A date with Frankie could disappoint her if it didn't work out. This was a casual meeting...

Then he started stroking her hand, and it became a date. "Your ex-husband had it all, and he missed it like an exit on the highway." Frankie blinked, showing off his killer blue eyes and thick dark lashes. He was tracing little circles on her hand as he spoke, and she imagined what that would feel like on her breasts.

"He never had much of a sense of direction." All she could think about was where Frankie's hands were going.

"Some people can't stay the course, and they get lost... you have such soft skin," he said, running his fingers along hers.

"It's nice to feel appreciated," she said, enjoying his touch.

His phone rang. Frankie mouthed that it was a doctor, and she hoped it was nothing that might stop them from kissing before the night was over.

"Are you sure?" he asked. "Really, Doc? Now? But it's so early!" He ended the call with a huge grin that exposed the kind of straight white teeth actors coveted.

"What did the doctor say?" Fordham asked, holding her breath a little.

"My wife is in labor! I'm gonna be a dad! Sorry, beautiful. I gotta jet."

Frankie Tancredi left without even paying the check. Fordham trekked back to the car. Maybe she would never learn enough about cars to be a mechanic, but one thing Frankie Tancredi had taught her was to never invest in a smooth ride and to always be in the driver's seat.

But moping in the driver's seat was doing nothing for her just then. She got out of the car, ignoring the persistent rain, and looked under the hood again. Maybe Frankie was wrong. She went to the glove compartment and got the manual. The initial checklist was geared toward dull-normal.

Okay. It might just be that simple. She wiped a few hoses with a paper towel, tightened a loose cap, and got back in the driver's seat. The car cooperated. She cranked up the heat and headed home. *Screw you, Frankie Tancredi.*

Once the car started, Fordham went back to wanting to ring Margo's neck and scream at an imaginary Abe. She barely had the energy to take out the box of Junior Mints she had stashed in her seat pocket. But once she managed to get them, she was immediately soothed by the oozing goodness as the candies melted in her mouth. A new, unfamiliar job was not on her agenda, especially with Gil out of town and Whitty feeling neglected by him. It was going to be difficult to explain to Whitty that now Fordham would be less available too. She wondered how she was going to manage with there being even fewer hours in the day. Somehow, she was going to have to make Whitty understand that she had to do this, that everything happened for a reason, and that even though there was no logical explanation for them to be so thoughtlessly inconvenienced, someday there might be an answer.

Short answer: she would take her to O-My Sushi for miso and her favorite ikura hand rolls and then to Kiki Sweets Café for the richest, gooiest, most delicious brownie sundae on the planet. If nothing else, Whitty would have no room to be angry and might be too gripped by nausea to think about their new predicament.

By the time she approached her pristine tree-lined street in Bardonia, a hamlet in Rockland County about twenty-three miles from Manhattan, the rain had stopped and the moon had begun to peek through the fading clouds. Driving down the block, she could practically taste a Diet Coke and feel the welcome of her new queen-sized bed and Posturepedic pillow. It was late, and she was sure that Dorie and Whitty had eaten and were watching TV. She would say a quick hello and pass out. But as she drew closer, she noticed a plumber's van sitting in her driveway.

Fordham parked on the street and rushed through the front door. "Hello? What's going on?"

A chaotic mess of papers and cartons was spread around the family room. Fordham was only half-sure she wanted an answer. She didn't see any water. Maybe whatever had brought the plumbers would not cost her the spa weekend she'd planned with Evie. If they could quickly fix what they had to, she could go to sleep and deal with the mess in the morning.

Her mother came in from the garage, carrying a carton. At sixty plus, Dorie Price was anything but a senior citizen. She was staunchly independent and highly opinionated. Her best friend, Gloria, had once described her as a cross between Golda Meir and Shirley MacLaine, possessing intense wisdom, wholesome beauty, and a strong desire to control a nation, the universe, and everything in between.

Under normal circumstances, Dorie would have been reluctant to entertain guests or leave the house unless her hair was done and she'd "put on her face," an expression that used to make Whitty innocently ask her where it was so she could bring it to her. Dorie's style wasn't quite definable. Some days, she went for an Ann Taylor look, and other days, she seemed to have been dressed by gypsies.

That night was an exception. Dorie had allowed Gallo Plumbing to come in to fix the pipes even though she was in sweats and Fordham's father's old black T-shirt, a souvenir from Las Vegas that read, "God Kissed My Dice. Now I'm a Holy Roller." She said she still wore it because no matter how many times it was washed, it always smelled like Arnie Price. Arnie had worn that T-shirt the night he persuaded Fordham to join him for bingo at the synagogue in New City. She was home from college for the weekend, and Dorie was away, visiting Gloria. Arnie didn't want to go alone. Fordham lost, but he won a hundred dollars and took her out for sushi at Nobu in Tribeca to celebrate. They drank sake and talked about luck—how some people came by it naturally and how others made their own. He'd said he was among the luckiest because he had it both ways. And she'd believed him.

"Hi, honey," Dorie said, breaking the memory. "Glad you're home. I tried your cell phone, but I couldn't get through." Dorie continued to organize the mess without stopping to notice Fordham's reaction. "We had a little accident. Whitty and I didn't even get the chance to go out."

"A little accident?" shouted Whitty, who was working beside her grandmother. "Me and Mom-Mom have been moving boxes forever! Mom, how many times have I told you—you can't run the dishwasher and the washing machine and take a shower all at the same time! We have old pipes."

Fordham had passed cranky at the driveway and was now working on miserable. "It's 'Mom-Mom and I,' not 'me and Mom-Mom,' and I can promise you, young lady, now is not the time to be lecturing me about anything!" She zipped around Whitty to check on the condition of a large box marked Divorce.

Whitty wasn't finished. "It's just that sometimes you—"

Fordham flashed Whitty a disdainful scowl, and Dorie prudently intervened. "Sometimes, a smart young lady should go to the garage and see what else she can bring in. Go on. Listen to your grandmother."

The plumber and his assistant came in from the garage and went over to the toolbox they'd left in the family room. They didn't seem to notice Fordham, which might have bothered her if she hadn't been beyond exhausted. The younger of the two men was bending down intently to watch the older man fiddle with a pipe. His jeans were falling, revealing a slight dimple right at the top of his butt. She didn't mind the momentary distraction.

"Fine," Whitty said. "I get it. Even if I am right." Frustrated, she headed for the garage as quickly as her labored gait would permit.

Fordham stopped staring at the younger plumber's butt and opened the Divorce box. Even the sight of the top layer made her cringe. As difficult as their marriage had been, their divorce had been even worse. Eric Darnoff, her lawyer, had promptly bought a vacation home in Costa Rica on what she was sure was her dime.

Dorie said, "Honey, it's like your father always used to say. 'Shit happens. Our job is to make it stink less.' For what it's worth, Whitty has been a real help." She must have noticed Fordham's despair.

Fordham watched the younger plumber heading to the garage. "I'm sure. I just hate when she corrects me. You seem to think that's your job, and I don't like it much then, either. And after today, I'm not even sure how to do my job."

"Why? What's going on?"

"Margo left. Now I'm the editor of *Flowers from the Heart: Love Online*."

The older of the two plumbers started for Dorie. "Not me." She tilted her head toward Fordham. "Her."

The plumber was holding a pipe that could have been yanked from Abe Lincoln's house. "Lady, can you come with me? I wanna show you something."

Fordham followed the plumber—whose shirt pocket introduced him as Tony—to the garage, where a healthy inch of water was pooling around paint cans, garden tools, and assorted other items Fordham never used but knew were there for a reason. All the important boxes appeared to have been moved to the family room. It was a big job, and she now understood why Whitty had snapped at her.

There was no sign of her in the garage. *Poor kid must have slipped into the kitchen for fortification.* Fordham tiptoed around a piece of equipment that she imagined could suck up a swimming pool for lunch and still have room for dinner. Of course, her shoes were history, but that was just another thing to add to the list. And it wasn't even Friday the thirteenth.

Tony led her to a corner of the garage where some pipe had broken off because of a water-pressure valve that must have been designed during the Civil War because...

She wasn't listening. She wanted to say, *How much and how long? That's all I care about.*

Tony seemed to have gotten the message. He stopped talking and went back to work. Fordham examined the mess she had to walk over to get back to the house.

"Jerry, gimme the hose." Tony's *th* sounds all came out like *d*, but at least now Fordham knew the name of the guy with the butt.

"Which end?"

"The one you can grab!"

Tony smacked Jerry on the head and sighed. He appealed to Fordham for sympathy. "My brother's kid. Got some girl pregnant, quit school, and now I'm stuck with him."

Fordham's disastrous day got the better of her, and she gave herself permission to take Tony's lead and go off on his nephew. "Oh, really? Is that what happened, Jerry? You just woke up one sunny morning and said, 'It's a beautiful day—I think I'll knock up my girlfriend, quit school, and make my poor uncle clean up my mess'?"

"Um, not exactly. Like, it was raining a lot, and she wasn't my girlfriend... yet, anyway. When she said she was on the pill, I didn't know she meant Zoloft."

Jerry shrugged and continued working on the hose. Suddenly, there was a lot of gurgling. Tony panicked. "What the heck... be careful, Jerry! Oh shit!" Ice-cold water shot out of the hose, hitting Fordham in its line of fire.

"Shit!" She was dripping from head to toe.

"Jerry, you didn't turn off the freakin' water? I told you to turn off the freakin' main valve. Gimme that! I'm real sorry, lady. The kid is wet behind the ears."

"Yeah, me too," Fordham said, shaking herself off.

"You know," Jerry said, staring at her as if he'd just had an epiphany, "you remind me of a Sophia Loren poster my dad has hanging in his toolshed. She's coming out of the water, and she's wearing this shirt, and you could see her—" He lifted his hands to his chest and cupped imaginary breasts.

"What the hell is wrong with you?" Tony smacked Jerry on the back of the head. "That's not the way you to talk to a lady. Do you talk to your mother like that?"

Fordham was more mortified at being likened to Jerry's mother than at the crude comment. "Okay, I'm going to change now." She paused then added, "Jerry, why is Sophia Loren in the toolshed?"

He shrugged again, "Guess she's one of his tools."

FORDHAM NEVER EVEN got the chance to talk to Whitty. The poor kid fell asleep on her homework right after the plumbers left. Luckily, she was light enough to carry to bed. Dorie had also turned in early, and the house was totally quiet by the time Fordham was out of the shower and ready to unwind. She threw on sweats and laughed about how crazy the day had been, starting with Margo's belly and ending with Jerry's butt.

It was after nine, and Fordham hadn't eaten anything since lunch. Her stomach was gurgling. She couldn't decide between Cheerios and leftover cold noodles in sesame paste. Neither was grabbing her, but she got a pair of chopsticks.

Something about seeing her mother in her father's T-shirt was making her uneasy. She thought she had made her peace. His death had been from an accidental overdose. The "accidental" part was suspect, since he'd been swimming in debt, but that was the final conclusion. Either way, it was over, and there was no purpose in conjuring up the anger and disappointment. Sure, she had defended him when she was talking to Margo. A dead man couldn't speak for himself. But deep down, where she wanted to feel loyalty and respect for her father, she found resentment and emptiness.

Maybe a cup of tea would help. Her grandmother always said, "A good cup of tea is like a bath for your soul."

She switched on the light fixture over the center island. It was unusually modern for a turn-of-the-century piece, with four hanging pendants connected to one central unit. She and Dorie had found it when they were shopping in Nyack, a quaint little town near the Hudson River. Arnie had only been gone a couple of months when Dorie had called, requesting mother- daughter time. She suggested a waterside lunch and a shopping trip. Dorie, who normally didn't want to go out much during that time, sounded insistent. Fordham wondered what was up. Anyone who mattered was in good health, and Fordham's third cousin being elected as president of her chapter of Nutrisystem didn't warrant a celebratory meal. Maybe her mother had already found someone new. Fordham wasn't sure how she'd react to that so soon after her father's death.

But lunch had nothing to do with family or a new man. Dorie was trying to find a pleasant way to tell Fordham she was flat broke and then some. She'd been a stay-at-home mom, and since Arnie had insisted on being the breadwinner, the situation had never changed. But now, Dorie was stuck. She told Fordham that having to ask to move into her home was making her crazy, but she had no choice. A new light fixture and lunch wasn't much, but it was the best she could do under the circumstances. Fordham didn't understand. Arnie had to have purchased insurance policies and other assets. Their house had been in freakin' Dellwood, a posh old neighborhood in New City.

The kettle whistled, disrupting Fordham's thoughts. She got her mug and accidentally added enough honey to make her teeth hurt. She didn't mind. Somehow, the sweetness seemed like a good idea. She adjusted the dimmer switch to make the room glow as if it were basking in candlelight. She smiled, remembering the over-the-top candelabra Dorie had brought home during one of her redecorating phases. Arnie had griped, "Who does your mother think I am—Liberace? We don't even have a piano." But Dorie had loved it, so it found a home on a marble end table.

There was no denying that Arnie Price had a good heart and was loved by everyone. Especially his bookie. Dorie had known he enjoyed gambling. They used to go to Atlantic City with Gloria and her husband—and after the divorce, her second husband—at least once a month. Fordham and Gloria would play the slots, and the guys would hit the tables. Arnie never won big or lost much, or so he said. He liked the horses. They went to Monticello Raceway a few times during the summers but spent more time at the flea market than at the track. Even their trips to Belmont had been more about finding new restaurants in Queens than about the horses. Or so she presumed.

Dorie was crazy in love with her husband, who was almost fifteen years her senior, and she never questioned his actions. He treated her like gold, gave her anything she wanted, helped around the house, and watched soap operas with her. She was more satisfied than most women she knew, she told Fordham.

So it was all the more shocking when Dorie got a call from her attorney, after Arnie passed away, saying he had to meet with her immediately to discuss how to proceed. Arnie Price was a good soul who had spent every penny they had and every penny they didn't have to support his gambling addiction and secure the life he knew his adoring wife wanted. And as a grand finale, he had cashed in his life insurance policy.

Dorie blamed herself. During their lunch in Nyack, she said, "Your father may have fumbled here and there—no one is a saint—but bottom line, it was my fault. I chose to look the other way. I had to. Besides you, he was the light of my life. Some women love hard, and when it catches up with us, we deal with it."

Maybe Dorie could explain it away that cavalierly, but Fordham, having accepted Arnie's gambling as a passionate hobby, wasn't inclined to be as generous. Maybe she wasn't the first daughter who was ever betrayed by a father she'd adored and built Popsicle-stick castles for. A father she idolized and brought to school for show and share. A father who walked her down the aisle when she was making one of the biggest mistakes of her life, telling her, "You can still run if you want to, no questions asked." A father who cried when his granddaughter was born and said her imperfection was God's way of making her beauty more unique. A father who left her and her mother with a raging mess and no plan to clean it up. No, the betrayal was not unique. Things like this happened to other families, and to save face, they kept their mouths shut and went about their business.

She had loved her father, believing he was the beacon of reason in a world that often seemed to have gone nuts. Now she realized it was a ruse, and she was left with the daunting task of having to reinvent him in a more workable, realistic template. She had to learn to memorialize him as a man who'd been fallible, insecure, and incapable of picking up the pieces of her fragmented life. In time, she expected that she would find a way to forgive him, but she wasn't there yet. She was amazed at how easily Dorie had been able to think of it as one of life's tests without ever uttering a cathartic, "Fuck you!"

Tea finished, Fordham shut off the light and headed back to bed. Maybe she would meditate. She needed to figure out a way to make *Love Online* a bestseller. Abe had said that commercial success would translate to more money in her pocket. With just a little more confidence in herself, she could do it. She had to do it. From where she was standing, it was the only way to ensure she wouldn't end up on Whitty's doorstep someday.

Chapter Five: Bell, Book, and Scandal

Fordham couldn't sleep. She had, as her grandmother used to say, *too many knishes crowding her kishkas*, which was like *pain in the tuches* but more serious and with a greater range of angst and discomfort. She did have a lot on her plate, and there didn't appear to be much relief in the near future. She glanced at the clock for the ninety-sixth time. It was almost one in the morning. She'd hoped to get into the office early to check for submissions and go over some eventual layout options. That wasn't happening, and Abe would have to understand.

Since sleep was axed from the agenda, she got up and headed to the kitchen. There was nothing quite like one-floor living. "Open concept," her realtor had told her. Fordham wasn't sure if that was the case, but it didn't matter. A house without stairs was safer and easier for Whitty to get around, and that was enough.

Outside the cozy kitchen, a motorcycle revved its engine. Fordham went to the pantry for the second time and got out the Sleepytime tea, the honey, a spoon, and her favorite mug, which was tall and decorated with in a colorful Parisian street scene. She glanced over at the business card on the counter. Tony Gallo had successfully fixed her pipes, called her beautiful, and asked to take her out for the best *saltimbocca alla romana* she had ever tasted, as if assuming she was worldly enough to know what he was talking about. He'd probably faint if she told him that not only had she never tasted it, but she also wasn't even sure what was in it. She closed her eyes and tried to imagine a date with Tony Gallo, but she couldn't keep a straight face.

Fordham brought her tea into the family room and sat in the corner of the big taupe sectional. It had seemed like Barbie furniture in her old house. She didn't care. What this house lacked in space it made up for in warmth, and that was something that couldn't be measured.

A group of boxes rescued from the flood still had to be sorted, repacked, and stored, but that would have to wait. Maybe it was lack of sleep or the ungodly hour, but the huge carton marked Nostalgia seemed to be willing her to open it. At first, she resisted. Revisiting the past didn't seem productive. But since the box was within arm's reach, Fordham made a game of challenging herself to get it without leaving her seat. After a few good tugs, the box proved no match for her determination. She downed the tepid tea as if it was a belt of whiskey swallowed before a confrontation with a masked bandit then opened the flaps at the top of the carton.

"Okay, breathe," she whispered to herself.

She picked up the first folder lying on top of an enormous pile of stuff she couldn't throw out but wasn't sure she ever wanted to see again. Research papers from college. That wasn't so bad. Professor Hayley Stone had given her an A-plus for her "insightful contemporary account of the complex economical, political, and sociological conditions existing in Victorian London that perpetuated prostitution and led to the betrayal and ultimate dissolution of the family unit."

She was relieved to find documented evidence that she could write. She put it aside, thinking she might show it to Abe if at some point he gave her a hard time about her content or style. There were tons of similar papers and files, and she was sure that this box was strictly schoolwork until she noticed her high school yearbook and a small photo album covered in hearts and peace signs.

Yearbooks were tough, especially when life promised one road and somehow replaced it with another, which was what had happened to her. For Evie, the Spring Vale High School yearbook was further proof that she had always been a smart girl who knew what would work for her. She chose the right boyfriend, who became the right husband, the right dentist, and the right father to her daughter. For Fordham, it was a slap in the face for having been foolish enough to have irrational expectations when everything told her she was, as Dorie put it, "cruising for a bruising."

She threw the book down on the coffee table, but it still commanded her attention like a good horror movie—despite the lurid screams and the looming knife, she wouldn't be fulfilled until she saw the kill. *Fine, a page or two will satisfy my morbid need to connect with ancient history.* Fordham read a few entries then came to Evie's. Beneath a picture of Eve Gross and Marv Weiner sitting side by side on the bleachers at a football game was the label, "King and Queen of the Prom." She had almost forgotten how long and dark Evie's hair used to be. Nowadays, it was cut to her chin with caramel highlights. And Marv, except for a few stray grays, seemed untouched by time.

Dear Fordham,

Hey, sister—We've been friends forever and always will be. You're the only person I've ever shared chewed gum with—and I guarantee it will stay that way. You're beautiful, smart, and funny, and I love you so much I'm not even jealous. You're the only one who really understands me, and when Marv and I get married, I want you to be godmother to our kids. See ya at the party. Tell Aaron to remember to bring a bathing suit this time! Love ya always, Evie.

And there it was in print: the name Aaron and a reminder of the time he'd shown up at Marv's pool party without his bathing suit and convinced her to go skinny-dipping when all the guests had gone. Although they'd been dating all through high school, they didn't have the chance to have sex very often. That night, Aaron was pretty clear it was going to happen again. She didn't have to close her eyes to remember his voice.

"You gonna stay in the pool?" he'd asked from the deck. Aaron was perfection. He had soulful eyes, dimples, longish dark hair that feathered back, and just enough facial hair to enhance his chiseled features.

"Yeah, why not? *I* remembered *my* bathing suit." The moon was high and bright, and as she swam, her arms created little eddies that sparkled like swirls of glitter. She stopped to splash him, but he was too far away to reach. She closed her eyes and went underwater until she hit something hard that forced her up. It was Aaron.

"At least I have my birthday suit." He kissed her, and in seconds, her bikini was floating on top of the water.

"In the pool?" she asked.

"In the pool now, and in my bed later."

Evie and Marv were too busy making out at the other end of the pool to even notice they had company. Certainly, they would never have known Fordham and Aaron were naked if Marv's mother hadn't rung her famous cowbell to let them know the pool was closing for the evening. Aaron flew out of the water and into his pants before Fordham even realized they'd stopped kissing. He might not have been gallant, but he was fast and had her wrapped in a towel, bikini in hand, before the last of the clanging.

She had been head over heels, heels over head in love with Aaron Karp. It was the kind of love that made her stomach tumble when she said his name and her heart race when he said hers. They dated for two years—an obscene amount of time to emotionally invest in a fantasy that included a down-on-one-knee, two-carat brilliant-cut diamond proposal, a split ranch with an in-ground pool, an oak fence, and a toy poodle named Fifi. Not to mention a spacious music room where Aaron—a wannabe musician turned sound engineer with a soft spot for oldies—could store and listen to all the precious eclectic albums he obsessively collected and frequently quoted from. Friends said they looked like they belonged together and that someday they would have beautiful children. She remembered thinking she was good for two children, maybe three, as long as labor and delivery weren't really like the movie they'd had to watch in health class.

Fordham slammed the yearbook closed. This was silly. She did have a beautiful child, just not Aaron's beautiful child. But she couldn't kick the habit. She picked up the little photo album devoted to the summer after high school graduation, the last time they'd been a couple. It held picture after picture of her and Aaron smiling at the beach, at each other, on carnival rides, on his bed. Her heart hurt to remember being so in love with Aaron Karp.

She opened another photo album, hoping to numb the memory by jumping into a different decade. But somehow, Aaron's yearbook picture fell out of a collection of photos ranging from Whitty's first meal to her preschool graduation. Maybe the universe was challenging her.

Fordham opened the yearbook, flipped a few more pages, and spotted Aaron's unmistakable signature on the back cover. She wanted to slam it shut, but something that felt like a dare from one of her childhood sleepover parties wouldn't let her. *Fine. I'll read it then shove the past back in the carton.* The familiar script read:

To My "Golden Lady"—

You came into my life like a "Summer Breeze," and you made me feel fine. I was in "Bad Company," but you could sure "Make Me Smile." I was just a "Piano Man," but you made me a "Happy Man." "From the Beginning," I said, "Could This Be Magic?" And since then, it has been. Seriously, Fordie—I love you, and even though I'm "Leaving on a Jet Plane" to study in Spain, you'll always be "My Girl." Please don't ever tell me to "Beat It."

Love, Aaron

He was gone for three weeks and then sent her The Letter. She wanted to laugh, remembering Aaron's corny sense of humor, but instead, a few tears of humiliation and regret stung the corners of her eyes.

Enough. There was no room in her life for *coulda-woulda-shoul-da* memories. She smacked the book closed and tossed it to the other side of the couch, willing the past away from her. She returned to her tepid tea and stared at the blank television. She barely noticed when Dorie came in, also holding a cup of tea.

"It's late. What are you doing?" Dorie asked.

"Entertaining Brad Pitt, but he couldn't make it. Why are you up?"

"The usual. Online Scrabble. This time, I had a great seven-letter word, *z-e-a-l-o-u-s*, and he blocked it." Dorie shook her head in disgust.

"Who blocked it?"

"That one pain in the ass I told you about who always beats me. I don't want to talk about it." She noticed the yearbook. "Memories?"

"Yeah. I don't even know why I keep this stuff."

"Stuff is good. Things give us pieces of a puzzle we already started, and if we're smart, we keep them in place and move on. Did you learn anything new?"

"Yeah. Apparently, I had great-smelling hair and a laugh like Woody Woodpecker and could win any argument."

"I believe that. And you wonder where Whitty gets it. Good night, darling daughter. Try to get some sleep. You don't want to end up with Aunt Bertha's luggage under your eyes."

"Thanks, Mom."

Dorie paused as she was about to leave the room. "I almost forgot. Here you go." She retrieved a letter she'd stuck on the fridge under the Empire State Building magnet and handed it to her daughter. "Wear the coral sweater. It hides your little tummy and brings out your eyes." Dorie left the room before Fordham could comment.

She read the note and sighed. *Back-to-School Night. Tomorrow.*

She was too wired to sleep but too tired to sort through any more boxes, either. A laminated painting of Whitty's hand transformed into a Thanksgiving Day turkey was hanging off the side of one of the cartons. Fordham tilted her head to examine it. Even when Whitty was in preschool, she'd been artistic. She still liked to draw, but her passion was poetry. Fordham's little girl carried so much in her heart that deserved to be recognized. If anyone knew about getting over hurdles gracefully, it was Whitty.

Fordham had to make this book work. The sooner it was done, the sooner she could get back to spending time with Whitty. But for the moment, she would do her best to show Whitty that anything could be achieved with a little confidence and tenacity. Never mind that Fordham considered the sentiment a crock of shit. People failed all the time, and she was likely to be one of them, but her daughter didn't have to know that. Smart mothers lied to their daughters to protect them from their insecurities.

She went to the kitchen and got more tea, using the minutes while the kettle came to a boil to pick up her phone and see if there were any responses to the submission request she'd posted on Craigslist. *Holy shit!* There were seventy-five of them. The good news was that the post had worked. The bad news was what Margo had said about the arduous process of skimming, sifting, and tossing was true. The first dozen submissions made Fordham blush and worry that people were mistaking her call for submissions as an ad for a porn site. The last thing she was interested in reading was cyber sexcapades from horny teenagers who either fabricated their experiences or belonged in therapy. Some emails missed the point entirely and seemed to assume she was a matchmaking message board:

I cook, clean, do laundry, and can tie a cherry stem with my tongue. I also bake chocolate chip cookies from scratch. My womb is ready for a place in your house. Please write.

Unsurprisingly, this woman was still single.

Others seemed to have stories to tell but didn't offer enough information:

I met Earl on Facebook in a group called Sweet Cheeks. He said "Hi," then I said "Hi." Then we met for real at the Offal House in Kenawonga County. He had brains in sauce and mashed potatoes. I had pan-seared heart over wild rice. He said between his brains and my heart, we were a feast to be reckoned with. After some tripe ice cream and kidney cake, he proposed. It was quite a meal, and we've been married five years. But we're vegetarians now.

Fordham nixed the tea, sat back down on the couch, and kept reading. Some stories were mildly amusing, but nothing was tugging at her heart, saying, *I belong in your book...* until the second-to-last submission.

AFTER THE FIFTH RING, Fordham was about to hang up and go to bed when Evie's voice popped out over the line.

"Hello?" Evie yawned.

"Hi! Evie, don't kill me," exclaimed Fordham.

"No, it's okay. Marv went to the office—an emergency. Some boxer chipped his front teeth. They'll be bonding for hours." A note of confusion followed by panic crept into Evie's voice. "Did you have a date tonight? Oh my God. Did he hurt you? I'll come over there and kill him!"

"No. Evie, calm down. Everything is fine. I've been home, working. I had some trouble with—forget it. I didn't call about that. I called because I got a submission I have to read to you."

"A submission?"

"Yeah, it's a long story. I have to edit a book for work. I'll tell you about it when I see you, but I have to read this to you now."

"Okay. Wait, I need my glasses."

"Why? I'm reading it to you."

"I know, but I'll hear it better with my glasses on." Evie rustled on the other end of the line. "Go ahead. I'm ready."

Fordham felt herself tremble as she began to read. "Stephen Stills once said, 'There are three things men can do with women: love them, suffer for them, or turn them into literature.' I've already loved… and suffered, so it seems fitting to complete the journey now that I'm ready to move on.

"Several years ago, my first wife decided her guru's home was more fulfilling than ours. I came home one evening to a babysitter, a note, and an empty box of granola. Our daughter was only a few months old, and the idea of being a single dad terrified me. I was betrayed and alone. How could this have happened to me… to us?"

Evie sighed. "Awful, right? Choosing a guru over a baby."

Fordham continued reading. "I spent a lot of time online, hoping to find something that would help me make sense of it all. One night, I found a support group called Baby Games. The administrator was a single woman who couldn't have children, so she taught others how to be better parents. With her support, I became closer with my daughter and happier than I had ever been."

"Oh, that's nice," Evie said.

"Just wait," Fordham cautioned then picked up where she'd left off. "Paige was amazing. We'd sit online for hours, laughing, crying, and sharing our stories. I couldn't stop thinking about her. But when I finally got up the courage to ask her out, she turned me down. She said I was too young for her. After some serious pleading on my part, she decided to give me a chance. From the moment our eyes locked, I was hooked. A few months later, she agreed to marry me. On our honeymoon, she gave me a copy of *Flowers from the Heart: The New Family*. She loved me and my daughter in a way I never knew existed. Things were better than wonderful."

"Fordham," Evie said, "please tell me this fairy tale has a happy ending."

Fordham said she was almost finished then continued reading. "Of course, she had quirks. She would worry about ridiculous things like crow's-feet and wrinkles. Sometimes, she would look in the mirror just to point out the little lines to me. I told her they were my love-lines. As they would deepen, so would my love for her.

"But we never got to grow old together. Two years into our marriage, she went to visit an old friend, and a drunk driver ended it all. That was almost three years ago, and although my daughter and I are doing well, I feel I owe my Paige the chance to grace one of your pages."

Fordham allowed herself to sob as Evie did the same. "Do you know who this guy is?"

"No. All our submissions are sent straight to our legal department. They have details, but for the sake of impartiality, everything is set up to be anonymous to editors and consultants. Actually, I'm tasked with deciding on names for each story. They're even grouped together regionally to ensure that we appeal to a wide demographic. I just get them from my designated inbox.

"That's a shame," Evie said. "Prince Charming could probably use a date."

"Hey... good title. But the only date I'm interested in is with my publisher. I'm too busy for men."

After the call, Fordham lingered on the couch and read over the submission. Maybe someone in legal would be willing to share this guy's info. She'd call in the morning, giving herself yet another reason to find sleep an impossibility.

Chapter Six: It's a Blunderful Life

ordham was just about asleep when Whitty's alarm clock went off. Too tired to move, she decided to let Dorie give up her dawn Scrabble game to handle the morning. There would be plenty of time to face the day later.

Within minutes, she was drifting through a sea of flowers and climbing up a mountain of dictionaries. A man in a turban was sitting on a cloud, watching her... and then there was an annoying tug at her blanket. She went to swat it, but a gentle, kind voice got it to leave. Then a hugely pregnant Margo tied a rope around Fordham's waist and told her to keep climbing. Margo clenched the rope tightly as Fordham struggled with each step. Margo assured her she was safe and could do anything she wanted except marry the right man and eat fewer than fifteen hundred calories a day. Fordham's head hit the wall with a clunk when Margo let go of the rope, and the phone rang.

Groggy and cranky, she kicked off her comforter and picked up the phone. "Why did you let go?" she asked in a stupor.

"Fordham? Is that you?" said a voice that wasn't Margo's.

"It's me. Who are you?" she asked, still not awake.

"It's Abe. I'm in my office," he said, clearing his throat. "And you should be in yours. Have you been drinking?"

Fordham wondered what happened to her mug. "You stole my coffee."

"Fordham. Wake up and get over here. It's important."

FORDHAM SAT IN THE black swivel chair in front of Abe's desk while he finished up a call. She wasn't sure what he needed to discuss, but she did know she was too tired to process anything. All she wanted to do was spin her way into a long nap, but she doubted Abe would be that accommodating.

"Fordham," Abe said in a tone that reminded her of *Mission Impossible*, "negotiations are underway at our central office. The entire Flowers from the Heart series is being reevaluated."

She immediately recalled her dream.

"If the next book doesn't generate significant revenue, they're going to hire new staff and try a cookbook series," Abe said, shaking his head and shrugging.

"Cookbooks?" She couldn't imagine Abe agonizing over Beef Paprikash recipes. "So what are you saying?" Fordham said, still a little slow on the uptake.

"What I'm saying is if this book... you and the entire department may..." Abe was wringing his hands. "Make sure the book isn't just good. Make sure it's great."

The intercom buzzed, and Myra reminded Abe to take his stool softener. She must have thought Abe was alone. Fordham wondered if that was really part of Myra's job description.

"Seriously?" Fordham grabbed a big fat doughnut from Abe's desk. "This isn't even what I do, and now you're telling me I could be out of here altogether."

Fordham stomped out of Abe's office before he could get a word in edgewise and went straight to the ladies' room. She placed the doughnut on a piece of paper towel on the stainless-steel counter adjacent to the sinks and splashed some cold water on her face. She stared at her reflection in the mirror with horror. She'd used the too-light foundation she was planning to return, and there was gray hair at her temples that hadn't been there before this project had been dumped in her lap. Unfortunately, there was no time to indulge in self-pity or to make voodoo dolls in Margo's image. She was going to have to find a way to make this work.

A few minutes later, she was at her desk, staring around the room, hoping for inspiration as she nibbled on the overly sweet doughnut. She wasn't sure where to start. She got up and peered out the window. The weather was dank, but the sun kept trying to nudge its way through the dense clouds. A small crowd of people was watching a guy play bongos, and more than anything, she wanted to join them. She was too tired to get anything done anyway.

A knock at the door thwarted her plans. Abe immediately parked himself on the empty corner of her desk. "Don't make me feel guilty. I feel guilty enough without you giving me puppy-dog eyes."

"I don't do puppy-dog eyes. Too needy," she said, tossing her hair to the side. "No one said you have to feel guilty. But if you do, I'm certainly not going to stop you." She sat down at her computer. "You're doing your job. I'm struggling to figure out how to do mine."

"I spoke to Margo," Abe said, standing up. "She's getting married. She asked me if I would give her away."

"Oh, please, let me."

"I'm sure you'll be getting an invitation."

"I don't care. I'm not going." Fordham crossed her arms and returned to the window.

"You're being childish, and besides, weddings are a good place to meet people."

Fordham spun around. "Did Margo put you up to this? Did she ask you to do her bidding, for a change?"

"No. I told her you were upset about the way things were handled."

"I'm upset about the way *I* was handled." Fordham wiped away a few tears of frustration before they could be subjected to comment.

"She apologized," Abe insisted. "Said she was superstitious and didn't want to jinx anything."

"Nothing except our friendship. She found that dispensable."

"Fordham, what if this is fate at play? What if this is a good thing, and you're missing it?"

"The only thing I plan to miss is the wedding. When is it?"

"She's still working out the details."

Fordham sat back in her chair. "Abe, not to be rude, but I have a lot to do, and planning what I'm not going to be wearing to Margo's wedding isn't high on my priority list."

"You should reconsider, Fordham. That sour-grapes philosophy doesn't suit you."

"For you, I'll think about it. If it ever happens. But for now, I really have to get back to work."

"I have faith in you, Fordham. Just find it in yourself—quickly." Abe eyed Fordham's doughnut on a small paper plate, picked it up, and copped the best part on his way out. "Sorry, but you took my favorite." He left, closing the door behind him.

The phone rang just as she was licking chocolate glaze off her lips. She had forgotten all about Back-to-School Night, but Whitty hadn't.

"Aw, Whitty, honey, I have so much work to do, and you don't come with me anyway. I'll go next year."

"Next year, I'll be in middle school."

"I knew that." Fordham said defensively, even though she'd already entered the date in her planner for next year's Back-to-School Night.

"Mom, it's my last year at Crestwood, and it's not like Dad is going." Her daughter knew exactly how to play the guilt card. "And you need to meet my new principal. He likes me."

"Of course he likes you. You're smart and talented and funny and—"

"Mom!"

"I'm not buttering you up. I mean it, but... you're right. I'll go. I want to go."

"Good, and wear the coral sweater. You look pretty in that."

FORDHAM PLANTED A SMILE on her face and walked into the familiar entry of Crestwood Elementary. Dorie always told her, "What you show on the outside is your calling card." Sometimes she wondered what people thought of her, but that night, she was too tired to care. She was wearing the coral sweater and had just finished two weeks of teeth-whitening strips. That seemed like sufficient effort for a night of, "Oh, hi, so good to see you. Anyone special in your life yet? They say it's so hard out there."

She said a quick hello to her favorite security guard, who directed her to Whitty's classroom. It was crowded, and Fordham assessed that she and two other women were the only ones there without mates. No seats were available except for the one right up front. A very young, very pretty, very curvy, very new woman was seated behind the teacher's desk. There was something about her vibe that Fordham immediately didn't like. Standing at the blackboard was an extremely attractive man about Fordham's age, with a full head of light-brown hair and soft blue eyes. He waited for Fordham to sit before speaking.

"Welcome, parents. Thank you for joining us. As you can see, I'm not Lenore Hudson."

A few people chuckled. Fordham was too busy checking him out.

"My name is David Prince, and I am the new principal of Crestwood Elementary. And since your children are in the oldest group, I wanted the opportunity to talk to you first."

There was mild applause. In the ten minutes that followed, Fordham discovered that the youngster sitting at the teacher's desk was Pam Lesley, a substitute for Whitty's homeroom class until the regular teacher, Debbie Kessler, returned from maternity leave. She also learned that *Dr.* Prince—a title he humbly and nonchalantly revealed—was passionate about kids and education.

"It's overwhelming to think about how much the world has changed since we were the same age as our children are now," Dr. Prince said with a hint of regret. "I'm bummed when I think that my daughter will never experience the comforting smell of a worksheet fresh from the mimeograph machine."

So he has a daughter, Fordham mused. Maybe he was divorced. There was a fifty-fifty possibility. If so, it had to be recent, or he'd already be taken. Or he could still be married. Not all guys wore wedding rings. She couldn't get a solid read on him. His socks matched, and he spoke with confidence, but his smile seemed to struggle as much as hers.

"Or that she'll never be overjoyed about having thirteen channels of television," he continued.

Their eyes met for a brief moment, and she turned away before he had the chance to realize she was attracted to him. Playing hard to get had always been her most effective tool in getting guys interested in her. A few people were talking about the Jerry Lewis Telethon and how exciting it had been to be able to watch television overnight. Someone mentioned how the Beatles used to have an animated show and how the FCC would have a field day if Eminem ever became a Saturday-morning-cartoon subject. David Prince beamed. He had the group—Fordham included—in his pocket, and they were ready to hear anything he had to say. After a few more stories, he returned to the discussion of education.

"Today, everything is high tech. You can actually hula hoop without the hoop as long as you have the right game box. But the last thing we want is for our kids to lose their identities as living, breathing creators. It's too easy to sit behind a screen, big or small, and shut the world out. They must be encouraged to be participants, not reactors, in their lives. And we must keep in mind that in many ways, our kids are our teachers as much as we are theirs. They teach us to understand the prospects of the future as we continue to reinforce the importance of identity."

He picked up a bright-yellow piece of chalk and wrote on the blackboard:

I-dentity vs. i-dentity.

He sat on the desk, blocking Pam Lesley—which was not a crying shame.

"We must constantly remind our kids that the little *i* behind their iPods and iPhones doesn't diminish who they are. They must learn that the *Pods* and the *Phones* mean nothing without the *I* that they invest to make it all happen."

Everything he said resonated with her. There was loud applause that evoked a dimpled grin from him, and he began to pass around copies of an article. Fordham's phone vibrated.

Evie had texted: *How's it going?*

Fordham began writing: *The new principal is a real hotti—*

She dropped her phone just as Dr. Prince was laying papers on her desk. Like a gentleman, he picked it up, but his eyes were looking right at the text. His face reddened, but the glint in his eyes was unmistakably appreciative. As the parents scooped up their papers, he thanked them for their time and sent them on to the remainder of the evening's events.

Fordham was considering going over to say hello and thank him personally for his insight and for being so damn yummy, but Pam got to him first, and it was hard to ignore their body language. She stood so close to him it would have been hard to slip a credit card between them. To add to the show, each time he said something, she giggled, patted his arm, and squealed "You're too much!"

Fordham surmised that Dr. Prince was not married, but Pam had already staked her claim.

Chapter Seven: Track to the Future

"So, first I got hosed at work, and then I got hosed at home!" Fordham said to Evie through a mouthful of salad. "I mean it. My house was ready to swim upstream."

It was Fordham's idea of a perfect lunch—warm enough to sit outside but cool enough to not leave pit stains. The waiter came with their iced teas and a breadbasket. He squinted against the glare and flipped the sunglasses down from his head as soon as he left their table.

"The only saving grace was the plumber's nephew's ass."

"Salmon are ready to spawn near your snowblower, and you're busy admiring an ass," Evie said with a touch of envy.

Fordham missed Evie. Except for her hair, height, and the few extra pounds she fought with, her friend had changed very little since the two had met making Play-Doh hot dogs in kindergarten. She still had mops for lashes and round coffee-colored eyes that could say things words would miss. They used to get together all the time, but then Fordham's schedule had required her daily presence at the office, and Evie took over the reception desk for Marv's practice. Lately, they had to rely on texts and phone calls, except for the rare times when she was working from home and they could do lunch.

"So what happened to your stuff?"

"My mother and Whitty managed to save most of it," she said, opening a package of crackers. "You'll be happy to know that my high school yearbook is safe and sound, along with a bunch of photos that confirm we once wore training bras."

"Some of us still could." Evie gave her chest a disappointed grimace.

"I wouldn't sweat the small stuff," Fordham said with a wink.

"Very funny." Evie eyed the breadbasket. "Something is wrong. You ordered extra dressing, and you ate all your crackers. Tell me what's going on."

Fordham chuckled. It could be unnerving, but it was nice to be known. "The book," she said with a scowl. "It is really driving me crazy. I'm still trying to find my footing, and if I don't, I could lose my job."

"Don't worry. Margo has done this kind of thing before. She'll be back. You're going nuts for no reason. She's probably off somewhere getting liposuctioned or reconstructed. I doubt she's actually pregnant."

"No. This time, I'm sure she's telling the truth. I got an email from her this morning: 'Darling, hope all is well. I'll be in for a visit in a few weeks. Betsey Johnson just came out with a new line of mid-size handbags that will go perfectly with my second trimester.'"

"Oh, Fordham, I'm so sorry. You're right. She must be pregnant. Margo would never use Betsey in vain."

"I know." Fordham speared a tomato. "And I can't even stay angry at her. I mean, she should have told me, but I don't think she had a clue that the book would get dumped in my lap. I'm not even sure Abe told her."

Evie flailed a floss stick. "You know, Marv and I were talking, and we think you should become a hygienist. Less stress, and you meet so many people. You can tell a lot about a man by the way he takes care of his mouth. Like Gil, that good-for-nothing schmuck you're finally rid of. He had halitosis. That should have been a giveaway."

"Oh, it was. I told you, he clearly forgot to swig his Listerine after he went down on his secretary."

"And there goes dessert," Evie said, scrunching her face. "Just as well. I didn't need it anyway."

Evie was toying with her club sandwich when her phone rang. She apologized, saying it could take a while. Fordham didn't care. As she watched Evie walk to the lounge, she contemplated stealing a bite of her bacon, but a gas pain decided against it. The mention of Gil had given her indigestion and taken her back to the night they met.

HER PARENTS HAD BEEN away for the weekend, visiting Gloria and her then-husband, Sid. Fordham, a sophomore in college, had asked if she could throw a get-together, but Arnie said the only friend he expected to stay with her was Evie. He didn't like the idea of kids being in his home unsupervised. Dorie was younger and cooler than Arnie and said Fordham could have a few friends over, but Fordham had to make sure the house was clean and in one piece before they got back. Evie promised she would help Fordham take care of everything.

The guest list was long and eclectic. When Dorie said "a few friends," Fordham pretended that meant anyone she had ever met. One of her roommates asked if she could bring her boyfriend and his friend, Gil. Fordham said sure. She had seen Gil's picture in her friend's high school yearbook, and he looked like someone she might want to fall in love with. The only conceivable fly in the ointment was Joe Mathis, a guy Fordham had met at college and was casually dating.

The beer was flowing, and everyone was using the garbage bins for their intended purpose. Fordham was having a tolerable time with Joe, who was a sweet but ultimately boring guy. And of course, to make her feel guilty, Dorie and Arnie liked Joe. They said he was a fine young man who came from "good stock"—which was true, but Fordham wasn't as interested in a rich bouillabaisse as she was in a guy who could stir her passion.

Halfway through the party, that guy walked in. Gil Presser was everything his picture promised and then some. He had long dark wavy hair, a thin wiry frame, and scruffy facial hair. He looked like an even cuter Sly Stallone without the cut abs. The bonus was his winning smile that oozed *Catch me if you can* in a language that defied words.

Fordham, standing against the wall opposite the laundry room and talking to Evie, gaped at this paragon of desirability and nearly lost her footing. It was in that moment that she knew he was the one—the subject of her fantasies, the one she dreamed of having children with, the one who Aaron was supposed to be until he left for Spain and broke her heart.

"Fordham, how much did you drink?" Evie was helping her stay upright.

"One beer. Did you see him?"

"See who?"

"The guy that just got here. His name is Gil Presser. I saw his picture in my roommate's yearbook."

Evie glanced at him. "Okay, so...?"

"Come on, be serious, Evie. He's gorgeous."

"If you say so," Evie said, watching Marv playing bumper pool. "What about you and Joe?

"We're not official."

"I just found out official is in his pocket. He's giving you a promise ring at midnight."

"No way!" Fordham screeched, eyes fixed on Gil, who she could have sworn had also been keeping her in his view. "Now what am I supposed to do?"

"If you're smart, you'll take it and say thank you. He's a good guy, and he's joining his father's firm on Wall Street after he graduates. This is a gift, Fordham."

"Maybe, but it isn't meant to be mine."

Fordham liked Joe and didn't want to hurt him, but she was certain Gil Presser's arrival was no coincidence. He was sent by a higher power. No one could make her feel like a bowl of Jell-O and not be destined to be part of her life. Evie shook her head and went to find Marv. Fordham went to the kitchen to find answers.

Joe made it easy. She was getting a bag of corn chips from the cabinet when he came in and told her he was very sorry but he had to leave. His friend from out of town who'd come to the party with him had had too much to drink and wanted to go back to Joe's house. Then they were leaving at dawn to go on a camping trip for the week. Joe wouldn't be able to call her until he returned. He apologized profusely, saying he hoped she wasn't too upset since the evening hadn't gone the way he'd planned. She assured him, probably too zealously, that he had nothing to worry about. She decided it would be cruel to break up with him and ruin his trip. His disappointment could wait.

With Joe's heart safely out the door, Fordham was free to get Gil's attention. She wasn't sure where to begin other than to position herself under his nose and seem oblivious to his presence. She could feel Evie's eyes following her over to Gil and the small crowd of people he was talking to. Fordham glanced her way and rolled her eyes. She wished Evie could understand that there was no free will involved here—it was destiny.

Gil didn't seem to be as aware of their destiny. He was busy showing his friends how he could squeeze dip between his teeth. No one seemed as fascinated by his every move as she was. Having had his fill, he headed for the deck door. She knew the shortest route to it. If he wanted to go outside, he'd have no choice but to bump into her. That was the moment their eyes locked. She knew he felt it too.

"Hey," he offered. "I'm Gil."

"I know."

"What's your name again?"

"Fordham."

"Right. Like the street in the Bronx."

"Yeah. And like the university."

"Right." He set his eyes comfortably on hers. "This is a nice house."

"Thanks."

"Wanna take a walk?"

She wasn't sure where they were going, and she didn't care. Evie would make sure no one puked where it couldn't be cleaned. Besides, the party was winding down. A lot of people had already left, and there were others heading out. Gil told his ride to wait for him, which didn't seem like much of a problem.

The air was slightly damp and cool, as if the clouds had been kissing ice cubes. She shivered, and he instinctively put his arm around her. The moon took notice and framed his face so she could see his cheekbones more clearly. Beneath his scant beard, he had a little cleft in his chin.

She wanted to study his face more, but there was laughter coming from up the block that threw her off. As they came to a streetlight, she saw a guy carrying a girl on his back. He was galloping toward them, wearing a bra on his head. The girl was holding her top in her hand, and her large breasts jiggled each time the guy moved. He looked like an inebriated steed carting around Lady Godiva. Fordham wondered if they were a real couple, and in a quick fantasy, she pictured her and Gil swapping roles with them. The guy said something barely intelligible to Fordham and Gil about being sure to check out the cool party down the block, then he disappeared back into the night.

In the moments they walked around the neighborhood, she and Gil seemed to share a lifetime. They talked about everything—school, parents, the suburbs, politics, music, Atari, sugar, movies, and bad breath. He wanted to stay, but he was afraid to make his friends wait. They headed back to the house, and before they reached the driveway, he gently pushed her onto the grass and kissed her the way Burt Lancaster kissed Deborah Kerr in *From Here to Eternity* but without the beach.

As they got closer to the house, she realized the party was over. Everyone was gone, including Gil's friends. The only thing on the driveway was a heap of filled garbage bags. Gil checked his watch, which said it was one in the morning. Then he followed Fordham into the house and gasped. It was really four in the morning. He had to be at work by nine, or he was sure to lose his job.

There was only one thing Fordham could do. She had to drive Gil home. The car was in the garage, and the keys were in the ignition where they always were. It was no big deal. Granted, her father told her not to use the car because there was something wrong with the something or other, but it didn't sound serious, and she was sure he was just being extra cautious.

Gil was being a gentleman and kept telling her he would call a cab, but neither one of them had the cash, and she couldn't imagine how any of this would be a problem. She would drop him off, go back to the house, crash for a bit, get up, and clean before her parents got home. As she drove, he thanked her for the ride by taking her free hand and sensuously kissing each finger.

That was when the car stalled thirty miles from her house on the summer-busy Long Island Expressway. Dead. It wouldn't turn over for anything. Gil told her to put the car in neutral so that he could push it off to the side and onto the shoulder. He managed to get most of the car off the road, but the back end was still jutting out a little. The highway was empty, and there didn't appear to be many cops on patrol. Gil said they should leave a note on the windshield and try to find a phone. Fordham was too numb to panic and followed his lead.

They found a phone several miles from the car. Gil called the police and explained what happened. He told them where the car was and described where they were. The police said to hold tight and they would send a car to get them. There was nothing to do but wait. Gil rested his arm around her shoulder and drew her close to him. If it had been up to Fordham, the officer would have never shown up.

But he did, and he drove them back to the disabled car. It was still there, but now it resembled an accordion more than it did a vehicle. Someone had plowed into it at record speed and kept going as if nothing had happened. There were no remnants from any other vehicle in the area, and the officer deduced that either a van or a truck had been responsible for the accident. Fordham could see the prison bars being installed on the door to her bedroom. Her father, a mad dog when provoked, was not going to be okay with any part of this.

The cop went to his car to get the paperwork so they could file a claim. The tricky part came when the officer asked for license and registration. Fordham had her license, but the registration was not in her name, and the officer said it was necessary to speak with the owner of the vehicle before signing off on the report. A short ride later, they arrived at the moderately busy police station. Fordham summoned her courage and called Gloria's, certain that at nearly six in the morning, her parents would still be fast asleep.

After a lot of ranting and shouting, Arnie said they were on their way. To assuage her anxiety, Fordham focused on Gil. He was sitting on a chair, sleeping. She watched him swat a persistent fly away from his face and giggled when he seemed to shout at it in the midst of his dream. The amazing thing was that he didn't ditch her to go do whatever he had to do for himself. He stayed to make sure she was okay. He was responsible, caring, focused, and incredibly adorable.

Arnie didn't see him quite the same way. He waltzed into the station, screaming, with Dorie behind him, begging him to calm down. He was trying to swat her away, much like Gil's treatment of the annoying fly. He stormed over to Gil, who had just woken up, and grabbed him by the collar, pulling him to a standing position.

"So you're the punk that got my little girl into this mess!" His fist was in the air, and he was just about to strike Gil when Fordham jumped between them. Gil just stood quietly, as if that might mitigate the situation. An officer came and pulled Arnie to the side. He said if Arnie didn't control himself, he would end up in a jail cell. That was all Dorie needed to hear. Typically the more reasonable parent, she told Fordham to say goodbye to her friend and get in the car. They would go for a bite to eat and then come back to handle the particulars. Dorie pushed Arnie out of the station, motioning to Fordham to hurry.

Fordham went over to Gil. "I am so sorry about all this. And I'm even sorrier that my dad is crazy."

"Don't worry about it. It wasn't your fault. It isn't his fault, either. I met a cute girl at a party I was barely invited to, and I didn't want to let her go. I still don't."

"Good thing, because any guy so cool about all this is not someone I would ever want to give up."

They kissed again, this time more like Fred and Wilma Flintstone after a filling brontosaurus burger. But they both knew it was just the beginning of destiny.

FORDHAM DIDN'T WANT to think about the Gil she'd met and loved. It was a lifetime ago, and the boy—who she believed had the promise of depth, sensitivity, and a will to be judged for the strength of his kindness and character—had never really existed. She'd refused to look beyond his veneer to see the lost, insecure, egocentric man with an endless need to be fed and idolized. Her parents had warned her about his level of dysfunction, but she ignored them because she believed she could either save him or change him, a consuming job that proved to require too much work for too little compensation.

In the end, she realized he'd never been truly committed to her or inclined to fight for their relationship. He let whatever they could have had slip away with every dollar or new pleasure set before him. Everything about him was tired old news, and she was grateful he was tucked away in a new venture in Istanbul, far from her world and unable to taint the life she had been learning to build without him.

Evie came back to the table, beaming. "I just finalized the order for Marv's new office furniture, and what a bargain!"

Fordham nodded to acknowledge Evie's coup then wondered if the past was the only thing they had in common.

"What can I tell you, Fordham? The pleasure of shopping lasts a lot longer than the pleasure of coming."

And that was why they were still close. She could set her watch by Evie's candor.

"That text you sent me last night was pretty interesting," Evie said, salting her fries. "Did you talk to him?"

"It was nothing. Whitty's principal is"—she stabbed a large piece of lettuce—"very attractive. But I think he's with someone."

"What do you mean, *with*?"

"*With*, like Tums and heartburn." Fordham scanned the dessert menu. "Forget about it. I have."

Fordham got out a pen and a little memo pad from her bag. She began making a shopping list while she was talking then noticed she'd written, "Prince" instead of "Pringles."

"Anyway, I'm not sure which sites or apps to research for dating," Fordham said. "I've never done it. You've been setting me up, although after the last time, I'm really not sure I'm going to continue that arrangement."

Evie was the only one Fordham had trusted to set her up on dates. None of them ever worked out, but at least she always got home without making the headlines.

"Oh my God, Fordham! All this talk about Margo and Gil, and I almost forgot. You have a date tomorrow night, and as a favor to me, please go. It's Marv's cousin Paul. He's in from Detroit for a family wedding—not Marv's side, the other side, but he's staying with us."

"You're sending me to a wedding with a *Michigander*?"

"He's a nice guy. Once you get over the extra nipple."

"Cute. Anything else worth sharing?" Fordham always hoped to be wooed if not wowed.

"Honestly, I don't remember what he looks like. But here's the Paul Nudelman story in a nutshell. Recently divorced, two teenagers, PhD from Columbia, a professor of mathematics."

"Evie, you know numbers make me queasy. I would rather have root canal than figure out the square root of anything. I don't even like balancing my checkbook."

"You like books. You're editing a book. He writes books. The last one he wrote was about pi."

"Apple or cherry?"

TRAFFIC WAS BUILDING as she headed to the supermarket. Fortunately, she was still full from lunch and wouldn't be tempted to scarf down a bag of pretzels while shopping. She flipped on some jazz and tried to relax. But she was too wired. She should have said no to the date. Evie might have been disappointed, but she would have understood.

If Fordham was honest with herself—and she preferred not to be—she would have to admit that somewhere deep down, she was hopeful. It was illogical. All of her dates were dead ends that left her feeling cold and worried that she would never find anyone. But still, this little traffic light inside her kept leading her through the blinking yellow into new experiences. It was a dumb light that almost never flashed red, and the few times it went green, she remained cautiously optimistic.

A guy on a motorcycle cut into her lane, and even though she yielded, he gave her the finger. *Typical male. Even when you give them what they want, they still give you grief.*

She turned the radio off since all it was doing was adding to the noise in her head. The more she ruminated about going to this wedding, the more anxious she became. She should have told Evie she couldn't make it. She wasn't even sure her black dress was back from the cleaners after the last date disaster a few months back. That one had been with a nutjob friend of Evie's from sleepaway camp who'd found her in the French Woods group on Facebook. Evie was giddy with glee when Donald asked if she knew a nice woman he could go out with. She hadn't seen the guy in decades, but she remembered that he smelled like Pop-Tarts and didn't make fun of her for having a crush on David Letterman. Why she believed that was a legitimate enough endorsement to send Fordham on a dinner date was not something Evie could ever adequately explain.

Fordham met Donald at a small café outside of town. He wasn't attractive and had an unusually large mole on his forehead that she couldn't help but stare at while they spoke. He had been away for several years, teaching English to kids in the jungles of Peru. It was very rewarding, and while he was there, he'd not only found inner peace, but he'd also found Christ. For the rest of the evening, he assumed what one might call the missionary position and fully shared the precepts of the New Testament with anyone who even inadvertently glanced his way, including the busboy, the cocktail waitress, and the older woman with silver-blue coiffed hair sitting at the table next to them.

"But," he told her in a whisper, "in order to lead a truly spiritual life, I must abandon the sins of the flesh." He would no longer enjoy the physical company of men and would marry a woman who did not place a high price tag on the "meaningless mingling of bodily fluids."

Fordham wasn't sure how to react, so she had a few sips of her drink and let him talk about the Second Coming then excused herself and went to the ladies' room. Just before she got back to their table, she deliberately bumped into a waiter so that everything on his tray strategically spilled all over her dress. The waiter was clearly confused when she thanked him and handed him a twenty. She apologized to her date for her clumsiness and ran out of the restaurant before he could say good night.

What if Paul was just more of the same—a well-educated, babbling lunatic with a penchant for scripture and an eye for hot guys? But it was too late. She'd already agreed, and there was no way to get out of it gracefully. This wasn't really a date—it was a good deed. As long as she kept it in perspective, she had nothing to worry about.

Fordham drove down Route 59 and decided it was a deli-and-baked-beans night. She had to work, especially if she was going to be busy over the weekend. Whitty loved turkey sandwiches and had been pretty agreeable about food since Back-to-School Night. Luckily, Stop & Shop was less crowded than usual. She was so exhausted that she didn't even do her typical makeup-and-hair check before heading into the store.

Milk, eggs, apples, and a package of sorry-I'm-neglecting-you-tonight Oreos for Whitty. As she headed to the deli counter, she wondered if the cute kid, Brandon, would be there. He had a little crush on her. At first she knew that because he would always give her at least a quarter pound more of anything she asked for. A couple of months earlier, he'd gone so far as to ask her out. Of course she said no—she was old enough to be his mother—but it had become a familiar game between them. She was actually in the mood for a little extra rice pudding that night.

He wasn't there when she got to the counter, and she was annoyed at herself for feeling disappointed. She pulled a ticket and got on line. *Number sixty-nine. Ironic, considering I haven't even come close to that number in ages.* There were still a few people ahead of her, so she decided to check out the international-cheese section. When she returned, Brandon was at the counter. As soon as he noticed her, he smiled and gave her a small nod. He was about twenty, and his body suggested that he should never wear anything more than tight, skimpy briefs. His white smock was open down the front, and the wife-beater shirt he had on underneath clung to every ripple of his six-pack. She was so engrossed in her fantasies that she almost didn't hear him call her number.

"Sixty-eight?" Brandon asked, widening his cat-green eyes. No one came forward. "How about sixty-nine? Anyone for sixty-nine?" Brandon gave a mischievous grin.

"That would be me," Fordham said, not sure if she wanted to sound playful and lead him on.

"Guess it's my lucky day." Brandon smirked.

"A pound of roast beef, a pound of turkey, a pound of coleslaw, a sliced rye, and three sour pickles," she said without a breath.

"Come here." He motioned her down to the end of the counter while he got her order together. And when she followed him, he said, "Have dinner with me tomorrow."

"We've been through this. I can't. You're too young for me."

"Just give me a chance. That's all I'm asking for—a chance."

"I'm sorry, I just don't—" She was considering leaving when a much older counter guy motioned to speak to Brandon. After a few minutes, she began to feel self-conscious.

"Are you almost done? I'm running late," she said, feeling like a diva.

Brandon gathered up her order and held it in his arms. "Fordham, you are... the ideal sandwich. Soft, but a little hard around the edges. And inside, you're filled with everything real men are hungry for: class, brains, and a warm heart."

She was taken aback. He had never been that eloquent. "Tomorrow night I'm busy," she said.

"Okay, lunch."

And before she even realized she'd forgotten the rice pudding, she said, "Fine, lunch. Nicky's in Suffern at twelve."

She caught Brandon and the older guy sharing a high five as she walked away.

Chapter Eight: Close Encounters of the Absurd Kind

Fordham was thrilled that before she even got out of bed, Whitty and Dorie had left to go shopping. *Two dates in one day.* She wondered if she could pull it off. She hadn't told anyone about her date with Brandon, and she wanted to keep it that way. She was too embarrassed. Maybe going out with the just-started-shaving set was working for Madonna, but Fordham wasn't a celebrity, and her behavior had to answer to three higher powers— her mother, her daughter, and her best friend.

It wasn't just the age difference that bothered her. She also didn't like the idea of going out with someone she would rather jump on than speak to. They couldn't possibly have much in common. He was just a kid working around a lot of meat. She barely ate meat anymore. The decision screamed "desperate" in a voice she no longer recognized as her own. She wondered if she was a terrible person for wanting her ego stroked by a gorgeous Adonis. Maybe she was. And worse, maybe she had actually abandoned hope of finding true love.

"No," she told herself out loud. "Not all hope." Her common sense might be on vacation, but the submission from Prince Charming kept her from being totally jaded. She read it every day—sometimes twice a day. Sometimes more, depending on how miserable she was feeling. It was a testament to love that reminded her that there were good men out there and in time, if she was sprinkled with fairy dust, she would find one of her own. Until then, she gave herself permission to be a little aggressive on the playing field.

She checked the clock. She had less than an hour. Without hesitation, she grabbed the coral sweater that had been hanging over a chair since Back-to-School Night. The skinny jeans were in the closet in first position next to the black dress. She clipped her hair back on one side and let the rest fall forward, perfect for how she was feeling. She studied her face in the mirror. There wasn't enough concealer in CVS to cover the twenty-plus years between her and the kid waiting to be her date. She was just going to have to suck it up.

THEY SAT AT A SMALL table near the front door of her favorite Italian place on the other side of the county. There was much less of a chance she'd run into anyone she knew there, and she could relax a bit. Recessed lighting gave the room a lift that compensated for the cloudy day.

A waiter handed Fordham the wine list. "Soda for your son?"

Brandon blushed and said a quiet, "No, thanks."

Fordham was less mortified than she expected to be. Brandon *was* just a kid. He went through every roll in the breadbasket, licking the butter off his knife when there was no room left on the bread. He couldn't seem to figure out when to talk and when to eat, so he did both at the same time. Every other sentence, crumbs would tumble out of his mouth onto the table. The waiter could have easily assumed he was fifteen and tall for his age. Fordham felt sorry for Brandon and was suddenly thinking more about him in a diaper than a condom.

"Wow, so you were, like, married for a while," he said, trying to inconspicuously sweep the table with his napkin.

"Yes, not even *like*. I really was."

"Yeah, so what was it like?"

"The Pamplona Run."

"Um, I don't... um, I'm not sure what you mean."

"It's the charging of the bulls. I avoided red nighties and sudden movements."

"Your husband must have been bummed. Red nighties are hot. I once met this crazy Spanish girl on Tinder. She tried to choke me with hers."

"No..."

"Yeah!" he said, his eyes lighting up. "Oh man, it was scary. I threw up right on her floor."

The waiter came with Fordham's side salad and Brandon's linguini marinara. Fearing the ruination of her coveted sweater, she put on her jacket. Brandon frowned.

"I'm just chilly."

Brandon heaved a sigh, which Fordham interpreted it as, *Cool, she's old. She just has iron-poor blood, which isn't my fault.* He loaded a massive helping of linguini around his fork.

She casually shifted her chair, pretended to shiver, and zipped her jacket up to her chin. "So, Brandon, tell me... do you still look for dates online?"

"No, I like the deli counter. Potato-salad girls are usually pretty available."

That was interesting news, since Fordham rarely ordered potato salad. Maybe he was into her for being a coleslaw girl.

"My mom used to be the online-dating queen," he said.

"How so?" She retrieved her always-handy pen and memo pad from her bag.

"She wanted to get married. Badly. She was on all kinds of dating sites. One was really weird—Bruncheon-Bunnies-dot-com. People would go to Sunday buffets to meet and stuff their faces. Ever hear of it?"

"No. Doesn't sound like my thing."

"Yeah, well, that's good. My mom gained, like, ten pounds meeting different guys over eggs Benedict and Belgian waffles. She stopped going."

Fordham jotted down some notes. If she needed another source for submissions, this site was a possibility. "Fascinating. Is she still searching?"

"No. She found a husband. Only took a few months. They were both on some dog lovers' site. Which was kind of weird 'cause we never had a dog." He pointed to her notepad. "What's that for?"

"It's a project for work. You think your mother would mind if I interviewed her?"

Brandon paused to consider. "How 'bout one date in your red nightie for one date with my mom?"

Fordham tossed her notebook back into her bag. "Listen, Brandon—"

"Uh-oh. I don't like sentences that start with that. I got thrown off the football team in high school cause my grades sucked, and that's how the coach told me. He said, 'Listen, Brandon—'"

"I'm not your coach. I think you're sweet and cute, and you slice a mean corned beef, but this isn't going to work. I'm just not the Mrs. Robinson type."

"Why? Is she a vegetarian?"

Fordham chuckled as she got up, leaving money for the bill on the table. "Thank you, Brandon. I really needed this, but I have to go."

He got up to give her what she anticipated would be a romantic kiss, but his foot got caught on the base of the table and forced him back into his chair. Fordham was relieved that no lines had been blurred or crossed and was almost out the door when he shouted, "Come in early next week! We're having a big sale on bologna!"

FORDHAM HAD THREE HOURS to get out the door and into her car. She scanned her room in disgust. There were stockings, shoes, and clothes everywhere. "Whitty in a few years." She sighed, comforted by the fact that her daughter preferred reruns of *Full House* to *Keeping Up with the Kardashians*. She didn't have time to get maudlin about Whitty growing up. She still wasn't sure what she was going to wear.

Dressing for a wedding was challenging enough without the added stress of it being a blind date. She touched a little zit on her chin and checked the mirror to assess the damage. The pimple was nothing, but missing the mustache hanging over her lip before she'd left for lunch was unforgivable. The lighting in her room could have been bad, or maybe she needed glasses. She wondered if Brandon had noticed it. Not that it would have mattered, but if he had, she could only imagine what he would tell his friends. "Hey, I went out with an older woman who looked like Mark Twain." They might not even know who he was talking about. She didn't care.

She found the tweezers hiding under the finishing powder. The doorbell rang just as she was twirling a big chunk of hair around a brush. She considered not answering it. But it kept ringing.

"Just a minute." The brush wouldn't unwrap. It was strangely affixed to one side of her head. She caught her image in the hallway mirror. *Very Lady Gaga.* She opened the door, relieved to find Dorie and Whitty.

"Sorry, sweetheart." Dorie had the garage-door opener in her hand. "Needs new batteries. Whitty, honey, go find a couple of double-A batteries, and a little later, I'll take you to the movies. "

"She has a Scrabble tournament," Whitty said to Fordham as she headed into the kitchen. "She's letting me watch a movie so I don't bother her while she loses."

"Thank you for the vote of confidence, dear granddaughter," Dorie called after her.

"Guess she has you figured out, Mom. But don't you always win?" Fordham was still playing with her hair.

"I usually do, but I told you, there's this one guy I can never seem to beat. I think I'm playing him later."

"Well, I have faith in you." The brush was finally out of her hair.

"And where are you going?"

"To a wedding. Remember the favor I'm doing for Evie and Marv? Marv's cousin, Paul Nudelman." Fordham stood at the mirror, closely inspecting her tweezed mustache. "Do you need me for anything else? I have to finish getting ready."

"No, go do your thing. I have to call back the chairwoman from the Y Group, anyway. You know, the gal who sets everything up so she can take anything she wants."

"The one with the tattooed eyeliner and the hairy birthmark who swiped the dessert platter when we were sitting shiva for Daddy?"

"Her. Sometimes it's cake, sometimes it's someone's husband. Whatever's available. She wants me to donate your father's clothes for the next auction."

Fordham winced. Arnie's clothing was the only thing they had left of him after the creditors were finished. "What's *she* donating—bad taste?" Fordham asked, raising her voice. "Why do you bother with this woman?"

"I have no clue. Habit, I guess. I've known her for years. By the way, she wants an invitation. She keeps complaining that she never sees you and Whitty."

"You can tell her we're still recovering from our recent flood, but when the ark is built, we'll find another ass and invite her on board."

Dorie laughed so hard she got the hiccups and had to get a glass of water.

Whitty came back into the room with an Xbox controller. "What were you talking about?"

"Nothing important," Fordham said. "Do me a favor and play later. I need you to help me figure out what to wear."

"Because *that's* really important," Whitty said smugly.

"Don't be mean. I need to be in a good mood."

Whitty gave Fordham an apologetic kiss on the cheek and followed her into the bedroom.

"Wow, your room is a mess. Maybe I should tell Mom-Mom to come in and ground you!"

Fordham giggled as her daughter inspected the dresses on the bed.

"I think you should wear the pink one," Whitty said, holding up a candy-pink satin dress with a row of crystal beads under the bust. "Pink is a happy color. It works for a wedding."

Fordham gave Whitty a kiss on the cheek. She was lucky to have her daughter's support no matter how many times she disappointed her.

"I was thinking of wearing the black one," Fordham said, holding it up to her body.

The dress was the best hundred dollars she ever spent. Clingy and short but tummy-bulge forgiving, with just the right amount of cleavage showing, it said *Take me to bed* or *Introduce me to your grandmother* equally well.

"You always wear the black one. It's so cliché."

"Exactly why it's perfect. I don't want to stand out in any way, shape, or form. Besides, we've been eating all that ice cream I bought last week, and black will help me hide some of the aftermath."

"You don't look fat." Whitty studied Fordham's image in the mirror. "You just always think you do."

"Come on. You can tell me the truth," Fordham said hesitantly.

"Okay, you look fat, since you won't believe me anyway." Whitty sat at Fordham's vanity and braided her hair. "Do you think you'll like this guy?" she said, fastening a ponytail holder.

"I expect to finish the ice cream when I get home."

If Brandon had been any indication of where her dating life was headed, she could bring along a sweat suit to change into after the appetizer and be home in time to watch *Cake Masters* with Whitty.

"Guess you'll be keeping the black clothes at the front of the closet." Whitty undid her braids and twisted her hair into a bun with a metallic clip. "Mom, do you think Dad will be back from Istanbul for my graduation?"

"Oh, honey, I don't know. That's a long way off. I'm sure he wants to be there."

"I'm not," Whitty said, taking the clip out of her hair. "He's been gone for over a month, and he only called me once, and he never emails me at all."

"Well, you know, in Turkey, if they catch you stealing, they chop your fingers off. So look at the bright side."

Whitty sneered at Fordham.

"You know I'm only kidding," Fordham said. "Sort of. Whitty, your father loves you very much, and I'm sure when he has the chance, he'll be in touch." Fordham wasn't sure she was telling Whitty the truth, but it seemed a good time to see the glass as half-full.

"I guess."

"What made you ask?"

"The dream I had last night. We were on a plane, and I was eating a turkey sandwich—don't laugh—and you were sitting next to Antonio Banderas, flirting and doing that hair-toss thing you do." Whitty started batting her eyes and tossing her hair in different directions.

"This sounds more like *my* dream," Fordham said. "Did Antonio have a little goatee?"

"Shhh! And Dad was the pilot, and he said he was landing right away so he could fly someone else's plane—and then we had to find a new pilot."

"Well, anyone could wear that uniform better than your father. Whitty, honey, I know you miss your dad, and I'm sure he misses you too. But honestly, I think we're floating along just fine." Fordham held up the pink dress and then the black dress for the fifth time.

"Wear the black one."

"Thank you!" Fordham said, utterly relieved.

THOUGH SHE HAD NO CLUE how it had happened, Fordham was dressed and ready to go with time to spare. The conversation with Whitty about her graduation was still weighing on her mind, and there was no time like the present to do something about it. She scrutinized herself in the full-length mirror and comfortably decided a video call to Gil's emergency number would be in order.

"Fordham, it's two o'clock in the morning," Gil said with his eyes half-closed. "Someone better be dead."

"Charming, as always," Fordham said, trying to determine if the lump next to Gil was a person.

"What the hell do you want?" Gil yawned away from the camera.

"I want you to be civil for a minute and listen to me. It's about Whitty."

Gils eyes opened, and he shook his head a few times as he started to look more awake. "Is she okay?"

"Yeah, she's okay, but she misses you."

"Please don't tell me that's why you called!"

"So you'd rather I called to tell you she's dead?"

"Fordham, you know damn well that's not what I meant."

The lump beside Gil stirred, and Fordham was surprised at how little she cared. "Are you coming to her graduation?"

"She's in fifth grade. What the hell graduation is that?"

"The kind they have after fifth grade."

Fordham could see a bottle of champagne and two glasses sitting on a table near Gil's bed. *Now I'm jealous.* It appeared that Gil had moved on while she was still taking baby steps, getting ready to meet Evie's catch of the day.

"I doubt I'm coming," he said, tossing the blanket to the side.

Their camera signal wasn't great, but a pink blurry thing caught her eye. She did a double take and realized, though it had been years since she'd seen it, Gil's mouse was out of the house. If things on screen were supposed to appear bigger, his mouse had missed the memo.

Fordham continued without missing a beat, empowered by his sudden exposure. "She wants you there. And if she means anything to you, you'll figure out a way to be there."

"When is this friggin' thing?"

"June."

"It's September, and you're throwing this shit at me now?"

The lump growled something inaudible, and Gil yelled at her to shut up.

Fordham smiled with gratitude that she was no longer on the receiving end of anything he had to offer. "She was practically crying, Gil. She thinks you care more about work and money than you do about her."

"Yeah? Where'd she get that from, Fordham?"

"Hey, don't shoot the damn messenger. You haven't emailed her. You haven't called her. I was ready to do you a favor and tell her you had malaria or something, but that would have upset her too much."

Gil let out a stream of breath that rumbled between his lips. "I've been pretty busy here."

"So I see," she said, hoping not to sound as if she cared.

"Screw you and your self-righteous bullshit," Gil shouted. "If you had played your cards right, things might have worked out differently for us."

Fordham wasn't sure if he meant sex or money, but it was getting late, and she'd had enough. There was her evening with Paul Nudelman to consider. "I'm thinking I'd have given you the royal flush under any circumstances." Fordham ran her finger over her chin and immediately covered a small pimple with her hand.

"Yeah, right. Believe what you want. Who do you think you're talking to, a moron?"

Fordham held back the obvious answer. "You sound angry, Gil."

"A lot less since I left you."

She wanted to call him out on his misinterpretation of events, but with all the coke he'd been doing back then, he probably didn't remember the truth. "I just called to say your daughter misses you, and she'd like to be penciled into your agenda when you can find some time between business and pleasure."

"Yeah, go fuck yourself, Fordham." He was seething. "I'll let my daughter know when I can."

Fordham let Gil end the call then went to the kitchen for a drink. She was fairly sure she had won that round, but it was pretty clear that they were both still stuck in a state of resentment. She had some water then slipped into her heels and let go of the last ten minutes.

SHE FELT CONFIDENT in her black dress, even if her sweaty palms made the steering wheel harder to maneuver. She turned on the radio and tried to get into the music. There was no reason to be nervous. This date wasn't going to be any different than any of the others Evie had sent her on. She was going to walk in feeling hopeful, see him, be immediately disappointed, and find a way to cut the evening short. Even if it meant leaving a wedding, if she was miserable, she'd find a way out. She knew the drill all too well, which totally explained her persistent anxiety.

"Stop this bullshit already," she said loudly enough to drown out the traffic update. In a few more turns, she'd be there. She steered with one hand and used the other to freshen her hair. Suddenly, she yelped in pain. One of her big dangling hoop earrings hooked onto the lacy strap of her dress. If her outfit ripped, she'd have a valid reason to turn around and go home. She was tempted, but she couldn't do that to Evie.

She challenged herself to fix the problem without pulling over. The cars behind her kept honking, and as each driver passed, there was an exchange of obscenities. The release felt good. She set the earring free just as she pulled into the parking lot.

"I'm not doing this for me. This is for Evie." She spoke to the rearview mirror as she checked out her face. But she wasn't ready to leave the car. She opened the glove compartment, pulled out a copy of her favorite submission, and read it—twice.

Stephen Stills once said, "There are three things men can do with women: love them, suffer for them, or turn them into literature." I've already loved... and suffered, so it seems fitting to complete the journey now that I'm ready to move on...

As always, reading those words produced a sense of calm. Her true love might not be at this wedding, but he was out there somewhere.

There was no valet in front of the large, gaudy catering mill, so she had to park near the dumpsters. It was drizzling, but she didn't bother to cover her head. The damp air felt good against her cheeks. This would all be a joke by morning. She was pretty relaxed and not the least bit flustered when she tripped at the entrance. Luckily, the doorman caught her and let her lean on him as she checked her shoes. If she and her clothes got home in one piece, she'd consider the evening a success.

Chapter Nine: The Wedding Zinger

"Paulie, what's your date's name again?" slurred Paul Nudelman's sister—and Marv's cousin—a plain, chubby woman in her forties with drinks in both stubby hands. "Something about toys... Fisher Price?"

"It's Fordham. Fordham Price," she interjected before Paul could answer.

"Yeah, that's right. This isn't a name," the woman said with conviction.

Paul rolled his gray eyes and continued buttering a dinner roll.

"I'll let my mother know. And the IRS," Fordham said with a cautious smile.

"The IRS," Paul said, mocking a serious Southern drawl. "There's no ducking those guys. When they shoot, they win because they all... hail from Taxes!"

Paul laughed heartily. Fordham worried that his slight frame would fly off the chair.

"Paulie, why isn't your girlfriend laughing?" the chubby woman asked as she dragged her wiry husband onto the dance floor. Fordham followed the couple with her eyes as they found a place to do the twist.

"So what makes you laugh, Fisher?" he squawked. "You know I mean Fordham, right?" Paul wiped his black-framed glasses with a dinner napkin then placed them on the skinny bridge of his long nose.

She wanted to say, *This date*, but held her tongue. "Oh, you got me." She laughed to buy time. She wasn't sure how to continue their conversation.

Paul surveyed the table and motioned for the waiter. "Waiter, I need five waters, four dinner rolls, three napkins, and two lemon slices."

"Of course, sir, but just so you know, we're all out of the partridge in a pear tree."

Paul ignored that. Fordham caught the waiter's wink.

"We should probably dance," Paul said, "I can dance. It's just that last week, I pulled two tendons. Then I aggravated my fifth lumbar carrying a dozen file boxes. And then—"

"Actually, I need to use the powder room," Fordham said, getting up from her seat.

Paul followed, making a beeline for the dance floor.

She wanted to go home and relax, watch TV with Whitty, and be done with this day of double Mr. Wrongs. But she couldn't. It would make Evie look bad if she left before dinner. She resolved to deal with it a little longer, a task made more daunting watching Paul do the Chicken Dance with his parents.

The walk to the ladies' room was a good opportunity for Fordham to clear her head. She was happy to see a lounge area with a loveseat. The room was empty except for the attendant wearing a black uniform.

"You need anything, sweetie?" the woman said. "My shift is up."

"Yes, actually I do. Do you know anything about online dating?"

"That is a question I can safely say I have never been asked in here." The woman laughed.

"It's for a project I'm working on."

"Can't say I know much. I've been married to the same guy since chatting was something you did on the telephone. I got lucky. He works and still has a full head of hair. The only reason I'm handing out toilet paper on Saturday nights is so I can buy him a home theater for our anniversary. My sister's the one who knows the computer stuff. She met a guy on some dating site for people who are into stocks—or stockings—I don't remember which, but they're getting married. It's her fifth and his seventh. Me, I think marriage gets cheaper by the dozen. Here, sweetie." She pressed a packet of aspirin into Fordham's hand. "You look like you could use these."

There was only so long she could stay in the ladies' room. After a quick check in the mirror, she was laboring her way back to the party when her heel gave out. Despite her spontaneous balancing act, she tripped forward right into what she immediately recognized as a man's zipper. Horrified, she quickly lifted her head only to have her earring latch onto his belt buckle. To make matters worse, she couldn't maintain her balance and fell to her knees. She closed her eyes in utter embarrassment as the man cupped her chin to raise her head and set her free. But his attempt didn't work, and she had no choice but to face her unwitting target. Her heart skipped a beat when she found herself gazing at Whitty's principal.

"Dr. Prince! Oh, I am so sorry!"

"I know you." He paused for an eternity. "Whitney Presser's mother. The woman with the text. From Back-to-School Night."

Fordham swallowed a gasp, despite Dr. Prince's easiness at having her hitched to his crotch. She would have felt less awkward if he'd just left his epiphany at "Whitney Presser's mother."

"Fordham. Fordham Price. With earrings I'm returning to Nordstrom's tomorrow."

They worked together efficiently, and in moments, she was detached and upright on one foot. The other damned shoe was useless. The heel was broken clean off.

"Interesting to meet you again, Fordham. Great name."

"Thanks. I never got lost at a playground."

"Now what?" he asked.

Fordham went into her bag and pulled out a tube of Krazy Glue. "Usually for broken nails," she said while doing a quick repair job on her shoe.

"I'm impressed," he said, taking her hand when she was done.

Fordham wasn't quite sure what the gesture meant, but she wasn't about to pull away. "Thank you so much, Dr. Prince."

"I'm David," he said, taking the shoe and checking the repair, "and I've always believed you can tell a lot about a woman by looking at her sole." He handed the shoe back to her.

Fordham laughed. "Got to hand it to you, I've never heard that one before."

"Pretty bad, huh?"

Nothing could be that bad when she was staring into David Prince's warm blue eyes. But he didn't have to know that, at least not yet. "Yeah, but I've actually heard worse."

"Well, now I feel redeemed."

"You should, considering you've been helpful from head to toe."

"So what brings you here tonight?" David asked.

"A huge favor for a very close friend. What about you?"

"I'm at a bar mitzvah in the Loring Room."

"I'm at a wedding in the Boring Room."

They chuckled in unison.

"Long night?" David asked sympathetically.

"If the marriage lasts this long, they'll be in good shape."

Fordham put the shoe down to step into it. David got down on his knee to help her. It could have been a Cinderella moment, but then Pam showed up.

"David?" Pam said, her voice icy. "The boys want you. I wasn't sure where you went."

"Pam, this is Fordham Price. She's Whitney Presser's mother."

"Yeah, we've met," Pam said curtly.

Fordham wondered if it was past Pam's bedtime. The women shook hands limply as a young boy came running out of a room.

"Uncle David! Come here! They want to lift Big Mike up on a chair, and they need you. Come on!"

"Okay, I'm coming." He waved at Fordham while Pam wrapped her arm around his. "Have a good night."

"You too," she said.

She headed back to the room, trying to avoid anything that could make the evening get any worse.

IT WAS A JOY TO BE home in sweats and slippers, accessorized with a carton of Ben & Jerry's. *Sleepless in Seattle* had gotten to the part where Rob Reiner was telling Tom Hanks about the importance of his butt. Fordham licked the spoon. *Sleepless* always worked after bad dates. Somehow, it cleansed the offending aura. If love could work out for Meg Ryan, Fordham still had no shot in hell, but fate and destiny were universal constants, and that comforted her.

After that night, she was going to have to talk to Evie and reconsider this whole matchmaking business. It was too forced and unnatural. People shouldn't just be thrown together like broccoli and onions in some wok concoction. They should get to discuss their ingredients before attempting to become a dish. Her analogy brought Rachael Ray to mind. She paused the movie and went into the kitchen to add pretzels to her ice cream. Whitty was sitting on the couch when she returned.

"You're watching *this* again." Whitty was holding an empty glass.

"Hey, monkey. What are you doing up?"

"I dunno. Guess I had a dream I was thirsty. Bad night, huh?" Whitty said, searching Fordham's face for clues.

"Get a spoon. I'm indulging in guilty pleasures. Phish Food and I are having a heart-to-heart. Is Mom-Mom sleeping?"

"Yeah. So come on, tell me about your date."

"It wasn't a date. It was a favor. We ate. He danced. I laughed, mostly at him, and then I left. And now your Aunt Evie owes me big."

"Oh, one of those. Was he *really* ugly?"

"No, not ugly. But definitely not my type."

Fordham wasn't sure she even had a type anymore. Her type used to be long hair, beard, mustache, medium build, and a confident swagger. Now she'd be best served switching her criteria to just a nice guy that didn't make her gag when facing him over dinner.

"Was he rude? Was he pond scum?"

Since turning ten, Whitty had shown a greater interest in Fordham's dating life and often asked her to share highlights. It was cute but also reasonable for Whitty to want to know about who might take on the role of a dad while hers was absent. So far, there'd been no one who even came close to filling that role, but Fordham wondered how Whitty would react should that time come.

"No... more like plankton. Very bland, very boring plankton."

"Sorry. You sound disappointed."

Whitty was half-right. Fordham was disappointed about men in general. She sensed Whitty wasn't crushed by the news of her bad date.

"There's only one more pint of chocolate chip left in the freezer." Fordham gave Whitty a nudge. "Kidding. I'm fine. Just tired. Oh, you know who I saw tonight? Your principal."

"Dr. Prince was at the wedding?"

"Not exactly. He was at a bar mitzvah in the next room, and we kind of bumped into each other in the lobby." She snickered. The next time they saw each other, she would be embarrassed, but she was looking forward to it anyway.

"Cool. Did you talk?"

"A little bit. Nothing much. He actually belonged at his party. He was with your homeroom teacher."

"Her? Really?" Whitty sounded bummed. "I think he's nice."

"Yeah." Fordham steered the conversation elsewhere. "Did you have a nice time with Mom-Mom?"

"It was fun. She bought me a couple of shirts. She was pissed 'cause that guy won at Scrabble again, but she was in a good mood by the time we went to the movies and had pizza."

"Hmmm, pizza. So we both had a cheesy time!" Fordham tickled Whitty.

"Eee! That was sooo lame!" Whitty said, tickling Fordham back.

By the time the credits were rolling, Whitty was fast asleep. Fordham got a tissue to dab her teary eyes and then watched Whitty dream. It was hard to believe her preadolescent daughter was once a baby, totally dependent on her to make every decision, from what to eat and what to wear to where to go and how to get there. These days, she rarely asked Fordham for help or advice. She seemed to thrive on doing her own thing, which made Fordham both proud and wistful.

But for Fordham, little had changed. The moment Whitty was born, she became the center of Fordham's life and inspired her to want to be everything a good mother was supposed to be. When she was a toddler, that meant moving to a new house. There was no question that a ranch house would be far more convenient than the colonial they lived in. Those steps were too much for any toddler to handle, and for Whitty, they were exceptionally frustrating. One day, when she was about two, Whitty threw all her toys over the safety gate. They formed a mound and blocked the front door. Gil insisted that they put up a For Sale sign the next day.

Gil could be impulsive, but Fordham had agreed with him that time. And finding a new house would mean they would have to spend more time together. She wanted that. He was always so busy working that they were more like roommates than spouses. She had difficulty remembering the last time they had sex. Moving, she'd decided, would make them closer and get them on the same page.

It was strange, especially after their conversation, to think of Gil as anything but an adversary. She could hardly remember that at one time, she'd wanted to be closer to him. She didn't think about it of-

ten, but she had to admit that he'd seemed to want to be a good father, at least in that moment.

The house with the too-steep stairs had sold quickly. She and Gil
hit the market at just the right time and netted a huge profit. Gil was
more than ready to show the world how important he was.

"This is it," Gil said when they arrived at Mont Blanc Estates.

Since they'd been to a dozen houses he didn't like, Fordham was
prepared to make an effort. It was, however, tough. "Do they do anything other than cobblestone driveways? And with all those security cameras, I'll feel like I can't step outside to get the mail without putting on makeup." When she saw the house itself, she said,
"This place doesn't feel homey, Gil. It feels tense. Like people throw
tantrums more than they do parties." Fordham had hoped to get her
husband's attention. She'd succeeded.

"Stop being such a snob. You're condemning these people because they're rich."

"It isn't that. It's just a feeling."

"I want it, Fordham. And it'll be great for Whitty."

Which really meant, *Get used to it. We're moving.* A month later,
the papers were signed, and the house was theirs.

FORDHAM'S PHONE WAS buzzing, and she grabbed it before it
woke Whitty. It was Gil again. A very small part of her was glad that
she still hadn't taken off her makeup. She clicked on the call, but it
was dark, and she could barely see him. She went into the kitchen for
privacy.

"I had a date, and I'm still awake," she said, realizing she sounded
more like a child than she had intended.

"I'm not playing games," Gil said unconvincingly.

"Sure. What do you want?"

"Whitty."

"She's sleeping. Now it's two in the morning here, but I'll spare you the obscenities."

"That's not what I mean." Gil sounded businessman serious. "I was thinking about it when we hung up, and it would be good for Whitty to come live with me. I got the bucks, and she could experience another culture."

"I work full-time. I'll take her out for Mediterranean food more often."

"You're afraid to ask her," Gil said.

Fordham hadn't seen that one coming. Maybe he had a point. She and Whitty were close, but the allure of a whole new world could be an offer too appealing to pass up.

"She needs consistency, not just joyrides in a Ferrari or whatever you're doing there." Fordham found a moldy lemon in the refrigerator and chucked it out the side door into the yard. "We've been down this road before. My uncle still works for the IRS, and you still have plenty to hide. Give it up."

"You're jealous. I make good money—I get it. That's why you're threatening me. But think about it, because it sounds like you're busy with work, screwing around, and whatever. You could use the break."

"Thank you for caring, Gil. I really find it touching."

"What can I say? I'm a good guy."

"I gotta go. The cat just threw up *for* me."

FORDHAM SANK BACK INTO the couch. Ella, their frisky tabby, leapt into her lap to get to the remnants of her ice cream. After a few licks, she was purring and gave Fordham an affectionate nudge. Fordham kissed Ella's nose before the cat jumped away to pursue a fly. Fordham clicked off the movie and realized she had to stop dredging up the past every time she watched a happy ending. Sure, she was lonely, but she had made the right decision, and it was foolish to get maudlin just because she hadn't found the right man. More importantly, she had email to read and a book to edit. The quicker she got through the submissions, the sooner she would be done with this project. At the last check, there hadn't been much to choose from. She printed out a few to have a closer look.

Her cell phone buzzed, and she shuddered at the notion of going another round with Gil. She was ready to dance when she realized it was Evie calling.

"Are you okay?"

"Yeah, don't kill me," Evie said. "Marv just interrupted my afterglow for an emergency. Paul's sister fell on the dance floor and broke her tooth. Did you meet her? Paul's not even back yet." Evie's voice got higher. "Oh my God, Fordham. Are you with him?"

"No, I'm not with him! The date's over. I met his sister. I met his uncle. I chatted with his aunt. My evening is beyond complete."

"So on a scale of one to ten...?"

"I swear, Evie, no numbers. None. Is that why you called—to find out if I was with Paul?"

"No, that isn't why I called, but if you wanted to tell me something, I'd listen."

"There's nothing to tell. He was everything I expected him to be, and we really don't have to do this again." Fordham was scanning the submissions as Evie spoke.

"Fine. Whatever. Listen, I just got tickets to R.E.M. for tomorrow night. A patient of Marv's can't go, and Marv isn't into it. Wanna go?"

"Yes. But I can't. Sorry. I barely have time to go to the bathroom, much less a concert. Actually, if you have time, I want to read you a funny submission."

"Good. I could use a laugh."

"Okay. Her name is Wendi." Fordham began to read. "I was at my wit's end with the dating scene. At forty-five, I had exhausted every possibility for a human relationship. I preferred my cats. They didn't give me a hard time as long as they were fed. The guys I had been choosing were losers. And worse, I allowed each of them to hurt me in his own special way."

"Oh, yeah. This is really hysterical," Evie said. "Tell me when she puts the razor blade to her wrist."

"It's going to get better. So shhh." Fordham continued to read. "I did some soul-searching to figure out what message I was really sending out to men. Based on my experiences, what did they see as my wish list? What I discovered was truly appalling, but for fun, I decided to make it public. I wanted to keep it very low-key, so I selected a totally obscure dating service. This was my post: *Are you seemingly calm and charming on the outside but seething uncontrollably inside? Do you take refuge in mind-altering substances? If so, we must talk. I am a single forty-five-year-old woman seeking an obvious control freak who brings new meaning to the word 'critical.' If you have a problem with the way I breathe, all the better. Your disdain is my ambrosia.*"

"She must have known Gil," Evie said.

Fordham definitely wasn't ready to get into any of that part of her evening. She continued with the woman's ad. "*Insensitivity and an overall cynicism toward humanity are crucial. A hot temper and a rebellious, stubborn streak make me cream. If you're too self-absorbed to think you're not self-absorbed, we must meet for an evening of empty, meaningless sex.*"

"I'm telling you, Fordham, it sounds like she was dating Gil."

Fordham shushed her and read the next part. "*Also, make sure you have an array of cute mannerisms and catchphrases for when we meet. I am totally shallow and get sucked in by inane bullshit all the time. Please, please call now. Begging is one of my specialties.*

"PS. Anyone who responds to this is either sicker than I am or has one hell of a sense of humor. Since I can never tell the difference, let's talk!"

"Pretty funny," Evie said. "Is there more?"

"A little." Fordham went back to the page to read the conclusion. "Man, was I shocked when Pierre, a normal, wonderful Parisian living in Paramus, New Jersey, contacted me. He said I had the funniest, most sincere profile he had ever read. We met almost a year ago and have been together ever since. Last night, he proposed! There really is a lid for every pot. My story needs to be shared."

"That was great," Evie said. "But be honest. Did you write it?"

"No, of course not," Fordham said. "I wouldn't do that, and besides, I don't know any men from Paramus."

"It really does sound like this woman had a relationship with Gil."

"Who knows, and who cares? She belongs to Pierre now. Anyway, I have to go back to my big push on the submissions. Have fun at the concert."

Fordham returned to her pile of papers. They were stacked by age group, and the pile for the over-forty set was substantially thicker than the others. She continued to read the submissions, and once again, the over-forty pile grew. It seemed the book was trying to tell her there needed to be a shift in direction. She would have to discuss it with Abe.

She let Whitty stay on the couch and covered her with an extra blanket. As Fordham headed to her room, she shut down her phone.

Chapter Ten: The Draw-Blank Redemption

Fordham was tired—crazy, wicked tired. A row of empty coffee cups lined her desk like trophies on a mantel. And if anyone asked about the dark rings under her eyes, she planned to say it was a new MAC shadow in asphalt gray. *Call me a trendsetter.* It was a little before eight, and she had already been at the office for two hours. She polished off her fifth cup of coffee and read over yet another submission. Somehow, they were reproducing spontaneously, and most of them still weren't worth her time. She was happy to hear a distracting noise.

"Hello." Abe was holding a briefcase and a bag of bagels.

"Morning!" Fordham said, meeting him in the hallway and grabbing the bag out of his hand as she followed him into his office.

"What are you doing here at this hour?" Abe raised his eyebrows as Fordham dunked a salt bagel into her coffee as if it was a doughnut.

"My brain keeps asking me the same thing. Maybe it was the stormy weather, but I got so many submissions over the weekend that my inbox is rejecting new mail." She laughed at her double entendre.

Abe flinched.

"Sorry. It was a crazy weekend," she added quickly.

"Sounds like it. But not my business. Fordham, I have to tell you something you're not going to like very much."

"L'Oréal stopped making Voluminous in Very Black?"

"The date has been moved up."

"What date? I told Evie, and I'll tell you: no more dates!"

"The book. It has to be finished by Valentine's Day or—"

"Or what?" She ripped off a piece of her bagel. If it weren't mid-September, she would have guessed it was April Fool's Day and this joke was on her.

And Margo had whined about a summer completion date being tight. Close to a year was the norm for editors to compile information, compose, edit, and decide on layout and cover. Fordham was near tears. "Don't tell me. I don't want to hear it. I have no idea how I'm going to give this any more of myself than I've been giving it, Abe."

"Fordham, you can do this. You'll eat, sleep, and breathe submissions. Work in the bathroom if you have to. You're very talented, and this is just the thing to get you out of your comfort zone."

"Abe, *out of my comfort zone* is ordering ziti for lunch instead of a garden salad."

"Do you think I would've given you this project if I weren't one-hundred-fifty-percent sure you could do it?"

"Yes, especially after everyone else said no."

"False. Stop being so negative." He moved around some papers on his desk. "Really, Fordham, do you think I'm some kind of an idiot?"

"How truthful do you want me to be?" she said with a smirk.

"Funny. I'd like to say you get your sarcasm from me, but I can't take credit. Listen to me. You are a smart, sensitive woman with a good head on your shoulders—just the kind of person I need for this project. You've been wading in the shallow end of the water for too long. It's time to jump in and swim." Abe handed her a bunch of files containing cover designs for upcoming books in the series.

A memory distracted her as she riffled through the papers. *Swim, honey. Come on, Fordie, you can do it. Come swim to Daddy.*

She'd been five, almost six, when they went to the Nevele Grand Hotel in the Catskills to celebrate her parents' anniversary. She spent most of the time in the camp program they ran for guests, but when it was swim time, she refused to participate. She didn't hate the pool, but there was something about it that scared her. The bottom was too far away, and she feared her feet wouldn't be able to stay firmly planted. If she wasn't careful, the weight of the water would carry her off or swallow her whole.

She didn't mind sitting on the steps, but that was as far as she was willing to go. Her father, who had won medals for his high school swim team, refused to watch his daughter sit on the sidelines. He spent hours with her from morning to night, teaching her different strokes, carrying her in his arms at different depths, getting her used to the feel of the water in a tube she called Myrtle the Turtle. Dorie didn't mind. She brought her crossword puzzles and occasionally would get in the pool, too, but most of the time, she seemed content to just watch.

By the end of the week, Fordham could swim without a tube, and not just to Arnie but to the other end of the pool as well. Finally, she could go to camp and stay for swim time. Everyone would be so surprised and impressed. But Arnie got some phone call, and their vacation was cut short. Dorie wasn't sure why. Arnie, a professor, said it was something about a program he was running at the college. He was apologetic and told Fordham he would take her swimming when they got home. But by then, his mood had shifted, and Fordham's glory in conquering the water had turned to mud.

"Fordham, you can go," Abe said, shuffling a stack of papers in his hand.

Fordham, still deep in memories, ignored his cue.

"What?" he asked, sounding guilty. "Something else is bothering you. You're crinkling your nose and furrowing your brow. It's subtle, but it's there."

"No, nothing. Something you said reminded me of a guy I used to know," she said, finishing the last of the bagel.

"Considering how many guys you've known, I hope he was one of the more interesting ones."

"He was," she said wistfully.

"Good. Then get back to work. Myra and I are leaving early. You know, that cockamamie conference to get me to do something I'm not interested in doing."

This time, Abe handed her an everything bagel—a subtle doughy reminder of what was at stake. She wanted to grab it like a gauntlet, but she was still stuck sitting on the steps of the pool.

Fordham stood in front of Abe's office and watched him strut down the hall, focused and confident. This was a man who would happily boast that no one could describe him as enigmatic. He knew who he was and was comfortable with what he believed he could and couldn't expect from himself and others. He always shot from the hip, so like it or not, everyone always knew where they stood.

She mindlessly gobbled an oversized piece of the bagel as she watched Abe disappear into the lounge and winced in guilt when she imagined how life might have been if he'd been her father instead of Arnie. Dragging herself through the muck of her disappointments was unproductive, but she couldn't control the impulse to keep doing it. Her cheeks flushed with a familiar suppressed rage. Somehow, her father had managed to be two different men, and her mother had been so enamored by one that she'd remained oblivious to the other.

Fordham wished she could be distracted by some gorgeous male model who was in town for a photo shoot. She was a grown woman. It was time to let go of the draining issues of her past and move on. But she couldn't. Perhaps there was some unwritten law that said that as long as she had to struggle in her professional life, her personal life was fair game as well.

To calm down, Fordham tried the *ujjayi* breathing technique she'd learned from a yoga app. She returned to her office a few minutes later, feeling recharged and ready to tackle whatever the day had in store. But there were some things that didn't include.

Margo had called, at least according to a neon-pink sticky note affixed earlier to her computer screen by Myra. She was "hunting for a wedding dress, darling" and would love Fordham's opinion on a few she'd picked out. Fordham tossed the memo in the trash can. The idea that Margo wanted her input was ridiculous. The woman never appreciated her fashion sense. Her favorite observation had been, "Darling, you don't always have to blend in with the office décor. Everyone already knows you belong here."

Maybe this was her passive-aggressive idea of an apology. Fordham wanted no part in dispensing advice. But the vision of Margo's flamboyance translated into a wedding gown was too tempting to let slide. Fordham would love to see her friend saunter down the aisle in a big, poofy nightmare that would live on in cocktail party conversation for years to come. No, she wouldn't really let that happen... but she might... no, of course she wouldn't.

As she debated with herself, Fordham perused her inbox. And there it was, tucked in among more no-doubt useless submissions: Margo's email with attachments. She clicked on it.

On the screen were four of the most stunning, tasteful wedding dresses she had ever seen. Margo had not only managed to find a husband, but she had also found the perfect look to celebrate the event. Fordham sighed at her own immature jealousy. She wasn't angry with Margo for dumping the project in her lap—she was angry with her for finding love when all Fordham could find was an endless run of first-and-last dates.

Grow up, she told herself and sent Margo an email congratulating her on the selections and assuring her that any of them would be spectacular even with baby weight. Since *spectacular* was not a word Fordham would ever use lightly, Margo would feel particularly complimented, and Fordham's guilt would be assuaged.

She checked the new submissions. Only one was promising, but after checking her phone, she decided to review it later. There was a text from Whitty, reminding her that Dorie had an appointment and couldn't pick her up from school after poetry workshop. Fordham knew that if she reflected on it long enough, she would hate how much she depended on her ten-year-old to take care of herself. She settled on the notion that self-reliance was an admirable trait and that Whitty was lucky to be indoctrinated early.

By two o'clock, Fordham realized that she had been reviewing the same submission for hours. And it wasn't even one she could use. She got up for her version of a seventh-inning stretch and went to the lounge. It was empty. *Right. Abe and Myra left early to go to the conference about social networking in the workplace. Like anyone could convince Abe to create a profile on Facebook.* Not long ago, Abe had said, over a corned-beef sandwich, "Anyone I know, I choose to know. Anyone I don't, there's probably a good reason."

Back in her office, she realized working was futile. All she could think about was Margo walking down the aisle in each dress and how pathetic she was for feeling envious. Fordham's heart palpitated, and she hoped this wasn't the time a higher power was judging her thoughts. She pulled out her compact to see what she needed to adjust—besides her attitude—before showing her face to the world again. There was nothing that couldn't wait, save a few flecks of dried mascara pooling in the corners of her eyes. She put on her coat and left to run errands.

The crisp air was refreshing. Maybe it wasn't really jealousy. Maybe she was concerned for Margo's welfare. After all, Margo was a bit old to be changing her life and her body so dramatically. No. That wasn't it. Jealousy was a closer match. But maybe it was even worse and she was afraid. What if she was destined to meet one loser after another until liver spots and saggy knees forced her to pick one? She didn't want to be alone forever. And she would never want Whitty to feel as though she had to take care of her. Being dependent was something Dorie had to deal with because she'd trusted the wrong man. That mistake was a learning tool, not a legacy.

She opened her bag and consulted her phone. The rest of the day loomed large. She had to get Whitty at school, pick up her dry cleaning, reschedule her hair appointment, get an oil change, return books to the library, call Evie back, shovel down some dinner, and knock out a working outline before bed. Staring at the list was even more depressing than usual. *Work and errands.* The bacon drippings tossed in a gumbo at the Suburban Diner was having more fun than she was.

Fordham watched a few couples walking arm in arm down the street as she approached her parking garage, and she wondered if she should ask Evie to set her up on another date. She needed a better diversion than an evening of pairing orphan socks—preferably, a diversion that would honor the fact that she used a depilatory religiously.

It was probably a bad idea. There was no room in her schedule for the endless conversations she'd want to indulge in to describe just how disappointing a date could be. Her timing was off.

She handed the parking attendant a tip and got into her car. After an easy ride home, with a bout of local traffic on Route 59, she stopped off at a drive-through for a self-soothing latte and a doughnut. With more cars in the line than expected, she was running late by the time she was on the road again. *Rushing. Always rushing.* She despised days like this, when all she wanted to do was stuff her face and cry. She had to get in a better mood, if for no other reason than to not bring Whitty down with her.

Fordham got to the school earlier than she expected and parked in the first spot of what experience taught her would be a long line of cars waiting to pick up kids. She considered taking a picture of the parked car to show Whitty she was a good mom, but she decided to instead use the time to check herself out in the visor mirror and was surprisingly pleased. She had done a good job of touching up her foundation. And even though she'd gotten no sleep, her cheeks still had a peachy glow. She was pushing the mirror back in place when she noticed that she was wearing the same earrings she'd worn to the wedding. They were too pretty to return. She giggled, thinking back on her encounter with David Prince.

With time to spare, she checked her phone. No new messages, just more submissions. She read one about a woman from Norwalk who was stationed in Iraq and had met her Norwegian husband in an online class run through the University of Connecticut.

The story was so engrossing that she jumped at the tapping on her window. David, oozing sexiness in a black silk T-shirt under a pewter sports jacket, was mouthing an apology.

"Don't be silly," Fordham said, opening her window. "I'm the one who's sorry. I'm working on a project, and I guess I... um... how late am I?"

Fordham could swear her heart was racing, and not because she feared she was late. She wondered if any of the other mothers found Dr. Prince uncomfortably distracting.

"Not to worry. You're actually a little early. We had a fire drill that screwed up our schedule. Whitty had to get her books, so I told her I'd wait for you. She's a great kid. Funny too. We've been analyzing nursery rhymes."

"That sounds like fun. Personally, I've always wondered why the old woman lived in a shoe, when clearly she would have had more room in the box."

"Oh, so Whitty gets her charming wit from you."

"Don't tell her that. She thinks I have no sense of humor."

"Kids." David chuckled. "They know everything except what they don't know."

"I like that," she said just as her daughter showed up. David helped Whitty get in the car.

"Thanks, Dr. Prince." Whitty was glowing. It was obvious she couldn't be happier to see Fordham and her principal together.

"You are quite welcome, Whitty." He closed the passenger door. "By the way, Fordham, I like those earrings."

"EVIE, I'M ALMOST POSITIVE he was flirting with me. He has a girlfriend, and he's flirting with me." Fordham's phone was propped against her ear as she straightened up her room before tackling more submissions. Sure, she was flattered, but if he was taken, this was a tease she could do without.

"Maybe she's not his girlfriend." Evie sounded frustrated.

"No, she is. They were together. At a bar mitzvah."

"So? You were at a wedding with Paul. What's the difference?"

"Between the flowers and the band, about twenty thousand dollars."

"Seriously, Fordham. Are you and Paul a couple?"

"No. Not even in an alternate universe."

"Then I rest my case," Evie said.

"Fine. I'll take your assertions under advisement."

Chapter Eleven: Mothering Heights

Fordham was reading her prized submission when Dorie burst into her room, angst ridden about not being able to find brown sugar. "Fordham, if this is a senior moment, I swear, shoot me, because I know I just used it to make the baked apples."

Fordham could understand her mother's panic. Gloria was going to be in town the next day for a funeral and planned to come for brunch when it was over. She'd asked for Dorie's famous cinnamon rolls. It was an easy request—Dorie could make them in her sleep. But Fordham's mother always wanted everything to be just so when Gloria came to visit.

Of course she did. While Gloria was leading a charmed life—traveling, designing her home to optimize the feng shui, and planning dinner parties with Ina Garten and her Hampton friends—Dorie was running to get Whitty from school, finding throw pillows to make her room cozier, and scanning flyers for the best deals on brisket. Except for their stories about the very old days, their lives had gone in opposite directions, and Dorie acted as though there would be consequences if she were the one to disrupt her friend's glorious karma, no matter how small the infraction. If she had known Margo forever, Fordham would have been in the same boat as Dorie. Luckily, they didn't have the inconvenient bond of childhood to dissuade her from still wanting to wring Margo's neck.

Fordham followed Dorie into the kitchen. "I forgot, Whitty and I used the last of the sugar for the oatmeal cookies. You're not having a senior moment this time. Guess I'll have to find another reason to shoot you."

"Why didn't you say anything?"

"Mom, it's sugar. I wasn't thinking FEMA had to be notified to intervene. If having Gloria over is making you so anxious, why are you bothering?" Suddenly craving oatmeal, Fordham took out a saucepan.

"Just because I like to know what's in the pantry doesn't mean I'm anxious. But the truth is, she hasn't visited me here since your father passed away, and I guess I don't want her to think that I forgot how to entertain."

"She's just a person, Mom—dripping in Gucci and the Harry Winston collection but still just a person."

Fordham poked around the fridge and was tempted to use whole milk for her cereal, but a disapproving internal voice had her choose the twenty-five-calorie cashew milk instead. "You're right. And Gloria's wealth doesn't impress me. Her luck, on the other hand—*that* impresses me. Speaking of which, you should talk to her about using her story for your book."

It certainly was a decent idea, and Fordham was a little annoyed she hadn't thought of it herself. Gloria's dating success wasn't typical. Single women over forty usually had a tacit obligation to go out with a myriad of losers whose excuses could range from, "My mom told me my ex wasn't good enough for me" to "It's just herpes—it's not like I'm balding or anything." A woman would know this going in and make the proper adjustments. If she had no clue what he looked like, she might decide to set up two consecutive dates with two different men. If she questioned the age of a man's most recent photo, she might come to the date armed with a story about a surprise visit from her aunt or a simple, "I'm sorry, but I can't stay very long."

Whatever the case, most older single women were prepared to suffer the indignity and humiliation of trying to find an emotionally available man who was ready to commit and whose looks didn't induce vomiting. But not so for Gloria.

Fordham stood at the stove, stirring the cereal. Like a lot of men she'd met, quick rolled oats promised instant gratification but delivered only when they were good and ready. After getting divorced, remarried, and widowed, all within a short period of time, Gloria had insisted three years back that she was not interested in marrying again. She'd get invitations, but she was too youthful to be trapped in a house in Miami tending to some guy's overactive prostate or red-hot gallbladder. But her daughter had other ideas and secretly posted Gloria's picture and profile on different dating sites. Fordham had to laugh. If she ever did that to Dorie, she'd have to join the witness-protection program.

Enter Bill Finkelbaum, once a poor kid from Brooklyn who cut school to hustle in pool halls, now an entrepreneur who'd made his way from behind the eight ball to craft and manufacture pool tables and accessories. Bill had millions, and when he found Gloria on Jew-WannaWed.com, he was immediately smitten.

Gloria's daughter arranged the meeting, and Bill did his part to make the encounter seem like a happy coincidence. After one night of jazz, martinis, dancing, and osso buco, the two were an item. He presented the ring on the sixth date, and by the time he and Gloria said their vows, she'd ordered new window treatments for all twenty rooms of their cozy love nest. To top it all off, she was genuinely crazy about the guy.

Although Dorie insisted she wasn't ready to date, she loved telling Fordham every detail about Gloria's fairy-tale romance. Fordham wondered if her mother secretly yearned for someone to care about again. If she hadn't been so busy worrying about her own life, Fordham might have picked up on a clue here and there about her mother's state of mind. She certainly had to admire Gloria's daughter's ingenuity.

Fordham couldn't imagine how Gloria managed to manufacture all that lucky energy. She wasn't jealous—she was fascinated. If there really was an answer, she too needed to know how to attract a healthy relationship. Gloria's missteps were no better or worse than hers or Dorie's, yet she was able to unleash the magic of lessons learned to find meaning, happiness, and of course, a skilled commodities broker.

"Mom, relax. I promised Whitty I'd take her to the library to get a biography for her report. I suggested Hillary Clinton. She said Hilary Duff. We settled on Derek Jeter. Don't ask. But I can pick up the sugar on our way back, okay?"

"Thank you, sweetheart. That would be a big help," Dorie said, taking out a mop and a bucket.

AFTER HER USUAL TOSSING and turning for most of the night, Fordham was exhausted when she woke up. She got out of bed reluctantly. It was Saturday, and she toyed with the idea of staying in her sweats and watching movies instead of visiting with Gloria and going over the latest batch of submissions. As she lumbered into the bathroom, she caught a deep whiff of the fresh coffee with a hint of vanilla and the warm, sugary cinnamon rolls. That was all she needed to convince herself to stick to her original plan.

She dragged her tired body into the kitchen to get a jump start on the coffee and gasped. Dorie had designed a tablescape that even a pro couldn't pull off. She'd spread a purple-and-sage tablecloth with matching napkins and gold runners and set out bone china dishes and Swarovski-crystal goblets that Fordham hadn't seen since she and Gil had thrown their first and only formal dinner party. Platters and bowls were filled with exotic dips, salads, and spreads that had nothing in common with Fordham's usual breakfast of V8 and an energy bar. Everything looked opulent and grand, as if Dorie were celebrating a holiday that no one had ever heard of.

Fordham's initial impulse was to ask Dorie if she had lost her mind, but then she realized this was something her mother had to do. It was her Flowers from the Heart, with just as much ego at stake. Fordham gave her a kiss on the cheek and told her she'd done an amazing job and that Gloria was lucky to be her friend.

The doorbell rang shortly before one o'clock. Dorie went to answer it, beautiful as ever in a cream-colored three-piece outfit that clung in all the right places and showcased her hazel eyes. Fordham stood off to the side, waiting for the rest of the fashion show. The door opened, and there was Gloria, looking as though she stepped off the pages of *Vogue*. She wore a black double-breasted pantsuit with subtle metallic stitching that for most would have said *inappropriate* but for Gloria said *cemetery chic*. Her hat matched her suit, and her shoes were probably shocked that she had the audacity to subject them to any surface but marble.

Fordham was happy to see Gloria. Sometimes, she could be a bit much, but they always got along, and Fordham knew it would be nice for her mother to spend time with someone who also loved doo-wop music and actually knew what a New York egg cream tasted like.

After hugs and hellos, Dorie and Gloria strolled arm in arm into the kitchen, cackling like a pair of schoolgirls. Fordham was glad that the two of them were managing to maintain the status quo despite Dorie's initial meltdown. Dorie's initial concerns were wasted on Gloria, who ran straight to the fridge after dribbling buttery cinnamon down her jacket, snatched a bottle of seltzer, and cleaned it before anyone could get up and make her feel like a guest. It wasn't typical of Dorie to relinquish that kind of control, but in this case, she seemed relieved.

Brunch was delicious, and Gloria marveled appropriately at Dorie's skills as chef and hostess, saying she'd have to tell Ina about the cinnamon rolls and arrange a time for them all to meet. Fordham and Whitty were about to leave the table when Dorie got a call from her cousin that she had to take. She apologized for the interruption and asked Fordham and Whitty to stay a bit longer to keep Gloria company until she got off the phone.

"It seems Dorie and I were doing all the talking," Gloria said, helping herself to another gooey roll. "What's been going on with you girls?"

"Not so much." Whitty had no problem being the first to chime in. "I'm still waiting to get my period."

Fordham was taken aback. She'd had no clue that was even on Whitty's mind.

"Don't rush it," Gloria said. "Tampax is making plenty of money without your help."

Judging by the diamonds around her neck, Fordham figured Gloria knew that financial information firsthand.

"And you, Fordham?"

"She has a crush on my principal," Whitty sang.

"What?" Fordham shouted, feeling her cheeks flush. "I do not!"

Gloria nodded in each of their directions, an amused expression on her face. She remained silent as if waiting to see what would happen next.

"She does." Whitty nodded directly at Gloria. "Whenever they're together, Mom gets all hair tossy, and she giggles way more than she does in real life."

Fordham was floored. Aside from having always thought of herself as an equal-opportunity giggler, she was unnerved that Whitty had called her out on what she'd hoped was a well-hidden secret. She wasn't sure how to respond. If she protested too much, she'd be lying, but if she agreed, she'd be indulging Whitty's fantasy—and her own.

"There are worse things in life than finding a man attractive," Gloria offered, trying to bridge the sudden divide.

"Of course," Fordham said, taking a deliberately slow sip of coffee. "And just because you think a guy is cute doesn't mean you like him romantically."

"Sure, but that's not what happens in all the lame movies you watch." Whitty wiped her hands on a napkin.

"I like those kind of movies," Gloria said enthusiastically.

Whitty got up and kissed Fordham on the cheek. "Sorry for embarrassing you, Mom. I have homework to do."

Fordham was about to respond, but Whitty left as Dorie came back, and the moment was lost. Dorie immediately got Gloria involved in a conversation about some mutual friend who'd become a nun and joined a convent. If she weren't a confirmed Jew, Fordham might have happily considered that vocation.

BACK IN HER ROOM, FORDHAM tried working, but more often than not, her thoughts were diverted to Whitty's claim about her crush on Dr. Prince. If Whitty was right, and she was sending those vibes out into the world, she could only imagine what he must think of her. She shuddered, but the sound of laughter from the kitchen caught her attention and drew her out of her worries.

She went to stand in the hall by the kitchen to hear what had was making her mother cackle. No matter how well-adjusted Dorie seemed, it was obvious she missed her old life. She missed Arnie. Fordham could hear it in the lilt of her voice whenever she said his name. To Dorie, he would always be her knight in shining armor, no matter what he had done to dull and corrode the finish. And Gloria, the most outspoken person on the planet, said that Dorie was lucky to have had a man so crazy in love with her that he forgot about everything else just to try to make her happy.

Fordham wondered if she was the crazy one to think her father's reckless abandonment had more dire consequences. Dorie couldn't pay her bills or have a roof over her head by simply holding onto the memory of love. But Fordham had already said her piece more than once, and it was time to make her peace with her mother's choices. Nothing was going to change the past. Luckily, she was managing, and she would have to respect her mother's feelings even though she couldn't understand them.

It was almost dinnertime when Gloria said she had to get going. Dorie had tears in her eyes as she hugged her friend. Gloria's life typically kept her too busy for visits, and even though Skype was better than nothing, it wasn't the same. But this time, Gloria promised she would find a way to be around more often. She said it was her place to help Dorie move on, not by helping her forget Arnie but by encouraging her to keep her heart open to possibilities. As she was leaving, Gloria told Dorie, in her most convincing fairy-godmother voice, that she had a feeling life was going to surprise the Price women in wonderful ways. Dorie watched as Gloria's Mercedes pulled out of the driveway.

"Truly lucky people, like Gloria, count their blessings and make a point of being optimistic," Dorie said, closing the door and patting Fordham on the back. "Most people I know are shallow and negative, and they take their good fortune for granted. Not everyone can turn the world on with a smile like Mary Tyler Moore. Most just grin and bitterly bear it, like many of the women in my group, whose names I will not mention. They have nothing better to do than worry about the off chance that Villeroy and Boch will discontinue their china patterns. I'm telling you, Fordham, most people have no inclination to wish others well." And with that, Dorie headed for her room and closed the door.

Fordham knew Dorie was talking about the women in the Y Group, an overly Botox-enhanced crew of self-proclaimed do-gooders who would sooner stick their necks out for a chemical peel than to do anyone a favor. Shallow as the day is long, these women had never considered burning their bras or marching to promote anything but gel manicures and fake eyelashes. The few times Fordham had been around when Dorie was hosting a meeting, she could feel their beady myopic eyes scrutinizing her jeans and balking at her Nice 'N Easy ponytail. For them, a day wasn't complete if they didn't find time to swap gossip and antidepressants. This group wasn't Dorie's cup of tea, but on the rare occasion that she bought a new outfit, it was a good place to go for feedback.

Fordham wished her mother had a friend like Gloria to share her day-to-day life with—someone like her Evie, who really understood everything she'd been through. None of these women could ever know her the way Gloria did. They'd never known her when she was in love. They never knew her on her wedding day when she stood with Arnie in front of the rabbi, hoping no one would notice her tiny baby bump. They didn't know her when Arnie surprised her with a new house and a private tutor so she could finish her degree without having to leave her newborn. They hadn't been around when she and Arnie went through three miscarriages after Fordham was born followed by the hysterectomy that would end their dream of having a big family.

No, they could never know *that* Dorie. They only knew the present-day Dorie with the cautious heart—the one who lived with her daughter, clipped coupons, hid her disappointment in online Scrabble games, and never spoke about men or dating. The cold, hard fact was that Dorie, who had once been a vibrant, sexy woman, was nearing extinction and was being replaced by a practical, systematic automaton. And if that was where her mother was headed, Fordham had a lot to consider about her own lot in life.

Several hours later, well after Dorie and Whitty had gone to bed and Fordham had confronted a few demons, she was thinking that a big bag of popcorn and a Diet Coke with lime had made an adequate dinner, especially when she'd indulged in such a decadent brunch. She even left her funky mood long enough to find a few more good submissions for the book. They might not be perfect, but they were good enough.

She glanced at the wall next to her bed and mumbled a little mantra: "Dreams can come true if you believe." She had laminated and hung a copy of her prized submission right next to her pillow and routinely read it, determined to keep her heart open. She hadn't had the time or the nerve before, but now she decided to do it. She would to call her friend in legal and find out who had written *her* submission.

Chapter Twelve: On the Daughter Front

Halloween. A sneezing fit had Fordham searching for a tissue as a metallic rust Rogue zipped into her lane. Then a blue Civic had the same idea. They were all out that day. Maybe there'd be a full moon later to celebrate.

"I'm too old to get dressed up like a stupid bride or something," Whitty had complained the day before, "and what am I supposed to do with a bunch of lollipops and vampire teeth?" She'd been saying for weeks that she had no interest in trick-or-treating.

A stupid bride. Fordham wondered if that was a slam. Regardless, she was unconvinced and had told Whitty she would come home from work early in case she changed her mind and decided to go. After a curt "Suit yourself," Whitty had gone back to her homework.

Ten-year-olds are coming in sassy models these days.

Fordham stopped off at a farm stand on her way to work and picked up a couple of decorated pumpkins. If she wanted Whitty to celebrate, it was up to her to provide the inspiration. She'd considered getting her a costume but decided that would be too presumptuous. Instead, she grabbed some cider and caramel apples for the house and for the office too.

The light was on when she got to work. Abe greeted her. "You trying to catch the worm again?" he said, checking his watch.

"I have to leave early—Halloween. I promised Whitty I'd be home to persuade her to go trick-or-treating."

"Persuade her? Why? She doesn't find going door-to-door and begging for a sugar coma fulfilling? Tell her I applaud her good sense."

"I just want her to be more of a kid. I think she's missing out on a childhood."

"Does she watch too much television?"

"Yes," Fordham said emphatically.

"Does she eat cookies right before dinner?"

"Yes."

"Do her clothes lie in a heap on her bedroom floor, and does she yell at you when you try to wash them?"

Fordham nodded.

"I wouldn't worry," Abe said with a reassuring smile. "She's having a childhood."

"Thanks, Abe. Maybe you're right," Fordham said, handing him the cider.

Adequately reassured, she spent the rest of the day buried in work, except for the call she got back from the legal department about *her* submission. The news was disappointing. The only information she could get out of anyone was that it had come from the Pacific Northwest, which meant the odds of her meeting him would be somewhat improved if she were an Eskimo.

Maybe she'd try a different route, but for the moment, she was ready to call it a day. With a couple of dozen submissions in her Accept file, for the first time in weeks, she was actually making progress.

COME THREE O'CLOCK, she rushed out the door and got into the elevator just in time to meet a masked and costumed group of politicians, mass murderers, and belly dancers. There was a big party on the eighth floor at the temp-agency office, and both Donald Trump and Freddy Krueger asked her to join them for a drink. She declined politely, but one of the belly dancers, who didn't seem too thrilled with Trump, slapped his misguided hand away from her rear end. As Fordham was getting off at the ground floor, someone asked who she was supposed to be.

She answered, "A public relations manager, but they handed me this editor's suit instead."

Luckily, traffic was light, and Fordham got to the door just as Dorie was handing out peanut butter cups to a group of smiling bunnies and chicks accompanied by Old MacDonald. Whitty was lying on the couch, watching television, and even when Fordham showed her the pumpkins, she didn't budge.

"Cute," she said and went back to watching the Halloween episode of *Chopped Junior*.

Fordham was pleased that Whitty was at least celebrating in her own way. Dorie came in, frazzled, holding a giant empty bowl. She offered a quick hello just as the phone and doorbell rang in unison.

"Fordham, please get that. I have to take this call." Dorie went to the kitchen, leaving Fordham searching for treats. The bell rang again.

"Okay, coming! Just a minute." Fordham opened the door to find David Prince standing next to a little girl dressed as a witch. "Dr. Prince?"

She tried to hide her elation. The man didn't seem to have the capacity to look anything but gorgeous and smell anything but sexy.

"*David*, please. And this is my daughter, Lily."

The insistence on her using his first name seemed like an invitation to take their relationship to the next level. Fordham could feel her palms begin to sweat.

Fordham shook the little girl's hand. "It's very nice to meet you, Lily. Dr. Prince, do you live around here?"

"David," he said warmly. "Not far. Is Whitty out collecting loot?"

"No, she's being a pumpkin pooper."

Whitty muted the TV and headed toward the door.

"Ah, here comes the Scrooge of the jack-o'-lanterns. Whitty, look who's here."

Whitty offered a small wave. "Hi, Dr. Prince. Hi, Lily. I love your costume."

"Where are my manners? I'm sorry. Please... come in." Fordham didn't know what to make of David's surprise appearance, especially without Pam glued to his side. *Maybe she's out trick-or-treating with friends.* She led them into the den and fished out packages of candy from a nearby shopping bag.

Lily's eyes lit up. "Thank you," she said in a tiny voice when Whitty handed her a candy bar.

The girl poked David with her broom, motioning that she wanted to tell him a secret. He bent down and Lily tugged at the back of his hair to whisper in his ear. He nodded and stood up.

"Whitty, Lily wants to know if you'd like to go trick-or-treating, and I'd be happy to have you join us... if it's okay with your mom."

"What a nice invitation," Fordham said enthusiastically. "Whitty?"

"I don't have a costume," Whitty said, seeming disappointed.

"Really? You'd go?" Fordham exclaimed. "Don't worry. We'll figure something out."

"I have an idea." Whitty got up from the couch, laboring to walk more quickly than usual toward Fordham's room. "Mom, come on—your closet."

Fordham was about to follow Whitty when Dorie walked into the room. "Mom, Whitty said she'll go trick-or-treating!"

"Well, isn't that nice!" Dorie said. "Good to see you again, Dr. Prince."

"Again?" Fordham did an about-face.

"We met briefly at the library board meeting," Dorie said, taking a seat.

"Oh, well, that's nice," Fordham said. "You'll have to excuse me. I'm not sure what Whitty is coming up with."

She found Whitty in her closet but was distracted by the on-going conversation between Dorie and David, which she could still hear.

"You had some great ideas, Dorie. As a matter of fact, we're going to start the Scrabble Club after the holidays. And please, call me David."

"Thank you, David. Glad I could help.

"So, David, how do you like being the principal at Crestwood?"

"Well, it's never easy stepping into popular shoes, but I think it's been going pretty well."

"Absolutely. I've heard only good things about you. But no one expected Lenore Hudson to retire. I think she was as surprised as anyone to get a husband for her sixtieth birthday."

"Lives often change in the name of love," David said.

"Are you married?" Dorie asked as if on cue.

Fordham didn't understand why her mother needed to interrogate every attractive man who crossed their doorstep. Whitty went to the bathroom, and Fordham thought about interrupting her mother, but she didn't want to be a buzzkill. Anyway, it wasn't that big a deal. Everyone expected mothers to be inappropriately overinvolved in the lives of their children.

"I was—twice," David said.

"I lost my husband almost a year ago. It certainly isn't easy."

"No, I'm sorry, it certainly isn't."

Fordham returned to the matter at hand, finding the material to turn Whitty into a witch. An old black nightgown that had once been intended for an amorous evening was sitting in a Macy's bag with the tags still attached, and a black felt hat that she and Gil had bought at the 1994 Dutchess County Fair was begging to be used for something other than collecting dust. *Perfect.*

"Whitty, why did you decide to go tonight?"

"I don't know. I like Lily. She's cute. You'll be busy tonight, anyway."

"How do you know?"

"You'll either have a stupid date or be working on your book."

"Ouch. Guess I deserved that."

"I understand about the book. But let's face it—the guys you go out with are pretty basic. The good news is, you only need three dating outfits. No one ever gets to see four."

"And this is my fault how?"

"I'm not blaming you." Whitty took a black eyeliner out of Fordham's makeup bag, faced the mirror, and began drawing wrinkles on her cheeks. "It's just... remember when I was little and you used to read me *The Three Bears* every night?"

"Yeah?" Fordham was baffled.

"Well, sometimes I feel like the baby bear. Mom-Mom is like the mama bear, and you're kind of like Goldilocks. You keep trying to find something that's just right. But there's still no papa bear." Whitty faced Fordham with a look of concern. "Mom, I hate to break it to you, but Prince Charming is in a different story. And in that story, *he's* the one that finds the girl."

FORDHAM WAS STRAIGHTENING up the family room, thankful that Whitty was finally out doing something kids were supposed to do, other than criticize their parents. If she hadn't had so much work on her plate she would have loved to tag along, but making this book work was her priority, especially if she wanted job security.

Fordham fluffed the couch pillows and filled both bowls with more candy. Instead of dwelling on what she was missing, she thought about how Whitty was consumed with concern for her dating life. She decided it was high time for her daughter to create the chapters of her own book rather than fairy tales for her relationship-challenged mother. Besides, Fordham wasn't trying to find Prince Charming. Evie was trying to find him for her. That had to be creating different karma.

It wasn't her fault all the men she'd been set up with hadn't been marriage material. The luck of the draw kept her in a three-outfit-maximum dating position. *And maybe that's what's meant to be*, she thought as she walked into her room and glanced over at the submission on the wall.

Thinking about romance was an impractical distraction when she needed the time to work on the book. Dorie screamed a few select curse words, and Fordham gathered that another Scrabble game was underway. Knowing Dorie, there was no chance of this feud ending till she'd beaten her rival, and from the sound of things, the competition could go on indefinitely.

Fordham took out her phone, checked her calendar, and called Abe. She got his machine.

"Hi, Abe, it's Fordham. I forgot to tell you I'm going to be late tomorrow. Doctor's appointment. You're not answering, which means you're either ignoring me or being attacked by trick-or-treaters who did not appreciate your prune-juice boxes. See you around lunchtime."

There was a faint tap on her door. "Fordham, are you napping?"

"Are you kidding? Come on in, Mom. It's open."

"I know if you're not sleeping, you're working. I shouldn't be bothering you with this."

"No, it's okay," Fordham said, seriously needing to come up for air. "What is it?"

The next half hour involved two visits from Dorie. The first was to ascertain whether Fordham knew the word *z-o-u-k*. She said it was a tropical dance. The second was to subject *f-a-r-t-l-e-k* to the same scrutiny. It had something to do with training runners. And yes, Fordham agreed that maybe Dorie's opponent was a plant used to taunt regular players.

An hour after Dorie took a two-point lead on her Scrabble opponent, the doorbell rang, and Fordham found Whitty and Lily standing on the porch, pretending to be too weighed down by their Halloween bags to move. David was behind them, holding their hats.

Standing there all scruffy with five o'clock shadow, he was unnervingly delicious. If she were a different kind of woman, Fordham might have concocted a way to get him to stay for the night, or forever, but that would be weird for Lily. And she wasn't that kind of woman.

They were barely in the house when Lily spotted the cat and went running after her. "Kitty!" she shrieked as her costume got caught on one of the corners of the coffee table and all her candy went flying around the room.

She was just about to cry when Whitty cleverly tripped to pretend the same thing had happened to her. There was candy everywhere, but Lily was still more interested in the cat than anything else. She ran after her with renewed vigor as Whitty tagged closely behind.

Fordham and David scanned the room in disbelief. They were mired in an ocean of candy, snacks, and scary little rubber toys. Neither of them made a move until they both eyed a big Nestlé Crunch bar and went for it at the same time.

"Go ahead—it's yours." David said gallantly.

Fordham refused, having come up with an innocent way for them to touch, if just for a moment. "Rock, paper, scissors?" she challenged, staring into David's eyes. "I like to earn my victories."

They played several rounds until David won fair and square. In what she deemed a naturally selfless gesture, he offered her the candy.

"No, that's okay," Fordham said, making a puffy face. "I'll be happier in the long run if you take it."

"You don't have anything to worry about."

"Thanks. I should probably try to keep it that way."

David broke the bar in half. "Here you go." He held her half up to her mouth.

She took a healthy bite without even considering the calories. "Very diplomatic," she said, finishing her half.

As she and David gathered the rest of the candy mess and tossed it back into the girls' bags, she said, "Thanks for tonight, David. It was nice to see Whitty have fun. She doesn't seem to do that enough." Fordham picked up a wrapper from the floor. "Oh, and thanks for sharing your candy with me."

"The pleasure was all mine." David said.

Fordham was feeling freer to be playful. Maybe Evie was right. David hadn't said a word about Pam the whole time they'd been together. She even caught a glimmer of disappointment in him as he was getting ready to leave.

"By all means, feel free to drop Lily off here anytime," she said.

"Thanks, Fordham. I just might take you up on that." He picked up one of the newly filled Halloween bags. "Come on, Lily, let's go. It's getting late, and we still have to de-witch you."

Lily came into the room, carrying Ella. She held her gently and gave her kisses on her head that the typically skittish kitty seemed to appreciate.

"I love you, Ella," Lily said then turned to Whitty. "And you too."

FORDHAM WALKED OUT to the car with David, said good night, and headed back into the house, where a giant bag of garbage was waiting to be tossed. She went to the side of the house to drop the trash into the pail and watched as David safely secured Lily in the car. In the dark, she knew she was obscured from their view. It was so quiet that she could hear their conversation.

"I like Whitty's mommy. She's pretty," Lily said, "like my Barbie before I cut her hair."

"Yes, she's nice," David answered.

"You don't think she's pretty?"

"Yes, she's pretty."

Fordham's heart skipped a beat. David had said she was pretty.

"As pretty as Mommy Pammy?"

Fordham winced as if Lily's words had pierced her skin.

"Yes, very pretty."

Fordham continued to listen in case there would be more information she needed to know before making a complete fool of herself over David Prince.

"What's wrong with Whitty's leg?"

"Something from when she was in her mommy's belly."

"Will it go away?"

"I don't think so."

"Daddy, can we get a cat like Ella?"

"Lily, honey, you know that Grammy is allergic, and when she visits us, we don't want her to get sick."

"I know, but I really want a cat like Ella."

"Maybe you can go to Whitty's house sometimes and play with her."

"Yay! Daddy, when are we gonna be home? I really, really have to pee!"

Of course, Fordham would have Lily over, but not if Mommy Pammy was going to be any part of the visit.

FORDHAM SPENT MOST of her gynecologist's appointment thinking about what it would be like to have another child. The visit with Lily had reminded her of all the things she enjoyed about motherhood, and the picture Margo had emailed, showing her growing belly, had cemented it. She even went so far as to fantasize about going to a sperm bank and ordering a shot of Brandon. He wasn't father material, but he was stunning.

A sperm bank and in vitro. That was her most realistic option. She wasn't exactly using her equipment these days, and there was nothing quite as sobering as stirrups and latex gloves topped off by a cold probing speculum to serve as a harsh reminder of that. To top it off, it had taken her and Gil years to decide to have a baby and even more years to finally get pregnant. If she was serious about having another child, she would have to do a lot of soul searching.

She needed to get her head out from between her legs. She had too much going on to dwell on her nonexistent sex life or to indulge in dreams about pink dimpled babies. Her appointment was uptown, and if she hurried, she could get back to the office in time to meet with Abe and go over her notes about the length of the submissions. Work would save her from herself.

Fordham took out her phone and was checking her messages as she exited the examination room. When she got to the central waiting area, a door shut, and she automatically looked up. Staring right at her was the last person she had ever expected to see.

Chapter Thirteen: The Good, the Bad, and the Bubbly

"Aaron?"

"Fordham?"

"Wh... uh... what are you doing here?"

"Business..."

Fordham couldn't stop staring at him. He certainly wasn't a lanky kid with a mop of unruly hair anymore. His eyes were a deep, penetrating shade of cocoa. She remembered them as being simply brown. The mustache and goatee were new, too, and gave him a sexy edge that hadn't quite been rooted when he was a kid.

"Don't you live in Florida? In Boca? With your wife? And your ob-gyn shingle?"

"I do, sort of... still..." He lowered his voice, forcing Fordham to stand closer to hear him. "Well, not exactly."

"I promise that wasn't a trick question."

"It's complicated," he said, gazing down at the floor. "And now I'm a fertility specialist. How do you know all this, anyway?"

"Facebook. LinkedIn. Twitter. Evie. We're still close, and she still knows everything about everyone."

"I'll have to keep that in mind," he said, sporting a grin. "Last I heard, through the grapevine, you were married."

"That grapevine is yielding raisins."

"Oh. Sorry. Well, you haven't aged a day since the last time I saw you." He seemed to be deep in reflection. "I remember! You were naked, at Marv's house before he left for college!"

Several people in the waiting room dropped their phones, eyes trained on Fordham and Aaron as if all that was missing were buckets of popcorn. Fordham was uncomfortable enough without strangers peering at her history before she could process it herself. One hugely pregnant woman was staring at them particularly hard.

"Can we talk outside?" Fordham asked, scanning the room.

"Oh, please, stay!" the pregnant woman said, pulling out a candy bar. "I'll give you this!"

Fordham started to walk away.

"Please!" the woman cried, "I could be here till I deliver!"

"YOU LOOK ABSOLUTELY amazing!" Aaron ignored the pigeon crapping on his expensive shoes. "Seriously, when was the last time we were together?"

Fordham didn't hesitate for an instant. "Your house, the morning you left for Spain. I came to say goodbye and to give you back your U2 tape. You kissed me while you were ironing your black Levis with the hole in the right knee."

"But what did I have for breakfast?"

"Pancakes. Your mother whipped up your favorite—blueberry pancakes. A little butter, Log Cabin syrup, and coffee light, two sugars." Uncomfortable, Fordham shifted her head to the side just in time to see a young couple kissing goodbye at the bus stop.

"Wow! You're scarier than turbulence."

"You forgot I have a good memory." Recalling Aaron's breakup letter, Fordham took a few steps away from him.

"You have a machine that should be shared with central intelligence."

"Actually, I forget a lot of important stuff, like where I parked," she said, scanning the crowded street—anything to not focus on how incredible he looked.

"Have lunch with me," he said while pressing her into a familiar hug.

"I can't," she said, pushing him away.

"Can't or won't?"

Fordham found his question curious. Maybe he realized she had good reasons not to have lunch with him.

"I-I don't know, Aaron," she stammered. "I just don't think it's a good idea."

"Come on. It's been a long time." He cupped her chin and lifted her face toward his. "I've missed you."

THEY WERE SEATED AT a small table next to a window overlooking a pretty garden dotted with pink and yellow flowers. Fordham couldn't pronounce the name of the restaurant or anything on the menu except à la carte. She didn't care. They were on their second bottle of champagne, and she couldn't tell the difference between the *foie gras en croute* and Mrs. Weinberg's chopped liver on a Ritz cracker. She focused on a delicate pink flower hanging on a nearby tree when she didn't want Aaron's eyes to meet hers, which worked until a gust of wind swept it off and carried it away. The important thing was to stay safe and keep talking. Silence was the key to true connection. With words on hold, everything said in a look or gesture could undress her heart.

"I liked my job. But then Margo, my old friend, revoked her claim as Manhattan's most confirmed bachelorette, fell in love, and got pregnant. Maybe even in that order. I didn't know I was the designated pinch hitter, but now I have her job. And this book has to sell or"—she took another sip of champagne—"I don't want to think about it."

Champagne always ensured her chattiness. She wondered if Aaron remembered that as he poured her another glass.

"Margo. You're not talking about Margo Flax, are you?"

"Why? You know her? Please don't tell me you're the father!"

"No. But I got her pregnant."

"Um... I'm buzzed and... nope, still makes no sense."

"Come on, take a guess."

"Okay. I like games. Sometimes. Let's see... your profession," she mused. "You're a gyno—no, wait, you're a fertility specialist... and"—her eyes popped wide open—"it was you! You did the deed!"

"I did, and she's doing incredibly well."

"That's wonderful. You ruined my life." She almost said *again* but had the presence of mind not to open that can of wriggling worms. They had been kids when they were a couple, and it was ridiculous to still care about how it had ended. *This is just a catch-up lunch with an old friend,* she kept telling herself.

"Don't be silly, Fordham. You'll do what you need to do. You're tough. Some people fall apart when a marriage ends."

Fordham took a roll from the breadbasket and slathered it in butter. "I couldn't. Too many responsibilities. I have a daughter."

She took a bite of her roll and wondered what he thought about that. She also wondered how much their relationship had meant to him. If it had been up to her, she'd have gone straight from her cap and gown into a wedding dress. They could have honeymooned in Spain, and now she wouldn't have an aversion to paella. But that hadn't happened.

"I'm really sorry about your divorce," Aaron said earnestly.

"Much appreciated. But I was relieved when Gil left. Finally, there was some oxygen for me."

"You're lucky. The last time Denise let me breathe was right before we cut our cake." He cleared his throat. "Anyway, I'm sorry you had to go through all that."

"Well, there's always an upside. I couldn't eat, so my skinny jeans fit, and I even learned how to fix a leaky toilet."

"That's my girl," he said, sending a shiver from the base of her spine right to her swimming head.

"Aaron, are you sure that you and Denise are really over?" Her ego wanted him to say that he and Denise never even had a chance... that after Fordham, he could never love anyone else... that she was more beautiful than ever, and he wanted to try again. Her mind pointed out that he'd crushed her heart and reminded her to be practical. "Maybe counseling could help?"

A server in a tuxedo shirt and tie came over to fill their glasses with sparkling water. Fordham noticed he had the same color eyes as David Prince and coughed a little as if that would purge the thought.

"This marriage has seen more triage than the Red Cross. I'm done."

"Do you have anything in writing?"

Aaron stabbed a cherry tomato so hard it burst, sending a stream of seeds into the air before hitting the tablecloth. He fumbled with his napkin to clean it but gave up and motioned to the server for help. "I haven't signed anything yet, but I decided to give her the power tools for when she's in between contractors. Literally."

"You sound angry."

"I am. Our vows turned from 'I do' to 'I don't.'"

They exchanged a glance, and each took a bite of something without commenting on the food. Fordham barely tasted hers. A busboy came to the aid of the tomato stain with a small spray bottle, and in seconds, there was no trace of the incident. Fordham made a quick mental note to be on the hunt for the infomercial.

"Aaron, this feels strange."

"Why?"

She couldn't say that the smell of his cologne and the sight of his precious dimples were making her more light-headed than the alcohol. *Play tough.* "I don't know. Maybe because even though you said the words, we were both strongly invested in our goodbye."

"We were kids."

"Maybe, but I was the kid who believed she was an adult, and I guess I expected that you were going to pretend to be one too." Fordham gazed out the window, suddenly aware of how many buds were right next to flowers that had already bloomed. She wasn't sure what it meant, but it spoke to her about aligning the past with the present, and that eased her mind.

"I think I did. Remember the time you dragged me to Macy's to window-shop for dishes?"

"I did not drag you. I invited you. And you kept on threatening to use a salad plate as a Frisbee."

"I did not!" he said, smirking.

"And I really enjoyed when customer service blasted, 'Will Aaron Karp's mother please report to the service desk. Your son is looking for you.'"

"Yeah, that was a good one. Guess I couldn't pull off being an adult quite the way you could. But I always hoped I'd see you again." He put his hand on hers.

"And so you have." She pulled her hand away and checked her watch.

"I'd like to do this again," he said, undaunted by the gesture. "Listen, I'm going to be around for a while. I'm staying at the DoubleTree in Tarrytown. I have all kinds of meetings going on, but I would love to get together again." He gently wiped a smudge of chocolate off her lips with his thumb.

Fordham hoped he hadn't felt her tremble. "I don't know." She sighed. "I was pretty comfortable leaving you as a well-worn memory."

"And now?"

"And now, I'm not sure what an adult who feels like a kid is supposed to make of any of this."

"Maybe you should let the kid lead, for a change."

THERE WAS NO WAY SHE could go back to the office. It was late, and her head was still swimming in champagne bubbles. She could spend the rest of the day sitting on the bench near the restaurant. It wouldn't matter. She couldn't concentrate on anything except Aaron. He was all grown up, and the years had been nothing but kind to him. He had no need for a comb-over and a smile not even the dentist Marv Weiner could replicate. And he still smelled great. She used to love when he dowsed himself in Drakkar Noir when they were kids, but now he sported an even sexier, more sophisticated scent. *Burberry maybe?* And best of all, a guy like him—with no rap sheet, unsightly moles, protruding incisors, or training pants—wanted to spend time with her.

She was still uptown and, after nearly tripping over an errant sneaker lying on the street, decided she was too buzzed to drive. She'd splurge and take a Lyft home. That would give her time to relax and process the afternoon. If she got lucky, no one would be around, and she might have the chance to sneak in a much-needed nap. And if she got even luckier, maybe her whole life would simply fall into place. *Fat chance.*

When she arrived home, Dorie was front and center, straightening out the hall closet. "Fordham? What are you doing home so early? Are you feeling okay?"

"I'm not sure if *okay* cuts it."

"What is it? Work? Abe again?"

"Aaron."

"Aaron..." Dorie hesitated and let the name sink in. "Aaron"—a bunch of wire hangers in her hand fell to the floor—"Karp?"

"No, Mom, Aaron the brother of Moses. Of course Aaron Karp." Fordham retrieved the hangers and stuffed them into the garbage bag parked by the closet door.

"I don't know. To me, one is as likely as the other. What about him?" Dorie turned back to the closet and began pushing the clothes on the rod from one side to the other at record speed. After the breakup, when she'd witnessed Fordham's despair, Dorie had said she never wanted to hear Aaron's name uttered in her presence again.

"I saw him," Fordham said nonchalantly. "I was leaving Dr. Ratisher's office, and he was leaving Dr. Dvorkin's office, and we met in the middle of the waiting room."

Dorie, holding a toddler-sized baseball glove, shifted to face Fordham. "He was at the gynecologist's office. Oh my God! Is he a woman now?"

"No, he's not a woman!" Fordham exclaimed. "He's a doctor, a fertility specialist. Get this—he's the one who got Margo pregnant. I said a whopping thank-you to him for that one."

"Isn't he in Florida—with a wife?"

"He was. He's getting divorced. He's up here on business."

"Sounds like a pretty involved conversation for a waiting room." Dorie dropped the glove into a white bag marked For Donation.

"We had lunch."

"Lunch? Is that all you had?"

"Jesus, Mother! Yes, that is all we had."

It might have been all she'd had, but it wasn't necessarily all she'd wanted. Fordham could still smell Aaron's cologne in her mind, and it was hard not to think about how his professional training might have enhanced his lovemaking skills.

"Just remember, Fordham: you can't see a leopard's spots if you close your eyes."

"You used to like Aaron."

"Yes, I used to. Until he hurt you."

"That was ages ago."

"I don't care how long ago it was. A mother can forgive many things over time but not her child's pain. I'd be careful if I were you."

"I get it. I'll be on my toes."

"It's when you'll be on your back that worries me. Fordham, be smart about this. You have Whitty to consider now."

"Mom, I said I'll be careful, and I will be." Fordham gathered clothes for the cleaners from the hamper in the closet while keeping a close watch on Dorie's grimace. She didn't understand why her mother was making such a big deal out of this. So she bumped into an old friend unexpectedly. There was no reason to get so bent out of shape.

Dorie left and came back with a couple of wrinkled shirts to be ironed. "Fordham, you come from a long line of bright women who all had the same problem: we fell hard for the wrong men. I'm not saying that I didn't have a good marriage." Dorie went into the closet on her tiptoes and grabbed the iron off the top shelf, followed by a small folded ironing board. "Your father did his best to give us everything, as you well know."

Fordham's heart was pounding. She didn't want to deal with this now. She was still feeling the effects of the alcohol, and anything she said was liable to come out in a way that would lead to consequences. She swallowed hard and forced herself to keep her mouth shut.

Dorie kept talking as she set up the ironing board. "But as in love with him as I was, I know I would have been better off marrying Seymour Nageldorf."

"Who is Seymour Nageldorf? He sounds like a Jewish lawyer in a Dickens novel."

"Close. The accountant my brother set me up with. He was a very nice man but too bland for my taste."

Fordham didn't remember hearing about an accountant. She wondered what had happened to Seymour Nageldorf, this accountant who could have saved her mother from financial ruin.

"Instead of listening to my mother, who sized Arnie up as a charismatic dreamer and said one day I would pay the price for my Price, I listened to my heart and my hormones."

Dorie stopped ironing and went over to the hanging photo gallery. She paused at a framed picture of Arnie and her sitting at a table, ushering in 1969. "And I married your father anyway. It kills me to say it, but we're all paying for it."

Fordham was shocked by her mother's disclosure. Dorie had finally admitted that Arnie was not some demigod they had to pay homage to on a daily basis. He was just a regular guy whose problems became his family's burden. Fordham knew how difficult it was for her mother to have nothing to call her own except the people she loved. Maybe that was why she was being irrational about the lunch with Aaron. She was probably thinking about what would happen to her if her daughter's life changed.

Fordham wanted to give Dorie an appreciative hug, but the woman would not give her the chance and kept pouring out her thoughts about choices. "I'm not even sure what I'm trying to tell you, sweetheart. I just know that my Grandma Becky, who I absolutely adored, used to say that a hell of a good time was worth a hell of a good lickin'. But, Fordham, it was truly the most ignorant piece of advice she ever gave me." Dorie returned to the ironing board.

"I got it, Mom," Fordham said, placing a hand confidently over the half-wrinkled blouse. "Thanks."

"Do me a favor and finish ironing this for me." Dorie kissed her on the forehead. "I'm beat," she said as she left the room.

Fordham was confused. Her mother could have married an accountant but had ended up penniless because she loved her father. Maybe since Fordham had already been married to the wrong guy, she was due to make a better decision this time around. And no one had uttered a word about marriage, which meant that many of her mother's concerns were ludicrous. Fordham had met Aaron Karp for an innocent lunch that meant nothing more than the chance to resolve things so that this time, she could part with him on a better note. He felt they still had more to discuss and asked for her number before they left the restaurant. She'd given it to him. There was no harm in exploring a more definitive resolution.

A COUPLE OF HOURS LATER, when the champagne buzz finally wore off, Fordham remembered that she'd left her car in the city. Luckily, Dorie hadn't picked up on her daughter's touch of inebriation and was too engrossed in a Scrabble game to question why Fordham asked to use her car to get Whitty. Fordham resolved that she would quietly walk to the bus stop in the morning and never mention that she had gotten too drunk to drive home. It seemed ridiculous to have to make excuses for her choices at this point, but her mother was not one to squelch her opinions, and it was easier to be a sneaky child than a confronted adult. She didn't particularly like the bus, but it was a small price to pay for having shared champagne and escargot with Aaron Karp.

The school was fairly empty by the time Fordham arrived to pick up Whitty from the poetry workshop "Share Your Candy" post-Halloween party. It was an idea Fordham totally supported since she had spent the last couple of nights succumbing to the call of miniature

Snickers and peanut butter cups from Whitty's bag. She hoped she hadn't been too out of it and gotten the time wrong. Feeling impish, she toyed with the idea of calling David to find out, but giving him the idea that she was irresponsible didn't seem like the best option. Just in case she really had screwed up, she decided to meet Whitty inside instead of waiting in the car.

The school was quiet. She lingered in the halls, browsing the artwork and projects from all the different classes. One particular finger painting of a cat with big purple eyes sitting on a couch next to a pumpkin caught her eye.

"I like that one too," David said from behind her. "Lily's interpretation of Halloween."

Fordham greeted him. "I'm not a critic, but I think your little girl has talent."

"Thank you. Certainly wouldn't be from me. I can't draw a straight line without a ruler."

"We must have gone to the same art school."

He was dressed casually in Dockers and a blue sweater that made his exquisite eyes stand out. She could have sworn he'd gotten even more attractive since the last time she'd seen him.

"I was headed to my office. Come join me." He motioned for her to follow him. "I want to talk to you about something."

For a split second, she imagined him sweeping her into his arms, pinning her against the colorful bulletin board, and kissing her passionately. Maybe she was still buzzing from the champagne and just didn't realize it. A dreamy, nostalgic lunch with Aaron, fantasies about David, considering sperm donations from Brandon—clearly, there was something off about the energy in the universe and, even more clearly, something hormonally pervading her status quo.

David's office was warm and inviting. It screamed "I am normal" with a dash of "And you should be too." The walls were painted a pale gray-blue, the perfect backdrop for a few photos, a framed Chagall poster, a drawing Lily had done of a rainbow, and all the degrees and certificates that had led him to this office. Fordham found herself staring at a photo of David standing in the middle of small ocean waves, holding Lily. The sun was setting behind them, and their heads were touching slightly. They had the same warm smile, and it was evident they were feeling safe and content. She wished Whitty and Gil had a picture like that, something Whitty could hold on to when Gil wasn't around to let her know that he loved her. But the only pictures they had were the typical posed shots taken at holidays and occasions that told the story of the event more than of the people. And in most of them, Gil wasn't smiling.

"I love the beach," David said, noticing her staring at the picture.

"Me too. But I don't get to go much."

"You should try to change that. If you can." He grabbed a couple of mugs. "Want some lousy end-of-the-day coffee?"

"Oh, no, thank you. I've had a few cups of that already."

He placed the mugs back on the shelf, and Fordham detected a slight frown.

"The party is running a little late," he said.

"No problem. I can use the time to clear my head."

"Busy day?"

"Every day is lately. I'm in publishing and up to my neck in work."

"Understood," he said casually.

Fordham was grateful he didn't press for further information. The last thing she wanted to do was talk about her job. "Do you know how Whitty is doing in the workshop?"

"She's doing great. That's what I wanted to talk to you about. Her writing has real depth and insight. It's hard to believe she's only ten."

"I know. If it were up to her, she'd be wearing makeup and driving. She loves to write, but lately, she never wants me to read anything. You're part of the workshop?"

"Yes, but I had a ton of files to go through today, so Pam Lesley is handling it."

"Oh, right, Pam." Fordham had almost forgotten about her. She wouldn't make that mistake again.

She flashed back to Aaron and his request to spend more time with her. She had to admit that despite her mother's disapproval, their possibilities were uniquely credible. She wondered what Whitty would think of him. She got out a pack of mints from her bag, took one, and handed one to David.

"Thanks." He popped it into his mouth as the secretary buzzed in and told him to pick up line one. "Oh man, really?" he said into the phone. "I can lend you my car. Do you think you could come over after? Okay, let me know. I'm still at school."

David hung up the phone and stared at his desk calendar for a moment. "Sorry for the interruption. What I wanted to talk to you about is a poetry contest coming up soon," he said, sounding like a principal. "I told Whitty she should enter."

"Really? She hasn't said anything."

"I think she has a good chance of winning. Her writing is that good, and I'd like to see her get the recognition."

David sounded paternal, and although he probably meant well, she questioned his motive. She worried that he was trying to subtly tell her that she wasn't supportive enough of Whitty or worse, that she was too self-absorbed to recognize that her daughter had talent. She could feel her head shaking in denial.

"Are you okay?"

"Yes," she said a little too curtly, "just a little headache. Thank you for filling me in. I'll talk to Whitty. How's Lily doing?"

"Good. She hasn't stopped talking about Halloween. Well, you saw her painting."

David's cell phone rang this time. "Mmm, really? Bummer." He sounded dejected. "No, it's okay. If you can't make it, you can't make it. We're still on for Thursday, right? Okay, good." He ended the call and jotted down a couple of notes on a pad on his desk.

Fordham was confused. Since Pam was busy teaching poetry, someone else's rejection had to be making David upset. Clearly, something was wrong, but since Fordham was wearing deodorant and sucking on a breath mint, it probably wasn't her.

"Actually, Fordham, I hate to ask, but is there any way Lily can stay with you for a couple of hours tomorrow night? That was my sitter on the phone. She has a driver's ed exam, and the board stuck me with a meeting."

Ah, the babysitter. Fordham was annoyed at herself for feeling relieved. "Of course, David. No problem." She'd wear the scoop-neck brown sweater set with the new leggings Dorie had picked up for her.

Whitty peeked into the office window, grinning from ear to ear. "Hi, Mom."

"Hey, monkey!"

"Shhh! Don't ever say that here."

"Sorry."

"Forgiven. This time. I'm starving."

"We're going," Fordham said.

David sat on the corner of his desk, chuckling at their exchange. "I'll see you tomorrow night."

She left, feeling redeemed. He obviously thought she was a fine mother, or he wouldn't have asked her to watch his daughter.

"You have a date with Dr. Prince tomorrow night?" Whitty sounded excited. "Finally, you're seeing your way out of the loser column."

"We don't have a date. Lily's coming over."

"Oh." Whitty sighed. "Well, at least that's a plus."

"Actually, there is someone I want you to meet."

"Yahoo," she said like an automaton. "I can hardly wait."

AS MUCH AS SHE WANTED to credit Gil for Whitty's sarcastic nature, Fordham knew he was not the only contributor. She was pretty good at wielding an acid tongue whenever simple declarative statements seemed wasteful. After all, a thought had only one good shot at making an impact so why not dress it to the nines? But children weren't supposed to do that. They were supposed to be innocent and carefree, not jaded and critical.

Fordham made herself a tuna fish sandwich. Whitty had been so tired after the party that she'd gone straight to bed, giving Fordham time to think about how far her little girl had come since the first shaky steps she'd taken as a toddler.

Fordham had known that Whitty was not an average child early on. She was saying actual words at six months old, and by one, she had the capacity to carry on a conversation. It was a little unnerving sometimes. One afternoon, when Fordham was changing Whitty's diaper, she noticed a brown smear on the wall, to which she said, "Thanks, Whitty. Nice chocolate on the wall."

Without a moment's hesitation, Whitty corrected her. "No, Mommy, nice *crap* on the wall."

Then there was the morning when the electrician was showing Fordham the new outlet he'd installed, and Whitty came crawling over, crying, "I want booby now, Mommy. Now Mommy." She was always big on *Now, Mommy*.

And since Gil wasn't around much, it was hard for Fordham not to compensate by being more available and yielding. There was the rub. Whitty was smart and intuitive. She knew Fordham was putty in her hands. Maybe that was why she'd been giving her such a hard time lately. Whitty wanted her home more often, and she couldn't be. As much as Fordham tried to explain how much this book meant to her and their future, Whitty didn't care.

She'd been born blunt and opinionated. By two, she had no problem telling Fordham exactly what she was thinking. One night, when Fordham had been too busy to make dinner, she offered Whitty a peanut butter and jelly sandwich with a sliced banana on the side. Whitty scrutinized the plate and said, "*That's* dinner?"

Fordham knew she had created her own little monster, but there were worse things her daughter could be than verbal, demanding, and critical. Whitty's negativity pained her. For someone whose needs were typically met without complaints and arguments, she should have been more affable and agreeable. But no, she was usually snide and cynical with a healthy dollop of judgmental, just the kind of emotional sundae that made Fordham's stomach turn.

Fordham hadn't yet spoken with Whitty about the poetry contest, probably because she wasn't sure how she'd react. She shut off the light in the kitchen, went to bed, and read the laminated copy of *her* submission that was tacked to the wall next to her pillow. Love was out there. Somewhere in the Pacific Northwest... or right under her nose, clear out of sight.

She tossed. Tossed and turned. Whether she was fretting over parenting misfires, worrying about deadlines, musing over Aaron, or wondering if David found her desirable, Fordham wasn't sleeping. Evie had told her to take some herbal preparation to help, but Fordham was worried it would take effect exactly when she didn't want it to. There was nothing that special about sleep, anyway.

Fordham wasn't sure what time it was when she finally fell asleep, but the stars were still twinkling when her alarm went off. That was the way it had to be, at least for the time being. With only twenty-four hours in a day and at least thirty hours' worth of obligations, the more time she used up with her eyes closed, the less time she would have to do anything else.

She would continue to worry about Whitty, but all the guys would have to be on hold. She had too many other things that needed her attention at the office that day. There were final decisions to secure about the last batch of submissions, and she had to start editing the ones she had already selected.

It was a short walk to the bus stop, and the early morning air had just the right snap to it to wake her up gently. A few deer were playing in a nearby field, and Fordham watched as they pranced around, poking at the brush. Their lives seemed calm and uncomplicated until Whitty's voice popped into her head, saying, *Mom. They're deer. Think about what happened to Bambi. Do you really think it would be easier to lose everything you love in a forest fire?*

Chapter Fourteen: Admission Impossible

Fordham actually fell asleep on the bus, something she hadn't done since she was eighteen, shuffling back and forth from home to college. She was having a dream about Margo buying her a bridesmaid dress that could pass for a canary-yellow cupcake prepared by Edward Scissorhands. Fordham was yelling at her for being inconsiderate and told her that if she wanted a sun or a son, she should call Aaron to get her pregnant again. Not to be undermined, Margo yelled back that Fordham was spoiled and smelled like a deli, which was when she opened her eyes to find a huge pickle landing between her legs.

A lady with short flaming-red hair a few seats in front of her was yelling at another woman, an otherwise attractive blonde with very crooked teeth, a few seats behind her. The redhead claimed the blonde was sleeping with her husband and threw the contents of her brown-bag lunch at the equally angry blonde. Fordham was hungry. For a moment, she contemplated eating the pickle and then figured she had to still be dreaming to even consider it.

By the time she arrived at work, people were busy making lunch plans. She tried reaching Evie—there was so much to tell her—but the call went straight to voicemail. *Oh well.* She had a bag of trail mix in her desk drawer and a banana in her bag. That was good enough. She could make up the time she'd missed by working through lunch.

She trekked briskly to her office, smiling when one of the girls ordered a corned beef on rye with extra pickles. She probably still had one in her bag. More importantly, no one noticed her, and she was relieved that she could start her day without any annoying inquiries.

The good news was that the book was coming along. The bad news was that she didn't see how it could be finished by Abe's decreed deadline. She took out a stack of papers and brought her notes up on the computer. No matter how much time Fordham dedicated to reading, writing, and editing, there were always more lovers in the pile, waiting to be scrutinized. It wasn't that easy to decide who would make the cut. She wondered if this was the kind of confusion the NFL went through when recruiting players. *Sorry, but you made an incomplete pass.*

And Fordham couldn't neglect her own mantra of late: this is too much for you to tackle. She'd never imagined that so many people could find love online and was even more surprised by how many of them wanted to share the details. Maybe she hadn't given dating sites a fair chance. Counting on Evie to find her dates had yielded the runts of the litter and made her feel even more jaded about her prospects. If her love life didn't pick up soon, she might consider writing a profile.

She was reviewing a submission about a sex-addiction therapist who'd met her boyfriend on a site for Christian singles. The guy had been admonished by the monastery when he was literally caught with his pants down, having sex with a conflicted nun in the church pantry. The clincher was when the missing jar of honey showed up on his nightstand drawer next to a pair of handcuffs. Rather than banish him from the church altogether, he was given the option of paying penance for his wayward behavior by attending therapeutic sessions to help purge him of his evil erotic tendencies. While in therapy, he decided that he was not so much a man of the cloth as a man of the sheets, so he opted to become a chef. Apparently, the pantry had been inspiring. He joined the same dating site as the therapist, and kismet had ensued. They were getting married in the spring and believed their chance encounter was truly heaven-sent.

Fordham was amazed that she typically didn't have to embellish any of the material she received. Some stories, like this one, sounded sketchy, but if legal approved, she was free to move forward with them. She wasn't sure this one was a keeper and was filing it away when her door flung open so hard that it knocked over her pencil cup. There was Evie, frazzled and peaked.

"Hi! I have something to tell you," both women said in a suburban Greek chorus.

"You first," Evie insisted.

"Aaron Karp is in town, and I had lunch with him," Fordham said without any telling inflection.

"No!" Evie said, falling into a chair.

"Yeah!" Fordham said with a Cheshire-cat grin.

"No!"

"Yeah!"

"Isn't he married?"

"Getting divorced."

"How does he look?"

Fordham gave an exaggerated sigh. "The dimples are still there when he smiles, even with his 'stache and goatee."

"Wow. Aaron with facial hair. So how was, uh... *lunch*?" Evie's question came with a snicker and a suggestive tone.

Fordham ignored the subtext. Evie had always liked Aaron. Like most of their friends back in high school, she'd thought Fordham and Aaron would end up together like her and Marv. When they broke up, Evie cried almost as much as Fordham had.

"Lunch was... interesting. He wants to spend more time with me."

"I swear, if you end up marrying Aaron Karp—"

"Evie, it was lunch and a stroll down memory lane, not a catered affair and a walk down the aisle."

"Does your mother know?"

"Yes."

"Do you still have a roof?"

"Just need to replace a few shingles."

"I can imagine. Dorie Price is not one to let anyone mess with her cubs."

"That's kind of what she said in her own inimitable fashion. So what's your news?"

"Dylan is pregnant, and the wedding is in a few weeks!" Evie groaned.

Dylan was Evie's oldest child, a born rebel who blasted her mother's conventional life and vowed she would never become an insipid member of the bourgeoisie. A confirmed individualist, she had wanted her bat mitzvah theme to be communism, but Marv put his foot down and said her point would be better served if they shipped her to school in China. She relented, and for her forty-thousand-dollar birthday party, they'd settled on the theme of Hollywood blockbusters.

"What?" Fordham screeched, knowing she was outdone.

"I know. I'm not sure which one of us has been throwing up more."

"Who's the proud papa?"

"Bob Kalinsky, computer geek and drummer extraordinaire. You met him at Dylan's high school graduation party."

"Right. It wasn't that long ago. Bob and Dylan?"

"Don't remind me," Evie said.

"It's not quite as funny as your wedding. 'Are you here for the Gross-Weiner party?'"

"Cute, Fordham. Cute."

"Do they love each other?"

"Dylan says they do."

"Is she happy?" Fordham asked.

"Ecstatic!"

"Mazel tov, Evie. You're going to be a nana!"

DYLAN WAS PREGNANT. Margo was pregnant. Aaron was getting women pregnant daily. And her date with Brandon had her contemplating getting pregnant. Babies were little gifts of hope and promise that made even the most crotchety soul pause and be awed by the miracle of life. But not always.

"What? Is she out of her mind? A baby?" Dorie was not inclined to mince words. "Dylan is barely out of her own diapers. I would have shot you if you had done that to me." She took a weary banana from a small wooden tree on the counter.

"To you?" Fordham said, grabbing a packet of nuts from the cabinet.

"Yes. I put my mother through hell when I got pregnant with you. She was the only one I told. She even kept it from Grandpa until I married your father, because she knew he would have sent me to a school for wayward girls who couldn't keep their legs closed!" Dorie pointed the banana excitedly at Fordham. "And all the while, she kept muttering about what a pity it was that my baby wasn't Seymour Nageldorf's."

"Could it have been?" Fordham's curiosity was piqued.

"Very funny. He and I barely dated, but I think about him from time to time."

"But you did go out with him."

"Once. We went out once. It was pouring that night, and he stood at the door, waiting for me. Your grandmother invited him in, but he was worried about getting mud on our carpeting. He kept say-

ing, 'Should I keep my rubbers on, should I take my rubbers off...?'
He never came in."

"Guess Dylan's fiancée didn't share that concern. He just left his
rubbers off." Fordham gave Dorie a little shove.

Whitty came into the kitchen, and the two women abruptly
stopped talking.

"Oh, don't let me stop you. I'm sure you were talking about sex
or something."

"Whitney Presser!" Whether Dorie was more astounded by her
granddaughter's insight or her brazenness was anyone's guess. "Okay,
I have a tournament to play," she added. "I will see you ladies in the
morning."

Dorie blew them kisses and left, and Fordham went to prepare a
quick dinner for her and Whitty. She could only imagine what Dorie
was thinking. Her daughter was divorced and dating indiscriminate-
ly, her granddaughter had no clue that she was only ten, and a woman
she loved like her own daughter was going to be a grandmother.
Dorie's world had certainly changed since Seymour Nageldorf wanted to take her for chow mein and a movie.

"So, what were you and Mom-Mom talking about?" Whitty
asked through a forkful of macaroni and cheese.

"Sex."

"I knew it. About who?"

"You're pretty nosy," Fordham said.

"I'm pretty bored. So who?"

"I may as well tell you since you're going to find out soon enough.
Dylan is pregnant."

"You're kidding. That is so weird. Aunt Evie must be having a
cow."

"Well, let's hope Dylan isn't."

"She isn't even twenty yet," Whitty said.

"Some people fall in love when they're young."

"Love? She's in love? I thought she just did it."

"No, honey. Dylan fell in love. That's the way it's supposed to be."

Telling Whitty about the birds and the bees had been easy. She'd used simple sentences and gotten straight to the point—something Dorie hadn't known how to do. At five, Fordham's friend from next door told her that babies came from people climbing on top of each other. That explanation didn't sound right to her, since she and her friend frequently played climbing games and neither of them had babies. Logically, Fordham asked Dorie for answers to quell her confusion. But the explanation sounded more like a lesson about gardening than one about sex.

"First, you start with the mommy's seed, and then the daddy waters the seed in a special way inside the mommy's tummy. It stays there and grows until it's ready to be born."

That conversation led Fordham to believe that babies started out as trees and somehow ended up looking like people on their way out of the womb, though by the time she was Whitty's age, the kids in school had set her straight. But this talk with Whitty was about romantic sex, and the idea of where the conversation could go left Fordham feeling queasy. Whitty was only ten, and there was no reason to get into a lengthy explanation about love, marriage, betrayal, and infidelity. No, she wasn't ready to have this discussion with her daughter. Not yet and maybe not ever.

Fordham set her plate in the dishwasher, poised to deflect the impending onslaught by going in an entirely different direction. "You'd better hurry. Lily will be here soon. I never even told Mom-Mom she was coming." Fordham assumed she was in the clear, but just in case, she went on. "Which reminds me, Dr. Prince said you should enter the poetry contest. What's happening with that?" Fordham was confident that she had dodged the sex-talk bullet.

"Yeah. I'm not sure."

"What's the problem? You know you're a good writer."

"I'm okay. I know a few kids who are doing it, and they're really good."

"Whitty, you're really good. And who knows? You might win."

"Maybe, but there's an opposite of winning," Whitty said.

"The only opposite of winning is not trying."

"Tell that to the Yankees." Whitty continued to pick at her plate.

Fordham shook her head but decided not to challenge Whitty and upset her before Lily's visit. There would be plenty of time to work on her later.

Dorie marched back out of her room, looking perturbed. "Okay, so now he wants me to believe that there's another 'droop' that's spelled with a *u* and an *e* at the end. I can challenge him, right?"

Whitty excused herself and went to the bathroom.

"No, Mom, it's a word... something about fruit."

"Ugh! I'd like to turn him into applesauce already."

Fordham patted her hand. "Chunky or fine?"

"Either would suit me." She poured herself a cup of tea then gave Fordham the once-over and raised an eyebrow. "Nice outfit, and no offense, but you don't usually smell quite this good by dinnertime. You're wearing the expensive stuff Margo bought you."

"Gee, thanks, Mom! Between bringing up Margo and letting me know I typically smell funky, I'm not sure which is more endearing."

Dorie chuckled uncomfortably. "Sorry."

"I'll live, and I forgot to tell you," Fordham said, wiping the counter around Whitty's unfinished plate, "Lily's coming over for a little while. David asked me to watch her."

"Interesting..." Dorie said, elongating the word. "In a good way. And now it all makes sense!"

"You're ridiculous," Fordham said as she wiped the gunk around the sink. "His sitter is busy."

Whitty came back into the kitchen, sat down, and poked at her plate.

"Well, if you want to work, I could always ditch the game," Dorie grumbled and sipped her tea.

"And disappoint Mr. Applesauce? Never," Fordham teased.

"Well, then, back to the torture chamber." Dorie huffed, leaving with a box of graham crackers in her free hand.

Whitty finished her last bite and pushed her dish away. "I don't get it. Why does Mom-Mom keep playing if it makes her so frustrated?"

"So no one can accuse her of doing the opposite of winning."

WITH LILY ARRIVING any minute, Fordham quickly got some things together she figured any kid would like for dessert. The doorbell rang just as she and Whitty finished setting up the sprinkles and whipped cream. Whitty got the door with Fordham following close behind. David was looking particularly handsome in a dark-green sweater. He even styled his hair differently with a little gel, giving him a casual look. He was nothing short of delicious—probably a little too delicious. She quickly remembered that Pam was likely to be at his meeting. For all she knew, Pam was waiting for him in the car. After the reality check, she saw he was holding a big bag that said LILY in pink marker.

"Hi Dr. Pr—I'm sorry, David," Fordham said.

"Hi, Ms. Pr—I mean, Fordham," he said, winking at her.

Fordham immediately distracted herself. "Hi, Lily," she said, giving the girl a hug. "Good to see you. Have you had dessert yet?"

Lily shook her head and ran off in search of Ella. Fordham went to check out the bag as David was unpacking items by the dozen. There were Band-Aids, pajamas, clothes, nail clippers—anything and everything a person might find in the Kids aisle of a department store.

"And this is Ms. Snuggles for when Lily gets tired. She sleeps with her every night. Oh, and here—*Cinderella*. It's her favorite book."

"David, this is a house full of women," Fordham teased. "We have it in every edition."

Fordham was impressed with how attentive David was to all his daughter's possible needs. Then she felt sad. Gil never overstuffed a backpack for Whitty.

Fordham called Lily into the room so she could say goodbye to David. He seemed less than anxious to leave. Even after Lily had hugged him and gone off with Whitty, he was planted in the same spot.

"You'd better go, or you'll be late," Fordham said, trying to be helpful. "She'll be fine. I promise."

"Oh, I'm not worried about that," David said.

"Don't worry about anything. We'll see you later."

He checked his watch and left. Fordham was just about to close the door when he darted back. "I can't believe I almost forgot to give you this."

He handed her a piece of paper. His cell phone number had been written on it with a neon-pink marker. She would file it under Perfection.

"Lily's favorite color. Well, I'd better go," he said, sounding reluctant. "Fordham, you're a lifesaver."

He finally left, and when she peered out, she noticed there was no one else in the car. If she let herself, she could easily build a case for why she should pursue David. But she couldn't presume Pam wouldn't be in the car with him the next time. She'd seen the way they were together with her own eyes, and stealing another woman's man was not on her bucket list.

A lot of noise was coming from the kitchen. Whitty and Lily were piling the ice cream and toppings Fordham had set up for them into their bowls. Something about pieces of chocolate chip cookie dough had the girls so hysterical that Fordham was laughing even though she didn't get the joke. Since they were happy and occupied, Fordham decided to check her email. There was a new submission, longer than most, that she found intriguing. She printed it out and knocked on Dorie's door.

"Come on in," Dorie grunted.

Fordham entered, unsurprised to see her mother sitting in her chair, pounding her fists on her desk.

"I'm losing," Dorie said, eyes fixed on the computer.

"I figured." Fordham sat on the bed. "Forget about that for a few minutes. I have a sinus headache. Can you read this to me?" She grabbed a box of tissues just in case. "It's a submission I just got."

Dorie grabbed the pages from Fordham, seeming to heartily welcome the distraction, and began to read.

"Hi, I'm Adele from Newton, Massachusetts. Some people would call me an older woman, but I don't believe in numbers. The only time they matter is when you're standing at the bakery counter. Maybe someone would ask, why is a woman her age writing to a book about love online? What could she know? To them I would have to say, a LOT."

Dorie peeked up at Fordham when she read, "a LOT," as if that part of the story was coming from her personally.

"Yeah, yeah. You're the relationship maven, Mom," Fordham teased. "Can you please continue?"

Dorie nodded and read on.

"Last year, my wonderful husband of fifty-five years decided it was time to join the other angels. I couldn't imagine my life without my Saul. He was such a good man. Unfortunately, he had never accomplished one of the most important dreams of his life: to find his twin brother."

"Oh no!" Fordham sighed. "It's going to be another sad one." She pulled a tissue from the box in anticipation. Her mother continued.

"Saul and his brother had been set on the doorstep of an orphanage when they were just infants. There were no real regulation laws in effect back then, and there were no records to speak of unless you got lucky. The only thing Saul's adoptive parents ever knew about their baby boy was that he had a twin brother who was taken a few weeks before they found Saul. Otherwise, they would have adopted both boys.

"Saul never wanted to tell our children he was adopted. I think he was a little ashamed since it was so uncommon in our day. He believed that once he could produce a genuine family member, he would tell them the truth."

"Mom, would you tell me if you were adopted?" Fordham asked.

Dorie shook her head and lowered the paper. "No, it wouldn't be necessary."

"Really? You'd keep it from me?"

"No, it's just that your grandparents would never have told me." Dorie raised the paper. Then she lowered it again. "I'm a duplicate of your grandmother, and you have my cheekbones and your father's nose, so if you were hoping for an out, I can't give you one."

"Mom, please just read!"

"Every night, Saul would sit at the computer and do searches for his brother," Dorie read. "He googled him, tried social networks, and got very close to finding him on a site for seniors who had been adopted. Someone had written that given Saul's description, he was pretty sure he knew his brother. But Saul never got the chance to contact the guy.

"A few months ago, I got up the nerve to pick up where Saul left off. I did some investigating, and sure enough, Saul's brother had been searching for him too. Instead, he found me. I told him what had happened, and we spent hours typing and talking. Finally, he said he'd had enough of the schmoozing and we should meet. He was in Arizona and flew to Massachusetts to meet me, the sister-in-law he never had.

"When I opened the door, I nearly fainted. He was a carbon copy of my Saul. Well, as you would expect, it was all very over-whelming. But one thing led to another, and in a very short time, George and I fell in love. It was a little awkward at first, but at our age, we don't have time for those kinds of worries. His kids lived in the northeast, and he decided to move to Massachusetts, saying he wouldn't miss the heat because our love would keep him warm. We had a lot to explain to our children, but in the end, it all worked out. Now we're one big family, and I feel like a kid again. My advice is never ever give up on the possibility of love. It can show up right on your doorstep."

Dorie and Fordham were dabbing tissues at their eyes when a piercing scream came from the kitchen, followed by uncontrolled sobbing. Dorie dropped the story on the floor, and she and Fordham sprinted toward the calamity. Lily sat on the kitchen floor, her mouth full of blood and a tiny tooth wedged inside a chewed-up gummy bear in a pool of melted ice cream on the counter in front of her. Fortunately, it was just a tooth and not a horrible story of ir-reparable negligence she would have to tell David.

Fordham stared at it wistfully, thinking it had been a while since Whitty had lost a tooth. Maybe she had lost them all. It was conceiv-able. She was turning eleven. Soon she'd get her period, and Fordham would get her AARP card in the mail. But for the moment, there was a little girl who needed to be assured that losing a tooth was a sign of growing up and that growing up was a good thing. Whitty was taking it all in stride, trying to be helpful.

"Oh, wow! We ran out of cherries, so Lily found her own topping for her sundae!" Fordham said, hugging her.

Lily smiled half-heartedly through her tears.

"You're fine, sweetheart. Promise."

Fordham tried to let go so she could clean up, but Lily clung to her the same way Whitty used to when she was scared. Dorie sent them all out of the kitchen, saying she would rather do anything than play in her tournament. Fordham mouthed "Thank you" as Dorie took out a fresh roll of paper towels.

Surprisingly, Lily hadn't asked for David. Fordham wondered if that was a good sign. Maybe she still had a knack for taking care of little ones. Whitty was only a few years older, but somehow it was hard to imagine her as ever being a little kid.

Fordham got a blanket, and they all sat down on the couch. She checked the time. It was still early, and David wouldn't be back for a while. Lily was still frowning.

"Lily, you're so lucky. You're going to have a visit from the tooth fairy tonight!" Fordham said, trying to distract her.

"Yeah. That is way cool," Whitty said. "When I lost my tooth, I put it under my pillow, and the tooth fairy gave me five dollars."

"And when I lost my tooth, I *paid* the dentist five hundred dollars," Dorie said, coming in from the kitchen. "And it wasn't nearly as exciting." She gave them each a kiss on the cheek and went to her room.

Suddenly, Whitty jumped up. "I'll be right back."

"But I'm not going to be home," Lily said, not missing a beat.

"You will be later, honey, and the tooth fairy only comes while you're sleeping."

Whitty came back with a pretty flowered ring box for the tooth just as Fordham was handing Ms. Snuggles to Lily. It was interesting to watch Whitty acting sisterly. She was so good at it, which prompted Fordham to think once again about having a baby. Maybe it was unfair to deprive Whitty of a sibling. Fordham had certainly missed that in her life. She knew about the miscarriages and understood that it wasn't Dorie's fault, but the void was there regardless. The timing couldn't have been more inappropriate, but the soft scent of baby lotion was on her mind, along with the billion other thoughts that kept her up at night.

"I have an idea. Why don't we all get comfy and watch TV?" Fordham craved an escape.

"Yay!" Lily said with a new tooth-missing smile. "Can we watch *Sleepless in Seattle*?"

Fordham was astonished.

Even Whitty was taken by surprise. "Really? How do you know that movie?"

"I watch it with my grammy," Lily explained. "The girl that's going to be the mommy is really pretty."

"Wow, Mom," Whitty said, "they've actually made another one like you in a smaller model. Lily, that's, like, my mom's favorite movie."

"It's my favorite too!" Lily exclaimed. "But Grammy's got broken."

Fordham pictured the three of them sitting on the couch with David, watching the movie and sharing a huge bowl of popcorn. Since the movie was rarely available for streaming on Netflix, she had her own DVD, which was still conveniently in the player. Fordham turned it on and went into the kitchen to get drinks. The opening credits were playing when her phone rang. It was Aaron asking her to go to lunch. Too distracted to get into a whole conversation, she quickly agreed to meet him in the park for a casual bite and ended the call.

A *casual bite*. Perhaps, or maybe she wanted a full course meal. It was still hard for her to get a handle on her feelings for Aaron. Fordham had pondered this for at least two full minutes before Dorie walked into the kitchen.

"How's Lily doing?" she asked, frowning.

Fordham felt a little guilty for being thankful that her mother was too preoccupied to discuss Aaron. Maybe she hadn't heard their conversation.

"She's fine," Fordham said. "Watching a movie with Whitty. What's wrong?"

"Nothing. It's silly." Dorie opened the pantry and scanned the contents. "Scrabble."

"He won again?"

"That's just it." She clenched her fists. "He always wins."

"Don't sweat it. I'm sure your pot roast has his beat."

"Comforting."

Talking about Dorie's pot roast led Fordham to think about all the times Aaron had eaten dinner at her house when they were kids. Maybe she was handling this all wrong. Maybe she needed to see how Aaron might fit into the fold again to decide if moving forward with him was the right thing to do.

"Mom, I've been thinking about having a little dinner party. Just a few people. You can catch up with Aaron. And I'll ask Abe and Evie to come too."

"If you want me to see Aaron, I'll see Aaron," Dorie said. "He doesn't have to be protected by a dinner party."

"No, he doesn't. I do," Fordham said with a smirk. "I'll check with everyone to pick a time."

"Fine. I'll make the pot roast," Dorie announced, walking away with an unopened box of oyster crackers.

Fordham went back to join the girls on the couch and found them leaning against each other, fast asleep. She covered them with a blanket and continued watching the movie, letting herself doze off as Tom Hanks headed off to find his son. Then the doorbell rang.

Whitty was the first to jump up, but Fordham quickly preened and got the door. David was smiling. The meeting had gone well, and there was a good chance he would get the funding for a writing lab he was anxious to set up.

"How did things go here?" His tone suggested he wasn't expecting much of an answer.

"Lots of excitement." Fordham got Lily's tooth box and handed it to David.

He inspected it curiously. "For me? This is a pretty big step," he teased as he opened the box. He took out the tooth. "Ahhh... another one bites the dust."

Fordham got the movie and put it in a case. As soon as it was quiet, Lily woke up.

"Daddy! See?" She proudly opened her mouth to show him where she'd lost the tooth.

"I know! I heard all about it," he said, cupping her chin in his hand.

"Dorie said I can get five hundred dollars now."

"Five hundred? I'll be broke before you're eight."

Fordham jumped in. "Uh-oh. I think she misunderstood my mother's little joke." She quickly retrieved the movie. "The tooth fairy doesn't like to carry that much cash on her. How about this before she comes?" Fordham said, handing the DVD to Lily.

"Fordham, you don't have to do that," David said, gathering up Lily's things.

"I want to. I was going to anyway."

Playing mommy to Lily felt natural, and Fordham wanted to give her something to let her know that.

"Thanks so much," David said, his eyes twinkling with gratitude. "I can't believe you have *Sleepless.* I was sure my mother had the only copy left, and since hers broke, Lily's been asking for it. I just never got around to buying another."

"Well, good," Fordham said. "Now you don't have to. I'm aiming to be indispensable." She had no clue why she let that last sentence tumble out of her mouth.

"So far, you're on target." David winked and patted Lily on the head. "What do you say?"

"Thank you, Fordham."

They were just about to leave when Whitty came to the door, carrying a folded piece of construction paper she said was Lily's. David glanced at it as Fordham was closing the door. It was a picture of a house, a smiling sun, and a family: two parents, two girls, a grandmother, and a cat. He quickly studied Fordham as if trying to place her in the picture, then he left.

Fordham was tidying up. Despite the loss of blood, Lily had fared well, and despite moments of self-doubt, so had she. The next day, she would see Aaron again, and the world would make more sense. He would say all the right things, and they would find their way back to each other. That had to be the reason he'd suddenly reappeared.

She went to her room and climbed into bed, still thinking about Lily. She wondered if the babysitter was a good enough substitute for a mother. *Doubtful*, she thought. But then, the mere thought of Lily calling Pam "Mommy" made her shudder.

Ahhh... sleep. That was what she needed to clear her head. But despite her resolve about Aaron and their upcoming date, she still found herself drifting off while reading the prized submission hanging on the wall.

Chapter Fifteen: Tunestruck

Deciding what to wear was always a chore, but that morning, it seemed even more critical. This was a planned lunch date, so there would be an inherent expectation that she'd look better than she had when she was leaving her gynecologist's office. But it was also a workday, which meant she had to look professional. She knew somewhere in her closet there was a compromise between salad sexy and publishing chic. Still, it was a challenge to find it amidst the confusing array of mix-and-match dating outfits at the front of the rack.

After nearly an hour of deliberation, she settled on a pair of tapered black pants in faux brushed suede and a clingy plum sweater that suggested cleavage but didn't actually announce it. She was reasonably certain she looked good, although after her recent slew of lousy dates, she'd done some serious overtime with Cherry Garcia, and her pants were tighter than they'd been a few months earlier. *So be it.* If things went well, she would be having sex again, and the unwanted pounds would melt into blissful oblivion.

After an easy commute into the city, she was in a good mood and prepared to take on the day. A few workers at an ongoing construction site near the office did a double take as she was passing and gave her a group thumbs-up. For the first time in a while, she was feeling confident. She hoped that vibe would spill into her workday.

As she sat at her desk, her waistband was mercilessly cutting into her gut. The only saving grace was that the sweater covered her little bulge, and unless Aaron made a move on her zipperless no-fly zone, he would be none the wiser. It was too soon for that, anyway. If she appeared too anxious, he'd think she was screwing everyone—or worse yet, he'd think she hadn't been screwing anyone, which meant she was either undesirable or frigid. There was no way of getting around the delay. She had to wait to get laid until she knew where she stood.

The morning dragged as she tried to focus on work. She ended up staring out the window, daydreaming. It was hard not to be consumed by memories. She'd fallen for Aaron harder than she had ever fallen for anyone since. There'd been something magical about the way he put his lips together when he was talking and the way his nose did this incredibly cute crinkly thing when he was about to sneeze. He'd been magnetic and irresistible to her when they were kids, and she remembered how good it used to feel to be in his arms and his life. One memory, in particular, kept drawing her attention.

IT HAD BEEN ONE OF those enchanting summer days when the sun spoke of fragrant breezes, frozen-yogurt sundaes, and whisper kisses. Fordham was due a long weekend and called in sick without compunction, quite certain Denim Palace had other girls anxiously waiting to fold jeans from dawn to dusk. Then she called Aaron. He was spending the summer getting paid by his parents to do odd jobs around the house and had plenty of free time. She knew he'd be psyched to hang out. But there was no answer.

Undaunted, she slipped on her tiniest bikini—fire-engine red with white swirls—and drove to his house. She arrived in record time and knocked repeatedly on the front door, but there was no response. She assumed his parents were at work and his little brother was at camp. Yet Aaron's car was in the driveway.

She let herself in. "Aaron, you here?" she called once or twice.

No one answered. He was nowhere to be found. Her mind drifted to all those slasher movies in which the unsuspecting ingenue wandered into a nightmare, but other than the usual horrific clash of plaid and paisley in the den, nothing seemed wrong.

Except the noise. A sound like a cross between an aggressive vibrator and a broken muffler was coming from somewhere outside. She went out through the sliding door in the kitchen and was now sure the noise was coming from the shed. The yard was full of raked acorns, lopped off branches, and debris from chipped trees and trimmed bushes.

Fordham was walking gingerly across the lawn when a wayward branch snagged her bathing-suit top, tangling it up in the dead tree. She tried to pull away, but there was no way to do it without taking off her top. She was trapped. She was not going to undress in the yard, especially with neighbors in such close proximity. The noise finally stopped, and she was ready to scream for help when Bad Company's "Feel Like Makin' Love" started blasting.

Determined not to spend the day tied to a tree like a naughty cocker spaniel, she tried a new tactic. By jumping, she hoped to dislodge herself from the offending branches. With one final leap, she broke free, but her bikini top still dangled from the tree like a proud ornament. She was topless when Aaron emerged from the shed, holding a small lawn mower.

He squealed with delight to see her standing poised next to the tree like a model on some pornographic version of *Let's Make a Deal.* "Whoa. Damn. Did I forget it's my birthday?"

She explained what had happened as she was untying her suit from the branches. But Aaron didn't seem all that interested in her explanation or in retrieving her bikini top. He scooped her up and brought her over to a tuft of grass in a well-hidden shady spot behind the shed. The music continued to play, and the sun continued to shine as they made love in what would later become the Karps' zucchini garden.

"FORDHAM?" MYRA WAS standing in front of her desk. "Are you all right?"

"Yes. I'm fine. Why?"

"Because Abe buzzed you three times, and you didn't answer."

"Really? Sorry about that. I was thinking about a submission," Fordham said. "A complicated one. Do you know what he wants?"

"No. He didn't say."

As it turned out, Abe wanted a comprehensive outline of all the submissions to present at a meeting later in the week. No big deal. She already had one. The day she'd taken over the project, she began structuring an overview of what she had, what she was getting, what she wanted, and a general feel for where everything was headed.

Their meeting was brief but informative. She headed back to her office, pumped. "Nice, Fordham, very nice," she repeated to herself as she sat down at her desk. That high praise had come from Abe, who was more impressed than he should have been. For someone who kept telling her how smart and capable she was, she didn't understand why he was so shocked that she'd come up with something useful on her own.

Another upside to the meeting was that Abe told her to take an extra-long lunch break, which then led to a discussion about Aaron. Fordham admitted that she'd been a little less focused since Aaron's arrival, but she assured Abe that her work wouldn't suffer for it. If anything, it would be motivating to have a romantic component to her life. Abe sounded cautiously optimistic and suggested that she take things very slowly.

"A leopard doesn't change its spots, Fordham," he said in an unexpected echo of Dorie's philosophical dictum. She knew Abe hadn't spoken with her mother, though it wouldn't have surprised her if Dorie had sent out a newsletter.

Suddenly, everyone was so protective of her love life. She'd been on dates with musicians, politicians, ex-cons, and possible hit men, and the reaction had been nowhere near as perverse. Aaron was a doctor. He was smart, financially stable, attractive, and almost available. There was no reason for him to be held up to such intense scrutiny. Nor was there a reason for her to be so vehemently defensive.

Lunch. They were going out for lunch. Fordham had to make a concerted effort to block out all the nagging and twisted assertions and simply follow her head and heart. She had to count on herself and *only* herself to determine what was best for her. So what if her mother had been right in the past? That was a long time ago, and a quick review of Dorie's relationships did not exactly promote faith in her choices or guidance. The best thing Fordham could do was check on the weather and, if it was warm enough, ask Aaron if he wanted to eat hot dogs in the park.

Fordham was coming out of the supply closet with a new pack of sticky notes when Aaron arrived at the front desk a little earlier than they had arranged. It was lunchtime, and the office was almost empty, which had led Aaron to wander. He looked so cute out of his element, and she was getting a kick out of surreptitiously watching him. She was about to greet him when Abe popped into the hall, apple in hand, and struck up a conversation with him that Fordham could hear from where she was standing.

"Can I help you?" Abe asked, munching.

"Yes. Where can I find Fordham Price?"

"Who are you?" Abe said, sending a spritz of apple juice at Aaron's face.

"Aaron Karp. Dr. Aaron Karp, a friend of hers," he responded, politely ignoring the drip on his cheek.

"The guy from high school?"

"Yes. I take it you two are friends," Aaron said.

"I'm Abe, her boss. She tells me everything."

"That's good. She's expecting me. We have plans for lunch."

"I know," Abe said.

"Is she ready?"

"For lunch, yes. For anything else, I'm not sure, but if you hurt her, you'll have to answer to me."

As much as Fordham was horrified by Abe's brazenness, she felt heartened to have someone like a dad protecting her.

"Are you a friend of her mother's?" Aaron asked.

"No. Why?"

"Just curious."

"I haven't met Dorie, but from what I've heard, she's quite something," Abe said, tossing the apple core into a nearby wastebasket.

"Yes, she is."

Once Dorie's name entered the conversation, Fordham quickly went to greet Aaron. "Hey, guys. Glad you two had a chance to meet." She gave Aaron a peck on the cheek. "When did you get here?"

"A few minutes ago. Abe and I have just been making small talk. You ready?"

Fordham realized she was still holding the sticky notes. "Yes. I'm just going to throw these on my desk," she said, holding up the package, "and get my bag."

She returned to her office but kept checking on Abe and Aaron. They seemed to have reached some kind of understanding that she couldn't ascertain from the conversation. As she came out of the office, they were shaking hands, a sign that Abe would offer his approval. The only person left to tackle was Dorie. Fordham sighed. *And Whitty.* It would be easier to win on *Survivor* than to get Whitty's support for dating Aaron.

Aaron took her hand as they left Haskins and headed out of the building. Holding hands had been such a big deal in the halls of high school, and it felt like an even bigger deal in the halls of the Starrett-Lehigh Building. The park was crowded for a fall weekday. The balmy temperature had everyone thinking summer was back for a command performance. Fordham was glad to get out of the office and away from the words and stale coffee that made up most of her day. She considered leaving work early to enjoy the warmth, but things were going well, and she didn't want to get off her game by letting the moment seduce her.

She watched Aaron go over to a vendor to get their hot dogs. He seemed content and more comfortable in his skin then he had been as a kid—a reasonable product of time and accomplishment. She'd been surprised when she found out that he'd become a doctor after all his talk of being a record producer. He seemed too wild and creative to be willing to yield to the rigorous demands of medical school and too rebellious to deal with administrators or anyone who could utter the word *no* in his direction. Maybe something had happened in Spain that made him think he had a greater aptitude to change lives than to revolutionize music. Whatever the reason, Aaron's life had taken off in another direction, and she was cautiously happy that the road still seemed to point back to her.

"Baby, do you realize how difficult you've made it for me to work?" Aaron said, handing her a wrapped hot dog with extra relish. "You're on my mind twenty-four seven. The other day at the clinic, I ordered a dozen cases of dinner napkins instead of sanitary napkins."

Fordham laughed so hard mustard spewed out of her nose. Aaron laughed, too, but had the presence to grab a napkin and wipe her face. It was a move that said he cared, something she hadn't experienced from a man in a very long time.

"Aaron, do you know how we got here?"

"Taxi."

"I mean it." She jabbed his arm. "I've been thinking about you, too, and I'm not even sure what I'm feeling. Maybe I want to be excited about us because I used to be."

"And this is bad because...?"

"Because we're not the same people anymore. We chose different paths that didn't include each other."

"Have you ever wondered if that was a mistake?" he asked.

"Yes. But not in a very long time."

"I didn't know what I wanted then."

"And you know what you want now?" she asked.

"Yes. What about you? What do you want?"

"I want... ice cream," she said, not wanting to sound committal before she had the chance to think all this through.

"Okay. Chocolate with chocolate sprinkles it is," he said, beaming. "See? I remember."

BACK IN HER OFFICE, she couldn't concentrate. Lunch with Aaron could have been called *a mild concussion* because once again, her head was spinning, and this time there hadn't been a sip of alcohol involved. Aaron said he'd be in touch, and she fought a feeling of disappointment that they hadn't cemented a plan. Abe dropped in to ask her if she'd had fun, and she gave him a quick nod to avoid a more complicated conversation. The moment he left, she brought up more submissions on her computer and began to mechanically go through each one.

"Fraudman?" a man bellowed from the corridor. "Anyone here named Fraudman?"

Fordham opened her door to a well-coiffed man in his forties wearing a white three-piece leisure suit, a black shirt with two buttons undone, and a guitar slung in front of his slight frame. He could have been auditioning to be the host of *Dance Fever*, a show her friends had forced on her when they had Saturday-night sleepovers.

"Are you Fraudman?" he said, staring her down, sounding miffed.

"Excuse me?" she said, taken aback by his impatience.

"Honey, are you Fraudman Price?" he said more politely.

"That depends. Did someone named Evie send you here?"

"Evie..." He looked puzzled.

If this was Evie's idea of a date, she was going to post her friend's impending grandmother status all over Facebook.

"Who's Evie?" the guitarist asked, bewildered.

She let out a sigh of relief. "I'm Fordham."

"Fordham! Oh, yeah man, you're right," he said, consulting his note card. "I'm Jeff. Sorry about that. Forgot my specs at home."

"No problem," she said, baffled. "So, Jeff, what can I do for you?"

"Nothin'. Just listen." He began strumming his guitar. "Fordham, this one's for you."

At the first chord, she recognized the song. It was Chicago's "Beginnings," a song from Aaron's parents' record collection that she and Aaron had danced to in his den. People were coming out of their offices left and right as the guitarist solidly played every note. A small crowd was huddled around her by the time he finished. Fordham was too flustered to know if she was flattered or unnerved.

Before he left, Jeff handed her a greeting card. The crowd let out a chorus of *oohs* and *aahs*. Fordham stood blushing, almost paralyzed. Abe handed him a tip and sent everyone back to work. She dashed back to her office with Abe at her heels.

"Not my style, but the guy sure knows how to make a statement," Abe said, closing her door. "You do know this could be a rebound deal, considering he has a divorce in the works."

Fordham swallowed hard and noticed her hands were trembling. Abe looked concerned.

"Well, what does the card say?" Abe asked.

She opened it. "Fordham, we met in 'September.' I know you remember. We're gonna have 'Fun, Fun, Fun' 'cause 'You're Still the One' who 'Knocks Me Off My Feet.' Baby—it's prom night. Again. Meet me at the front of the school tonight at eight. Aaron."

Abe snickered. "It sure sounds like you've got an admirer."

Chapter Sixteen: Of Advice and Men

If she was going to meet Aaron at their old high school, she didn't want to show up dressed like a lunch lady. She knew all too well what was in her closet, and there was nothing there that would stir him to think about her when their evening was over. After a brief chat with Abe, who told her to get lost for the rest of the day, she called Evie to meet her at Messengers, a privately owned unisex boutique whose name implied they should be able to deliver something. Their clothes and accessories were upscale and pricey but the promise of the evening was worth it.

The shop was more crowded than Fordham expected. She'd never realized how many people were free to shop midday. She had already tried and rejected a bunch of dresses from the sale racks when Evie came in looking pale and depressed. Her typical dewy shimmer was missing, and Fordham realized that without foundation, Evie just didn't glow the same way. It certainly wasn't worth mentioning. But Evie mentioned it anyway.

"I swear, Fordham, this menopause crap is for the birds," she said, blotting her face with an already wet tissue. "Look at me. My make-up is sweating all over my face." She consulted a mirror. "I look like Bette Davis in *Whatever Happened to Baby Jane?*"

"Don't be silly," Fordham said. "You're beautiful. But menopause? Really?"

"Really. All the women in my family started young. I think my hormones found out that Dylan is expecting and just assumed that I have a rocking chair and dentures on layaway. But don't worry. I plan to fight back." She dabbed at her face again, this time with a fresh tissue. "Do me a favor—let's not talk about it. It just makes me want to cry." She shoved the tissue in her purse, took out the compact of dewy foundation, reapplied it to her satisfaction, and started going through the dresses as though nothing had happened. Glowy Evie was back with the same vigor she'd had when Fordham first told her why she needed a new dress. She thought sending the guitar guy was the most romantic gesture she'd ever heard of. Fordham wasn't going to argue, even if she still wasn't quite sure how she felt about it. She felt reassured knowing she could count on Evie to root for Team Aaron.

Fordham was thankful she wasn't dealing with menopause yet, especially since she was still contemplating the idea of having another baby. She promised herself not to say a word about it to anyone, especially Evie, who was still in shock about Margo's pregnancy and in denial about Dylan's. Maybe that was part of the allure of Aaron being back in her life. Maybe the grand plan was that they were supposed to be parents together.

"What about this one?" Evie asked, holding up a strapless cocktail dress in a metallic fuchsia with a matching boa that Ray Charles wouldn't have missed.

"It's a date, Evie. He's not paying me to be Miss Piggy for the evening," she said, wincing, and continued her search on another rack.

"Fine. Be that way. But we both know how long it's been since you've—"

"Actually looked forward to going out," she said. Evie let the subject slide, and they went back to their search. Nothing was grabbing either one of them. Fordham was scanning a clearance rack when she noticed a familiar face shopping in the men's department.

"Evie!" Fordham squealed.

"What?" Evie jumped, and Fordham was grateful to see the tangerine jumpsuit she wanted Fordham to try on fall to the floor.

"That's Pam Lesley," Fordham said.

"Gil's old secretary?"

"No! I told you. The one Whitty's principal is seeing."

Evie followed Fordham's instructions to locate the woman and check her out. "No way. How did they meet—she was selling him Girl Scout cookies?"

"I told you she was young."

"Young is one thing, but I don't think she can vote yet. Fordham, are you sure they're dating?"

"She was ready to scratch my eyes out when she saw the two of us talking that night at the catering hall. Plus, I've seen them together at school. Oh, and this."

Fordham showed Evie an Instagram picture that Pam had posted of Lily, Pam, and David celebrating Lily's birthday, with the hashtags, #mommypammy and #luvinlifewithdavid.

Evie shook her head in disbelief and picked out a silver dress that had been a crumpled lasagna tin in a previous life.

"That's it, Evie?" Fordham asked. "No reaction?"

"Years ago, pictures were worth a thousand words. Today, they're worth a thousand questions."

Fordham continued to eye Pam, who was happily preoccupied with her own shopping. "Evie! She's buying him a tie. A nice tie. Oh. And a package of boxers. Funny, I pictured him as more of a briefs kind of guy. This is bad. I feel like a voyeur."

"So stop looking," Evie suggested. "Or go talk to her and do some digging."

Fordham went over to the section where Pam was shopping and began to poke around in men's wear.

"Mrs. Presser?" Pam asked, a blue robe slung over her arm and a lacy thong dangling from her wrist.

Fordham cringed. Pam could have just screamed *You're old* to address her.

"Oh, hi, Pam. What are you doing here?" Fordham could feel her cheeks redden. Obviously, the girl was shopping.

"Getting a few things for David." She giggled as if Fordham were an idiot for not knowing. "He loves when I shop for him."

"Is it his birthday?" Fordham asked, thinking she might pick something up for him too.

"No, it's kind of our anniversary," she gushed. "But what are you doing in this department? Whitty said you're divorced."

Fordham wanted to beat her with a hanger, but she didn't have the bail money. She was hoping for a supportive glance from her friend, but Evie wasn't in range. "I am," she said, forcing herself to stay calm. "My boss asked me to check something out for him."

"That's very smart of you," Pam said flippantly. "It's always a good idea to make your boss happy."

Fordham wasn't sure what the implication was, but she still wanted to beat Pam with a hanger.

"It's been a pleasure, Mrs. Presser, but I have to get going. David wants ziti for dinner."

"It's Fordham. Have a lovely evening."

She watched as Pam went to the register, the word *anniversary* screaming in her head. Then she went to catch up with Evie. She found her in the Scandalous section, picking out dresses that would make a prostitute blush.

"You shouldn't have made me do that," Fordham chided.

"I didn't make you do anything you didn't want to do." Evie admired a see-through lavender gown before returning it to the rack. "So what did you find out?"

"Nothing I wanted to know," Fordham said dejectedly. "They're together, period, end of story."

"I don't understand. What difference does it make, anyway? You want Aaron. Don't you?"

"Of course. I'm just playing around."

That wasn't entirely true. She did want Aaron. He was exactly what she needed in her life. But David was undeniably attractive, and Fordham resented that he had a girlfriend, even though she had absolutely no right to feel that way.

"Anything?" Fordham asked Evie, knowing they had exhausted every possibility.

"Nothing you'd be caught sober in," Evie said, motioning that she was going to the lingerie section.

Fordham went through one more section then spotted the perfect dress, which was exactly like the one she'd worn on her date with Paul Nudelman. The answer to her fashion dilemma was sitting in her closet after all. Evie came back with a couple of items for herself—two kinky black silk teddies and a peekaboo bra. Apparently, fighting back meant she was planning to take menopause lying down.

THE WHOLE RIDE HOME, Fordham was playing out the evening in her mind. Aaron probably wanted to meet at the school so they could sit in the parking lot and reminisce. It was a romantic notion, but she had so many mixed feelings about their past relationship that she preferred looking ahead to looking back. Sure, they had good times, but in the end, he broke up with her, saying they were too young to make that kind of commitment and that he needed to focus on school and had too many things to do that didn't include taking care of a girlfriend. She needed to get serious about her future, too, and it would be unfair of him to tie her down.

Blah, blah, blah. Evie and Marv had made it work, and if Aaron had really loved her, they could have worked through all their issues too. She spent days crying, puking, and torturing herself, listening to "It's Too Late" until it started to skip and incessantly repeat the same plaintive line over and over. At the height of Fordham's despondency, Dorie had sworn that she would never let "that nasty bastard" back in the house as long as she could breathe.

Fordham checked the time. *Good.* She had a couple of hours to regroup and get out of her self-imposed funk. She told herself it wasn't prudent to dwell on negatives and sabotage a potentially good thing. But despite wanting to be optimistic, she kept hearing Elmer Fudd imploring her to *be vewy, vewy careful.*

An unfamiliar car was parked in front of the house as she arrived, and she hoped Dorie hadn't invited any of her annoying Y Group friends for coffee. She didn't feel like dealing with their opinions about her neckline or the hairs in her nostrils. She planted a Miss America smile on her face and entered the house, expecting to make a quick exit to her room.

Dorie was sitting on a chair, facing Fordham, and the back of another head was sitting facing the opposite way. "Fordham, look who's here," she announced as David stood up to greet her.

"David." Fordham's pulse quickened.

"I called your mother and asked if she had time to discuss some ideas for clubs to run through the library."

Dorie had mentioned chatting with him about her different interests and ventures when she'd gone to pick up Whitty one afternoon. Fordham had assumed it was polite conversation that would have no consequence. She tried to form a response. Meanwhile, Ella surveyed the room, meowed, then jumped in David's lap and got comfortable. Fordham was ready to shoo her away, but David welcomed the tabby with scratches behind the ears.

"Well, my mother is very resourceful," Fordham said. "I'm sure she'll be able to help you out."

"Fordham, come sit with us," Dorie requested. "I'll call in for some takeout. It'll be fun."

"Oh. I would love to, but I already have plans I didn't get to tell you about." Although it was the truth, Fordham couldn't help thinking it sounded lame. "I don't mean to be rude, but I have to get ready."

"That's too bad," David said. "I was hoping we could all pow-wow."

Fordham's heart melted a little. Not only did he sound disappointed, but he also used quirky words just as she did. Still, she went into her room and wiggled into the slightly tight black dress, all the while wondering if she'd have a better time staying home.

David was leaving just as Fordham was on her way out. She kissed Whitty good night, told Dorie she wouldn't be too late, and let David hold the door open for them as they both left. She felt self-conscious, wondering if he remembered the dress.

"You look very nice," he said.

"Thanks. And thanks for including my mom in your... whatever. It's good for her to be active."

"She's smart. Smart is good for *whatever*." He lowered his head and seemed to be struggling to find something else to say. "Whatever you're doing, have fun." He paused. Then he turned back. "You look beautiful."

Fordham thanked him and got in the car. She primped in the mirror and watched him drive away. She wasn't sure why he seemed so awkward around her this time. He'd said she looked beautiful. Maybe he wasn't sure how to build their friendship. She wasn't sure, either. The good thing was that they each had a romantic interest, so their involvement with each other could stay focused and unencumbered by the weight of inappropriate expectations. Despite the wisdom imparted by *When Harry Met Sally*, Fordham believed that once men and women knew where they stood with each other, they could be friends.

She started the car and tuned in to classic rock. She and Aaron used to listen to music all the time when they were together. He liked everything from ragtime and swing to blues and pop. He even played her things he'd heard during engineering gigs in different studios. Whatever she liked, he'd mix on tape for her. By the time their relationship was over, she had a collection that spanned every mood and occasion.

She was singing, "I Think I Love You" along with David Cassidy when she arrived at the school. The lot was empty except for a limo and a truck. She parked under a streetlight, thinking it offered a sense of protection, though with the improved visibility, any crazy person hiding in the bushes would have a better shot at her. She got out of the car reluctantly. When Aaron got out of the limo, she felt better. He was wearing a black tux complete with a boutonniere. If he told her he had jumped off the top of a wedding cake, she would have believed him.

Aaron's motto in life had always been "Go big or go home." They'd met before high school when he was a stock boy at Music Den in the mall and she already had a sort of boyfriend. She went in to the store to buy a birthday gift, and the next thing she knew, this gorgeous guy was lip-synching to "Pretty Woman," which was piping through the speakers in the store. He asked for her number, saying she should forget her boyfriend and get used to being his girl. It wasn't her nature to be that bold, but she appreciated it in him. In most ways, she was glad his youthful spirit had grown along with him.

She had to admit, he was still magnetic. He planted a soft kiss on her cheek then slid an orchid on her wrist before helping her into the limo. She was about to thank him, but he motioned her not to speak. As she sat down, Aaron pushed a button, and Stevie Wonder was singing "Golden Lady," a song Aaron knew always tugged at her heart. He popped the cork on a bottle of champagne that had been chilling in a bucket alongside a pair of crystal glasses.

He poured them each some bubbly and gave a toast. "To a night of memories, laughter, and music, and to the girl who makes looking back a thrill and looking ahead a dream."

It took all her will power not to start tearing up. That would have definitely messed up her mascara. She was intent on keeping her wits about her for this date. After a few sips of champagne, Aaron proudly presented a platter of caviar and crackers from the compact fridge. He fed her one then ate one himself.

Fordham was certain she was having an out-of-body experience. She wasn't sure where the real Fordham was, but she was enjoying the moment too much to care. As soon as she finished her champagne, Aaron opened her door and led her into the school's auditorium. The lights were dim, and soft music was playing. A disco ball hanging above spun around, casting patterns on the stage.

"This is incredible, Aaron. How did you do it?"

"I used to tutor the head custodian. He owed me."

She was dazzled and in awe. "Not anymore."

He led her to a seat in the back row and showed her where he had carved a heart with their names inside of it along with the date of their "anniversary." She vaguely remembered Evie showing it to her at an assembly before Aaron had even told her about it. She couldn't believe it was still there after all these years. She paid a hefty school tax and couldn't understand why they had never remodeled.

"I carved that the second you finally agreed to go out with me. I still remember begging you to break up with that kid you were dating before I had the chance to ask you out. What was his name again? Mushroom? You know, the one I called the little Dutch boy…"

"Todd Goodman," Fordham said. "And he was nothing like the little Dutch boy! You were merciless."

"I was focused. I knew what I wanted."

He led her to the stage, and they began to dance as if they had been studying each other's moves for years. When the set ended, the custodian, dressed in a suit, wheeled out a beautifully set table like the kind her mother might arrange when Gloria was visiting. They sat down to oysters, lobster, prime rib, and an array of side dishes and topped it off with a dessert of baklava and pastries like the ones they used to get at the diner in the middle of the night. Aaron had thought of everything that Fordham could have wanted on her prom night.

After dinner, they spent what felt like only seconds reminiscing and dancing. Aaron was being a gentleman—affectionate but respectful, as though aware that this was the kind of evening that was more foreplay than *let's do it*. She was surprised at how okay she was with waiting. They'd taken it slowly the first time around, and since she deemed herself a born-again virgin, she decided it was reasonable to let nature take its course.

A couple of hours later, the custodian came back and began clearing away her living fantasy piece by piece. It had been a perfect evening, and she glided across the parking lot arm in arm with Aaron as if a magic carpet were delivering her to her car. But something was missing.

"Where's the limo?" Fordham inquired. A little Corolla was in its place—another piece of the fantasy gone.

"Custodian's son. It was a quickie loan."

"Oh. I guess everything comes to an end," Fordham said wistfully.

"You and I don't have to," he said, looking straight into her eyes.

"We don't?" she asked, meeting his gaze. "I'm not sure what else to say."

"Fordie, say you'll give us a try. Say you'll be my girl again." He swooped her in his arms and kissed her the way he had when she was sixteen.

"No guarantees," she whispered.

"None. Just hopes."

He kissed her again and helped her get in her car. She waved and pulled out of the parking lot, noticing in her mirror that he stayed there until she was gone.

THE HOUSE WAS DARK and quiet when Fordham returned to her real life. It wasn't that late, but she wanted to linger in the moments of not feeling time, a respite from her ordinary relationship with the world. She went into the family room and lit a rose-scented candle she found in the end-table drawer. Then she found her favorite Laura Nyro collection, an old gift from Aaron, and popped it into the CD player she refused to part with despite its antiquity. She poured herself a glass of pinot noir and tried to keep the evening's allure intact without the convenience of a custodian-busboy-waiter—and, somewhat ironically, without Aaron.

She wasn't sure how to feel. On the one hand, she was elated about the evening, and the prospect of making a life with Aaron seemed almost natural and inevitable, but on the other hand, she was afraid her willingness to dismiss the past meant she hadn't learned anything from their history. Maybe she was so enraptured by Aaron's persistence that she wasn't thinking straight. Or maybe she was falling in love with him again because he was wiser now and recognized her value. She didn't understand how a grown woman could not know her own heart.

The sound of footsteps from the hall caught her attention. Dorie burst into the room, bordering on frantic. Fordham surmised that her mother had been awake, playing in the dark, waiting for her to come home.

"Do you spell 'aeration' with an *e* or an *i*?" Dorie squealed.

"An *e*.

"Dammit! Fordham, he's done it again." She threw her hands in the air. "I have so had it with him." She started to leave then came back. "Uh-oh."

"What?"

"You're listening to Laura Nyro, which either means you and Gil are splitting up or you're upset about something. And since you and Gil are already divorced, my guess is you're upset about something." She sat down on the couch next to Fordham. "How was your evening?"

"Strange, but... wonderful."

"That's what you say about my fish cakes," Dorie said. "Explain."

"Aaron and I met at the high school. He hired people and transformed the auditorium into our own private prom night."

"You're right. That is strange. They wouldn't even let our group set up a bingo night. How'd he do it?" She sat on the couch.

"He has connections."

"I can only imagine." Dorie snickered. "So tell me why it was strange."

"It was so easy to be with him again."

"I can understand that. You were... friends."

"Mom, he wants me back," Fordham said.

"I'm not trying to rain on your adolescence, but isn't the man going through a divorce?"

"Yes, but that has nothing to do with me."

"Fordham, this has *rebound* written in neon letters all over it."

"Mom, one of the finest attributes a person can have is knowing when to just smile and nod."

"Sorry, but I'm your mother, not a dashboard bobblehead in a '65 Chevy." Dorie mimicked a bobblehead, forcing an unwanted chuckle out of Fordham, who was determined to stand her ground, regardless of how brittle it felt.

"I know, Mom. I know how you feel. You have made it clearer than a Swarovski piece."

"Fine. I'm not going to say another word."

"Can I have that in writing, please?"

"Only if I can ask you for the same. You know, someday Whitty is going to be all grown up, and when you see her heading into a storm, do you think the only thing you're going to do is give her an umbrella?"

Dorie left, but before she was out of earshot, Fordham couldn't resist having the last word. "I might throw in a slicker."

Fordham felt a little guilty about giving her mother a hard time, but it was the only way she knew how to assert her independence. Whether she was right or wrong, the decision about who she would be involved with had to come from her. She drank a few more sips of wine and dozed off...

HER MOTHER AND LANKY little Paul Nudelman were arm in arm, strolling through the house, holding paint cans and singing, "six geese a-laying, five golden rings, four calling birds, three French hens, two turtle doves..." They passed her bedroom door, blasting a crescendo. "And a partridge in a pear TREE!"

"Mom?" She couldn't grasp why the two of them were together.

"Oh, hi, dear. You remember Paul?"

"He's unforgettable." Fordham was thinking about his performance of the "Chicken Dance" at the wedding.

"He's your daddy now. I met him on the website I joined, call-me-cougar-dot-com. Can you imagine?"

"No. And what's *that* for?" Fordham asked, pointing to the paint.

"Oh. Paul wants to paint our room by numbers. Ours is going to be sixty-nine. It's a lovely magenta." She began swinging the paint can. "Fordham, dear, you really have to stop frowning. You're getting jowls."

The idea of Paul Nudelman being anything but a memory made a series of cannons go off on the front lawn. Fordham was thrilled when he and her mother finally exited. But then she found herself in a punk club. In the back, by the bar, was Whitty, decked out in Goth garb. She was standing with a hot guy who Fordham recognized as Brandon, dressed in his deli uniform. Whitty and Brandon began to make out passionately. Fordham ran over to separate them, but Brandon pushed her away.

"Um, like, Fordham, you had your chance, but you blew it. Your daughter is way hotter!"

"Yeah, Mom. While you were busy writing your book, I was busy getting salami from Brandon."

The two of them were holding a six-foot hero, each taking huge bites from opposite sides. Fordham wanted to stay, but after a blink, she was in a delivery room. There was Evie, hugely pregnant, her feet in stirrups, in labor. Fordham was at her side, trying to decipher what she was saying through her panting and moaning.

"Marv read *Flowers from the Heart: The Dentist with a Slow Drill.* Hee, hee, hoo. That man always has"—the contraction escalated—"something to prooove!" At the top of her lungs she grunted, "Thanks for the best seller, Fordham!"

The next face Fordham saw was that of Abe, who was dressed as the attending physician, positioned between Evie's legs. "Push! Push! It's time to deliver."

FORDHAM WOKE WITH A start. She got off the couch and went to check on Whitty. She was still fast asleep and, fortunately, still ten years old. Just to make sure she was truly awake, Fordham peeked at Dorie, who was sleeping alone, her room still a muted ecru. Satisfied that her dream had been just that, Fordham went to her room and clicked on her desk lamp, anxious to reread her comforting submission hanging on the wall. Somewhere in back of her mind, she believed she was replacing one dream with another. Or maybe she was trying to give herself the encouragement she needed to believe in what she could have with Aaron. After a few tears, she went over to her mirror and examined her face for signs of aging.

As much as she tried, there was no way she could sleep. She finally gave up and showered. Now was as good a time as any to work on the book. She went to copy a page, but it came out blank. She was going to have to buy more printer ink. Her desire for hard copies was an expense she would have to shoulder. She liked the feel of paper in her hands. Sure, e-books were more convenient, but turning pages was more engaging and exciting than pushing buttons. Convenience wasn't everything. After all, drinking was easier than chewing, but no one outside of LA was willing to give up food.

There were more submissions to review, and everything was going relatively well, but again, she noticed that only one pile continued to grow. She was hesitant to tell Abe at this point in the project, but if this was going to work, she didn't have much choice.

A couple of hours later Fordham entered Abe's office, carrying coffee and doughnuts, determined to get his approval.

"How nice. For me? How's the book coming along?" He sounded cautious, as if he sensed he was being played.

"That depends on what you decide. I think the best stories are coming from people over forty. I get erotica from twenty-year-olds who lost their virginity to hyperlinks. Thirty-year-olds haven't screwed up enough to be interesting. I want to change the title to *Flowers from the Heart: Love Online after Forty*.

"It's risky to be so specific."

"Abe, we did *Flowers from the Heart: The Golfer with a Low Handicap*."

"Yeah, I know. Don't remind me. Headquarters is still on my case about that one."

"But *Flowers from the Heart: The 'General Hospital' Fan* went into a second and third printing."

"That's true," Abe said. "You know this project better than I do. I trust you. If it works for you, it works for me."

Fordham toyed with the box and offered Abe another doughnut. "Now what?"

"I'm having a dinner party. I know you haven't wanted to go out much since you lost Harriet, but I'd really like you to come."

"You cook?" he asked.

"I garnish. My mother cooks."

"Your guy coming?"

"Yes."

"Ah, now I understand," Abe said. "Your mother doesn't like him, does she?"

Fordham wasn't sure how to answer that question. Maybe Dorie didn't like Aaron, or maybe she didn't trust that Fordham could make a good decision when it came to men. Regardless, Fordham didn't want to ruin her day by starting off with a conversation about either possibility.

"Will you come?"

"Sounds entertaining." Abe looked into the distance as if imagining the scene. "Okay, I'll come. Even without the coffee and doughnuts." He winked.

She returned to her office, glad that Abe was being so agreeable. It would be easier to work now that she was given more control.

Everything was headed in the right direction. Around lunchtime, there was a knock at her door.

"Come in," Fordham said, standing at the file cabinet, searching ferociously for stats on their last book about relationships. She glanced at the door and found a woman wearing a Blake Lively blond wig and a tight neon-lime minidress with sequins studding the deep neckline. She was also wearing matching fishnets and black stilettos. Fordham cringed at the thought that she was there to deliver a new singing telegram from Aaron. But then the woman spoke, and Fordham realized who it was.

"Evie?" she asked with a modicum of uncertainty.

"In the flesh."

"You could say that. Has there been a career change you'd like to tell me about?" Fordham tossed a file on her desk. "Why are you dressed up like you jumped off the cover of *Debbie Does Dallas*?"

"What's wrong with it? I lost six pounds!"

"And you are clearly thinner. But as a dental hygienist, you're marketing a whole new look for a cavity search."

"Fordham, you don't get it. When I look in the mirror, my face doesn't look happy to see me."

"Right now, your face doesn't even know you."

"I'm thinking of having some fat from my butt injected into my lips," Evie said.

"Why? So you can laugh out your ass?"

Evie was getting teary. Fordham knew she'd have to switch gears, or they were going to end up arguing. She realized Evie's whole getup was another way to try to deal with the sudden onslaught of extreme middle age. As a friend, she would have to be more supportive.

"So Dylan is having a baby. That doesn't mean you have to dress like a newbie at the Playboy Mansion." With no reaction from Evie, Fordham floundered for the next thing to say. "You're already beautiful and sexy—because you're you."

"You still don't understand."

"Of course I do. I just don't think you need to handle it this way."

"I have to go." Evie sounded hurt, bordering on angry.

"Evie, wait. I'm sorry." Fordham stepped in front of the door. "I'm having a dinner party, and I need you there no matter what you feel like wearing."

"Is Aaron coming?"

"Yes."

"Has your mother seen him yet?" Evie asked.

"No."

"I'll be there." And with that, she tossed the wig onto Fordham's desk.

Chapter Seventeen: Bless Who's Coming to Dinner

Fordham paced nervously through the supermarket. This evening was going to determine her future. She picked up a bag of romaine lettuce and inspected it for signs of wilting and bruising. Just because she felt like damaged goods didn't mean she had to serve any at her party. Her stomach kept growling as if to ask her why she had chosen to do this. She had no real answer other than to burp and continue pushing her shopping cart up and down the dizzying aisles.

She stopped when she got to the mushrooms. *Mushrooms.* Aaron loved her stuffed mushrooms. She'd prepared them for a New Year's Eve party at Marv's house, and everyone, including his mother, asked her for the recipe. Aaron was proud and told her that he was so lucky to have found a girl who had it all—beauty, brains, passion, and a touch of Julia Child. He found out it was a pretty small touch when she attempted lo mein a couple of weeks later, but until then, she was nothing short of a goddess, a role she didn't know she would ever have to relinquish.

She picked up the last box of gourmet whites and tossed them into the cart. Her stomach growled again. She was pretty sure it was telling her to just deal. This dinner party was going to be the pivotal moment of introducing Aaron back into her life. There was no better way than in one fell swoop. Evie and Abe would be open-minded, Whitty would see his potential, and after spending time with him, Dorie would understand why this was destiny at work. Fordham took a second glimpse at the box of mushrooms, hoping to see the word *magic* printed somewhere on the package.

The deli counter wasn't as crowded as usual, and for the first time in nearly two years, when her number was called, Brandon didn't jump to serve her. As a matter of fact, he ignored her. *Guess the sperm-donation idea is off the table.* She understood. Rejection wasn't an easy thing, and each person had a particular way of handling the disappointment.

Brandon's disappointment emerged from the back kitchen as a tall, thin, pretty brunette whose deli jacket tag said she was Olivia-Sue and whose T-shirt clearly stated in red capital letters that she was Property of Brandon. She asked Fordham for her ticket and her order. Her friendliness suggested that Brandon hadn't said anything to her about their date, and to his credit, he never gave anything away during the interaction. He seemed happy. Fordham briefly wondered if he had forgotten about her altogether, but he gave her a wink as she left the counter with her pickles and chopped liver.

She was amazed at how easy it was for kids these days to mend their broken hearts. Here she was, decades later, still trying to get over how badly she'd been hurt after Aaron had broken up with her. Her crushing heartache had been unbearable, leaving her vulnerable to anyone who could make the emptiness go away—the kind of pain that had led her to marry Gil just to forget how little she must have meant to Aaron for him to have dismissed her so cavalierly. Fortunately, that was a memory she could now forget. Aaron was being nothing but attentive, and she had no reason to question his intentions, though she had yet to figure out what they were.

The drive home was a blur. Sometimes, she wanted to smack herself. Those days were long over, and she was obsessing as if there was something she could do to change history. She had to remind herself that the upcoming dinner wasn't about bemoaning the past but was about acknowledging the present and guiding the future. As a hostess, she had to be a good poker player, assuming a confident air while keeping her anxiety hidden.

As soon as she walked through the door, her spirits were lifted. The house was enveloped in the sweet, aromatic smells of garlic, onion, and basil—plus a touch of vanilla, courtesy of a candle set on the end table next to the couch. Feeling inspired, she went into the kitchen and began preparing the mushrooms. She didn't remember if it had been the heavy amount of Parmesan cheese or the extra minced anchovies that had earned Aaron's raves. Since she wasn't sure, she added a little bit of both for good measure. When the mushrooms were all stuffed, she proudly placed them in the oven.

Dorie's roast had been in the oven for hours. The vegetables were cut up and ready for the skillet. The mashed potatoes were just about done, and all the hors d'oeuvres and cold appetizers were neatly arranged. Everything was going according to schedule. Maybe this evening *was* about changing history—not to alter what had happened but to show what might have happened had a different path been taken.

And if she had taken a different path, maybe she wouldn't feel like a sweaty bundle of nerves. If she hadn't already downed two glasses of wine, she might have popped a Valium, something she hadn't done since she had a slipped disc at fifteen. There was no reason for her to be so anxious. Everything was in order. The house was decked out in fine crystal, china, and candlelight, and except for the mothballs, it smelled like her grandmother's apartment in the Bronx on a Friday night.

Fordham went over to the CD player and tried to decide what to play. She settled on Gato Barbieri's *Caliente*, figuring the saxophone would be romantic, unobtrusive, and subliminally sexy.

Whitty bounced in wearing an oversized T-shirt, jeans, and a Yankees cap, whining, "I know it's an old game, but the Yanks are sucking." She threw her cap in the air, caught it, and stuck it back on her head. "Kinda like this music. Mom, why do you listen to boring stuff that doesn't have words?"

"It's a dinner party. We'll be using our own words. And it is not boring. It's jazz."

"Yeah, yeah. So where is everybody?"

"Should be here soon. Is that what you're wearing?"

"What's wrong with jeans? I see you're wearing outfit number two with a new necklace. Nice." She snatched a few crackers and went back to her room.

Fordham checked herself out in the hallway mirror. She liked outfit number two. It was jet-black, comfortable yet sexy, and most importantly, slimming. It was the outfit she'd planned to wear on *Oprah* to promote *Flowers from the Heart: The Oprah Addict* until the segment was cut due to some legal technicality. The change of plan was a disappointment to this day because Fordham believed she and Oprah were kindred spirits and would have become besties. For the dinner part that night, Oprah would have brought her signature gourmet key lime Bundt cake.

She went back to the kitchen to see what was left to do. Dorie was meditating over the pot-roast gravy while adding squirts of ketchup à la Aunt Fanny. Fordham checked the vegetables and was tossing the salad with her hands when the doorbell rang.

"Mom, my hands are oily. Please get that."

Dorie grabbed a sheet of paper towel and wiped her hands. "With a little luck, maybe he'll slip right through your fingers again."

"Mom, please behave." Not trusting her mother, Fordham peeked out of the entrance to the kitchen as Dorie opened the door to Aaron, who was wearing a long black leather jacket and holding a large cake box.

"Hello, Aaron." Dorie's reception was underwhelming as he handed her the box from Ferrara's, the sweetest spot in Little Italy. "Thank you," she said, eyeing him up and down as he hung his coat on the rack.

He was wearing an expensive-looking charcoal-gray Italian suit with a matching turtleneck. Dorie quickly inspected him again. She seemed unimpressed, as if she could have sized him up with a thimble.

"It's a Napoleon cake. I remember you and Fordham used to fight over the icing."

"We did," Dorie said, "and I remember you and Fordham used to fight over—"

"Mom-Mom, did you see Ella's squeakie? I looked everywhere." Whitty had appeared out of nowhere, still wearing her baseball cap and jeans. She was holding Ella and scanning the room.

Fordham, still manning her post, almost cheered at Whitty's timing.

"Aaron, have you met Whitty, Fordham's daughter?" Dorie asked, ignoring Whitty's plea.

He shook his head.

"Whitty, this is Aaron, Mommy's friend from high school."

Aaron sneezed, sending Ella jumping out of Whitty's arms and out of the room. Whitty wasn't shy about studying him from head to toe. Fordham could tell Whitty was about as impressed as her mother. Her eyes kept rolling from his perfectly gelled hair to his pointy leather shoes. Whitty wouldn't understand corporate casual. He should have worn jeans. *No, I should have told him to wear jeans.* She let out a long sigh. *So much for first impressions.* Unless she could find a way to turn things around, it was going to be a long night.

"Hi, Whitty," Aaron said. "Nice to meet you." He sneezed several times, making Whitty step away. "Sorry. Small allergy, big cat." He took out a packet of pills. "Dorie, may I please have some water?"

"Of course. I'll be right back. Why don't you and Whitty get acquainted?" Dorie giggled.

Seeing Dorie coming, Fordham quickly hopped back into the kitchen. "Well?" Fordham asked, pouring a glass of wine. "What do you think?" She drank a few healthy sips.

"I think too much alcohol will make your skin sag."

"That's not what I'm talking about." Fordham took another swig. "What do you think of Aaron?"

"I think he's allergic to cats. What do you want me to say? He looks like Aaron... he sneezes like Aaron. He's Aaron." She scrunched her face. "Is something burning?"

Fordham checked the oven and freaked. "Oh Christ—I burned the mushrooms. I burned the mushrooms! Dammit! They used to be Aaron's favorite."

"Well, now salsa and chips will be his favorite. Relax, honey. It's only food." She got Aaron's water but was sidetracked by the bland potatoes.

"Thanks, Mom. When I'm cooking, it's only food. When you're cooking, we're in *Iron Chef*'s stadium."

Fordham took out a bag of tortilla chips and a big colorful never-used ceramic bowl she and Gil had gotten as an engagement gift. "Mom, where's Whitty?"

"Talking to Aaron."

"Talking?"

"You know, that thing people do when words come out of their mouths."

"Funny, Mom," Fordham said, alternately shredding a block of cheddar cheese and slicing jalapenos. "You know Whitty hasn't exactly been open to the idea of meeting anyone I'm seeing. I just don't want her to give him a hard time."

"He's a big boy, sweetheart. If he can't handle her at hello, this dinner party may as well be a tasty bon voyage." Dorie changed to a more supportive tone. "Honey, I'm sure everything is going just fine. Relax. Nothing is worth crow's-feet."

"Thanks, Mom." Fordham went back to the kitchen doorway to see how Aaron was going to handle her mother and Whitty without her intervention. Perhaps it was a sneaky move, but it was also one of the primary reasons she was having this dinner party.

Dorie entered the family room with a glass of water for Aaron. Whitty was perched on the arm of the couch like a bird ready to fly. Aaron was a few cushions away and didn't seem to mind the distance.

"Here you go, Aaron," Dorie said, handing him the glass.

"Thanks," he said, struggling to smile.

"How are you two doing?" Dorie asked indifferently.

"Great. Just getting to know each other." Aaron swallowed his pills with a loud gulp.

"Good. I have a call I must make. I'll be right back." Dorie went into her room, and Fordham continued to stand like a prop against the kitchen doorway.

"So you're a Yankees girl," Aaron said. "Isn't the season over?"

"Duh, we have the YES channel."

"Ah, got it," Aaron said. "I'm kind of partial to the Mets, but a New York team is a New York team."

"No fans I know would ever say that." Whitty crossed her hands defensively. "What do you do?" she asked not bothering to feign interest.

"I help women get pregnant."

"Eeew! That's a job?" she screeched.

Fordham chuckled. Whitty did indeed have her sense of humor. She continued watching as her daughter jumped off her perch and got some pretzels from a bowl on a table nearby. After scanning the room, Whitty sat on a chair away from Aaron and turned on her tablet.

Dorie returned and headed to Aaron, who was sitting stiffly on the couch as if awaiting his next misstep. "She's something, that girl," Dorie said with pride. "Can you believe she's only ten?"

"I can certainly believe she's a Price girl. Maybe I should ask Fordham if she needs my help." Aaron stood up.

"I wouldn't."

The doorbell rang. Fordham decided to let Dorie continue to work the front of the house. She hadn't finished setting up the default food, and she wanted to give Aaron a chance to feel what he was getting into. If he still wanted to pursue her after this experience, she would be more inclined to take him seriously. As much as she needed to prepare, she needed to watch what was going on even more. She eyed the snacks on the counter and continued to stand by the kitchen door to watch this chapter of the evening unfold.

Dorie opened the door to Evie, who was dressed like her usual self but with more makeup. Fordham was impressed. Her look was chic and confident. She and Dorie hugged cheek to cheek, leaving room for the enormous cookie platter in Evie's hands.

As Dorie took the platter, Evie's eyes shifted to Aaron. "Oh my God! Aaron." Evie gave him a welcoming hug. "It's been... I don't know... forever and a half?"

"Something like that. So tell me Evie, how are you?"

"Still married, but Marv is working tonight."

"How are the kids? You have two, right?"

"No, just one. And another on the way."

"Really?" Aaron said, studying her as if trying to figure out how far along she was. "And you didn't even need me."

"Oh, no, not me. My daughter!" Gratitude for Aaron's error brightened Evie's entire face.

Fordham accepted that as her entrée into the evening and came in with the chips and salsa. She noticed Whitty quietly taking in the whole scene and seeming genuinely amused. She was in a room full of adults, and her life was likely more stable than anyone else's. Whitty ate with more poise than gusto, making Fordham wonder if this would be the moment she would always remember as her daughter's passage into full-fledged adolescence. With a push, maybe Whitty would even let Aaron in at least a little bit.

Aaron appeared relieved to see Fordham. Still, he gave her a kiss that didn't need to be censored. He was pouring her a glass of wine when Whitty accidentally grazed his arm, sending the liquid all over his suit.

"Oh shit!" Aaron grabbed a handful of napkins, but they were about as effective as trying to extinguish a forest fire with a water gun. "You have to watch where you're going, Whitty."

To that, Whitty offered a scowl the likes of which Fordham had never seen.

"It was an accident, Aaron," Whitty said, emphasizing his name.

She slowly stomped out of the room. Fordham knew Whitty had wanted to punctuate the sentence with *dipshit*—one of her father's favorites. Luckily, her daughter had held back, which—for better or worse—allowed the evening to continue.

"I am so sorry, Aaron," Fordham said. "I'm sure she didn't mean it."

"Of course she didn't mean it!" Dorie said, rushing to Whitty's defense. "Now you got her all upset." She left to check on Whitty.

Although it seemed like an accident, Fordham wasn't sure Whitty's motives were entirely pure. Maybe she'd subconsciously knocked the wine in response to Aaron's choice of apparel. But that was probably more Fordham's issue than Whitty's.

"Come with me," she said to Aaron. In seconds, they were in Fordham's bedroom. "You know it was accident." She opened her closet, immediately happy she'd organized it the other day.

"Okay. She's a kid. I get it," Aaron said, calming down.

"Yeah, and sometimes, because of her hip issue, she's a bit more on the clunky side."

"You're right. I'll apologize. I'm not used to kids."

She went into her closet and pulled out a men's jogging suit.

"What the hell?" Aaron was flabbergasted as he stared at the outfit. The fabric was printed with hundred-dollar bills. "Is this some kind of bad joke?"

"Yes! Actually, it was. Gloria—you remember, my mom's friend—bought it for my ex as a gag gift. But he was as amused as you are and never wore it."

"I have newfound respect for him."

Fordham wasn't even sure why she'd kept the damn thing, unless somewhere in back of her mind, she'd anticipated having a night like this.

"You really want me to wear that thing?" Aaron asked. "It's tacky as hell."

"Well, I hope you can't fit into anything of mine." She went through her closet for other possibilities but came up empty. Her last-ditch effort was a sweater box under her bed, but it yielded the same results. "Just put it on. It's the best I can do."

"Okay, fine, but it's on you to explain to your mother that I am not all about the Benjamins."

Fordham handed him the clothes. Although she was tidying up, she was able to catch a few peeks of his body while he was changing. There was no denying that the years had been more than kind in turning Aaron the kid into Aaron the man.

When he was dressed, he followed her into the party with the angst of a man on death row. Dorie did a double take when Aaron entered, and Fordham offered a quick announcement to everyone, explaining the new outfit. No one gave her grief, which was surprising since it wasn't her birthday.

Whitty gave Aaron a once-over. "That's my dad's."

"Yeah, your mother told me," Aaron said. "Listen, I'm sorry I got snippy before."

"Sure, whatever." Whitty parked herself at the snack table.

Fordham had drained a glass of wine and had a few chips with Aaron when a phone call took him into another room. She replenished her glass. Evie grabbed her arm and led her into the kitchen.

"Are you having a hot flash or is that cabernet invading your cheeks?" Evie probed.

"I can't do this." Fordham was hyperventilating.

"Do what?"

"Have a dinner party. Have Aaron here. Have a book to write and a daughter to raise and a mother to criticize me."

"But, Fordham, we're women. This is what we do. We clutch life by the balls and scoff when it tries to come in our faces."

Fordham stayed silent.

"Look around," Evie said. "What do you see?"

"A mess. I'm not even sure which dry cleaner is good enough for Aaron's suit."

"It doesn't matter. Honey, this is success."

"Thank you," she said through a few stray tears. "And on top of everything else, there's this." She went into the cabinet, pulled out a sheet of paper, and handed it to Evie.

"What is this?" Evie gave it a cursory review. "This is that submission you read to me from that guy. So?"

"So I have a few copies of it stashed here and there to read when I need a lift. I pulled the one off my wall just in case Aaron might end up in my room. Which turned out to be an excellent call for unforeseen reasons. Anyway, I still read it every night before I go to bed. I don't even know why. Aaron is great, and things seem to be working, so why do I feel this compulsive need to gush over it?" Fordham pressed her hands against her forehead.

"Maybe it's become your fairy tale. We're all entitled to fantasies. Marv would kill me if he knew that sometimes I close my eyes and picture George Clooney. Stop thinking so much. Come on. Let's have a party."

Evie's phone rang, keeping her in the kitchen. Fordham went back to the family room to find Aaron still on his phone and Dorie and Whitty watching *Back to the Future*. This wasn't exactly what she'd had in mind for a dinner party, but she decided to make the best of it. She sat down with a bowl of pretzels and joined them.

Aaron must have seen the expression on Fordham's face and realized he was being antisocial, because he quickly finished his call. He motioned her to meet him in the kitchen, where they found Evie filling an ice bucket. Though part of Fordham wanted to want to be ensconced in Aaron's sexy embrace, more of her was ready to call it a night and crawl into bed—alone.

The doorbell rang. Fordham went to get it, but Evie stopped her with a wink and said she'd get it on her way to the guacamole. She seemed almost excited to be on Team Aaron, which was odd, since she was usually the first one to say that Fordham was moving too fast or reading too much into a smile or a kiss. Evie's good sense seemed to have flown out the window just when Fordham needed her to be clearheaded and scrutinizing. Fordham certainly wasn't going to share any of her concerns with Dorie. That would be like begging to be smacked on the head by a two-by-four repeatedly. No, she would have to work this out on her own.

But Aaron didn't appear to be questioning anything. He wrapped his arm around her while she finished plating hummus. He must have been happy they were finally alone because he kissed her as if there would be no other chance for the rest of the evening. It was a promising kiss that encouraged her to make the evening work and see what the future could hold.

Aaron remembered something he needed from the car for a business call he was expecting. He promised to be right back and left through the side door. If Fordham hadn't been so busy, she might have cared more, but she knew the only reason he was in town was because of work demands. She got the plate of hummus and set it on the table in the family room.

Dorie said the pizza delivery guy had come with an order, but she'd told him it was a mistake unless Fordham had ordered backup pies because she didn't trust her dinner menu, which would have really upset her. After assuring Dorie that she had the utmost faith in her pot roast, Fordham poured herself the last of a bottle of wine she wasn't sure she had shared with anyone else. The doorbell rang again. Fordham, standing off to the side of the snacks while Evie was hovering around the cheese tray, was more than happy to let Dorie remain the official greeter. The door opened to Abe, who was all cheery though struggling to hold a majestic bouquet of flowers in one arm and a bottle of wine, paired with a gold box of candy, in the other.

"Hi, I'm Abe. You must be Dorie. These are for you," he said, handing her the flowers.

"These are gorgeous. How did you know I love pink roses?"

"Lucky guess. And for the little lady..." He handed Whitty the candy.

"Salted caramels. These are awesome!" She rewarded him with a kiss on the cheek.

Aaron came back into the family room, and Fordham led him to the door to greet Abe.

"Fordham, for you," Abe said, handing her the wine.

"Perfect," she whispered.

"Hi, Abe." Evie shook Abe's hand. "Nice to see you again." Before Abe could answer, Evie clutched her stomach and sprinted to the "powder room."

"Sorry. I didn't bring anything for you, big guy," he said to Aaron. "But you seem to be rolling in dough, so I don't feel that bad."

Dorie giggled and said she'd tell him about the clothes later.

"So you've met my mother," Fordham said.

"Yes, I have," Abe said with a broad smile. "Sorry I'm a little late. Traffic." He was trying to sound suave, but it was a wasted effort. "I'm lying. I stopped off to buy aftershave."

"Well, it was worth it." Dorie said. "You smell..." Dorie's face contorted. "Ugh—my pot roast!" She ran into the kitchen, clutching Abe's flowers to her chest. Fordham considered following her, but since she already couldn't take the heat, she needed to stay out of the kitchen.

The family room had grown quiet, and Fordham noticed that Whitty had turned off the TV. She couldn't normally get her to do that without a fight, but there she was with Abe, going through old CDs and giggling. Fordham was disappointed that none of that bonding was happening between Whitty and Aaron. Abe nuzzled the cat and handed Whitty a CD to play. Whitty obliged, and Abe led her onto the designated dance floor.

"In honor of Whitty's cat," Abe proclaimed.

They danced to Ella Fitzgerald singing, "All the Things You Are," a song Fordham loved that her father used to sing to her in the car late at night when they were coming home from just about any-where. Aaron asked her to dance. And in that warm memory of her dad, she not only danced, but she even managed to relax as well.

It might have been the wine and music, or perhaps the way Aaron was holding her close to him, but something was telling Ford-ham that everything was going to work out the way it was supposed to. All she had to do was have faith that nothing in life ever happened in vain. If she would just let herself meld into the soft, simple steps of the moment, she believed she would always feel safe and the pain of the past would wither away as all things did when they went unfed.

"Dinner will be ready very shortly," Dorie announced as she reentered the family room.

Their dance ended, and Fordham broke away from Aaron to talk to Dorie. "Mom, Aaron was just saying how well he remembers your delicious dinners. Isn't that sweet?"

Dorie gave her a curt smile. "Sweet."

"It smells great," Abe said, dipping Whitty, who told him to finish the dance with Dorie so she could check out how the Yanks were doing.

Abe took Dorie's hand. "I can't make pot roast. It's either too dry or too stringy," he said, leading her into a foxtrot.

"Getting it right is tricky," she said, comfortably accepting his lead.

"I like tricky," he said, dipping her.

Fordham was enjoying the scene, but as perfect as some moments might seem, there were always others conspiring to keep the laws of balance in check. Yes, their kiss had been reminiscent of the passion they'd shared in the old days. The problem was this evening had presented no opportunities for her to promote Aaron. Between his cat allergy, his wardrobe malfunction—which had been her and Whitty's fault—and his business calls, the party was turning out to be only an appetizer. She would have to find other ways to get Whitty and Dorie on Team Aaron.

Evie finally emerged from the bathroom a little pale and seemingly ready to add lactose intolerance to her list of middle-age maladies. Despite the setbacks, dinner was going okay. Everyone was eating and drinking, and the conversation, though topical and bland, was civil and endurable. If no one asked any probing questions or challenged the status quo, Fordham believed the night could be considered relatively successful.

"So, Aaron, how long are you expecting to be in town?" Dorie asked as if hoping to circle the end date on her calendar.

Fordham braced herself like a referee at the US Open, sensing this question was just the first serve of the match. Both of them could be hotheads. Any exchange would most assuredly snowball into a volley, and she had no clue who the ultimate victor would be.

"It depends. I'm researching a few offices, and we'll see. It seems like New York is the hottest ticket in town for fertility, but expansion is the way to go. What about you, Dorie? Any plans to relocate somewhere to bask in the sun? I hear Brisbane is beautiful and brimming with retirees."

Fordham wondered if anyone heard her gasp.

"Relocate?" Dorie uttered as if Aaron had stabbed her in the heart with his fork.

"I think he meant like a vacation—somewhere to have fun for a little while," Fordham offered as a bandage.

"I think he said relocate," Abe interjected, not realizing the incendiary implication.

"Me too," Whitty proclaimed with a big, telling smile that reeked of her agenda.

"I didn't hear him say anything because the almonds in these green beans are so incredibly crunchy and delicious that you can't hear anything that's not going on in your mouth," Evie said, munching away. Like a true friend, she had taken a large dose of extra-strength gut medication.

"Actually, I enjoy the seasons, Aaron. *All* of them. Always have. You know, we Price women have thick skin," Dorie said so casually it was cutting.

Aaron helped himself to more potatoes.

"And heavy furs. Right, Mom?" Fordham added, trying to lighten things up.

"I think it's mean to wear fur," Whitty said. "How would you feel if some mink was walking around in your skin right now?"

"Relieved," Fordham answered, sending her an accusatory look.

"I hear the Yankees hired a new pitcher," Evie said, taking a pickle.

Fordham had no idea how to facilitate that conversation.

"Mom-Mom, where is Brisbane?"

"Australia," Dorie said, glaring at Aaron.

Aaron seemed oblivious to Dorie's tone, which had Fordham quaking in her heels. "Mom, Aaron must remember that when we were kids, you told us you wanted to see the Sydney Opera House."

"I told you a lot of things when you were kids. Tastes change, dear. At least for some of us."

"You know, another place that's booming for seniors is Tokyo." Aaron continued eating. "You could corner the market on pot roast."

Fordham wished she could shut Aaron up without being too obvious.

"I'd still be a little concerned about Fukushima," Abe chimed in. "While the radiation risks are minimal at this point, why should a beautiful woman like Dorie expose herself unnecessarily?"

Dorie looked at Abe the way Margo had looked at her banana split at their last lunch date.

"When did Derek Jeter retire again?" Evie asked.

"Sorry to disappoint you, Aaron, but I'm not planning on going anywhere." Dorie scanned the table. "Fordham, we need more water."

Worried that she might miss something crucial, Fordham ignored her mother's request.

"No prob," Aaron said, getting up.

A loud shriek informed them that Ella had been under Aaron's chair until he stepped on her, which was precisely when he tripped and fell into Dorie's lap. Dorie stared down at his face as the tip of his nose met her nipple head-on. They both looked mortified and jumped up at the same time. Evie had her hand over her mouth, and Fordham could almost see the laughter between her fingers.

Aaron, white as a sheet, quickly apologized and sat down. Dorie rolled her eyes at Fordham and reclaimed her seat. It was a good time to get the water.

Fordham went into the kitchen to clean up the tattered shreds of her dinner party. Whatever hope she'd had of everyone getting along had been dashed by the will of the universe. It was going to take a miracle to right this sinking ship. Just as she was ready to give up, the sound of laughter from the dining room sent her into the hall. Obscured from view, she decided to listen in.

"Well, I, for one, think New York is the only place to live if you want to stay young," Abe exclaimed. "I have a friend who moved to Arizona. He came back to visit, and he looked downright coriaceous."

"What?" Dorie asked intently.

"Coriaceous. You know, like leather. Sorry, I have a thing for words. My late wife gave me a dictionary a few years ago, and I've been reading it for fun ever since. I think that's why Fordham and I get along so well. She's into words too."

"Well, she was raised on crossword puzzles. Her father and I used to do the *New York Times* puzzle every Sunday, in ink," Dorie said with a hint of cockiness.

"That's funny. My wife and I had the same routine. Usually over brunch."

"Lox—" Dorie said.

"Eggs and onions," Abe finished.

"We lived the same Sundays," Dorie said, forgetting everyone else in the room.

"What did you do the rest of the week?" Abe asked.

"I had Fordham and a lot of volunteer work to keep me busy. Were you always in publishing?"

"Pretty much. I worked for a newspaper when I was a kid. I was never into numbers, but I've always been a logophile," Abe said.

"What's a logophile?" Whitty asked. "Someone who likes commercials?"

"Close," Abe said.

"A word lover," Abe and Dorie said in unison.

Last time Dorie had played Scrabble online with her archnemesis, she had left an *l-o* opened vertically on the game board. Her opponent completed it using his seven tiles to make *l-o-g-o-p-h-i-l-e*. The coincidence was uncanny.

"Whitty, dear, is the music still on?" Dorie asked in an exaggerated tone. "I'd like to hear some..." She paused. "Zouk."

"Zouk? You mean, like, Caribbean dance music?" Abe sounded astonished. "I just had that word come to mind the other day when I was..." He rubbed his forehead. "This may sound ridiculous, but do you play Scrabble online?"

"Yes!" Dorie roared. "Now that I gave up running and have no use for fartlek—you know, interval training!"

"No! Get out of here!" Abe looked stunned.

"You, my anonymous opponent, have been driving me crazy for months!"

Well, son of a gun. Her opponent was Abe. Yet another man who could drive both Price women crazy but for entirely different reasons.

"Better you than me," Aaron said, inviting disapproval from everyone. "But seriously, do you know the odds of something like this happening?"

"Better than yours of turning me into a Mets fan," Whitty responded with a scowl.

All heads turned to stare at Fordham when she reappeared with a new carafe of fresh water. Deciding it would be infinitely easier to play dumb, she nonchalantly asked, "Did I miss something?"

Chapter Eighteen: The Way We Err

Fordham was fast asleep when the phone rang, forcing her out of Johnny Depp's embrace on top of a Land Rover in the middle of an African rain forest. *Nothing's sacred.* She fought with her puffy Vera Wang comforter—a divorce gift from Evie—and a pesky matching throw pillow to reach the phone, only to then drop it twice before it actually got to her ear. Aaron was on the other end, sounding distraught. He'd left Fordham's late and had decided to stay at the Hilton in Nanuet, a five-minute drive away, to avoid an accident reported on the Tappan Zee Bridge. He was waiting for her at Congers Lake, a park they used to go to for picnics where they would feed ducks and make out. He had a double latte waiting for her and wanted to know if she could get there while it was still hot—which, he specified meant she shouldn't bother with anything more than clothes.

She could understand if the night had been too much for him. It had been too much for her, too, but it was her life. He was probably going to return the hideous jogging suit and end whatever they had begun. She'd be stoic and understanding and—

She abruptly switched gears. It was possible he just wanted to see her away from the mix of too much food, Scrabble, the Yankees, and overzealous critics. He had toughed out the whole evening. Maybe he was a glutton for punishment and ready to take things to the next level.

It was too early for a weekend morning to begin, but Fordham was curious to hear what he had to say. She brushed her hair into a ponytail, threw on jeans and a sweatshirt, and uncharacteristically got to the park before she had a chance to think.

She found Aaron sitting on a bench facing the lake with two coffee cups next to him. His eyes were closed. He might have been meditating, but she had him pegged as a skeptic, an assumption likely confirmed by the two loud snores he let out before his eyes flew open. He wasted no time getting to the point.

"Denise called," he said, handing over her coffee.

He didn't have the jogging suit, and he was talking about his ex. *So far, so good.*

"Why?"

"The divorce papers are ready."

"That was fast."

Fordham envisioned walking down the aisle with Aaron. She was wearing a fashion-forward dress and giving Margo the finger. Realizing how childish that thought was, she stopped herself and focused her attention back on Aaron.

"Yes," Aaron said. "She also wanted me to know that she plans to turn my forceps into nutcrackers." He opened the plastic tab of his coffee lid. "Isn't there a five-letter word for that?" He looked at her for the answer.

"Bitch?"

"Precisely. Right on a triple-word score."

"It's too early for Scrabble," Fordham said, not wanting to revisit any aspect of her dinner party. "Aaron, I'm really sorry. Divorce is always difficult, even when you want it."

"Don't be sorry. I'm tough. I even survived dinner last night."

"I know. Things were a bit tense."

"Tense?" he said. "I've had easier nights delivering sextuplets."

"I don't know what to say."

"It might not have been so bad if your mother hadn't started me off as a sitting duck—"

"Yup. And then cooked your goose. I know. The whole night was a foul."

They commiserated and finished their coffee while watching a couple of swans do a pas de deux across the water. She appreciated the bucolic scene and, in that moment, wished she could fly away and forget about everything life seemed determined to teach her. There had to be a reason for all the madness. Between her romantic failings, Margo leaving her with the book project, Whitty on the fast track to maturation, her mother moving in, and even Evie becoming a grandmother, the energy around her couldn't produce more static if it tried.

Aaron was yawning when Fordham's phone rang.

"Hi, monkey, what's up? Lily's house? What time? Okay, get ready. I'll be home soon. Love you too." She ended the call. "I have to drive Whitty to a friend's house."

"Short and sweet, huh?"

"'Fraid so, but I'm all yours tonight if you're still into dinner."

Fordham got up and kissed Aaron on the forehead as if he were a little boy who'd just lost his puppy. He didn't seem to mind her maternal edge.

"Of course I am. It'll be nice—and quiet. And no worries about today. I have to work anyway. Welch's Pharmaceuticals just launched a new spermicidal jelly. Big mix-up. What we've got goes better with peanut butter."

IT WASN'T EVEN LUNCHTIME yet, and Fordham was exhausted. Whitty was being quieter than usual, and Fordham was relegated to staring at license plates and quietly cursing out-of-towners for not understanding the local traffic flow. She stopped at a light, and a silver Maserati from California on her right begged for entry into her lane. She smiled mischievously and let him in because he reminded her of Johnny Depp and the dream that had been yanked from her prematurely. She eyed Whitty, who was running her finger over a mark on the upper middle of the windshield.

"Is that a crack?" Fordham asked.

"Yeah. It's little, though."

"Well, I still have to take care of it." Fordham checked the Google map to see how close they were. "Why did you call Lily?"

"I didn't. She called me. She wants me to teach her how to write in script. And David said he would help me with my poem."

"David?" Just the mention of his name sent little quivers down her spine. That wasn't good. Whether she liked it or not, she was looking forward to seeing him.

"He said *Dr. Prince* makes him feel old. It's only when we're not in school, of course."

"Hmm. You know, you never even told me you entered the contest."

"I know. I wanted it to be a surprise."

"Okay. Are you going to show me your poem?"

"No." Whitty tilted her head at the phone to see the directions. "It's here," she said, pointing to a charming white colonial with a black roof and a red door.

Flower boxes holding an assortment of mums, marigolds, and yellow pansies hung below the windows, and a little footbridge crossed over a tiny creek toward the far side of the front lawn. It was the kind of house that, along with a blue sky, gigantic trees, and a refurbished tractor in the driveway, would be the subject of a jigsaw puzzle.

Fordham brought Whitty to the door and rang the bell. She could hear Lily running and yelling to David to let her get it. He was standing close behind her when the door flew open.

"See, Whitty?" Lily said, showing her a big sticky clump of matted hair. "Me and Daddy made Rice Krispie treats. I got marshmallow in my hair, and it was so yucky!"

David picked up scissors and a comb from off the top of a hall-way dresser and quickly stashed them in a drawer. He seemed a little frazzled, but not enough to cut through his basic calm.

"Yeah. I hate when that happens," Fordham said, speaking from experience.

"Believe me—me too," David said. "Please, come in."

"Thanks for having Whitty over. She said you offered to help with her poem. She—well, we—really appreciate the extra attention."

"What can I say? She's special. She must get it from her mom."

David's phone rang, and he went into a small study to answer it. Fordham was trying to analyze what he'd just said to her, but her attention was diverted by his conversation. She wondered if he realized she could hear him.

"I can't talk now," he said uncomfortably. "No, not now. Please don't come over. I will call you later. Promise."

He hung up and went back to Fordham, who could feel herself blushing. "I hope I'm not interrupting anything," she said.

"No! Not a thing."

"Okay. That's good. When should I pick Whitty up?"

"Why don't you let her stay and get her in the morning?" David retrieved the pen from behind his ear and put it in his pocket. "It would actually help me out. I have a quarterly report to finish, and with Lily busy, I might even be able to get it done."

"This is nice. You do me a favor and let me think I'm doing you one. I'm sure my mother will be happy to have the night off."

"Ah, you have plans." David sounded disappointed.

Fordham hadn't meant to invite the question. "Yeah, um, dinner. Nothing special. Just dinner with... an old friend. I should really go. I have to get my windshield repaired. There's this little crack. I don't even know how it happened."

"Well, you know what they say—broken glass means good luck."

"That's true, especially for the guys at Jose's Perfect Auto Body."

Fordham found Whitty and told her she could sleep over if she wanted to. Lily jumped up and down, and Whitty seemed happy with the arrangement. Fordham didn't want to intrude, but David assured her it wasn't an imposition. He had a stash of new toothbrushes for when his mother would come to visit and a big T-shirt Whitty could sleep in. He even offered to toss her clothes into the machine for the next day. Fordham left, realizing there was nothing she could find to obsess about except David's thoughtfulness.

THE GUYS AT THE AUTO body shop said the windshield would have to be replaced, and they could do it in the time it would take her to have a cup of coffee and do food shopping at the market nearby. She didn't feel like sitting there for that long. She mused over her options then called Evie, who was at Pettigrew's Bridal Salon, shopping for a wedding gown with Dylan. If Fordham wanted to join them, they would love to have her opinion. She was still having visions of Margo's dress selections, and it seemed crazy that no matter which way she turned, someone was either insanely in love or happily pregnant and planning a wedding.

There was only so much mirth and merriment Fordham could take. She told Evie that she had to work before seeing Aaron for dinner. It wasn't a lie. She didn't have all day to play *Say Yes to the Dress*, and her mood would have put a damper on all the *oohs* and *aahs* required when rating each froufrou frock. The fact that she wasn't in a better frame of mind troubled her. Maybe she needed to get a handle on what Aaron was expecting—or more importantly, on what she was expecting from him. She told Evie to have fun and was about to hang up when a wrench was thrown into her goodbye.

"So, Fordham, you never told me. How's the sex?"

That was a very good, very bad question. She walked outside for privacy and sat on a bench in front of the auto shop. "I couldn't tell you."

"Oh, you're not allowed?" Evie seemed earnest. "Is that some kind of tacit gyno rule?"

"No rule, I just don't—can't—answer," she stammered. "We haven't had sex yet."

"What? It's been at least a year since you've been with someone."

"You don't have to remind me. We just haven't had the time or the chance."

"Seriously, Fordham, how much time do you need?"

"It's been more than a couple of decades since we've been together. So I'm thinking I need a while."

"Honey, he's not twenty."

She listened as Evie told Dylan to try on the ball gown with the pink hearts and then the blue tulle. *On second thought, maybe I should head to the store to save the poor girl.*

"You don't get it. We're both really busy. Aaron is in meetings. I have the book and Whitty—"

"My concern is that *you're* not getting it. Period."

"I hear you," Fordham said. "And there's also the matter of the gatekeeper, who I'm more than sure would be willing to forgo Scrabble games just to sit between us and squelch every possible sexual impulse with a discussion about one friend's smelly yeast infection or another's hemorrhoid adventures. Honestly, Evie, I'm not sure how it's ever going to happen."

Despite how much she missed the intimacy, her life wasn't sounding or feeling very sexy even to her own ears. Fordham hung up with Evie, and with an hour to kill and nowhere to go, she wandered into a pet shop to see the new puppies and muse over her squelched libido. It wasn't lost, like her car key, but every time something came close to her ignition, there was a backfire. She picked up a baby Maltese that Ella, their cat, would have mistaken for lunch. It was into snuggling, and she held it close to her. As much as she wanted sex, as a single parent living with her mother, she felt the need to pursue it tastefully. She put the dog down, and it peed in retaliation. No great surprise—it was a male.

With still more time to kill, she stopped into the Five Below next door, figuring she would pick up nail polish for her toes. Two colors immediately caught her eye. Purple Passion might be a fun way to inspire possibilities for her evening with Aaron. And then there was Prince of the Sea, which, though dazzling, evoked her guilt for even choosing it. With hope in her heart, she went with the Passion.

Sex had been different when she was married. She and Gil were so into it at first that they used to take routine trips to the adult toy store to check out the inventory. They bought creams that smelled like French toast or snowflakes and oils that promised to soften and harden different body parts at the same time. If they were feeling really adventurous, they'd bring home an assortment of things that buzzed and hummed. Once Gil came home with a bag that should have been groceries but was filled with sexy gag gifts. She was pretty embarrassed one night when her parents were over and she acciden-tally prepared a box of penis-shaped pasta with meatballs for dinner. Arnie didn't notice, but her mother said on the sly that she felt like an obscene slut with every bite.

That spirit of adventure quickly disappeared, replaced by the same ruts, routines, and practical behaviors all couples vowed they wouldn't fall prey to when they were in the throes of passion and gratitude. No one cared about rubbery eggs or washing whites and colors together when there was a steady supply of orgasms on the menu, but those were the very things that crept inside a marriage when spouses became roommates, their bodies no longer revered as new territories of endless exploration. Everyone said it was natural for the sex to fly out of a marriage, which it did when Gil got pissed off and threw her favorite vibrator out the window at some very confused birds. But that hadn't happened until much later, when she figured out he'd been cheating and she wanted him to know that sex was mechanical for her too.

Maybe that was part of why she was feeling so hesitant about Aaron. She didn't want the fuss of being involved and hurt. When she was first split from Gil, she tried to protect herself by not caring about men. It was easy to gallivant and flirt without making an emotional investment. She'd have drinks or dinner, and most of the time, it was simple and pleasant. But after a while, like anything habitual, the experience became monotonous, and a date meant enduring another night of bad pickup lines:

"What kind of music do you listen to?"

"Ever had a threesome?"

"My Jag is in the shop, actually."

"My ex took everything but my sense of humor."

That last one was the real kicker, typically being the furthest from the truth.

The only upside of the casual-dating scene was that once she had her fill, she could move on. She didn't have to sleep with anyone unless she wanted to, and since most men were not worth sweating over, or under, she kept her legs and her heart shut.

The question she had to ask herself now was if she was ready and willing to let Aaron Karp back into her heart and her bed. If she were honest with herself, she would have to acknowledge her uncertainty. She had no legitimate reason to shy away from telling David about her plans for the evening. He didn't care. He had a Girl Scout or girlfriend or whatever. Fordham was the one being evasive. She was the one who was worried that things between her and Aaron were moving too quickly—although, her concerns could simply be a product of her insecurity. Perhaps it was time for her to accept that she wasn't a kid anymore and her prospects for a relationship that could lead to marriage were diminishing daily.

Even Brandon had moved on, she reminded herself as she left Five Below and spotted her car in the body shop garage, still being worked on. Although she'd never been serious about him, she didn't think he was the type who would willingly make a commitment to anyone. Maybe his deli darling was pregnant. That would explain it, and assuredly eliminate him from the backup-sperm position. There was no way she was going to share a baby daddy with Olivia-Sue.

The best option was to stop thinking so much. She needed to take matters into her own hands. It was time to provide Evie with the answer to her question.

RUSHING ON THE WEEKEND was particularly annoying. The car needed a special part and wasn't fixed until long after the guy had promised. Now Fordham was running uncomfortably late. At this rate, she would be meeting Aaron for dinner in a grease-stained T-shirt and sweatpants with a rip in the crotch, which he might not mind but would not go over well in a place like Carrelli's, where people were dressed up like patrons at the Met. She didn't like changing plans but had no choice. She called Aaron and was thrilled to find that he'd postponed their reservation until an hour later than they'd originally planned. He said his day had gotten screwed up and asked if she would mind meeting him at the restaurant. His rental, a Jag, was actually in the shop.

She was a few minutes early when she pulled up to Carrelli's, a brand-new place hailed by local critics as the quintessential modern supper club of the twenty-first century. She was in awe. It was exactly as the *Rockland Magazine* review sitting in her console had described:

"Set prominently in a mountain, like a jewel in the midst of a lush landscape, Carrelli's offers panoramic views of the entire Hudson Valley region. With nothing commercial in sight, the vision of the Catskills and its myriad neighboring lakes remains gloriously untainted by man's intrusion, leaving one to marvel that such perfection is possible in this day and age, when beauty is being eagerly corrupted by any marketable concept."

A tall, thin man with a strange handlebar mustache, wearing a baggy tuxedo, escorted her out of her car and into the entry. Her jaw dropped. The place was magnificent, with crystal chandeliers hanging from the ceilings and elaborately framed artwork decorating the walls. A life-size circular mural behind the ten-piece band surrounded the dance floor in a supper club scene from a forties movie, complete with musicians, well-coiffed waiters, capable busboys, and an array of patrons in haute couture. The décor complemented the mural by replicating much of its contents, giving the room a cohesive ambiance that blended the past and the present in a striking balance.

Aaron called, still stuck in westbound traffic on the George Washington Bridge. A short, somewhat sympathetic redheaded woman with a pudgy face and peony-painted lips took Fordham to a table in the bar area near a ceiling-to-floor window overlooking Bear Mountain. Aaron had mentioned he'd called the restaurant, and a few moments later, a server came over with a large martini and a dish of caviar and flatbreads, compliments of her tardy companion.

A man sitting alone at a nearby table kept peering at her over his menu. His face was blocked, and all she could make out were his pricey Versace glasses. She was never quite sure how to handle a situation like this, when it wasn't clear why she was being eyed. Maybe he recognized her from the supermarket or the bank, or—the most awkward possibility—a date. She ignored him, deciding it was not her place to make any overtures. Finally, the man lowered his menu, and she could see his face. It was Bingo Smack, Fordham's last client before editing the book had consumed her life.

"Fordham, honey," he said, walking over to her, "I thought it was you, but it's a little dark, and these are new specs." He gave her a hug. "It is so good to see you!"

"Good to see you too, Bingo. I'm glad your book is doing well." The Clotheser was a successful series about the hits and misses in the fashion industry. Abe had called it when he signed Bingo, saying it was the kind of topic that would never go out of style.

Bingo sat down at her table as he asked her if it was okay. She told him it was fine but that she was waiting for someone. She was sure he didn't believe her. Bingo waved his hand, and the same server who had given her Aaron's message came over. He scratched his head for a second as Bingo ordered drinks and mussels mariniere. If Aaron was running a tab, this was going to get complicated.

Bingo was fun to hang out with. He took her onto the dance floor and began telling her how positively his life had changed since they'd last spoken. He was genuinely happy now and grateful to Fordham for setting him in the right direction. He'd gotten a nose job and was busy writing another book in the series, which would be on her desk by the summer. But his most exciting news was that he was recently engaged to his partner, Adam, whose sister was having a baby for them. They were planning to wear matching tuxedos for their spring wedding, and he would be thrilled if she'd join them. At this point, Fordham was going to have to grow another hand to keep count of the boundless babies and marriages surrounding her.

Bingo was twirling her in a spin, which she was sure had him looking far more graceful than she, when she noticed Aaron standing in front of her. He seemed apologetic, but before she could say a word, Bingo pushed her into the center of the dance floor. He was enjoying spinning her every which way. She surmised that Adam was too tall to fling. The music continued, and Bingo didn't miss a beat.

Fordham tried to slow down, but that seemed to encourage him to hold her more closely and lead more fervently.

After the next spin, she couldn't find Aaron. He wasn't standing near the dance floor where he had been, nor was he at the bar or sitting at a table. She couldn't imagine that he would have left just because she was dancing with some strange man for no apparent reason. Certainly, he must have known there'd be an explanation. The music stopped, and Bingo excused himself to take a phone call from his agent. Fordham scanned the room but still didn't see Aaron. She went to the front and asked the redhead if she had seen her gentleman friend, but she pursed her peony lips and said she didn't want to get involved.

This situation had gone from annoying to amusing to ridiculous in less than an hour. She tried calling Aaron on his cell phone, but it went straight to his too-full-to-leave-a-message voicemail. She called the house and asked a particularly chipper Dorie if she had heard from him. She said she hadn't, but Fordham was reluctant to trust her answer.

"Why would I lie, dear? The sooner this relationship begins, the sooner it'll end."

She had to hand it to Dorie, the queen of non-diplomacy who knew how to take a bad situation and make it worse in an instant. There was no way Fordham was going to let this night be ruined because she had unwittingly become the star of *A Series of Unfortunate Events*. There had to be some way to get a hold of Aaron and salvage the evening.

She walked out onto the terrace to get some air and gazed up at the stars. Sometimes, it helped her to notice how small she was in the vast expanse of the universe. And there Aaron sat, talking on his cell phone. He was at a small table with his back to her, and she watched his body move as he spoke. His shoulders were much broader than they used to be. When they were kids having chicken fights in the water, and she was perched around his neck like a tie, she'd always been worried she'd fall. That would no longer be an issue. Aaron, the adult, seemed very capable of carrying her weight.

Fordham lightly touched his arm. He flinched at first but smiled when he realized it was her and told whoever was on the other end that he had to go.

"Ah, there's my girl. You are stunning." He stuck his phone in his jacket pocket.

"You disappeared," she said, sounding more concerned than she wanted.

"I got a call that I had to take. Besides, you were having a good time dancing with that guy."

She was disappointed that he wasn't jealous. Somehow, the possessive edge that sought to thwart competition and insist that she be his and his alone had gone missing. A man was not supposed to be so cavalier about finding his woman in the arms of another man, even if it was innocent. Of course, she was being unreasonable. Moments earlier, she hadn't even been sure she would qualify their relationship as a romance.

"I was having a good time," she said, hoping that would fan the flames.

"Good. I felt so terrible about running late. Between the car fiasco, traffic, incompetent lawyers, and meetings, I'm glad you weren't bored waiting for me." Aaron was cooler than a cucumber heading into a salad.

So that was it. Aaron was going to be the consummate good guy, considerate and trusting. Maybe he could tell Bingo was gay. It was too hard to accept that he couldn't care less that she'd been dancing with another man. But it would be even more foolish of her to waste the evening trying to rile him up so she could feel appropriately complimented. She had to get over herself. Most women would have appreciated having that kind of trust from their guys, and if in fact that was the role he was assuming, then his reaction was a good thing.

They were escorted to their table by the redhead, who acted as if Fordham had never approached her about anything more than a question about the dinner specials. The same confused server came back with a bottle of champagne and an assortment of fresh breads in a silver basket. She allowed herself a long, thin salt stick with a small pat of butter. She had one bite left by the time their entrées were served.

Aaron had taken the liberty of ordering for her as he'd regularly done when they were kids. Back then, he'd done it partly because he knew what she liked and partly because of limited funds. Tonight, the gesture was reminiscent and endearing.

"How's the tuna?" he asked, remembering that it had been one of her favorites.

"Delicious. Remember when I got food poisoning from the shrimp salad at Black-Eyed Sue's? I spent the night puking."

"I don't remember that."

"You wouldn't," she said, ribbing him a little, "You had an omelet and french fries."

"You want to know one thing I do remember?" he said, raising his eyebrow amorously.

"Okay..."

"The first time we made love. We were listening to Elton John."

"Wrong Yellow Brick Road. We were watching *The Wizard of Oz*. Your mother was upstairs, doing the dishes. The house fell on top of the Wicked Witch of the East, and since I was tired of being a virgin, I raised my hips just in time for the munchkins to start cheering."

"No way! Are you sure?"

"It was my first time!" she said. "Of course I'm sure."

"I remember it differently."

He didn't have the right to remember it differently, especially when she had every detail of that evening chronicled in a journal.

"Do you remember when we did it in the back of your convertible?" Fordham said in a sultry whisper.

"Of course I do. You had to dangle your legs over the side," he offered, seeming deep in memory. "You left a scuff mark."

"We never did it in that car," Fordham asserted. "See what I mean?"

"No," he said, sounding lost.

"Time plays with our memories. This is here and now."

"You're right, Fordie. But if I remember loving you, what's wrong with that?"

"Nothing. I just don't want us to get too caught up in the past."

"Past. Present. I never stopped loving you."

"Maybe you didn't," she said, beginning to believe him.

The band was playing a Beatles medley in the background, and people were making their way to the dance floor. Aaron got up from his seat and extended his arm. "Baby, dance with me. Not for the past, but for right here and right now."

He held her close as they danced to "And I Love Her." Despite their bickering and his challenged memory, Fordham was enjoying being in Aaron's arms. Maybe it wasn't so important for him to feel threatened by other men or even to remember every morsel of their relationship the way she did. He held her a little closer and nuzzled at her neck with soft kisses. Maybe he was right, and the only time that mattered was the present.

He whispered, "And maybe we did make love in the back of my Mustang, and you're the one who doesn't remember."

"I doubt it," she said with mild conviction.

"Well, now I have a BMW in the parking lot. What do you think?"

"I think I have a better idea."

Chapter Nineteen: Stunts upon a Mattress

"**O**uch!" Aaron yelped.

That wasn't good. She knew it had been a while, but *Ouch* wasn't *Baby, not so fast.* Or even, *Just use your hands,* which would have been insulting but not appalling. No, *Ouch* meant she was a complete sexual failure. It meant she no longer had the capacity to navigate his body with the reckless abandon that used to drive him wild and render him incapable of all speech save a few grateful shouts of her name. It meant that she not only lacked passion, but she was also inept and inflicted pain, possibly because she was still harboring hostility over their breakup.

"What did I do?" she said, mustering up the courage to face her incompetence.

"You didn't do anything. You're amazing, but what the hell is this?" He pulled out the laminated copy of Prince Charming's submission with a tack affixed to it from under his butt.

She quickly grabbed it out of his hand before he could decide to turn on the lights and read the offending weapon. *Damn!* She'd completely forgotten to take it down.

"It's nothing," she said, pushing the submission under the bed while still lying on top of him.

"Well, then, nothing just poked me in the ass. I think I'm bleeding."

She rolled over as he did, and sure enough, the tack had punctured his skin, leaving a tiny trickle of blood that she was able to blot away before it hit the brand-new Calvin Klein sheets she'd bought and saved for a night like this. She tossed away the tissue and began kissing him with renewed confidence.

"So are you going to tell me what that was?"

"It's a submission for the book."

"Are all the pages going to stab the readers?"

"No, I..." She wondered what Evie would have told Marv. "I hung it up... as an example. To help me format the others."

That response might not have worked so well if it had been a picture of George Clooney, but in this case, Aaron seemed satisfied to drop the investigation and began to unhook her bra. She was hoping that he wouldn't immediately ask her how long she had breastfed. He couldn't. He was a doctor. He'd taken an oath swearing he'd be tolerant and respectful, and besides, she was just a little pendulous. It wasn't as if she had hairy nipples. She was banking on that attitude as her bra hit the floor.

Aaron seemed nothing but pleased as he drew her close to him for a deep kiss. The music continued to play random selections as the lavender-scented candles continued to sweeten the air, and the foreplay continued to give her time to question whether she was making the right decision. She wondered if it was possible to pick up the past and move it forward so quickly. He was still a great kisser, and each brush of his lips against her skin was telling her that this wasn't such a bad idea. But if she was still able to think maybe she wasn't really ready to submit.

Aaron was now on top of her, and this time, "Goodbye Yellow Brick Road" was playing in the background, courtesy of the CD Aaron had chosen. She still wasn't sure what she was feeling, but she'd decided she was ready to go with it regardless when a loud crash came from Dorie's room. Fordham sprang up in an instant, threw on panties and a robe, and was heading out the door while Elton was proclaiming about rejecting the penthouse and embracing the plow.

Aaron jumped into his playful satin jock strap and grabbed a can of hair spray and a curling iron. Apparently, he was going to fend off the attacker by forcing him into an updo. She glanced at him quizzically, and he shrugged while pointing to his crotch as if to say *Cut me some slack—I'm dressed like Ron Jeremy.*

Fordham flung open Dorie's bedroom door and immediately wished she was a fainter just to have some relief from a scene she had no interest in being part of. There was her mother, lying on the floor next to her collapsed bed, wearing a sheer hot-red teddy with a snap crotch, holding her ankle in her hands and moaning in pain. Abe, wearing green silk boxers, was at her side, trying to comfort her. They could have been posing for an X-rated Christmas card.

"Abe?" Fordham cried.

Dorie moved a little and let out a few shrieks.

"Now is not the time to discuss this, Fordham," Abe said.

"We need ice," Aaron said, examining Dorie's ankle.

"Good idea," Abe said.

"And a scarf," Aaron added.

"Mine is hanging over my desk chair," Fordham said.

Abe quickly exited the room as if claiming his own white horse, while Fordham kneeled next to Dorie.

"Mom, what happened? Not that I'm entirely sure I want to know."

"That's okay," Dorie said. "I'm not entirely sure I want to tell you."

"Fair enough." A whooshing sound caught Fordham's attention. "Do I hear water running?"

"Oh my God, the Jacuzzi!" Dorie said, panicking.

Fordham opened Dorie's bathroom door to find the overflowing tub sending a storm of fragrant bubbles to the floor. She shut off the jets and released the stopper then gathered as many towels as she could find to hold the water back from the bedroom carpet. It was mostly working, but there was still some seepage, so Fordham whipped off her robe and deftly shaped it around the towels to create a stronger barrier.

"Well, I'll be dammed," she said, proud of herself for having completed her mission.

She marched back into the bedroom and watched as Aaron and Abe both tended to Dorie.

"What were you guys doing—reenacting *Titanic*?"

"Fordham!" Dorie said. "Where's your robe?"

Abe's eyes popped open, and he quickly bent his head in the opposite direction. Fordham glanced down at her bare breasts and decided that if everything happened for a reason, this was one for the books. "My robe is lying in a sea of love, saving your carpet."

"I will get you for this," Dorie said. "Go put something on."

"Bennett or Sinatra?"

His gaze fixed on the floor, Abe said, "Fordham, be a good girl—listen to your mother, and put a nice shirt on."

Fordham winced. Her boss, who she'd discovered was sleeping with her mother, had just politely admonished her. There was no time to emotionally process any of it, but at least her immediate thought had been practical. This was going to make one hell of a submission. She went to her room and threw on sweats and a tank top before returning to the excitement.

"I think it's just a bad sprain, but it may be broken," Aaron concluded, putting the finishing touches on Dorie's makeshift brace.

"Dorie, I'm so sorry, sweetheart," Abe said, near tears.

"It wasn't your fault," Dorie said. "I should have never tried to... well, you know."

"Oh, please don't say anything else," Fordham said.

"She needs an X-ray," Aaron said as if clad in his usual suit and tie instead of a jockstrap.

"I am not going to the hospital like this," Dorie said.

"Why? I made a diagnosis like this," Aaron joked, pointing to his near nakedness.

"You could say you were in a lingerie fashion show, Dorie, and you took a tumble on the runway," Abe said.

"And how did you come up with that, Abe?" Fordham asked.

"There's a *Cosmo* in the bathroom."

"Let's get her to the car," Aaron said, "before the swelling gets any worse."

"You have to leave," Dorie insisted, shaking her head.

"Who has to leave?" Abe asked.

"Both of you. Fordham is taking me. Alone."

Neither Abe nor Aaron seemed happy about that decision.

"Guys, I wouldn't bother arguing with her, or there'll be another man overboard," Fordham said.

Aaron and Abe found robes and helped Dorie to the car while Fordham got together a small bag of her mother's things in case they decided to admit her. Needing a coat, she went to her room, where Elton was still singing, the candles were still flickering, and the linens were still in a confused heap. The moment had clearly passed. Fordham stood at the mirror, half expecting to catch a glimpse of the girl who would have been crushed by a night that ended up this way. But she was a woman now, and rolling with the punches was the rule, not the exception.

Fordham went to blow out the candles and noticed the submission peeking at her from under her bed. She hung it back up on the wall then went back outside, where Dorie, in too much pain to care, was still in the teddy but was at least wearing a coat over it. Abe and Aaron helped her get into the car. Fordham followed and tossed the bag into the back seat.

Fordham got behind the wheel and opened Dorie's window for Abe.

"Dorie, are you sure you—" Abe was trying to ask her something, but Dorie seemed too embarrassed to listen.

"Thanks for everything. I'll text you." Fordham gave Aaron a peck on the cheek as he leaned down to her window.

"Please, just drive," Dorie said to Fordham, who waved and slowly pulled away from the curb.

The silence was awkward though still a blessing. Fordham preferred not to have a conversation about everything that had happened after a night that apparently had begun on a hopeful note for both of them. But it was too quiet, and Fordham needed music to make it seem as if they were sharing an activity.

She flipped to Sirius XM Love and nearly skidded off the road when Celine Dion started singing "My Heart Will Go On."

"Oh, Mom, listen—they're playing your song." She knew it was mean, but she couldn't help herself.

"I am so glad you're amused. But you must promise me you won't say a word about this. To anyone."

"Are you really going to plead the fornication fifth?"

"Fordham Ruth Price, I'm not kidding. I have a reputation to consider. If any of the girls from the Y Group find out about this, I'll never hear the end of it."

"I'm kind of curious to hear the beginning of it, but I still don't want to know."

"Fordham, enough. Ugh, the ice is leaking." She touched her seat. "Terrific. Now they're going to think I'm incontinent."

"Just flash them the nightie. That ought to shut everyone up."

IT DID. FROM THE MOMENT she arrived until when she was released hours later, Dorie was revered as the most entertaining patient the Nyack Hospital emergency room had ever admitted. The nurses marveled at how amazing she looked and asked her where she'd bought her lingerie and makeup. And when she told the doctors her age, they didn't believe her and said she must have had a head injury.

By the time she and Fordham left, Dorie had promised a host of nurses, doctors, janitors, and cafeteria staff members that she would set up a Facebook account and keep in touch. Luckily, her injury was just a sprained ligament, and in a few weeks, she'd be able to do the cha-cha with the best of them. Both Aaron and Abe had texted, but the signal was too weak for Fordham to respond. She'd get back to them later.

A new Dorie, brimming with affability and easiness, had emerged. Granted, she'd been a bit crotchety earlier, but Fordham had been unrelenting in her teasing. All things considered, Dorie had handled the situation well. A couple of drivers helped her get into the car, and Fordham drove home slowly, trying to avoid potholes.

Feeling particularly thankful she had no steps to navigate, Fordham got her mother into bed a little before dawn. Dorie was on enough pain medication to keep her knocked out for most of the day. Fordham set the vial of pills and a bottle of water on the night table and kissed her mother good night. She was already asleep.

Fordham got to her room and collapsed. She was exhausted from all the commotion and still thinking about her mother. She had seen a change in Dorie since the dinner party. She was glowing in a way that had nothing to do with Revlon, and she was calmer than usual. With no viable explanation, Fordham had assumed her mother was coming down with something. And now she knew the some*thing* was really a some*one*, and that someone was Abe. He was bringing Dorie back to life.

Fordham didn't get much sleep before the phone rang. It was Whitty telling her that she was having a great time. She didn't let on that she had completely forgotten that Whitty had slept over at

David's house. Exhaustion was not a viable excuse to duck out of parental responsibilities. Whitty had to get picked up, which meant Fordham had to get dressed. Despite her fatigue, she managed to find a presentable sweater to wear with her jeans. She even put on some makeup. If for some reason Pam was there, Fordham still wanted-ed to be worth a glance or two.

There was very little traffic, which made driving with her eyes ready to close much safer. She opened her windows, hoping the air would force her to stay awake. The good news was that David's house was nearby, and if Whitty was ready, Fordham could be home and back in bed before lunch. Aaron had off-Broadway tickets that he couldn't exchange, and she promised him she would be awake enough to go. He'd been so helpful and patient. Keeping that date was the least she could do, considering she'd left him high and dry.

She turned onto David's street and spotted a moving van next door to his house. The crew was carrying something large wrapped in a bunch of blankets and couldn't quite get it up the small set of steps in front of the door. When it fell, she could hear the guys cursing in different languages. *An obvious case of failure to communicate.* She parked in front of the house and noticed there were no other cars around. David was most likely alone. Unless, of course, Pam had parked her bicycle around the back. *Leave it to me to make a difficult morning even more vexatious.*

Embracing her insanity, she knocked on the door, half expecting Pam to answer. David opened the door, and the smell of his cologne was intoxicating. There was no sign of Pam, and Fordham was flattered that David's scent was all for her but then considered that it might be his typical routine or he might have other plans, in which case the cologne would have nothing to do with her. She hoped there was a direct correlation between her exhaustion and her irrationality.

"Sorry I'm late. I was at the hospital all night. My mother, uh, hurt her ankle."

"I'm sorry to hear that. What happened?"

"If I tell you, I'll be disowned, and I haven't written down all her recipes yet."

"Sounds intriguing, but I won't pry. The girls are inside playing. Would you like a cup of coffee? I have..." He paused, coming to a realization. "A mug with your name on it!"

"You do?" She yawned.

"I do."

Fordham followed David into the kitchen. It was a cheery room with butter-colored walls and tasteful white accents. There was a small center island that doubled as a breakfast bar. He pulled out a seat for her and brought over a basket of assorted mini muffins.

"Last night's project," David explained. "You didn't tell me Whitty could bake."

"I didn't know. She makes cookies with my mother, but... she never ceases to surprise me," Fordham said, feeling out of the loop.

She was a little bummed Whitty hadn't come to greet her, but the rich aroma of the coffee kept her from being too overwrought. David went into a cabinet, took out a large stainless-steel Yankees tumbler and a Fordham University mug, and poured two coffees. Milk, sugar, and anything else one might want in coffee were on the counter. She and David sat opposite each other for what was turning out to be breakfast.

"See?" he said, setting the mug in front of her.

"Oh, funny. I have the same one. Did you go there?"

"My freshman year."

"Really?" Fordham blurted. "My father was a professor there. That's how I got the mug. He taught Shakespeare."

"Shall I compare thee to a summer's day?"

"Sweaty and dehydrated?"

"I'd say sweet and warm."

Fordham could feel herself blush. "My mother was sitting in the front row of the classroom when my father recited that poem. She said she felt like—and I quote—'the class disappeared, and he was speaking straight into my soul.'"

"She must have been a good student with that kind of connection."

"She got an A, got pregnant, and got married. Whoops. I think I was supposed to say that the other way around."

"Our secret," David said.

"Anyway, when I was born, they decided to name me after the place it all happened."

"Good thing they didn't meet at the University of Buffalo."

"You're right." She shot him a glance. "It's grown on me over the years. It's like having a metallic mango car. You're always pretty sure it's yours."

"You certainly are unique," David said in an alluring tone.

Fordham ignored the goose bumps his words produced on her arms. "By the way, great coffee."

"Thanks. Great company."

Their eyes met again in what Fordham could only interpret as a romantic glance.

"I should probably get Whitty and go." She yawned. "I have theater tickets to an off-Broadway play, *The Illusion of Confusion*."

"Sounds enlightening."

Suddenly, there was a tremendous crash outside. Whitty and Lily screamed from another room as she and David ran to see what happened. They all ended up outside, where Fordham's car was in a compromising position with the moving van and resembling something an organ grinder would play while a monkey danced.

"Girls, go back in the house," David said as the driver approached them. Whitty and Lily happily ran inside.

"Sorry. I have a new driver," explained a guy in a *My Cousin Vinny* sweatshirt. He had a thick Russian accent.

"I had a new windshield!" Fordham said, near tears.

David put his arm around her shoulder and led her to the car to survey the damage.

"Maybe now's a good time to buy the wife a new car," the guy said.

"We're not married," Fordham said, holding her head in her hands.

"This might be a good time to consider it," the guy offered as he went back to his van to get business cards. "Hey, I'm really sorry. Call this number, and then call me." David read the cards while the guy continued his plea. "I have people who can take care of this, and it won't cost you a thing. I promise, and my word is golden. We can work this out."

David checked with Fordham, who nodded.

"We'll be in touch," David said, taking Fordham's hand and leading her back into the house. "The good news is no one was in the car when it happened."

"I know." She yawned a couple of times. "I'm sorry. I'm so exhausted. I was planning to sleep before going to the show."

"So take a nap. I'll call the service station and drive you home later."

She was tempted, and Whitty would be thrilled... "I can't do that," she argued, still yawning.

"Why not?"

"Because. You're Whitty's principal. And you have a—" She was about to say girlfriend, but David interrupted her.

"You can have Lily's bed or the guest room. Honestly, my bed is the most comfortable."

"All right," she agreed, "I can't keep my eyes open."

David took her to his room and came back with a blanket. Her eyes were closed, but she wasn't asleep as David covered her with the comfy throw. Whitty and Lily must have come into the room, because he was telling them to be very quiet. "Your mom's really tired, Whitty, so she decided to take a nap."

The girls giggled something about Goldilocks and said they would play in Lily's room. She could still smell David's cologne as she drifted off to sleep.

FORDHAM WAS DREAMING. At least, she thought she was dreaming. A man in a dark suit was chasing her. He had dark piercing eyes and a leather briefcase and kept saying he would never forgive her. She let out a scream, and David rushed into the room. He held her protectively, promising she had nothing to worry about. Next thing she knew, she drew his face to hers and kissed him with the kind of fervor that made her moan. He told her no one was going to hurt her, and it was safe to sleep.

Fordham jumped up with a start. Nothing about the cozy room was familiar. She didn't remember checking into a bed-and-breakfast. And then she remembered the dream. If it had been a dream. She wasn't sure. She knew she was at David's house and that her car had been crushed in a case of incompetence. David had spoken to the *My Cousin Vinny* moving guy about working something out. *That was this morning, and now*—she checked her phone—*it was almost dinnertime*. Aaron was expecting her to be ready to leave soon, and she wasn't even home yet.

Fordham got up, and as she folded the velvety blue blanket David had covered her with, a small thong of the same color fell onto the floor. She recognized it immediately—the lacy thing dangling from Pam's wrist at Messengers. If she left it there, David would know she'd seen it. Something made her shove it into her pocket.

She found David at his desk, listening to his iPod, his chair positioned to look out the window. "Hi," she said, touching his arm. "Sorry to disturb you."

"You're not disturbing me. Are you okay?"

She wasn't all that okay. Proof of David and Pam's relationship was stashed over her right butt cheek, smothering her Dentyne.

"Yeah, thanks," she said. "I can't believe I just conked out like that."

If she'd been dreaming and she'd kissed him in the throes of her angst, he would probably say something about it. Or not. There were panties floating around his room, so she couldn't be sure what he would or wouldn't disclose.

"I'm impressed you stayed awake as long as you did." He didn't offer the slightest hint about that kiss.

She decided to nudge him. "I feel like I was sleepwalking." She paused, giving him a chance to comment. "I had so many dreams."

"Well, you look none the worse for wear." David glanced at a business card on his desk. "I spoke to the moving guys and had your car towed to Jose's. It won't cost you a dime, but it could take a week or so to fix."

If anything had happened between them, David was clearly never going to share it.

"Thanks so much for taking care of everything." Fordham stretched a bit. "Where are the girls?"

"Watching *Frozen* again. Should I make popcorn? I'm sure we could talk them into something else."

"Sounds like fun, but I have to get home."

The thought of Aaron waiting for her made her anxious. There was no denying she and David shared a certain kind of chemistry, but that didn't mean they were meant to be together. And that thong probably meant he had great chemistry with Pam too. No, Aaron coming to town was destiny—*bashert*, as her late Aunt Fanny would say. This whole situation with David was probably just a test to see how she would stand up to the desires of the universe.

"Right, the show." David hit his head with his palm. "I forgot."

David got the girls into his Jeep in one take. Fordham usually had to ask Whitty three times before she would move at all. It was another case proving that familiarity bred contempt—or, at the very least, insubordination. Fordham wondered if having the camaraderie influenced Whitty to behave differently. She had to admit, her daughter did seem sisterly sitting in the back seat with Lily.

Being an only child had its perks, but it also had its disadvantages. Fordham had experienced the void growing up. Being alone meant there was no built-in playmate, no one close to her age who witnessed her life on a daily basis. What she had was hers to treasure or trash without argument or consequence. The result was quieter—though lonelier—days, and she often imagined how different her life might have been had a sibling been there to eat her candy or steal her toys or warn her when she was making foolish decisions.

David checked on the girls in his rearview mirror. They were engrossed in a TV show playing on Whitty's tablet. "They get along really well. You should have seen them making those muffins last night. It's amazing any chocolate chips got into the batter."

"Sorry I missed it. In more ways than you could imagine. But I'm sure this is not how you wanted to spend your weekend, David."

"You're absolutely right. I wanted to cruise down to Bermuda. But I had to settle for laundry and Chuck E. Cheese's. You ruined everything." David patted her hand in just the right way to make it impossible to read.

"Well, then, I owe you chicken nuggets or something."

"I'm just glad I could help. I feel terrible about your car."

"Can you believe it?" Fordham said. "More broken glass."

"More good luck." David pulled into Fordham's driveway.

It was late, and Aaron was outside, pacing. In the rearview mirror, Fordham caught Whitty grimacing. She suspected David had seen it as well. She jumped out of the car while Whitty thanked David and hugged Lily goodbye.

"What the hell happened? Where have you been?" Aaron demanded.

Aaron's jealousy was not all that flattering after all. Fordham went to stand closer to him as Whitty exited the car and walked past him as if he were invisible.

"And who is he?" Aaron asked, pointing at David.

Fordham signaled David to open his window. "This is David Prince, Whitty's principal. And this is his daughter, Lily. Whitty stayed at David's house last night, remember?"

"You mentioned that, but what took all day?"

He sounded like her father, demanding an explanation for her misbehavior. That didn't suit her at all. She dropped the thought before it could infect their evening.

"David, this is Aaron."

David got out of the car and shook Aaron's hand. Fordham was surprised at how easygoing he was. Then she reminded herself that there was no reason for him to be anxious. They were friends. And even though she'd slept in his bed, she'd been alone the whole time. Except for when she might have kissed him, which she still wasn't sure had happened.

"When Fordham came to pick up Whitty, a moving van hit her car while she was in my house. It's in the shop now," David offered.

"Why no phone call?" Aaron asked Fordham.

She had to think about it. Maybe he had a valid reason to be upset. She'd never even tried to call him.

"There wasn't much time between the car and the kids," David said before Fordham could offer a reply.

He didn't say anything about her nap. If nothing had happened, there'd have been no need for either of them to keep it a secret. The uncertainty was making her head swim, but considering how angry Aaron was, leaving out that piece of information seemed like a good idea.

"Well, then, thanks for taking care of my girl," Aaron said, not coming across as all that appreciative.

Fordham noticed that he said "girl" and not "girls." But then she considered the fact that Aaron didn't really know Whitty all that well yet. It would take time for them to build a relationship.

"Fordie, the show starts in an hour. Can we just go, please?" Aaron said.

"Fine." Fordham sighed, wishing he would give her time to change her clothes.

"I'm going to go," David said as if he were a third wheel. "Lily's getting hungry. Enjoy your show."

He got into his car and glanced back at Fordham. She caught his eye as he pulled away and wondered if he was going to take Lily for chicken nuggets without her.

Chapter Twenty: Journey to the Center of the Dearth

Her relationship with Aaron remained hopeful. They enjoyed the show—a silly farce about relationships, involving an obsessive-compulsive magician and a hairstylist turned veterinarian—then walked a few blocks under the bright half-moon to Playwright Bar & Restaurant for Irish coffee and cheesecake. They were seated at a romantic candlelit table near the bar, and a server with short black hair tinged with magenta tips promptly took their order. Fordham was glad Aaron hadn't said a word about David in the car as they were going into the city. She figured she was home free.

"This is fun," she said, taking a sip of water. "It's nice to be in the city for pleasure instead of business, for a change."

"The show was pretty ridiculous, but it was nice not having to share you."

Fordham wriggled in her seat and was thankful when the server came with their order. "Yum." She poked at the huge swirl of whipped cream with her long spoon.

"What's the deal with the principal?" Aaron asked.

"He's a principal with a sweet little daughter that Whitty likes. They're friends."

Fordham picked up the cocktail menu.

"*They're* friends? What about the two of you?"

"We're friends too, I guess," Fordham answered. "I haven't known him very long."

"No, you haven't. I could tell. Be careful, Fordham. This guy wants something." Aaron picked up his fork and helped himself to her cheesecake as if it were his.

So much for keeping their conversation light. At least he hadn't brought up anything about *the night to remember* or the fact that they still hadn't consummated their new relationship.

FORDHAM WAS UP AT THE crack of dawn and toyed with the idea of taking the day off. With everything going on, she was entitled to some time to herself. It had been the weekend from hell when all she'd wanted was an easy transition from the disappointing past to the promising future. And if she went in early and left early, she wouldn't have to see Abe, who'd sent a company email saying he'd be in late. The idea of another day between them and that ridiculous night was comforting. Try as she might, she wasn't sure she'd ever be able to look at him the same way again. As if the thought of him in those silly boxers, sharing pleasures with her mother, wasn't enough, she had to hold onto the image of herself in a bare-breasted frenzy, like Florence Nightingale performing triage on *The Love Boat*.

She went to the kitchen, found her Fordham University mug, and boiled water for a cup of Roastaroma tea, hoping for some soul-soothing magic. As was often the case, David came to mind. He was a good man. Pam was lucky. He was a bit of a flirt, but she didn't think it was in him to be calculating and hurtful. Sometimes, nice men with no particular agenda gave women the wrong idea. They didn't realize that by being attentive, they were sending out vibes that said they were interested. Even if he had kissed her that day—she still hadn't had any breakthroughs on that—it was probably just to calm her down. There was no legitimate reason to try to turn David into a bastard just so she wouldn't have to think about him. But it didn't matter anyway. He was probably counting his blessings that he had Pam, especially after Aaron's little scene.

The facts were clear. She was with Aaron now, and it was time to put everything in the proper perspective, which also meant addressing why their timing was always off. Sure, she was appreciative that he wasn't pressuring her to be more available. He was easy that way—so involved in his business that he didn't have the chance to dwell on her stuff or their stuff for very long. That was a good thing. This way, she could be her own person and never have to worry about getting swallowed up by his identity. If the key to independence was sharing a little bit less, she was headed in the right direction.

She decided to hang tough. She was going to get dressed, run a few errands, work through lunch and dinner, and not ruminate over what had happened with Abe and her mother. Just because they were older didn't mean they weren't entitled to a booty call every now and then. At least someone under her roof was finding the time for sex. It was a win-win situation, and Fordham was old enough and young enough to accept it and mind her own business.

She got a text from Aaron saying he'd be tied up. Had she wanted to engage in sexy banter, she might have asked him by whom. Instead, she responded with a benign *np* and got ready for work.

The trip to the office was therapeutic. The roads were as clear as the skies, and the leaves clung to the trees in pretty shades of purple, red, and yellow. If she had any artistic ability at all, this day would inspire her to paint. Things were good. The universe was telling her to relax and let life move her gently where she needed to go. She was more resolved than ever and ready to meet whatever the rest of the day would bring...

But when she arrived and found a note from Abe requesting her to come to his office, she stopped feeling ready. There was no sense in prolonging the inevitable or trying to hold onto the autumnal palette that had her smiling seconds before. She walked to Abe's office as resolutely as possible, hoping that her professionalism would usurp her tendency to get emotional. She was in no mood to confront Abe about his cavorting with her mother.

Myra stopped her. "You just missed him. He's meeting with Voltage Press. He should be back by three." She cleared her throat. "He asked me to make sure you wait for him," she said, taking out an extra-large box of cough drops. She offered one to Fordham, who declined. Myra needed whatever she had left.

Fordham went back to her office. She gazed out the window and watched the toddlers playing in Hudson Park. They were cute, climbing up and down little metal ladders and beams. *Their first hurdles.* Others would follow, but that day, they would conquer these steps and decide whether to choose Cheerios or Kix with their milk.

Maybe we never grow up. We're always checking out the lay of the land in search of ground that feels safe and steady. Fordham closed her eyes and imagined being on a swing as she munched on trail mix from a bag in her desk drawer.

There was a stack of submissions she'd printed out sitting on her desk, and she methodically read through each, reworking some of the text for flow and editing content when necessary. She had passed the point of feeling overwhelmed, and at times she actually had fun bringing these stories to life.

She checked her watch—almost four. If she wanted to make a run for it, she still could. Myra would be too consumed by phlegm to stop her. Or she could stay and be the responsible adult she was supposed to be, armed with a bevy of excuses if she needed any. The decision was made for her when Abe came through the door, calling for Myra.

Myra knocked and let herself into Fordham's office. "Please go talk to him," she choked. "He's a wreck, and I need Nyquil." She wiped her nose with a spent tissue. "I'll see you tomorrow, or whenever." She sneezed and left.

Fordham put her work away and finished off a few fortifying sips of exceptionally stale coffee. As she walked down the hall, she noticed there were only a few people still in the office. Maybe four o'clock was the new six o'clock. She was usually too busy to notice.

Abe was sitting at his desk, and for the first time since she'd met him, she noticed he had warm green eyes. *Maybe that's why he wore the green boxers*, she mused and instantly regretted that she'd let her mind wander in that direction.

"First things first," he said, handing her a postcard while she was still standing. It was from Margo.

Dearest One and All,

Exciting news—I am having twins! Yes, a boy and a girl. So now I am twice as thrilled and twice as bloated. We've decided to postpone the wedding until we don't have to buy a tent to dress me. I will keep you posted and will Skype as soon as my face doesn't take up the screen. Love You! M.

"That's interesting news," Fordham said. "She'll love all the shopping options. But I don't think she's coming back to work anytime soon."

Abe was stoic. Maybe he was going to tell her he needed a hearing aid.

"Have a seat, Fordham," he said in a low voice as he floundered for more words. If she was being laid off, this would be the worst timing in the history of timing. "I'm sorry about the other night."

"Forget about it," she said. "I'm certainly trying to."

Abe was pacing in the small area between the bookcase and the file cabinet. "Well, that's... kind of the point."

"What is?"

"I can't forget about it. And I don't want to. I'm not sure how to say this." Abe's pale had become a light shade of crimson, and he perched himself on the corner of the desk to face her.

It dawned on her that he might not be able to deal with seeing her every day, knowing what he had done with her mother. "You're going to fire me because you had sex with my mother?"

"No! Of course not."

"Okay, well... if you want my blessing," she cajoled, "you have it." She'd already resolved that she was fine with him and her mother spending intimate time together.

"Really?" he said with more gratitude than she'd anticipated.

"You're serious? You want my mother?"

"I love her. Really." He nodded. "I, who swore on my late wife's wedding ring that there could never be another."

"I've heard you say that." Fordham glimpsed at Abe's hand and noticed his ring was off.

"Last night, I went to the cemetery to tell Harriet about your mother. I asked her for her blessing and some kind of sign."

"You did?"

"Yes. I had to. Harriet was my best friend. It was only right. Later on, your mother and I were playing Scrabble online. It was the end of the game. I laid down my seven-letter word and picked up the last seven tiles."

He got a piece of paper, wrote, "I, H, T, Z, O, H, K," and handed it to Fordham. She stared at the page, confused.

"Ihtzohk? Like Perlman? Harriet played the violin?"

"Read it again. He doesn't spell it that way."

"Oh," she said.

"Correct! There is an *O*," Abe said enthusiastically.

Fordham tried sounding it out again, this time even less intelligently. If he wasn't firing her, she didn't understand the need for all the cryptic clues. Abe shook his head.

"I stink at this," she said, "but it's okay—I'm great at crossword puzzles."

"There! You said it!"

"What did I say?"

"It's okay!"

"Abe, this is becoming *Who's on First*. Just tell me: What's okay?"

"*It*. Fordham, that's what the letters spell out. *It's okay*."

Fordham read it again excitedly. "Ah, I get it! But what's okay?"

"To ask her to marry me."

"What?" She wondered if her shock was visible. "Why?"

Fordham's thoughts were as jumbled as the tiles shaken in a Scrabble bag. Her mother said she and Abe were talking all the time and seeing a lot of each other. Still, it was one thing to be a bed partner and quite another to be a life partner. Dorie had never been an impulsive decision maker with the exception of marrying Arnie—and even that had been out of necessity. Maybe a year of being alone had been enough to teach her that she didn't prefer it. Maybe some people could fall in love at first sight.

"Because I love her," Abe said. "Just don't ask me where or when, because that'll be up to her, if she'll have me."

Her state of having a lot to process had just become a whole new territory. Fordham didn't think she could handle the terrain. She hugged Abe. "Congratulations... Dad."

"It's about time." Abe gave her a hug. "I've always felt like you were my daughter."

She left his office, but she really didn't know what to think or feel. She just knew she had to run. She grabbed her bag and sped out to the elevator. It was atypically empty, and she was relieved to not have to make idle chitchat. All she wanted was to escape to the cushioned leather seats of her mother's car.

My car. She didn't even have that. She missed the welcoming scent of musky vanilla that emanated from the air freshener hanging on the rearview mirror. She also missed the chocolate stashed in the glove compartment. Dorie would never do that. Dorie would bake cookies, take one bite, and say she had to stop or she'd spoil her dinner. Fordham dissected the glove compartment anyway. Nothing but registration and insurance cards and... yes! In what must have been a moment of delirium, Dorie had caved and bought a roll of chocolate antacid tablets. No surprise, it was still unopened. Fordham sighed. Oddly, she was thinking about how much she wanted to talk to David.

A WEEK LATER, DORIE, having had what her orthopedist called a "miraculous recovery," was almost herself again. She'd left Fordham a note on the fridge, saying she'd be gone for the day and would pick Whitty up after school to get her a dress for the Poetry Awards.

Whitty had won first prize and still refused to let Fordham read her poem. "Mom, it's a surprise," she'd said.

Great, another surprise. Take a number. So much had already changed in a few short months. For the most part, she didn't like change. At least with Gil, she'd known with certainty that every day was going to be a depressing challenge. She didn't really want that life back, but she did crave terra firma.

There were more cars in the school parking lot for the Poetry Awards than there had been on the West Side Highway earlier that afternoon. Fordham had wanted to take the day off, but she'd had too much to do, and if she began taking more liberties, surely there would be gossip at the coffee counter. She didn't want her colleagues to start crying "nepotism." Although, the more she pondered it, the more she was enjoying the idea of Abe being her stepfather. The hard part was over. They knew each other, they liked each other, and they had already seen each other in compromising positions.

After combing the parking lot several times, Fordham finally got a spot and went into the auditorium alone. Aaron texted that his meeting was running late and asked her to save him a seat. Dorie left her a message saying she and Abe were on their way and to save two seats. If the requests kept up, she could start a company. There were surprisingly more seats than the traffic indicated, and she found a row of empties near the stage. Whitty had stayed after school for rehearsal and was nowhere to be seen. Fordham scanned the room. There was no sign of David, either. She hadn't had the chance to see him since the day of the *Was I dreaming?* kiss and found herself missing him. She wasn't proud of it, but she wasn't going to lie to herself.

With nothing to do but wait, Fordham checked her email. There was a text from Margo.

Fordham, darling, major update... we're exchanging vows at the Taj Mahal before the twins arrive. So much fabric my sari wants an apology. Miss you... and Abe. Kisses.

For a moment, Fordham found herself actually missing her spirited friend. So much was happening that she wanted Margo's inimitable take on. Some of the news was work related. A couple of stray submissions had caught her attention, but for the most part, she was satisfied with what she had. She was still perplexed about what to do with her Prince Charming entry. There was a part of her that didn't even want to include it in the book. It felt too personal, as if it was hers and too private to share. She was in the middle of reading it when Aaron arrived, and she quickly threw it in her bag.

He gave her a peck on the cheek and slung his coat over his seat. "Oh, good—your mother's not here yet," he said like a naughty child.

"What does that mean?"

"It means I get to have you to myself for a few minutes." He kissed her again.

"That's not what you meant, but I'll go with it."

Whatever their issues, his kisses were not the problem. Making time for anything else, however, was proving troublesome. Having been busy with back-to-back meetings for nearly a week, Aaron apologized for not seeing her. He promised to make it up to her and swore their sacrifices would be worth it. But they still had no set plans for even a moment of intimacy. She didn't have to disclose that she was so wrapped up in her own work she almost didn't care.

The auditorium was filling up. She wondered if any of the other parents were in her shoes and clueless about their children's poems. It still didn't seem right to her. Aaron was on his iPad, working on some kind of chart.

"Really? You're going to do that now?" she asked.

"Hey, beautiful, calm down." Aaron patted her shoulder. "Whitty's just reading something, and she isn't even on yet."

Fordham scowled and turned her head toward the doors as Dorie and Abe walked in. She stood up and waved to them while Aaron scrambled to pack his work away in his bulging briefcase. Before they sat down, Dorie flashed her hand under Fordham's nose.

"Can you believe it? Isn't he stunning?" Dorie said, beaming at Abe.

"Yes he is—and the ring isn't bad either," Fordham said, inspecting her mother's hand.

The ring was a big, shimmering, brilliant-cut diamond set high in an elegant diamond-studded band that gave Dorie license to serve brunch on paper plates next time Gloria was in town. Dorie's smile was so broad that the rest of her small features almost disappeared. If she hadn't just gotten over her foot injury, she'd have been jumping up and down. Abe's complexion was brighter, and he seemed calmer now that his girl was wearing his ring. His forehead was smoother, and his eyes twinkled in a way she'd never seen before.

"Abe said you gave us your blessing." Dorie got a little teary. "That means a lot to me. To us."

Aaron offered his congratulations. Fordham gave her mother the excited-bride hug she'd become accustomed to giving ring recipients over the past few years. Now that her mother was one of them, she worried about how their relationship might change.

A teacher in a burnt-orange suit and frosted hair announced that they were having some technical difficulties and that the assembly would start as soon as possible. Dorie asked Fordham to go to the ladies' room with her, and they left the men, who were already wrapped up in a discussion about politics. The bathroom was empty except for one woman applying way too much lip liner.

"You look really happy, Mom."

"Oh, Fordham, you have no idea. Abe and I just clicked like computer mice. Or would you say *mouses*?"

"I don't think it matters. The important part is the clicking."

They stood at the mirror and retrieved makeup at the same time.

"It's strange. I loved your father madly. But he was a lot older than I was, and even though we had a lot in common, we were still from different times." Dorie brushed on a layer of highlighter she didn't need. "Abe and I grew up on the same candy, movies, and music. It feels like we can be friends. And this time, no one can say he robbed the cradle and played Pygmalion."

Fordham was jolted back to a day when she'd been out shopping with her parents. They promised her a movie and Chinese food if she would be cooperative and let Dorie find a dress to wear to a friend's wedding. Each time Dorie would model a dress, Arnie would say she looked beautiful but then subtly add that one thing or another wasn't quite right. Finally, *he* picked out a dress for her to try on. It was a flashy yellow cocktail dress that had a fitted bodice and several tiers of feathery flounces. Dorie seemed to think it was very funny and took it into the dressing room as if playing along with him. She came out laughing, and Fordham remembered thinking she looked like Big Bird. But Arnie never got the joke. He patted himself on the back for his keen eye and said, "Now, that's the way I want my wife to look: like a million bucks." Without a peep, Dorie had worn the dress as if had been her choice all along.

"I never knew it was like that for you," Fordham said, feeling more enlightened.

Fordham had to admit that she and Gil had never been true friends. They enjoyed some of the same activities, had similar taste in movies and music, and even shared similar political views, but when push came to shove, he was more inclined to shove her to be what he wanted than push her to be herself. And she and Aaron had been so young that it was hard to know if their friendship was as strong as their attraction. She was certainly hoping so this time.

"Why would you know what it was like?" Dorie said. "Children seldom think past their own experiences." She looked at Fordham quizzically. "What else is going on? That face you're making has nothing to do with me and Abe."

"I haven't read Whitty's poem. She's been very secretive."

"Are you worried she's going to rat you out about the Ben & Jerry's?" Dorie teased.

"No. Not that I'd like that, but it's just not like her to keep things from me."

If Whitty was being secretive about her poem, maybe there were other things she wasn't sharing. She could be resentful of Fordham in deeper ways than she'd typically express. Maybe between the granola bars for breakfast and the string of horrific dates, her little girl didn't trust her judgment, and maybe one day she would get fed up and take Gil up on his standing offer to live with him—though it was unlikely to actually happen. Gil, true to form, still hadn't tried to connect with Whitty, and the more he continued to neglect her, the less she discussed his participation in anything going on in her life.

"You were ten once too," Dorie said, raising her eyes.

"Yeah, but, Mom, I told you everything, unfortunately, and still do."

"Like the time you paid Beegie Moser a dollar to show you his—"

"How'd you find out about that?"

"His mother noticed that he was two candy bars over his allowance."

"And he ratted me out just like that." Fordham shook her head. "The damn candy will get you every time. Why didn't you say anything to me?"

"I didn't think it was necessary. I figured you were normal and curious, and if you needed to talk, you would. Although I did cut back on your allowance."

"I guess I gave you a good reason to worry about inflation," Fordham said.

Dorie and Fordham got to their seats just in time to see David adjust the mic at the podium. Aaron's shoulders tensed. Fordham hoped it was because he'd slept wrong.

"Good morning, family and friends. Please rise for the Pledge of Allegiance led by Whitney Presser."

Everyone stood up as Whitty recited. When she was done, she left the stage and disappeared behind the curtain.

"Mom, she never even told me she was leading the pledge."

Dorie shrugged. There was nothing diplomatic she could say anyway. *Too bad your daughter doesn't confide in you* would be harsh, and *Too bad you don't know if she has her own Beegie Moser* would be even harsher.

Fordham nudged Aaron, who swore to her that his eyes were closed so that he could pay more attention to the words. She could tell he was bored. This wasn't his world. His job was over after the baby's first breath, when the hardest part was just beginning. More than ever, she was impressed that he was willing to change his whole way of life for her.

David stepped back up to the podium. For a second, Fordham could smell his cologne. He was in a navy-blue suit and a great purple tie that brightened his face. *That tie from Messengers.* The girl had taste. It was conceivable that playing with Barbies was informing her sense of fashion.

David appeared very much at home as he began to speak. "Today is a special day for Crestwood. We are the very first elementary school in the state to host the National Young Poets Awards," he said amidst applause and cheering. "The world is a busy place. AI is pushing its way into our daily routines. Yes, modern technology is forging ahead at a pace we have never experienced at any other time in our history. We can buy food and cars from our phones with our faces, we can watch our favorite movies and TV shows anytime and anywhere with an app, we can chat with our friends while scuba diving—at least those of us who can scuba dive—and we can gather information about ourselves just by plugging our names into a search engine."

You could hear a pin drop in the auditorium. Fordham was once again impressed by David's keen ability to engage his audience. It was a similar speech to the one he'd given on Back-to-School Night, but as always, he was speaking from his heart, which made him all the more effective... and attractive.

"With such intense change challenging us from one moment to the next, it's easy to lose sight of other valuable riches—the riches born from our hearts and souls, not just from our heads. For this reason, I am especially proud of all the students who participated in the National Young Poets Contest. Their efforts illustrate that words, feelings, and ideas are alive and well and that pen and paper still, and will always, remain the most powerful tools of our society."

David called students, waiting backstage, up to the podium one at a time to recite their winning entries. Some were cute, others more imaginative. Fordham had no idea what to expect when it was Whitty's turn. She leafed through the program. As with the Academy Awards, Whitty, the overall winner, would be the last one called.

David spoke with what Fordham detected as personal pride when he introduced Whitty. "Our final presenter today is the first-place winner of the National Young Poets Awards, whose poem, 'My Shoes,' will be published in the *National Young Poets Anthology*. It is with pleasure that I invite back to the stage our own fifth grader, Whitney Presser."

There was enthusiastic applause, but even after several moments, no sign of Whitty. David spoke to a teacher nearby then returned to the podium. Certain her daughter hadn't been kidnapped, Fordham was more distressed than panicked. She had no clue why Whitty wasn't going up to the mic.

"Whitney is feeling a bit under the weather and is unable to present her poem today. Please welcome back our runner-up, fourth grader Layla Fox, who will read another poem entitled, 'My Dog Rocks.'"

As Layla approached the podium, David exited, looking more resolute than concerned, and Fordham took that as her cue to find Whitty. "I'm going to see what happened," she said, jumping out of her seat.

"I'll come with you," Aaron said, standing up. "I'm sure it's nothing serious. She was fine for the pledge."

"No, please just stay here. I want to talk to her myself."

"Babe, take it easy. Whitty has a way of being dramatic," Aaron said.

Fordham flashed him a look of antipathy and stormed out of the auditorium. *Dramatic. You don't call your almost-lover's child dramatic. It's not good form.* She tried to put herself in Aaron's shoes and softened when she decided that, in his own way, he'd meant to be helpful. He still needed more time to get to know and understand Whitty. But she didn't want to have to deal with that. At the moment, she wanted effortless support from someone who didn't need to be taught how to give it.

Fordham was walking up and down the halls when she spotted David talking to Pam. For a moment, she wondered if Pam was missing her panties. Whatever they were discussing could wait. Fordham drew near and was relieved to see that Pam suddenly had somewhere else to go.

"David! Where's Whitty? Do you know what happened?" Fordham asked.

"I do know. Don't worry—she's fine." He nodded. "Come with me first. I need to show you something."

They walked to David's office in a comfortable silence. He escorted her in and closed the door. "You haven't read her poem, have you?"

"No," Fordham said. "She wouldn't let me. Which really isn't like her because we're very close."

"I know. But Whitty wanted to wait till today. She said if it won something, maybe it wouldn't hurt as much."

"Hurt?"

"Sometimes kids don't want to burden their parents. Whitty adores you, but she knows you have a lot on your plate."

Only a few weeks earlier, she'd told Fordham not to worry about going to Family Game Night at school because she knew Fordham had to work and would have to stay up later to make up the time. She even told her they could wait on shopping for her first bra until the book was done, claiming that no one cared about boobs until middle school anyway.

"But she knows she always comes first," Fordham said, aware of Whitty's sacrifices.

"Of course. But she loves you, and she puts you first too."

Fordham couldn't argue that. "She told you all this?"

"Kids share a lot over pizza and ice cream." David opened a drawer and handed her a typed sheet. "Here. You'll understand."

Fordham hesitated, not wanting to intrude on her daughter's privacy, but decided it wasn't a page from her diary and continued.

Fordham read the title aloud. "'My Shoes,' by Whitney Presser." Then she quietly read her daughter's poem.

Sometimes late at night,

When I'm

Lying in my bed,

I think about the day

And the things that people said.

Sometimes they spoke the truth,

At times they chose to lie

But some of their nasty words

Have been enough to make me cry.

Fordham dabbed at her teary eyes with a tissue she retrieved from her jacket pocket.

It's not easy to be different

In a world that's filled with same,

When people stare and look at me

They box me in a frame.

I wish that I could say

I have two feet on the ground,

But God made me this way,

And one I drag around.

I hope one day I'll wake up

In a world where I won't lose

Because people will finally see

The girl who stands inside my shoes.

Fordham was crying, and David went to console her with a hug. His arms, wrapped around her, felt healing, protective, and familiar, just as they had in her ambiguous dream scenario at his house. She lifted her face and was overwhelmed by the unabashed compassion in his eyes. In that moment, they understood each other in a pure, uncomplicated way. She was about to give him a very wide-awake kiss when the office door flung open.

Aaron was clearly upset, and she quickly broke away from David.

"I don't see Whitty in here," Aaron sniped.

"David needed to show me something," Fordham said with a tinge of guilt.

"That seems pretty obvious," Aaron retorted.

"I think you're getting the wrong idea," David said calmly.

"I think I don't care what you think." Aaron got right in David's face.

"Aaron, stop it. This isn't about you or any of us. It's about Whitty."

"Come on, Fordham. I'll take you," David said, walking out of his office.

"I'm coming too," Aaron insisted. "The thing is over, and I don't need to continue to play dartboard for your mother."

She wondered how badly Dorie had been treating him in her brief absence. "No! Just go back to the hotel," Fordham said, pushing him away. "I'll meet you later. I promise."

Aaron threw his hands up in the air as if he were releasing footballs and stomped his way down the hall without looking back. With Aaron gone, David led Fordham down a series of corridors until they got to a classroom door bathed in silver glitter. The sign on the door was made of words cut out in the colors of the rainbow.

"This is the poetry workshop. The kids voted on the design," David said. "She's in here." He pointed to a tie-dyed curtain that was closed, sectioning off a part of the room.

"Whitty?" Fordham called, pulling back the curtain.

Sure enough, Whitty was sitting there, holding a box of tissues and crying. Fordham had seen her in the exact same pose after she'd told her that Gil was moving out and they weren't going to be married anymore. Fordham hadn't been able to shield her from that kind of pain—try as she might—and this was no different. Whitty had her cross to bear, and the only thing Fordham could do was help give her the confidence she needed to handle it. Fordham gave her daughter a hug, and David seemed to take that as his cue to give them some time alone.

"Don't go," Whitty said.

"Um..." David looked to Fordham for confirmation then sat on the writing table.

She was encouraged that Whitty seemed to trust and care about David. With no father figure around, Fordham worried there'd be a void in her daughter's life that she'd be reluctant to allow anyone to fill. Even if this relationship wasn't meant to be enduring, it was good to know she had the capacity.

"Are you all right?" Fordham asked. "You feel okay?"

"I'm fine," Whitty declared. "I'm a woman. I changed my mind. I didn't feel like reading my poem."

"Well, not just any woman could have written such an awesome poem," Fordham said, kissing her forehead.

"You showed it to her," Whitty said to David, sounding betrayed.

"She was supposed to hear it today, right?" David asked.

"Yeah."

"And, Whitty, what do we always say in PW?" He mouthed to Fordham, "poetry workshop."

"Beautiful poems are meant to be shared, especially with those we love." Whitty sounded like a robot that had said that line dozens of times before. "But it's not beautiful. Sometimes I messed up the rhyming."

"Whitty, it's wonderful," Fordham said. "I am so proud of you for writing it." She kissed Whitty on the forehead. "All this hide-and-seek has my stomach growling. I need a hot-fudge-brownie sundae. How about you, monkey?"

"Can David come?" Whitty pleaded.

"Well, I—" Fordham stared at the floor.

"I wish I could, Whitty, but I still have things to do here," David said.

"Okay," Whitty said sadly. "I'm sorry I ruined the assembly."

"Are you kidding? You didn't ruin anything. And Layla Fox will probably want to be your best friend now."

"You always know how to turn something bad into something good," Whitty said.

"That's a very nice thing to say," David replied.

"I'm not really sure how to thank you," Fordham said.

"Maybe one day we'll figure it out." David walked out the door.

Whitty was okay. That was the most important thing. Fordham watched David walk away and realized that for the first time all day, she was smiling. She and Whitty were holding hands and making little jokes as they strolled through the empty halls. Dorie and Abe were sitting on a bench near the auditorium. Aaron was still there, standing against an opposite wall and talking on his phone, which he swiftly pocketed when he saw Fordham.

"Finally," Aaron said, exasperated.

Fordham was surprised he hadn't left. If he had caught the desire in her eyes when she and David were hugging, which she was pretty sure he hadn't, he'd have a reason to be concerned. She supposed she should be concerned, too, but then she caught a glimpse of David at the end of the hall, walking, with Pam clinging to his arm. She reminded herself that people could get caught up in the moment, especially when it came to romance, but moments were often just meant to serve the immediate and nothing more.

"Whitty, sweetheart, are you okay?" Dorie asked, giving her a hug.

"Do you feel a little better now?" Abe patted her head.

Fordham was touched that Abe was being so affectionate toward Whitty. He'd listened while Fordham talked his ear off about her daughter, but that was different than actually spending time with her. Since Abe and Whitty had met, it was as if they had never been anything but close. Fordham was fascinated by how quickly they'd bonded and thrilled that Whitty could grow up with a warm, caring grandfather after all.

"I'm fine. I just need ice cream," Whitty said, brightening at all the attention she was receiving.

"Ice cream—now? For what?" Aaron checked his watch.

"For eating," Whitty said as if addressing a cretin.

Aaron ignored Whitty's tone. "Fordham, we have reservations for dinner."

"Not until later. We have plenty of time, and I don't really care whether we make it or not."

Aaron shook his head as if he would never understand her. Fordham wasn't sure why he was being so ornery. Even if he had seen her hugging David, she'd offered a logical, specific reason for it that she willingly shared with him. The problem had to be something else. Her best guess was that their relationship was being threatened not by David but by her. She was a parent, and Aaron wasn't. It was strange that he and his wife had never had kids, but he was a doctor, not a superhero, and it was possible that the issues with his ex had extended beyond his abilities. She softened as she thought about Aaron missing out on fatherhood.

"Aaron, I still want to go. Maybe we can call and go a little later?"

"Sure, I understand. Why have champagne and caviar when we can have butter pecan and rainbow sprinkles?" Aaron said through a half-hearted smile.

"Yuck! I'm not getting that!" Whitty groaned.

Fordham escorted Whitty out the door. Aaron was a few steps behind, back on his phone. The parking lot was almost empty. She, Abe, and Aaron were parked at opposite ends of the lot. Abe told Dorie to wait while he got the car. He didn't want her to put excess strain on her foot. Whitty nudged Fordham, saying she wanted to go with Abe and Dorie, and Fordham couldn't see any reason not to let her. Grandparents were safe, especially when parents were impossible to figure out. It would also give her a chance to speak with Aaron and sort out the mess of this event.

Fordham told Dorie to meet her at CC's Ice Cream Castle. She had coupons for free sundaes that she'd left at home. Dorie said that was fine as she watched Abe walk hand in hand with Whitty to his car.

Fordham was near Aaron's car when he opened the window to tell her he had to run to meet a colleague about a "pressing issue." Suddenly, he wasn't as concerned about her eating ice cream sundaes and delaying their dinner plans. The meeting was one he'd been hoping to set up since he'd gotten into town. Soon, he assured her, all his phone calls and crazy scheduling would make sense.

It was just as well. Fordham was too tired to get into a relationship chat, and Aaron always seemed to perk up when he had business to tend to. There was a better-than-likely chance he'd be pleasant by dinnertime. Besides, he was too practical to enjoy dessert before dinner.

"Have a good time," he said, after he gave her a peck on the cheek. "And don't worry—I'm going to take care of everything."

Fordham was happy to have a few minutes to decompress. She got into the car, cranked up Sirius Classic Vinyl, and let the music take her home.

Chapter Twenty-One: The Jazz Zinger

Fordham was officially full. The steering wheel was closer to her stomach than it had been a couple of hours earlier. The brownie-fudge sundae had done more than hit the spot, and she'd selected outfit number three—brown corduroy pull-on pants with a matching sweater set—to hide where it had landed. The neckline was deep enough to help make up for its monochromatic tedium, and a few choice pieces of jewelry made it passable for a Friday night out in the suburbs. A side salad was about all she could handle, and convinced that Aaron's meeting would be foremost on his mind, she knew he wouldn't even ask why.

It had been Fordham's choice to go to Indigo—not for the food but for the music. The restaurant had an upscale menu, but for her, the draw was the live bands that would perform weekly. Piermont wasn't the East Village, but it was close to home, and most of the musicians who played there were as talented as any she'd heard elsewhere.

Although she was reluctant to acknowledge it, there was a good chance David would show up. Their school district was sponsoring a month-long fundraiser for the music program, and Indigo was one of the sponsors, donating a percentage of its proceeds to the cause. Fordham knew that David liked jazz—she was pretty sure he'd been listening to Coltrane the day her car was smashed, and there was a jazz band playing that night. In a county as small as theirs, it was possible he'd want to show his support and be there.

The parking lot was pretty full, and she recognized a couple of cars belonging to staff from Crestwood. Exhausted from the day's dramas, she hoped Aaron would be waiting at the front to keep her mercifully spared from any small talk that would keep her from a much-desired martini.

As she walked through the heavy wooden door, she was glad to see Aaron where she'd hoped to find him. The hostess with long hair and a too-large-diamond nose ring apologized as she led them to the back of the restaurant. Since Aaron had canceled their reservation, all the small, intimate tables were taken. The two of them were seated at a table that could accommodate a much larger party.

The band had just gone on break, and Fordham was listening to a piped-in version of Diana Krall singing "Just One of Those Things" while Aaron excused himself to take a "vital" phone call. Fordham stirred her filthy dirty double-vodka martini, which was brimming with enough stuffed blue cheese olives to make it a meal, and considered leaving. She was tired and wanted to be in her bed, finishing her latest Beverly Swerling novel, casting herself as a nineteenth-century socialite who could navigate any chaos New York threw at her. She was about to get up when Aaron ended his call.

"Sorry, baby. It might be that kind of night," he said.

"What kind of night? The kind where you knock my daughter's accomplishments? Insult my mother? Or misinterpret a platonic hug?"

"Either you've had one martini too many, or you need another," Aaron said.

If he bottled his calm, he could sell his practice. She supposed she was coming on a bit strong. She could retract the claws and still get her point across.

"I'm upset," she said. "You weren't being very supportive."

"You're right. I've been very focused on work, and today it made me cranky."

"You're being insanely reasonable," she said, hoping she didn't sound as disappointed as she felt. There was no fun in bickering without a partner.

"By the way, did you get through to your mother?" he added.

"On your behalf or on the phone?"

"Touché," Aaron said.

"Yes, I did. They went out for sushi."

"Japanese penicillin. Works every time. When I was a kid, I never thought I'd want to eat flounder before it hit the batter and the frying pan. And for the record, I'm glad Whitty's okay."

"Thanks. Me too."

"You seem tense."

Now, that was an understatement if ever there was one. She'd had a taxing, emotional day and gone out that night to escape or have some kind of release. She assumed Aaron would leave work behind to spend quality time with her, but it wasn't going to happen. And she was still annoyed with him, so neither of them was catching a break. They were just setting their stress to music.

"It's been a long day, and I bet you forgot that Dylan's wedding is at noon tomorrow."

"Noon?" Aaron grimaced.

"Yes. Is that a problem?"

"I'm supposed to meet with Feingold about the design for Ovary Park Place. I already cancelled on him today to hear Whitty recite the Pledge of Allegiance."

"Well, I'm so sorry for inconveniencing you. Next time, I'll tell Whitty to make sure her feelings don't interfere with your schedule."

"Don't start with me again. That's not what I said."

"No, but that's what you meant."

He shook his head. She scooped up a handful of mixed nuts from the bowl in front of her. Aaron's phone rang.

"I have to take this," he said, touching her hand.

"By all means," she said, pulling away.

Aaron went to a lounge area away from the bar and the band. Fordham downed her drink and ate all the olives. The band came back in and was getting ready to play again when Fordham got up to leave. She'd say a civil good night and head home. She was bending down to get the napkin she'd dropped when someone tapped her on the shoulder.

"David," she said, standing up.

"Lose an earring?" he asked coyly.

"No." She blushed. "Just clumsy."

"How was your brownie sundae?" David asked.

"Delicious, thank you. I'm still full."

"How's Whitty?"

"She's still full too." Fordham chuckled. "She's doing better. I'm really glad you were there for her. Please, join me."

Charged again after their last exchange, Fordham knew if she wanted to argue with Aaron, she had just found a way to call "bingo." She felt a little flushed and tingly. She blamed it on the alcohol.

David sat down next to her. "Where's Aaron?" he asked, scanning the room.

"Business call," Fordham said coolly. "So what brings you here? The fundraiser?" She noticed Pam standing by the band and answered her own question with a muttered, "Ah—date night."

Pam looked gorgeous in a tight little black dress that hugged every non-maternal curve of her body. She was braless, and Fordham could see the form of her perky nipples from several feet away. Even Pam's dark hair was coiffed to perfection as it hung down her back, screaming "Take me now" by any worthy pornographic standards.

"The fundraiser," David confirmed, "and my buddy is the sax player, Jake Lesley, Pam's brother. Do you know him?"

"No. Should I?"

She had dated several musicians, and for a split second, she wondered if Jake had been one of them. She studied him more closely, and to her relief, she didn't recognize him. But what she did notice was that he was wearing the same tie that David had worn for the poetry awards. She wasn't sure what to make of it. Maybe men secretly shared clothes, too, and having women think it was some gender-specific phenomenon was merely a clever ruse. Fordham had a sip of another drink that had magically appeared before her. There were some things she would never know.

"Oh, yeah, he's excellent. He's played with the best and even studied with one of my favorites, Gato Barbieri," David explained.

"You're kidding! I love Gato. *Caliente* makes me..." She giggled.

"Makes you what?" David teased.

Fordham smirked and shrugged. She scanned the room but didn't see Aaron anywhere and assumed he'd stepped out to continue his call. Pam was spending a suspicious amount of time with the piano player, but it didn't seem to bother David.

"You don't have to answer that," he said. "Music is important to me. I used to be a DJ in college. I did some sound engineering and worked the concert crew."

"I had no idea."

"You wouldn't. People usually don't wear their lives out in public."

"True. It's a bitch to accessorize them and impossible to find matching shoes. And those 'I'm with stupid' T-shirts are way too tacky to be telling." She was feeling a buzz, but she didn't let it bother her. "Actually, I find it fascinating to learn more about people I think I know."

Fordham was enjoying the conversation. She almost didn't care that David had a girlfriend. She had Aaron, and it didn't matter. There were all kinds of relationships. She thought about *When Harry Met Sally* and wondered if she and David could be friends the way Harry and Sally were before they slept together. *Yes*, she decided, but she definitely couldn't think about that part.

"I've shared, so now tell me something about you that I'd find fascinating," David said, provocatively leaning toward her.

Fordham was thinking of a response when Aaron returned to the table, visibly annoyed to see David sitting in his seat.

"Look who's here," Fordham said.

"Yes. I see. Hello again, David," Aaron said curtly.

"Hello, Aaron," David said, getting up to leave.

David's tiny grin and quick wave told Fordham he viewed Aaron as more of an annoyance than an adversary.

"Oh, please. We have this big table. Stay," Fordham insisted.

David sat down again. Pam ended her conversation with the piano player then slammed down two shots and a bottle of beer before coming over to sit next to David. She was wearing high heels but wasn't very tall and seemed a little wobbly on her feet. *Forget about walking. How can she could hold all that liquor without popping the seams of her dress?*

"Pam Lesley," David began, "this is Aaron—"

"Karp. Dr. Aaron Karp," Aaron filled in, politely taking in the newest member of their party.

"Hi, Aaron," Pam said in a Marilyn Monroe whisper. "You know, Fordham, David never shuts up about you and your daughter."

Fordham found that curious and wanted to muse about what David might have said, but the conversation was moving along too swiftly for her to give it ample attention. His blush gave her enough information, at least for the moment.

"Well, isn't that nice," Aaron said, downing his drink.

"Aaron, David is friends with the sax player, Pam's brother." Fordham pointed to Jake. "I love jazz," she added passionately.

"Yes, Fordham has always loved her jazz, but I'm more of a classic-rock kind of guy," Aaron admitted.

"Oh! Me too!" Pam interjected. "If it weren't for Jakie and free shots, you'd never catch me in here." She was talking right in Aaron's face.

Aaron seemed to be enjoying the attention, and Fordham was oddly undisturbed by his enthusiasm. If anything, she was finding their exchange amusing, and a glance at David conveyed that he was similarly entertained.

"Classic rock?" Fordham chimed in. "Maybe, but Aaron is one of the only people I know who owned a copy of 'Billy, Don't Be a Hero.'"

"I was being supportive. My cousin Billy was a firefighter," Aaron argued.

"That's true," Fordham conceded. "But what was your excuse for 'The Night Chicago Died'?"

"I love those!" Pam started singing a mishmash of the lyrics to both songs. She got up and twirled her way back to the band's table like a dehydrated ballerina.

"Excuse me. I'd better take her home," David said, looking concerned.

Fordham watched as David talked to the band. He and Jake joked for a few minutes, then Jake led Pam out of the club. Fordham was surprised when David came back to the table.

"Sorry," David said. "It was a long day."

"You can say that again," Aaron said, agreeing with David for the first time since they'd met.

"Pam's not usually like that," David said gallantly. "Jake's on a break and wanted to take her home."

"Fordham and I will understand if you want to follow them," Aaron said, carefully confirming their status as a couple.

No one seemed comfortable, and they all drank at the same time.

"No, it's better this way," David said.

"I understand," Fordham said, forgetting about Pam being a rival. "Kids can be so difficult. I can't tell you how relieved I am that Whitty feels better." She took out a compact mirror from her bag and inspected her face. "I think I sprouted new crow's-feet and a frown line from all my worrying today."

"Baby, you have nothing to worry about. I know more plastic surgeons than Cher, and they all owe me," Aaron said generously.

Fordham sipped her drink, ignoring Aaron's remark.

David gulped his scotch. "That's wild," he said, sounding wistful. "Fordham, you just reminded me of my late wife. She was always talking about the little lines on her face. I never even noticed them. To me, she was beautiful." He drained his glass. "I told her she had no reason to worry—that they were my love-lines, and as they deepened over time, so would my love for her."

"And she actually bought that?" Aaron asked.

Love-lines. Fordham felt the stuffed olives come up in the back of her throat and swallowed hard. This had to be someone's bad idea of a joke. Evie had probably gotten bored and signed her up to be on some new web series. She looked around, but there were no cameras in sight. There was only David's sweet face, innocently declaring that he was Prince Charming, the secret owner of her heart.

"What was your wife's name?" Fordham asked.

"Paige."

FORDHAM PULLED BACK the curtain of the window in the bridal room. It was still pouring. Aunt Fanny used to say rain on the wedding day meant the bride was going to be fat. Dylan was a beanpole, so that myth likely wouldn't hold water. But given that Dylan was pregnant, Fordham could grant Fanny a slight victory. It was a silly superstition, anyway, like all of Fanny's sayings. The previous night, when Fordham had been too tipsy and overwhelmed to think about their argument, Aaron had kissed her on the steps of the restaurant. Aunt Fanny always claimed that a kiss on the stairs was a sign of a misstep in the relationship and predicted a life of discord. It was all silliness. And this day was about Dylan and Evie, not about her. Her news would have to wait for the right time. If there ever was a right time.

"So, is it still raining?" Evie asked, feverishly wrapping the guest favors Dylan had forgotten about. Nearly two hundred scented candles had to be wrapped in festive paper and placed into little gift bags before the guests arrived. She had gotten through ten of them.

"Yeah, it's still raining," Fordham said, coming over to help her.

"Good. Maybe people will come late." Evie sounded hopeful. "You know, we're never going to get these done in time. And Dylan would have just left them sitting on the floor if Marv hadn't seen them when he was packing up the car."

"Don't worry. We'll get them done," Fordham said.

They had time. Dylan and Bob were busy taking solo and couple pictures. The photographer was a friend of Bob's and wanted to try different kinds of poses and techniques to use on his web page. He planned to shoot the bridal party next. Evie and Marv had already taken a bulk of their pictures.

"Where's Marv?" Fordham asked.

"He went to pick up his grandmother. I swear, Fordham, the woman is so old that Marv's father said it was more fiscally prudent to rent her food than buy it." Fordham assured herself this wasn't the time to bring up her ironic news about David literally being Prince Charming. Evie seemed to have enough on her mind.

"Can you believe it, Fordham? Can you believe Dylan is getting married and having a baby of her own? It feels like yesterday that I grounded her for dyeing her hair blue and getting a henna tattoo around her belly button."

"And don't forget about the nipple piercing. I know I won't," Fordham added.

"I try to forget about that one," Evie said, continuing to wrap favors. "How will I do this? How can I let my baby go?"

"You'll bring brunch to their place on Sundays to remind them of how much they still need you," Fordham said, confident of her practical answer.

"*Their* place? Marv and I finished our basement. That's *their* place." Evie tore open a new package of tissue wrap and examined Fordham's face. "What's up with you? Underneath all that bronzer, you look like you've seen a ghost."

"I don't want to talk about it now. It wouldn't be right."

"Right? I think we snuffed out 'right' ages ago when we shoplifted tampons and Hershey's kisses. Tell me what's going on."

"I can't," Fordham said, near tears.

"Why?"

"Because if I do, it'll be real—and I'm not sure I'm ready for that."

"I'm not ready for this. See what Marv got me?" Evie heaved a sigh and pulled a copy of *Flowers from the Heart: The New Grandmother* from an enormous bag that held a seemingly endless supply of hair spray, stockings, safety pins, Advil, and handheld fans. "So I don't understand. *What* will be real? Your book?"

"Sort of," Fordham said.

As much as she feared her news would upstage Dylan, it was now or never. She reminded herself that Evie had a big heart with plenty of room to spare. Maybe this news would serve as a decent diversion from the wedding frenzy.

She finally let it out as if she had been holding her breath to get rid of hiccups. "I know who he is."

"He *who*?" Evie asked, grabbing a stack of gift bags.

"The guy who wrote the submission."

"Prince Charming?" Evie dropped the gift bags. "You tracked him down?"

"No, that's the crazy thing. He found me."

"How? Who is he?" Evie asked, sitting down on the overstated floral loveseat.

Fordham sat down next to her and inhaled deeply. "Whitty's principal."

"What?" Evie was suddenly pale and began fanning herself with her hand. "Are you sure?"

"I'm sure."

"The one who drove you home after your car was hit?"

"Yup," Fordham said, getting up to check the weather again. The sky was clearing, giving Dylan a fighting chance to lose her baby weight with relative ease.

"You slept in his bed."

"And I drank his coffee, which was delicious, by the way."

"Does he know you're the editor?"

"No," she said, shaking her head. "He knows I'm in publishing, but we never got into details."

"Does anyone else know?" Evie asked.

"No. Not even my mother. Especially not my mother."

"What about Aaron?" Evie asked, more relaxed now that the favors were nearly half-done.

"Nothing about Aaron. Nothing yet, anyway. He'll be here soon."

"What are you going to do?"

"Finish the book and get on with my life."

"But your life just changed," Evie said, going back to the favors. "Fordham, you need to tell David."

"Why? He's seeing someone. A young someone."

"Well, it can't be that serious. He always seems to be one step behind you." Evie went over to her bag, got out a pocket fan, and waved it under her chin. "Fordham, you're at a wedding. You're supposed to be celebrating honesty and love. Face what's right in front of you. We all have to," Evie said, letting the fan relieve her hot flash.

ONE OF THE BEST THINGS about a wedding was that it was distracting. It was very hard to concentrate on old loves, new loves, deadlines, or even love-lines when a roomful—or in this case, a stadium full—of people were gathered to celebrate love on the grandest scale known to man. It was obvious that Marv's dental-implant service was thriving, and Fordham was certain there was not one extra the catering hall had offered that he'd refused.

The place looked regal and magnificent, like the kind of setting one would expect to find inside Cinderella's Castle in Disney World, except that in Disney World, the castle was merely a shell. Everything in this mansion was decorated elaborately—from lighting to candles, linens to place settings—and each table in the main ballroom was adorned with a beautiful crystal vase perched high on jewel-studded stanchions, holding elaborate arrangements of roses, tulips, orchids, and other flowers Fordham couldn't name.

Fordham and Whitty were enjoying the cocktail hour, going to each food station and marveling at how many ways chicken could taste like anything but. Dorie and Abe were drinking mimosas and talking to Pearl, who at ninety-five years old looked remarkably youthful in makeup, a professional hairstyle, manicured nails, and a pale-pink gown. She sipped champagne as if she was royalty. Fordham hoped that someday she would be older than old and treated with the same admiration and respect.

Whitty was becoming antsy and told Fordham she was going to get a drink. Fordham checked her phone. Aaron was delayed, but he would be there before the ceremony and was thrilled that everything was going just as he'd hoped. She was glad he sounded happy, given how grumpy he'd been the night before. It wouldn't be much fun to be at a wedding with someone who couldn't bring some of his own joy. Abe and Dorie left their chat with Pearl and went to talk to Evie's parents. Fordham went over to Pearl, hoping to cull some of her insight and wisdom.

"Hello, Pearl. I'm Fordham—Marv and Evie's friend. It's a pleasure to meet you," she said, extending her hand to shake Pearl's.

Pearl wiped the sour cream off her mouth and slapped the soiled napkin into Fordham's hand. "Who are you?" Pearl asked as if Fordham hadn't said a word to her.

"I'm Fordham. A friend," she said, thinking an abbreviated introduction would be more manageable.

"I don't know you," Pearl said, spearing a piece of her cut-up potato pancake, dipping it into more sour cream, and trying to get the fork into her mouth. She stared at Fordham earnestly. "Where's Hymie? Is he at the moving pictures with that whore?"

THE CEREMONY WAS ABOUT to begin, and Fordham was sitting with Whitty, Abe, and Dorie. The entire wedding party walked down the aisle to Bob Dylan's "Forever Young," assuring everyone that the couple was good-humored and well aware of the coincidence. Evie and Marv were more jittery than Dylan as they brought her down the aisle to meet Bob, who presented more preppy than Fordham had remembered. They were just under the *chuppah*—the Jewish wedding canopy—when Aaron arrived and promptly sat in the empty seat next to Fordham.

She was glad he'd been late. It had given her time to think about Evie's advice. Maybe she did need to tell David and let the chips fall where they might. At least she'd know definitively where she stood, or where he stood, or where they stood.

The rabbi chanted several prayers then handed the mics over to Dylan and Bob who had written their own vows. Bob began, "The first time I saw you I was in line in the school cafeteria, waiting for my chicken tenders. You were sitting with friends at a table, eating a bagel, and the way your dimples celebrated each bite was the most beautiful thing I had ever seen in my life. I was clearly out of my league—I mean, look at you—but all I knew in that moment was that someday I wanted to make you happy. When I finally got up the courage to ask you out, months later, you smiled and said, 'What took you so long?'"

There was warm laughter from the guests. Fordham found it hard not to think about what would have happened if she and Aaron had married when they were kids.

"I guess what took me so long was that you were already living in my heart and soul, but I wasn't sure if you were going to like the furniture. It was a leap of faith that got us here today. Well, a leap of faith and a bagel. Dylan, you're the love of my life. You always have been, you always will be, and I promise to spend the rest of my life making sure the furniture is always comfortable."

People were dabbing at their eyes. Somehow, these young kids were getting all this so right. Fordham was ready with another tissue for Dylan's turn.

"Girls are silly," Dylan began. Dressed in a long white A-line with a bejeweled belt under the bust, her hair long and curly, Dylan could have passed for the princess bride, except for the baby bump. It was a sweet understated look that led Fordham to believe that Dylan had really grown up and Evie hadn't been involved with her dress selection.

"We stand in front of our mirrors and think of ways to show the world how different we are. We paint our faces, our hair, and our nails, and we pretend that we don't care what people think. But we do. The mistake we make is that the last thing we show the world is who we are. You never let that happen. Like a shirt out of the laundry, you turn me inside out whenever you look at me and make me feel beautiful from the core of who I am. I usually don't eat bagels. I'm always too worried about the carbs. But I'm glad I lost my head and bought one the day you found me. How lucky I am to be the one who gets to live in your warm smile, your gentle touch, and your gorgeous soul. I promise to spend each day honoring the special person you are and appreciating the lovely furniture."

The rabbi put the glass down, Bob stepped on it, and the couple kissed. Fordham glimpsed over at Dorie. She was teary, and Abe gave her a little squeeze. Very possibly, they would be the next ones down the aisle. Fordham shivered a little bit thinking about it.

She wondered what Margo would say about Prince Charming. The woman was as straight a shooter as the arrow would permit. Maybe she'd agree with Evie and convince Fordham to have the courage to tell David. One way or the other, she knew she had to do something. Life was changing by leaps and bounds, and Fordham could only hope that one day she wouldn't be sitting in a chair, sipping champagne, eating potato pancakes, and wondering if Hymie was out somewhere playing with a whore.

Chapter Twenty-Two: Floored of the Rings

Fordham was happy to be home and thrilled to kick off her heels after spending hours on her feet. And that stupid lace thong Evie had talked her into buying to avoid panty lines went straight into the trash. All day long, she'd had to keep stopping herself from tugging at the persistent wedgie. There was only one place for floss, and that was between her teeth. Another lesson learned the hard way.

Aaron was at a meeting—he'd left as the bride and groom cut the cake—and Dorie and Whitty had gone back to Abe's house to watch the Giants game. Fordham poured herself a glass of wine and called Margo. It went straight to voicemail: "Sorry, darling. Eating for three is consuming all my time. Leave your message at the beep and I'll try not to eat your words..."

She considered calling Evie, but that would smack of insecurity on top of being egregiously intrusive. She thought about Aaron and how dashing he'd looked all decked out for the wedding. They'd danced, eaten, and had some laughs with a few old friends, but before the clock struck four, he was out of there. It was nothing she hadn't become accustomed to. He'd told her that once this major deal was finalized, he'd have more time, but he'd never said how he'd use that free time. She wasn't even sure if he was planning to stay in town.

She made herself a pot of coffee to sober up. A piece of her fairy tale was dangling like an errant participle. If she wanted to start the next chapter, it was time to find out what was going on in between the lines.

THE WEATHER WAS CHILLIER than she expected, and the flimsy light-purple sweater over her new not-so-skinny jeans wasn't doing much to keep her from shivering. She switched on the heat but hesitated to put on music, in case one of her songs with Aaron came on to make her feel guilty. In truth, she wasn't going to David's for anything more than clarity. Why she still had the thong from his bedroom shoved in her bag next to the lipstick vibrator she'd forgotten about was not a question she could answer.

The roads were empty, and the ride seemed shorter than it had the couple of times she'd driven there before. The house was pretty dark. Maybe they were sleeping. It was probably a silly mistake to just show up at his doorstep. It was also possible he was out, or worse, that he would come back and find her parked where the *My Cousin Vinny* guy had hit her car. He'd think she was a stalker, which was borderline truth at this point.

She was about to leave when a soft, low light flipped on in what she remembered was David's office. She got out of the car and sprinted up the driveway toward the house. Before she got too close to the door, she saw David go into his desk drawer and pull out a small box. The room wasn't bright enough for her to see more than that, but the contents of the box became increasingly apparent when Pam, wearing pajamas, entered the room. Fordham could feel her pulse racing as David opened the box and, though not down on one knee, put a ring on Pam's finger. The girl was apoplectic with joy. She jumped up and down a few times and threw her arms around David. Then she spent a few seconds focused on her finger. She mouthed something that made him laugh then gave him what Fordham would have considered more of a thanks-for-the-blender kiss. He turned off the light, and the two of them headed to the kitchen, probably ready to make dinner.

The scene wasn't exactly what Fordham had been seeking, but it gave her clarity: David was engaged to Pam. She was shocked. Despite Pam's blathering on about her relationship with David at the store, Fordham hadn't seen a proposal coming. He seemed too mature to want what Pam had to offer. But Fordham had been wrong about people before. Some things never changed. At least now she could go back to her life without obsessing over every nuance between her and David.

It's over. Done. Finished. Say when. Stick a fork in it.

FORDHAM'S DECISION to not bother setting her alarm had been a bad move. It was Monday morning, and while both Dorie and Abe had brought Whitty home after her visit, Dorie still wasn't back. The sad truth was that Fordham had gotten used to Dorie taking care of the morning rush, the after-school running, and the dinner prep. She'd never intended to take her mother for granted, but while she was simultaneously brushing her teeth and making Whitty a peanut butter and jelly sandwich for lunch, she realized that was exactly what had happened.

Between the divorce, the loss of Arnie, her mother's financial ruin, and her daughter's growing up, Fordham had received an implicit call to action, and a new order had been established before any of the terms were defined. Maybe it had been more comfortable for the three of them to just fall into roles and never address their wishes and expectations. Up until that point, it had all seemed to work, but now Fordham had to question what she had been seeking and what she really wanted.

Rifling through her closet in search of the gray jacket with the black piping that Dorie said she had picked up from the cleaners, Fordham became acutely aware of how dependent she had become on her mother. Maybe too dependent. Dorie made her daily life effortless. She had told Fordham that she hated being a burden and that the last thing she'd wanted was to step on Fordham's toes while she was in the midst of reshaping her life. Instead, she'd become indispensable and did everything to make Fordham's life easier. It was possible that neither of them had been giving unconditionally, but Fordham decided the most constructive thing she could do was to start weaning herself off of her mother's help.

Fordham quickly made Whitty oatmeal in a microwaveable cup and threw in a plastic spoon so she could eat en route to school. It wasn't exactly the breakfast of champions, but it was better than the Snickers bar she had initially contemplated. Whitty didn't seem to mind and wanted to talk about the wedding again. She remembered Dylan's blue hair, and even though it was definitely cool, she liked her better as a brunette.

"Mom, what would you say if I wanted pink hair?" Whitty asked, primping in the visor mirror.

"Cotton candy or hot magenta?" Fordham asked flatly.

"Would it matter?"

"No. I just wanted a visual for when I asked if you were out of your mind."

"That's not funny, Mom."

Fordham dropped Whitty off as the last bus was pulling away. *Pink hair, of all things.* Whitty was only ten and already bent on driving Fordham crazy. There had to be some kind of natural law that stated she was supposed to be menstruating before demonstrating her rebellious streak and being confrontational. If only Dorie could put off her marriage for another decade or so, just until Fordham could get the hang of being the kind of mother Whitty needed her to be. On the plus side, despite the world not always affording Whitty the sensitivity she deserved, she seemed happier and more confident since the poetry awards. Somehow, the recognition and honor for her talent had given her a boost and added a lilt to her cumbersome steps.

The ride into the city wasn't bad, leaving Fordham enough time to pick up a light latte and a fat-free corn muffin at the new organic takeout place around the corner from her office. It was her ritual to eat the top and around the outside then pitch the gritty leftover guts to the pigeons hanging out on the High Line. She agreed with Dylan: carbs were for the birds. After a few bites, the muffin's flaws outweighed its merits, and remembering her intake at the wedding, Fordham ditched the whole thing, offering the birds a cocktail hour of their own. Just then, a lone sparrow came, gave a few pecks, and before flying off, issued an angry squawk. Criticism seemed in abundant supply from everywhere. Fordham rushed to the office, certain a Hitchcockian flock would soon be assembling to assault her.

Fordham was on the elevator, heading up to her office, when her phone rang. It was Aaron speaking a mile a minute, asking if she'd be around. He needed to see her with news he couldn't wait to discuss. When she said she'd be in and didn't have any meetings scheduled until the next day, he sounded relieved. She wasn't sure where he thought she was going to go.

All Fordham did these days besides obsess about one thing or another was work. Work was the panacea that could take her away from pink hair, Dorie's future, gritty muffins, and her perfectly executed self-pity parties. Even if the book kept her imbued with the lunacy and wonder of love, at least it wasn't about her, and she could distance herself from any direct challenges.

The only expectation was that she made each story sound remarkable yet attainable and placed it strategically to ensure its impact. Fortunately, her touch of OCD had enabled her to finish the first round of edits in her Definite pile. While there was still plenty to do, the light at the end of the tunnel no longer warranted her throwing Margo onto the train tracks. With the exception of David's submission, which she reread and still didn't know what do with, she was comfortable with her choices. If she were smart, she would omit his, especially since she had no idea why it originated from the Pacific Northwest. It would be a reasonable cut to make, and David would get a standard rejection letter and never be the wiser. Of course, then she'd have to live with the knowledge that she'd betrayed him and his past and cheated her readers out of an inspiring story.

A knock at the door let her temporarily drop the dilemma. Myra was holding a pile of cover designs Fordham needed to check out, a responsibility Fordham hadn't anticipated. Myra very matter-of-factly added that Abe would check in with her later, after his breakfast date with Dorie. That was it, although she did want Fordham to know that Abe had picked the engagement ring out on his own and that her only part in it was sending him to her brother, a jeweler in midtown. Myra left the office, grinning with satisfaction.

Fordham riffled through the designs for what seemed like an eternity. Some had artwork and some didn't. She wasn't sure which route to take. She was leaning toward one that had the title set in a kitschy old-style font inside a computer screen. It was light and playful but tasteful, which was just the feeling Fordham believed would draw readers.

A sudden clamor outside her office was making it difficult for Fordham to concentrate. *People can be so inconsiderate.* She'd opened the door to quiet the offenders when she spotted Jeff, the same guitarist who had come to the office before. This time, he was dressed in a tux T-shirt and was once again being dutifully followed by a throng of bored coworkers anxiously awaiting his next move. He recognized Fordham and asked her to step back into her office, where he leaned his guitar off to the side and began to set up an iPod and speakers.

Fordham couldn't determine what Aaron was thinking this time and surmised that it was either an apology for being incessantly busy or some version of "Leaving on a Jet Plane." Either way, this was an annoying interruption, and she wanted to go back to work.

Abe pushed his way through the crowd and into Fordham's office. "You again?" he said to Jeff, bewildered. "Is this really your day job?"

"Yeah man." Jeff nodded. "Like, I used to can sardines, but my old lady kept accusing me of cheating on her. She's a wrestler, and I'm walking a lot straighter doing these gigs."

"Charming," Fordham commented.

Jeff picked up his guitar and played "Colour My World" by Chicago along with the recording. When the song was over, he pulled a long-stemmed red rose from a bag and handed it to Fordham. There was a high school ring attached to the ribbon. Aaron's name was inscribed inside the band. It was the ring she used to wear around her neck when they were kids. She hadn't seen it in years, and the memory of how important their love used to be brought tears to her eyes.

Jeff strummed a few warm-up chords and prefaced the next song. "Fraudman, this is for you." He sang "Follow You, Follow Me," by Genesis. When he was done, he went back into his bag to retrieve a satiny black box. Just then, Aaron flew into the office, grabbed the box from Jeff, and got down on one knee.

Fordham held her breath. This was the moment she had wished for all those years ago, yet all that came to mind was that David hadn't gotten down on his knee to propose to Pam. It was not exactly the reaction she had anticipated, but many things had her confused these days.

"Fordham, you are my love and my life. You are my inspiration," Aaron said, reminiscent of his younger lyric-quoting days. "My divorce is final—'Signed, Sealed, Delivered I'm Yours.' Baby, marry me."

He put the ring on her finger so fast she wasn't sure what hit her. There were a lot of *oohs* and *aahs* and then a round of applause. She just stood there, frozen, as if time had taken a holiday.

"Okay, this is an office, not the Wedding Channel. Everyone back to work and let these two have some privacy," Abe said, giving Fordham a supportive nod while closing her office door.

With everyone but Aaron gone, Fordham was left staring down at her sparkling finger. The ring was everything she never wanted. The center stone was round and probably a little over a carat, and the band was thick, chunky, and sporting a clunky, curvy cluster of pavé diamonds that looked almost as overwhelmed as she was.

"What is this?" she asked, stalling for time.

"A proposal. I love you, baby. You know that. The deal I've been working on—it finally came through!"

"That's great news! I'm so happy for you, Aaron."

"Not just for me—for us. It's our time now. We're breaking ground in LA. I have to leave tomorrow morning, and I want you to come with me. We'll get a place, set up—two weeks tops—and then we'll get Whitty and bring her back with us."

"What? Get a place? Move? What about my job?"

"I'm sure you could work from home if you wanted to, but with the kind of money I'm expecting, you wouldn't have to work at all. Listen, baby, forget all that. Let's just make this happen. Everything in our lives has brought us to this moment. Don't you feel it?"

All she felt was queasy and an incredible urge to fart. Aaron got up from his knee and took her hand.

"I don't know what to say," she admitted uncomfortably.

"The word you're looking for is... yes!" he said with puppy-dog eyes and an air of certainty.

She searched his eyes. It was her Aaron, the kid who had made her heart melt before Spain, separate paths, and scruffy facial hair had come between them. She had a quick flash of the future and pictured Dorie packing her things and moving to Abe's house. She envisioned days of rushing Whitty out to the bus or car with a Special K bar in one hand and a box of Mott's in the other. Fordham gazed at her gleaming hand. The ring wasn't her style, but it was beautiful, and Margo would have been proud that her nails were manicured for the occasion. It was not her place to tamper with the will of the universe. Everything so far, including David's engagement, had been leading up to this moment. Maybe the timing was right and she had been too caught up in work and a myriad of distractions to realize it.

She looked up at Aaron and said a barely audible, "Yes."

He kissed her and went to the door. "I've got to run. I have a lot of loose ends to tie up. The limo is all set for the morning. I love you, baby."

Abe found her sitting on her desk dumbstruck. "So what's the word?"

"Yes... I think."

"Do you think you meant it?"

"I think I might have."

"Fordham, go home," Abe ordered softly, "and when you think you know what you might have meant, you can explain it to me."

SHE NEEDED TO THINK, and that meant going anywhere *but* home, where her news was sure to be met by a whining chorus of scorn and derision that would have her heading out the door anyway. Her head was spinning, and she had to digest the logic of her decision before she could even think of selling it to Whitty and Dorie. It had all happened so quickly and unexpectedly. Even her coworkers were taken aback and had jumped up to surround her during the experience. Then again, they had left their desks the previous week to watch new paint dry in the lounge area. Regardless, engagements were supposed to be exciting, and this one felt rushed.

Fordham checked her phone. There was no one to call. Evie and Marv were on a monthlong second honeymoon, exploring tantra with a private instructor in Koh Pha-ngan, and Margo was self-sequestered until her delivery. Relatively certain of her support, Fordham toyed with the idea of calling Gloria, but that would be dirty pool, and she didn't want Dorie to feel slighted. She could talk to Abe, but he was marrying her mother, and she didn't want to saddle him with any confusing deterrents.

She just needed some time... plus a box of Junior Mints, a glass or three of pinot noir, and Laura Nyro. Fordham stared at her ring and wanted to be happy, but something was holding her back. She had dreamed of this moment from the time she and Aaron had first met. There had to be a reason why wasn't she jumping up and down like a contestant on *The Price Is Right*. Once she sorted things out and her mind was in a better place, she would pop open the champagne.

With a full tank of gas and no plans, all she needed was a destination. She stared at the stack of book-cover designs piled in the back seat. She could go to Barnes & Noble and have a cup of better-than-mediocre six-dollar coffee and review the covers, or she could head to Bridges Bar in midtown, have a glass of wine, some of their sweet-and-salty nut mix, and try to forget why she was there. Neither sounded appealing, but there had to be somewhere she could go to find her own celebration. And in a moment of sudden clarity, she knew exactly where she needed to be.

"SWEET TEMPTATION, TO win," Fordham said, handing two singles to a slight Asian woman with short gray hair and a chronic frown.

"Long shot. Risky. Bet on next race—good money," the woman said in a thick Chinese accent, handing her a ticket. "You have husband?" She raised her chin.

Fordham looked around to see if the woman had assigned her anyone specific. The men nearby looked as if the last time they'd consulted a mirror was during the Reagan years. She also noticed there was no one else in her line.

"No. Not anymore," she said, not sure why the woman had asked or why she had chosen to answer. Then she eyed her ring and understood.

She kept her bet despite the ticket lady's disapproval, figuring it was a reasonable place to draw the line. With almost an hour before the first race, she decided to walk around. Yonkers Raceway was not a place Fordham imagined she would go to share her life story. Situated somewhat randomly off the Cross County Parkway in the middle of the area's best places to shop, it presented more like a big off-black department store than a gambling mecca. Although it was only a short car ride from the grandeur of many of Manhattan's buildings and establishments, there was nothing aesthetically pleasing about the exterior that would beckon tourists to visit, making it feel more like a community center than a destination on a must-do list. As far as she was concerned, its biggest perk was the boundless parking, which seemed to cover as much ground as a small city.

No, this was not a place she'd call home. She was so far out of her element that she could have created her own periodic table. Right in front of the block of *Wheel of Fortune* slot machines was a large woman in a tight bright-orange tube top with a denim overshirt and yellow spandex leggings, sporting a camel toe and a head full of curlers covered by a kerchief. Margo would have fainted.

The woman was arguing with a nearby ATM machine that didn't want to give her any more money. A uniformed security guard, who looked like an Anthony but was in fact named Melissa, told the woman emphatically to quiet down or she would be escorted out the door. The woman gave the guard the finger and grabbed the hand of a short man in a dirty white undershirt and ripped jeans, who looked as if he hadn't eaten in a month. She stomped away, complaining in a language Fordham didn't recognize.

Most of the couples looked like mismatched socks. There was no unifying factor that offered a clue about the unions, but one had to assume there was some basis that extended beyond their being strikingly unattractive together. Fordham felt sad and perplexed that people dressed as if they'd forgotten to do laundry. If Officer Melissa could hand out citations for fashion infractions, there would be ample funds to reduce the state deficit. But alas, spandex, Lycra, denim, and polyester were being heinously abused, and there was no recourse.

Fordham knew she wasn't one of them, and the people knew that she knew. In her brown suede heels, matching shoulder bag, and beige tailored suit with round gold buttons, along with her perfectly coiffed hair, she looked like some kind of alien interloper who'd wandered away from her planet and gotten stuck on theirs. But she didn't care. She had a lot riding on this visit. She just wasn't quite sure what it was yet.

The whole place was unfamiliar. She hadn't expected to remember it well, since the only time she'd been there was when she was five, the first and only time she and her father went to the track together. Still, she hoped to feel some sense of connectedness. Another security guard explained that the casino was where the betting windows used to be. That sort of fit into her scant recollections. All she could really remember was watching the horses and kicking the losing tickets lying on the ground.

These days, there were slot machines, roulette wheels, craps tables, and a variety of ways to slowly or quickly clean out one's wallet and bank account. She wondered if that was what had happened to

Arnie. Maybe he'd been seduced by the hum and glow of the moment and robbed of his keener senses. It could have been like that. Over and over again.

She read her ticket. *The long shot. To win.* It figured. Fordham hadn't even checked the odds. She never did. She believed the magic was in the name. She'd rarely gone to the track, but anytime she'd ever placed a bet, the horses always seemed to know if they'd been saddled with an inferior moniker. In keeping with a study known as the Rosenthal Effect, a horse with a good name such as Studley Do-Right or Mr. Lucky was expected to outperform a horse with a bad name such as Limp Biskit or Charlie Horse. It wasn't exactly a science, but somehow, it worked.

The race was about to begin, and Fordham wanted to see if she could locate where she and her father had sat. She found a spot that seemed familiar and opened up her program. In an instant, she could smell the Aqua Velva and see Arnie popping a couple of Sen-Sens in his mouth. He offered her some, but when he said they weren't Chiclets, five-year-old Fordham lost interest.

It had been a hot June day. They'd walked close to the track to look at the horses, and the smell of manure was pungent.

"Daddy, it smells like a toilet," Fordham said, holding her nose.

"You're right," Arnie said, chuckling. "The horses go potty before they race, but we're going to sit where it doesn't smell."

"Good," she said, still pinching her nose shut.

"The horses have to go around the track really fast to get to the finish line, and whichever horse gets there first wins. They poop so they don't have a bellyache while they gallop."

"But, Daddy, what do we do?"

"We watch them, sweetheart," he said.

"Why?"

"To see who wins."

Fordham still wasn't sure of her role. "But I want all of them to win."

"Our job is to pick the horse we think will win."

"Do we win the horse?" she asked hopefully.

"No. We win money."

Arnie stared at the program for a while then read Fordham the names of all the horses. She giggled at some of them and decided on KaptnKangaroo. Arnie laughed, saying hers was the long shot, but he indulged her and even let her hold the ticket. He picked Foolforlove, who he said had a good steady gait and decent odds. He led her to the ticket window to place their bets. It was fun, but she had no idea that this little world was slowly ruining his life.

They finally found seats Arnie was happy with. He liked being somewhere midway so that they could take in the entire track but still close enough to see what he called the "look of determination" on the horses' faces. Fordham thought the horses looked more like they wanted to eat than anything else.

Finally, the horses were lined up at the gate. Then the bell sounded, and they were off. Fordham watched all the people standing and cheering. Some guy was talking really fast over a speaker, telling everyone which horses were running the fastest. She kept hearing the name of her horse. Arnie was standing and cheering, and she stood up and cheered right along with him. The next thing she knew, Arnie picked her up high in the air like a trophy and kissed her cheek as KaptnKangaroo crossed the finish line first and Foolforlove followed.

They went to the window to collect their winnings and then to a little concession stand for a Coke. Arnie asked her if she wanted anything, and amongst all the little toys and trinkets, she showed him a ring with an adjustable band.

"Fordie, do you know what kind of ring that is?" he asked, sounding amused.

"Pretty. Like Mommy's," she answered, handing it to him to buy.

"It's called an engagement ring. Someday, when you're all grown up, you're going to get a real one from a lucky man who will ask you to marry him."

"I'm going to marry you, Daddy." She kissed him.

He gave her a hug, bought her the ring, and asked if she wanted anything else. But in that moment, there was nothing else she could ask for. Her father was beaming and happy to be with her. And even better, he told her that seeing the horses was only supposed to be for grown-ups. It was their special secret that no one, including her mother, should ever know about.

They returned to the ticket window and Arnie asked her to pick another horse.

"Why are we staying, Daddy?"

"Because we won. You picked the right horse. You're lucky."

They each chose another horse and went back to their seats to watch the next race.

"You see, honey," Arnie explained, "you pick a horse because it looks like a winner, and you hope really hard that you're right. Sometimes it works, but sometimes the horse you think looks best isn't."

This race was one of those times. At the end, Arnie muttered a couple of words her mother had told her never to say.

"What's wrong, Daddy?"

"We lost, Fordie."

"Does that mean we're leaving?"

"No, honey. We need to stay."

"You said we had to stay because we won," she said.

"Well, now we have to stay because we lost. Daddy doesn't like to give up, and you shouldn't either." He gave her a hug and promised her ice cream if she behaved.

Fordham was less than pleased with his decision and was getting fussy. She told Arnie to pick the next horse for her and whined that she was getting hungry. He told her to quiet down and that he would get her something to eat after the race was over.

Fordham could not stop fidgeting and playing with her ring. She kept putting it in her mouth and back on her finger until she decided to throw it up in the air then caught it on her tongue before it slid right down her throat. She tried coughing to get it back up, but it didn't work.

"Daddy," she cried, "I swallowed my ring."

The horses were at the gate, but when Arnie saw the tears rolling down her face, he picked her up and rushed her out of the park. While they were in the car, he kept asking her if she could breathe, and she kept answering that she was fine. But he still brought her to the emergency room of a nearby hospital. Every case of poison sumac or poison ivy was waiting along with them, and after a couple of hours, Fordham had had enough.

"Daddy, I'm hungry," she whined.

Arnie surveyed the room then looked at his watch. "Here have some of this," he said, bringing his Timex up to her mouth.

FORDHAM HAD KEPT THEIR secret and held that day in her heart as a gift she would let herself open from time to time. She finally accepted that Arnie had been an addict who fought a daily battle to overcome the pain of his feelings of inferiority. He lived under the delusion that his success had something to do with what he could offer from his hand instead of from his heart. It was a mistake that cost him his self-respect and undoubtedly pieces of his soul, but that was the deal he'd made in his moment with the unsympathetic devil he'd invited to invade every corner of his happiness.

Cheers came from the crowd, breaking Fordham's memories as her horse crossed the finish line in first place. Instinctively, she stood up and honored her unexpected victory. A long shot—Arnie had probably arranged it. Maybe he owed it to her. One could never accuse him of being passive when he wanted something. Like the old man in *The Old Man and the Sea*, he'd clung to the hope that someday, he would reel in the big one. In truth, Fordham realized, he'd been no more imperfect than any other father who struggled to be the man his family wanted to see. For some, being that man came with a heavier load and a higher price tag than for others. Arnie might have faltered, but his determination to be the unwavering hero had remained steady.

As she hurried to the window to collect her money, Fordham searched the crowd. All the faces were unfamiliar. Some looked pained, others joyful, but there was no one who could give her answers or guarantee what the road ahead would yield.

On her way back to the car, Fordham paused to take in the night sky. She had come to see her father somewhere in the middle of his heaven and hell to let him know that she forgave him. She was ready to let go of the past and move forward in life and in love. It was probably the last place he'd expected to find her, but when she saw the first star of the evening twinkle, she knew Arnie was there, sending her his love.

FORDHAM NEEDED TO MAKE one more stop before heading home and sharing her news. Her old high school parking lot was full. That night was registration for adult-education classes. She had gotten a pamphlet, and Whitty had mentioned that David was teaching a class. All the classrooms would be open, giving her the perfect opportunity to visit the school on her terms.

Fordham entered through the main entrance. At her prom date with Aaron, they had been confined to the auditorium, and she'd been too invested in the moment to care about visiting the rest of the school. But now it seemed vital for her to go up and down the familiar halls to visit the past and connect with the history that had influenced her decision to make Aaron her future.

Fordham never wanted to move away from home. She'd always imagined Whitty tracing her footsteps down these very same halls and wondered if she would make friends like Evie and Marv, each of whom was still a constant in her life. She wanted Whitty to experience the same sense of comfort and belonging that she had, and even though Fordham knew that most of that came from within, she still equated familiarity and continuity with security.

Fordham passed by the main office and lingered at the display cases hanging on the wall. Several were dedicated to the school's history and included pictures of each class president through the years. Aaron's picture was there, showcasing his dimples and his muscular frame in a royal-blue Qiana shirt. There were trophies and pictures chronicling sports and academic events, including a picture of her winning an award for the debate team. It amazed her that this wall could speak so richly to her about the past.

She glanced down at her ring and remembered how much she had wanted Aaron to propose to her before they went away to college. Evie told her she was out of her mind to think of making that kind of commitment when they were so young and inexperienced. Marriage was romantic but unrealistic. She and Marv were being mature and practical. They'd agreed to see other people when they went away to school, and if they were meant to be together, their relationship would be stronger after that. Of course, all that went out the window when neither one of them could stand to be apart. They'd ended up getting married while they were still struggling students, and to this day, they never hinted at missing the adventures they had voluntarily forfeited.

Fordham continued down the hall to the cafeteria. A few people were sitting at tables, drinking cans of soda and eating bags of chips from the vending machines. There'd been no vending machines when she was in school. She was standing at one machine, toying with the idea of getting a candy bar, when a hand dropped coins into the slot.

"So, what are you signing up for?" a familiar voice asked as the hand retrieved a Reese's Peanut Butter Bar.

"Hi, David," she said, unsurprised. "Nothing. I'm just visiting. This was my high school. Whitty mentioned you were going to teach 'grown-ups.' What course?"

"Poetry," he said, offering her a bite of his candy.

He was being his usual pleasant, friendly self. It was a good thing that being engaged hadn't changed him much.

She bit off a corner. "That makes sense." The candy bar was in perfect range, and she boldly chomped off more of it.

"Funny. We always seem to be at the same place at the same time," he said, unwrapping the candy bar a little bit more.

"I was just thinking that," she said, watching him take another bite.

"Guess it's fate," he said, gazing into her eyes a little too deeply.

"Could be, but this is a pretty small town." She brought her hand up to her mouth to brush away a crumb.

David cupped her fingers to look at the ring. "That new?"

She doubted it looked anything like the ring he gave Pam. "Yes, it is," she said, slightly taken aback by his gesture. "Aaron proposed. His business deal came through, and we're leaving for California. To-morrow."

David tensed his lips in something like a scowl but ultimately refused to be that judgmental. "Wow. That's a pretty big step. How does Whitty feel about this?"

"She doesn't know yet," Fordham admitted sheepishly.

He didn't seem to want to share the news of his proposal to Pam, and she certainly wasn't going to admit she was stalking him and had watched it unfold firsthand. "He was my first love," she offered as if trying to excuse herself.

"Does that mean he has to be your last?"

"At this stage of the game, how many chances do you get?"

"I don't know. Maybe as many as you need." He moved his face closer to hers.

Her heart quickened, and she was almost certain he wanted to kiss her. "David, I should tell you something." She wasn't sure if this was the right time or place, but before she stepped into her new life, she needed to tell him how much his submission had meant to her.

A security guard came over to them to tell David that there was a group waiting for him in a classroom down the hall and that they needed him there immediately.

"Sorry, I have to run. What did you want to tell me?"

There was nothing more to say. The universe had stepped in yet again. David was a good guy. He had already gone through more than his share of difficulties, so why burden him with her complicated life? Pam was young and simple with a family David already knew and loved. She would be an easier package for him to handle. Eventually, he would forget about her and whatever had been developing between them. Fordham had to assume they both would.

"Just... goodbye. I'll see you... when I see you," she said wistfully.

"Bye, Fordham," he said, hugging her. "I'm going to miss you."

David walked briskly down the hall, and Fordham whispered, "I'm going to miss you too," wondering if she would ever see him again.

Chapter Twenty-Three: Some Like It Not

There was no sense delaying the inevitable any further. Fordham was going to go home and calmly tell Whitty and Dorie that she was about to yank the new foundation they had been building right out from under them. The move was a matter of practicality, and it came with the realization that life had its own schedule, and not everything happened when she would have wished. In this case, Aaron's proposal was more than a couple of decades late, but at least it had come, and in that spirit, she would accept it.

She said it out loud: "I am going to marry Aaron Karp." It didn't sound bad. It just sounded dated.

Fordham pulled up to the house and sighed in relief when she saw the lights off. In all the chaos, she had forgotten to charge her phone. Maybe Dorie had taken Whitty out for ice cream when she couldn't reach Fordham. Had Fordham been younger, Dorie would have already sent a SWAT team out to track her down.

She was retrieving the book-cover samples from the back seat when the lights flashed on. *It must have been one of those stupid brownouts again.* Her heart flip-flopped, and she had to remind herself that it was her life and she was in control. Her decision was final, and as long as her resolve remained steady, she would get through this conversation and still have time to pack.

Fordham bounced through the door like Judge Judy entering her courtroom, but when she heard Whitty and Dorie laughing in the kitchen, she couldn't help but soften. She tossed her things down on a table and debated letting her news wait until the morning. She even considered writing a letter, keeping her explanation short and the goodbye quick. Granted, it would only be delaying the inevitable, but the extra time was tempting. Then she had a flash of *Sex and the City*, when Berger left Carrie a breakup note on a Post-It. Carrie had been traumatized for the entire season. Granted, the situation was different, but the cowardice would be the same. Fordham couldn't do that to Whitty or her mother. It would be unfair and unforgivable.

She put on Bon Jovi's "It's My Life," opened a box of Raisinets, and tried to pump herself up again before facing the jury. Whitty and Dorie were almost on cue, greeting her before she got to the kitchen. Whitty was holding a large piece of oaktag, and Dorie was carrying a bowl of cherries.

"Mom, look at this. I'm making it for my family project for school," Whitty said, handing Fordham the sketch. "Where did you get *that*," she continued, pointing at the ring, "the downtown flea market? I hate their junk."

"I have to tell you... tell you both something," Fordham said, the words spilling out like a drum roll.

Whitty and Dorie looked at each other, raising their eyebrows in unison, then shifted their attention to Fordham.

"Aaron proposed, and I said yes."

"Why would you do a dumb thing like that?" Whitty challenged.

"Really?" Dorie's eyes were about to pop out of their sockets.

"Mother, some support here, please," Fordham pleaded. "Aaron is a good man, and he'll give us a nice life. In California."

"California?" Whitty shrieked. "There is no way I'm going to live in the smoothie capital of America. Do you know there are bars there where you have to pay to breathe?" She picked up her poster, crying, "Go if you want, but I'm staying with Mom-Mom. I'm sure you'll have lots of fun getting helium shots in your forehead and flirting with pool guys while Aaron is busy getting women pregnant." Whitty stomped out of the room.

Fordham ran her hand across her forehead and sighed. Whitty's reaction had been even more intense than she'd expected.

"Sweetheart," Dorie said, taking the same tone she'd used when Fordham was a child and skinned her knee, "have you really thought this through?"

"Sometimes thinking clouds your judgment."

"And what are you planning to do about *this*?" Dorie said, crossing over to a drawer and pulling out a copy of David's submission.

"Where did you get that?" Fordham snapped the paper from Dorie's hand.

"It was stashed under the pot holders in the utility drawer. Don't worry—there's another one hanging on the wall in your room. I noticed it when I was trying to find my slippers." Dorie crossed her arms. "I thought someone might have left them there... that night. It was right there, so I read it."

"Okay... so?" Fordham asked.

"I know it's David's."

"How do you know? The only one I told was... ugh, Evie. She told you!"

"She had to," Dorie said.

"How many bullets were in the gun?"

"She loves you, Fordham. We all do."

"I know, and I appreciate it. So the submission is David's. What does that change?"

"Quite possibly your life," Dorie said, cupping Fordham's chin in her hand. "I see the way he looks at you and how he shows up where he thinks you might be." Dorie shelved the cherries and moved out heavier artillery: a box of crumb doughnuts. "He's falling for you, Fordham, if he hasn't already fallen. It's as obvious as one of these"—Dorie held up a doughnut before taking a bite—"at a Weight Watchers convention."

"Mom, Aaron loves me," Fordham explained, pulling away to get a bottle of Advil from the end-table drawer. "He's loved me since we were kids. He helped lay the groundwork for me to become who I am."

"The cement is still wet. He can leave his footprints, but he doesn't have to claim the whole block."

"You don't understand. Aaron and I have history. He gives me everything I need."

"Fordham, you're the one who doesn't understand. You only *think* you need to turn back the clock. The truth is that everything Aaron gives you—the memories, the financial security, the love of music, the confidence in your beauty—well, maybe not that one. But most of those are things you've already given yourself."

FORDHAM SPENT A RESTLESS night awake, even after downing a guggle muggle—the mixture of warm milk, honey, and butter her grandmother had sworn could cure insomnia. All those calories, and not one dream to show for them. She wondered if Whitty was feeling any better. She'd fallen asleep before Fordham had the chance to talk to her again.

It was 7:15 a.m. Aaron would be picking her up in a couple of hours. Fordham slammed off her alarm and got up to start packing. Fortunately, the crux of the showdown was over. Other than some last-minute sniping, Fordham didn't anticipate any major setbacks to impede her plans. She went on her computer to check her emails. Abe had sent her a cute e-card of a kitten doing a crossword puzzle to wish her well. The book was pretty much done, and he had no problem with her working remotely to deal with the finishing touches.

He said they would Skype, and she was proud that he'd conceded to opening an account.

An email from Margo was more astonishing. "Fordham, darling, I'm thrilled for you and Aaron! Abe told me the good news. I didn't want to say anything, and I swear Aaron didn't have a clue, but I was the one who set up the deal that sent him to NY. He and I became friends while I was trying to get pregnant, and when your name came up, I knew I couldn't depend on fate, so I decided to intervene. I realized I'd left you in the lurch and figured surprising you with a gorgeous rich guy you used to love might help. Let's face it—a man is only a good catch if he's netting a profit. All's well that ends well, and you can thank me when I visit after Brandywine and Slick finally emerge. Meanwhile, I've completely lost sight of my toes. Gotta run. We're having brunch with a snake charmer. From one Cobra plan to another..."

Margo strikes again. Of course, the whole connection had seemed uncanny, but life being a strange string of coincidences was kind of the norm for Fordham. The secrecy, however, was baffling. She wasn't sure why Margo had held back—unless she'd figured Fordham would be too mired in anger to appreciate the gesture. That did make sense.

It was getting late, and Fordham didn't have the time to ruminate over how she'd ended up engaged to Aaron. She clicked out of her email and onto the weather in LA. She wasn't surprised to see that an unusual influx of rain was forecast for most of the time she was going to be there.

Fordham had just gotten out her luggage when Whitty came into her room. "The bus is coming soon," she said, stoic.

"Monkey, I'm going to miss you sooo much," Fordham said, hugging her close. "Please be good for Mom-Mom, and try to understand that I'm doing this for us."

"Sorry, but that's a lie you're telling yourself, Mom. I think you just got tired of no one ever seeing the fourth outfit."

"Whitty, you're not being fair."

"I'm not being fair? You want us to live with Mr. Babymaker in a place where a deep conversation is, 'Like, oh m'God, did you see her highlights? I think she bought them in a box. Like, oh m'God,'" she said, imitating a Valley girl.

Fordham was about to defend her decision but decided against it and let Whitty continue to vent.

"David is right," Whitty said.

"David?" Fordham asked, confused.

"Yeah. In PW, he says sometimes people make choices to try to make their poems sound true, but for a poem to really mean something, you can't force the truth."

Fordham heard honking from outside.

"There's the bus." Whitty gave her a perfunctory hug. "I have to go," she said, walking out with her head hung low.

Fordham stood motionless, trying to grasp what Whitty had said. She was a wise young girl, but Fordham had to focus on her own truth. The best thing to do to get in a better frame of mind was to move forward and pack.

There was a knock at her door and Dorie appeared, carrying a small package. "This just came for you," she said, handing Fordham the box.

"I didn't even hear the doorbell," Fordham said.

"There's a lot you're not hearing," Dorie said.

Fordham rolled her eyes.

"It's from Aaron," Fordham said, opening the box. She had no cause to think David might send her a going-away engagement gift.

"Shocking," Dorie mocked.

Fordham opened the package unceremoniously. A pair of designer sunglasses in a fancy case was accompanied by a note. She read aloud: "These are for when our days are 'Sunny,' but I'm going to love you 'Come Rain or Come Shine.' 'The More I See You,' the more I want you, and soon the bells are going to chime."

"Judging from your track record, you won't hear them," Dorie teased.

Fordham ignored Dorie's comment and tried on the glasses.

"Are you sure those lenses are rosy enough?" Dorie wasn't pulling any punches.

The phone rang, and Fordham picked it up as Dorie sat with her morning coffee in hand.

"Hi, Aaron, thank you for the gift," Fordham said. "Yes, they're very cute. Yes, you're very cute. Uh-huh. And the card is very cute. Yes, Aaron, everything is cute, but if you want me to be ready, you have to let me hang up... you're right. I'm sorry for snapping at you. I just have a lot to do. Yes. I'll be ready. Yeah—I know you love me. Me too you." She hung up. "I need coffee."

"You're in luck. I just perked some. And have a muffin. Whitty baked them by herself yesterday, and they're delicious."

Fordham remembered David saying how impressed he was with Whitty's baking. David was impressed with Whitty, period. Fordham followed Dorie into the kitchen.

"Oh no. Whitty left her project," Dorie said, seeing it on the counter.

"So she'll take it in tomorrow."

"She can't," Dorie said, admiring the poster. "They're having the school fair today. Just stop by the school on your way to the airport. I'm sure Aaron won't mind."

"Of course he won't mind." Fordham thought, *He might mind*, but she was confident he'd happily concede to her wishes.

"Are you ever going to tell David the truth?" Dorie asked.

"I saw him last night. I wanted to tell him, but I couldn't... I have to finish packing."

But instead of packing, Fordham rerouted and went into Whitty's room. Where pictures of Disney princesses had once hung, there were now Yankees posters, prized artwork, and her recently framed award-winning poem. Fordham picked up a stuffed elephant off of Whitty's bed. Gil had bought it on his way home from work on Whitty's first day of kindergarten. It was pink and fuzzy and just plush enough to use as a pillow. Whitty called it Elly-Smelly because a new bottle of Gil's cologne had been in the same bag and leaked on its head. Whitty would never admit it, but she still cuddled with Elly when she was going to sleep.

That was another reason this move was a good idea. It would give Whitty the chance to build a better relationship with a father figure. It was natural for her to resent Aaron, but in time, they would find a way to appreciate each other and become close. Whitty needed a man in her life, and even though Aaron was clearly inexperienced at fatherhood, Fordham believed he was willing to make the effort. That had to count for something.

Fordham was done packing and left her luggage by the front door. With nervous energy to spare, she decided to straighten up the house. She was in the backyard, shaking out a small area rug, when Dorie stepped out from the side door and interrupted her.

"Gil is on his—oops, I mean, Aaron is on his way. I was on the phone with Abe, and Aaron beeped in."

"Mom, Aaron is not Gil. Not at all."

"I know that. I'm getting old. It was an innocent slip."

"Fine. I'm not going to argue with you," Fordham said, heading into the kitchen. She laid the rug back in its place. "I know you don't like my decision. I know Whitty doesn't like my decision. But I do, and that's the bottom line."

"Maybe you're right. I mean, let's face it, you're not getting any younger. You've already lived through the marriage from hell, and you've spent the last three years serial dating, and no one has suited you. This could be your best shot at the kind of life you've imagined for yourself."

"Reverse psychology, Mother. What do you mean by *the life I imagined for myself*? I like my life. I just don't want—"

"To take any chances," Dorie said, waving the submission, which she'd stashed in her pocket. "I know. And with Aaron, you know exactly what you're getting."

"For your information, Mom, David is engaged."

"That's ridiculous. Who told you such nonsense?"

"No one." Fordham hung her head. "After the wedding, when Whitty was with you, I went to David's house to talk to him. But I didn't get the chance because while I was standing at his office window, he proposed to Pam."

"Had you been drinking?"

"My mother taught me never to drink and drive. I had plenty of coffee and was clearheaded before I went."

"Did you ask him about it?"

"No, I didn't ask him!" Fordham's cheeks grew hot. "He didn't say anything about it, so I certainly wasn't going to bring it up."

"Don't you think it was a little odd for him to not mention it when he saw the ring on your finger?"

Dorie had a point. He'd had the opportunity to tell her he was getting married, too, but he never said a word. If anything, he seemed more into her than ever.

The doorbell rang.

"It must be your limo," Dorie said. "Are you sure you're not leaving something important behind?"

Fordham rolled her eyes. The woman was relentless. She went into her room to see if she'd forgotten anything. There was nothing she needed that she hadn't already packed. She was only going for two weeks. Her eyes were fixated on David's submission, still hanging on the wall. She considered taking it along or at least taking a shot of it to keep on her phone. She would feel strange not reading it before drifting off to sleep. But she decided to leave the memory safely in its place. She went back inside to find Dorie sitting in the family room, chatting with a limo driver who looked too young to have a permit much less a license.

"So you're Fordham." The driver had a Liverpool accent. He gave her a brief once-over and grinned. "Awesome."

"You had five minutes, Mother. What could you have possibly told him?" Fordham scowled.

"That you're a brilliant editor," the driver chimed in.

"Oh," Fordham said, relieved.

"And a fool in love," the driver said, walking over to the luggage. "Will these be all, Miss?"

"Yes," Fordham said, glaring at Dorie.

The driver started to collect her bags.

The doorbell rang, and Aaron walked in, stressed. "Good morning, Dorie," he said, looking past her as if she weren't physically present. "Hey, baby." He kissed Fordham on the cheek.

Fordham wasn't feeling very responsive with her mother hovering, but Aaron seemed unfazed. "We've got to run. I have stops to make before we go to the airport. I was stuck on a conference call that wouldn't end. I sent the limo here so you'd be ready to roll." He looked at Fordham accusingly. "I had to take a cab." He checked the time and turned to the driver. "Is this her stuff?"

The driver nodded.

"Why isn't it in the car?" Aaron shouted at the driver. "You know what—go out to the cab and transfer my stuff first." He was texting as he spoke.

The driver exchanged an understanding glance with Dorie and left. Aaron finished what he was doing and followed.

Fordham took a long, loving look around the house. "Bye, Mom," she said, teary-eyed. "Thank you for everything and then some." Fordham hugged her and went toward the door.

"Wait a minute," Dorie said, walking into the kitchen. She came back holding Whitty's project. "Did you forget? You have to bring this to Whitty." Dorie handed her the oaktag.

"Oh, you're right. My head's not on straight today."

Fordham held up Whitty's work. It was a diagram entitled, "A Family through My Eyes," highlighting a replica of their house done in marker, crayon, glued-on tiles, and stapled wads of crumpled paper. A mother and father were presiding over the outdoor scene while two girls, one a little older than the other, were playing with a cat at the foot of two older relatives who were sitting on chairs in front of the house.

"She did a good job, didn't she?" Dorie smiled.

"She always does. I'll make sure she gets it. Bye, Mom."

"Goodbye, sweetheart. And whatever happens, I love you."

"I love you too," Fordham said, carrying the bulky project in her hand.

Dorie closed the door, but Fordham could see her watching through the window. She walked to the limo, carrying Whitty's project. Aaron was standing beside the passenger door.

"What's that?" he asked, perplexed.

"Whitty's project. She forgot to take it."

"So why can't your mother bring it to her?"

"Because I'm not going to ask my mother to do my job."

"Baby, I don't have time for this. I still have to go to Feingold's office to pick up lab coats, and I haven't even had my oatmeal yet."

"But this is Whitty's project, and she needs it now."

"She's playing you again, baby. You know that. She probably left it behind deliberately because she doesn't want you to go. You can't give in to that kind of behavior. She has to understand that things are going to be different now that I'm in the picture."

Fordham looked down at Whitty's project. The man in it clearly resembled David. He had light-brown hair and no mustache or goatee.

Pictures really did say a thousand words. This one wasn't calla lilies or Warhol. It was Whitty's way of telling her what she needed to hear.

"But you're not," she said with certainty.

"I'm not what?"

"In the picture. It's right here. In front of me. And it's not you."

"I don't know what you're talking about, baby."

"Aaron, I am so sorry," she said.

"That's okay. All's forgiven. Just tell Dorie to take that thing to Whitty so we can get out of here."

"That's not what I meant."

"We're going to miss our flight," he said, taking her arm. "We'll talk on the way."

"Aaron," she said, shrugging him off, "this isn't working."

"What are you talking about?" Aaron seemed genuinely confused.

"What I'm talking about is that I'm not the same girl I was in high school. I have a daughter now who means more to me than breathing. I watched my father take a nosedive from being the conquering hero to being the man who sold out to a bookie. I have a mother who I thought was shallow until I watched her make lemonade, not from the lemons but from the damn pits. I still love chocolate ice cream with sprinkles, listening to Chicago, and talking to Evie on the phone for hours, but I'm an adult now. And you really don't know me."

"That's ridiculous. Of course I know you. You just have cold feet."

"It isn't cold feet," she said with confidence. "I don't love you. I did, and then when I saw you again after all these years... I wanted to. But I can't use the past to build a future."

"I think you're scared. And if I go you're going to realize you've made a big mistake unless... unless there's someone else." He glared at her, realizing he could answer his own question.

Fordham nodded.

"So, what you're telling me is I'm not charming enough to be your prince?"

"No, you're charming, but"—she studied the picture again—"I have another prince in mind. I'm sorry, Aaron. I have to go."

"Seriously? You're going? Just like that?" he said, snapping his finger in the air.

"I'm almost as surprised as you are, but yes," she said, handing him back the ring.

"This is crazy, Fordham. Don't do this to us."

"Aaron, there hasn't been an 'us' in years. Good luck in LA," she said, carefully adjusting Whitty's project.

"You'll be back." He glanced at his watch. "Mark my words. This isn't over," he said, getting into the limo.

The driver winked at her in the side mirror. She realized he had never brought her bags out of the house. He raised his hand out the window, giving her a thumbs-up. She doubted Aaron noticed. And she didn't care. Fordham could see Dorie out of the corner of her eye, dancing by the front door.

As the limo turned the corner, Fordham realized she had turned one too. She was done looking back to agonize over failures, real or imagined. She could never change where she had been or the choices she had made. The past would always be a living lesson that she could return to at any time to fill in the blanks, quell her fears, or carry her to a dream she never allowed herself to have. It would be there to lean on or listen to, to ignore or expose, to argue or reckon with, or to simply enjoy for the clarity it brought. It was hers to own in all its glorious dysfunction if she ever needed the wisdom carved from her tears and triumphs. The past was her medal, and she would honor it in that spirit.

No magic or luck had brought her to this moment, just a willingness to listen to the beats and pauses of her life in an entirely different way. It was time to look ahead and take a terrifying gamble in which she had no inkling of what was at stake. There were no guarantees, but this time, she believed the odds were in her favor. This time, she was betting everything on her heart, to win.

Chapter Twenty-Four: Sleepless in Seattle—Really

Whitty's poster in hand, Fordham got in the car, anxious but happily prepared to tell David everything. She'd start with the submission because that would be the most benign introduction to her stalking him in his driveway. Then she'd explain her role as editor of the book. Hopefully, by that time, he'd be so engrossed in her confession that he wouldn't ask about Pam's thong that had gone missing. It would be even better if he didn't know about that at all. She wasn't sure how he'd react to any of it, but it was a semi-calculated risk she had no choice but to take.

Fordham pulled into the school like Danica Patrick and parked like James Bond. She didn't have sweaty, blissful sex to account for the weight loss, but she was still down five pounds and feeling confident. She grabbed the poster and marched into the school as if it were Oscar night and she'd been nominated. Maybe she'd win, and maybe she wouldn't, but she was there, and that had to count for something.

A couple of vaguely familiar administrators were standing outside the main office, exchanging Christmas vacation plans. They smiled her way but didn't stop talking as she entered the office.

"Hi, Robbin," Fordham said to the busy redhead behind the long front desk. "This is for Whitty."

"Oh, okay. They're in the auditorium for an assembly. Do you want me to get her?"

"No, don't bother."

If Fordham told Whitty about breaking up with Aaron, Whitty would insist on going straight home to bake a celebratory cake. Fordham wasn't quite up to that confection just yet.

She left the project on the desk and resolutely made her way a few doors down to David's office. One knock. Two knocks. There was no answer and no light through the crack at the bottom of the door. Her favorite security guard stopped to tell her she smelled heavenly then informed her that David hadn't been in yet. She had no idea about any of the particulars. Before going back to the main office, Fordham pondered the question of how to ask where David had gone without seeming inappropriate.

"Hi, Robbin," she said to the secretary. "I wanted to ask Dr. Prince a question about, um, the poetry workshop, but he wasn't in his office."

"Yeah, he left word that they wouldn't be in."

"They?" Fordham asked.

"He and his daughter and—"

"Oh well," she said too quickly to conceal her disappointment.

"And Whitty's homeroom teacher, Pam Lesley."

Panic set in, making Fordham's nerves tingle. Without a smidgeon of concern about what impression she was giving, she ran out of the school, holding back tears. If the pieces fit the way she was constructing the puzzle, David, Pam, and Lily were busy getting married and becoming a family. She had waited too long and had played it too safe. She would pay for that choice. Someday in the not-so-distant future, she was going to become a *yenta*—her grandmother's word for a gossip—with a dozen cats, too many cardigans, and a steady canasta game. Her bed would be in a permanent state of emptiness as birthdays came and went, unremembered and uncelebrated.

Unwilling to bear the sadness any longer, Fordham decided to take charge of her life. She'd go home, change her clothes, and tell

Abe to expect her at the office after lunch. When everything else failed her, work was unrelenting. She turned on the radio. It was tuned in to a station that was devoting a segment to "secret love." The disc jockey had a soothing yet irksome manner that nonetheless commanded Fordham's full attention.

"Is there a special someone in your life who doesn't know how special he or she is to you? Did 'Unchained Melody' just send you to the phone to call or text? Today on 'Live with Cecilia,' we're going to help you find the courage to share your feelings. Our number is 555-213-5550. Call and tell us your story. In the meantime, Robert Palmer wants to say he's got a 'Bad Case of Loving You.'"

A couple of weeks prior, she would have considered it a sign from the universe that she needed to find David no matter what. But those days had passed. She promptly mumbled, "Screw you," and clicked the radio off.

Ten minutes later, having settled for a Christmas CD stashed in the glove compartment, she was home. No cars in the driveway meant Dorie had gone out, probably getting the latest edition of *New York Weddings,* her new favorite publication. Fordham noted her luggage still sitting in the hallway by the door. Thinking about all the unpacking she had to do was exacerbating her already somber mood. She went into her room, and her eyes darted to David's submission, which she'd deliberately left hanging in its rightful home.

She recalled Margo's most recent advice about relationships. *Darling, love is only easy for ducks because they're ducks. You can't just quack and expect to be understood.* Fordham concluded that not much would help her handle her current situation.

She had to find a way to put the past behind her. She went to the wall and tugged on the submission until the tack fell to the floor. Then she went into the kitchen and pulled out that copy. She searched the house and collected every copy until she had a pile sitting on the island in the kitchen.

Dorie came in through the side door, humming "Chapel of Love." If she'd been anyone but her mother, Fordham might have tackled her.

"I'm so glad you're home!" Dorie gave her a peck on the cheek. "So what happened when you got to the school and talked to David?"

"I dropped off Whitty's project," she said stoically. "And nothing happened. He wasn't there."

"What's this?" Dorie rested a copy of *New York Weddings* on the counter next to Fordham's stack of David's submissions.

"Kindling. I'm having a bonfire of my insanities."

"You're not making any sense."

"Actually, I'm making more sense now than I have in months!" Fordham opened a drawer and took out a pack of matches.

"Fordham Ruth Price, put down those matches right now!" Dorie pounded her hand on the island. "Are you nuts?"

In an instant, Fordham threw down the pack just as she'd done when she was six and being admonished for trying to light a sparkler in the kitchen on the Fourth of July.

"I've had enough, Mom. I'm done with this fairy tale." Fordham picked up the top submission from the pile and waved it in the air. "It wasn't just David who wasn't at the school. Lily and Pam are out with him." She couldn't stop a few tears from streaming down her cheeks.

"I'm not old enough to give up on fairy tales," Dorie said. "Let me make you a bite to eat. You're looking a little gaunt."

That was music to her ears. The last time Dorie had told her she was too thin was when she was twelve and spending every dinner night as Bashful in the town's traveling theater production of Snow White and the Seven Dwarfs.

"Thanks, Mom. I am kind of hungry," she said, surprising herself.

Fordham picked up the wedding magazine, leafed through the first few pages, and tossed it aside in what she feared would become enduring ennui. Dorie was standing at the fridge and seemed fixated on several envelopes grouped in a large Bronx Zoo magnet clip.

"Oh, Fordham. I'm so sorry. I've been so busy with Abe and wedding plans that I completely forgot to give you this." Dorie pocketed the other letters except for one, which she tossed in front of Fordham. Not only was it from Crestwood, but the return address also signified that it was from David's office.

Fordham tore open the letter, barely noticing her mother making her breakfast. She decided to read it out loud.

"Dear Parents,

"As you know, Pam Lesley has been substituting for Debbie Kessler, who's on maternity leave. This situation will be changing again as Ms. Lesley has been offered a prestigious grant to pursue her graduate degree at the School of Education at Seattle University, effective immediately."

A sudden crash ended her recitation. Dorie had dropped a bottle of dressing on the floor, and shards of glass soaking in slick liquid covered a cluster of tiles near the refrigerator. Fordham jumped up and grabbed a wad of paper towels from the holder on the counter.

"You know what they say—besides, 'Dorie, you're a klutz,'" Dorie said, taking out a broom and dustpan. "Broken glass is good luck."

Fordham tossed the heap of used towels into the trash. "David said that when my car got messed up." She picked up David's letter. "Mom, were you listening?"

"Yeah. Hopefully, we won't be overwhelmed by fumes from the vinegar."

Dorie went over the floor with the broom, and Fordham continued reading.

"Ms. Lesley's service has been an asset to our school, and I personally cannot thank her enough for her expertise as my daughter Lily's caretaker for the past several months. In her place will be Lisa Oberlander, who comes to us from Chestnut Ridge Day School."

"So now what?" Dorie leaned the broom up against the wall.

"It doesn't sound like David's engaged to Pam." Fordham scrutinized the letter in front of her.

"No sugar, Sherlock," Dorie said. "When did you realize that?"

"While you were sweeping."

Fordham reread the letter to herself.

"Mom, I think it's a sign." She grabbed the laminated submission. "I've got to go."

A LIGHT SNOW BEGAN to fall as Fordham drove to David's house, and she was glad the ice scraper she'd gotten from her secret Santa the year before was still in the trunk. Being prepared was a gift that typically evaded her, but in that moment, with the smell of Christmas in the air, the frosty picture-postcard treetops, and her heart feeling hopeful, she was ready for anything...

Except for the abrupt stop and complete halt of traffic in both directions. She turned on the local news, and one smart-ass at the weather desk reported that Grandma got run over by a reindeer. Annoyed, she shut it off and spotted a cop walking in the road toward a long line of squad cars and emergency vehicles. Fordham opened her window and called out to get his attention. He stopped at several cars, finally reached hers, and explained the situation. Through a steady stream of noise from nearby equipment, she surmised that an explosion of some kind of gas line was the culprit. The one thing the cop made crystal clear was that she should sit tight because it was going to be a while before the problem could be resolved.

Sitting in traffic was the most annoying thing she could think of, with the possible exception of a poorly executed bikini wax. Her phone buzzed, and she read a new text. Crestwood was evacuated due to a suspected gas leak, and buses were taking the students to the middle school. Parents should arrange to pick up their kids as soon as possible.

Soon wasn't happening. Fordham called Dorie. Her mother didn't answer, so she left a text. Then she turned on her CD player and sang along with Aretha Franklin until the songs started skipping. Overuse was an ongoing problem with her collection. Returning to the radio, she found it set on the same station that it had been on earlier that day.

"That was Evan from Warwick, New York, hoping his secret love reads his submission in the upcoming book from the Flowers from the Heart series."

Fordham had no clue they already had advertisers for the book. She wondered if Abe had anything to do with this choice.

"It's 'Live with Cecilia' here to make your Christmas merry and bright. We've been having a weeklong segment on 'Secret Love,' and we're looking forward to your call. Next up, we have a woman from Boca Raton, Florida. Merry Christmas, you're on the air..."

"Hi, Cecilia," the caller said. "I'm afraid my Christmas isn't going to be very merry. I think I made a terrible mistake, and I'm not sure how to fix it.'

"Well, let's see if we can help. I'm sorry, I haven't even asked—what's your name?"

"I'm Denise, and this isn't exactly about secret love, but in a way, it is, because even though I just divorced my husband, he doesn't know I'm still in love with him."

Fordham nearly choked on the protein bar she was eating and stared at the radio.

"Okay, Denise from Boca Raton, tell us what's going on," Cecilia said.

"Well," the caller said, "a few months ago, I was feeling very lonely. My husband, Aaron—now my ex-husband—is a very prominent fertility specialist, and he was doing a lot of traveling to expand his practice. He left for a business trip when we were in the midst of having our pipes overhauled. One thing led to another, and I had an affair with the plumber's assistant. He was a sweet younger guy, and he was around. I'm not proud of what I did, but it happened because I missed my husband."

Fordham could feel a few tears building in the corners of her eyes. Aaron had never been hers after all.

"What would you say to your husband if you had the chance?" Cecilia asked.

"We have this silly little thing we do. We speak in song titles. So I would tell him, Aaron honey, 'We Can Work It Out,' and please 'Don't Give Up on Us, Baby.'"

"Aaron, if you're listening, this is Cecilia. It's Christmastime, and we hope things work out for you and Denise. Now, let's play those songs for you..."

Fordham dabbed her eyes with the sleeve of her coat. If she had married Aaron, it would have been an even bigger mistake than when she married Gil. He belonged with Denise, and her mother and Abe had been right all along. She'd been nothing but a rebound relationship to help him deal with his disappointment. And now she was stuck in this car, unable to move forward in every way imaginable.

She picked up her phone to see if Dorie had gotten back to her, but there were no new messages. She decided to call the middle school to tell them she was stuck in traffic seemingly connected to the problem at Crestwood and would be there as soon as possible. But the call couldn't go through. Her phone, along with her life, was overheating and powering down.

Fordham was about to burst into tears when the line of cars in front of her began to move. *A holiday gift.* Chanukah was all about miracles. She drove down a side road to head toward the middle school, the opposite direction from David's house. The snow was still light and, since it wasn't sticking to the ground, was more calming than menacing. In a few minutes, she'd get Whitty and take her home, and all the obstacles that kept her from talking to David would be history.

Her assumption that the middle school parking lot would be empty and holding a spot for her had obviously been a delusion brought on by wintery brain freeze. Cars were converging every which way. Fordham figured it would be easier to park at the farthest corner from the entrance than to fight the pileup. Her phone would still not respond to her efforts to turn it back on. As she neared the school, she spotted a couple of kids from Whitty's class, but she didn't see Whitty.

The main office was mobbed with anxious parents. People were buzzing about getting to Costco or the supermarket before the nor'easter buried them in a foot of snow. Fordham searched for Whitty but didn't see her anywhere. She went into the main office and asked to use the phone.

Dorie answered, sounding exasperated. She'd just gotten home after having gone out to pick up a few holiday gifts and hadn't realized she'd left her phone at home. She had more messages than Santa, and considering it was Christmastime, that was a lot of messages. She was going through them one by one while Fordham patiently listened on her end of the phone. The calls were from Dorie's nail place, her hair stylist, and her Y Group friend with the hairy mole, plus a few from Abe, reminding her how much he couldn't wait to be her husband. Finally, she got to the one from Crestwood.

"Oh my! They evacuated Crestwood! Fordham, Whitty's at the middle school."

"I'm at the middle school. She's not here." Fordham tried not to let frenzy get the better of her. "Mom, are there any other messages?"

"Let's see. Um, my dry cleaner won't have my silk teddy until next week. Um, they've extended the sale on kosher turkey—"

"Mom, anything relevant?"

"Okay, you're right, you're right. Here you go. David has Whitty."

"David has her?" Fordham said.

"He knows you're out of town, and he tried me but couldn't connect because I was being a forgetful moron—not his words—so he brought her to his house."

"Thanks, Mom. Don't text him. And if he calls, do the usual and ignore it. I'm going there, and I'll speak to him myself."

Fordham walked back to the car, laughing. Only Shakespeare's *Comedy of Errors* could compete. The day seemed so ridiculous when she replayed it in her mind, but the biggest act was yet to come, and since she wasn't the only player, she couldn't determine how things would go when she and David finally managed to speak.

Fifteen minutes later, she arrived at David's house. The silence had been golden, and she was as ready as she would ever be to explain her part in whatever feelings had been building between them. She assumed his car was in the garage and pulled up in front of the house. The snow was coming down hard as she trekked across his lawn to get to the front door. She knocked, infinitely grateful to not have to bear witness to an assumed proposal through his window. Several knocks later, there was no answer.

Fordham got back into her car, frustrated. She turned the ignition and hit the defroster to melt some of the snow off her windshield. With the way her day was going, it was possible David and the girls had joined the ranks of cautious consumers in buying up every last carton of milk and loaf of bread. If she waited, the snow could pile up, and she wouldn't be able to get home. If she left, she might be able to track them down at the supermarket. But maybe being snowbound at David's house wasn't such a bad idea. *Finally, a plan I can get behind.*

She was about to turn off the car when a Sienna pulled up behind hers. It wasn't David's car. She imagined David's neighbors telling him that a strange woman they'd seen before was parked in front of his house. Not wanting to take any chances, she was about to pull away when a large branch from a tree dropped right in front of her car.

She screeched to a halt, which produced a weird sound, given the snow. Fordham was about to back up when there was a knock at her window. In the past, she might have jumped, but somewhere in her heart, she knew it would be David. She got out of the car, slipping a little. He grabbed her arm to keep her from falling.

"That's not your car," Fordham said, leaning on him.

"It's a rental. Mine's in the shop. Broken headlight." David guided her to stand against the driver's door. "Was your flight delayed?" He made sure she was steady on her feet before letting her go.

"Indefinitely."

"What happened?"

"Besides you, not much."

"You broke off your engagement?" Despite sounding more surprised than anything else, David broke out into a broad grin.

"I had to," she said, wiping a snowflake from her eye.

Whitty and Lily got out of the car and came toward her.

"Mom!" Whitty shrieked. "You're here!"

"I am." She gave Whitty a hug and then gave one to Lily too. "Aaron and I broke up."

Whitty shouted something that sounded like "Hallelujah," and she and Lily went to the front lawn to have a snowball fight.

"Why did you have to break up with him?" David asked.

"Because it wouldn't be fair to marry someone I'm not in love with."

"You seemed very sure that was what you wanted when we spoke at the school." He kicked the building snow with his foot.

"I thought you were engaged to Pam," she blurted.

"Oh, I can't wait to hear this one," he said, crossing his arms in what appeared to be utter amusement.

"I came by to talk to you over the weekend, and when I was about to knock on your door, I saw what I assumed was you proposing to her, so I left."

David looked perplexed but then his eyes widened. "The ring! Her grandmother's ring. I had it fixed for her as a going-away gift. She lived here over the summer, helping me out with Lily and the house. It was the least I could do."

Some snow from a branch above them landed on top of David's head, and he brushed it off. "I guess in the back of my mind, I knew she had a little crush on me," he continued, "but she was so good with Lily that I didn't want to rock the boat. She seemed happy to run errands for me, so I let her. I didn't think much of it because I didn't want to. Now I see that was a mistake, but while it was happening, I just went with it."

"Well, now it makes sense, but—whatever." She licked her lips. "There's something else I have to tell you."

They both glanced over at the girls, who were building a snowman.

"I already know you're a chocoholic," he said.

She went to the car and got the submission but kept the text facing her. "Remember when I said I was in publishing?"

He nodded. "But we never talked much about it."

She handed him the submission. "No, we didn't."

He read it then looked at her quizzically. "How'd you get this?"

"You answered my post." She took in a deep breath and let it out. "And in a way, my prayers."

"*You're* the Flowers from the Heart editor?"

"In the flesh." She studied his face as he let the idea sink in. "My sources told me this story was from the Pacific-Northwest region, and I had no clue it was yours until recently. The thing is, David, it was your submission that got me through putting the book together. Your words inspired me and gave me hope about what love should be like. You touched me in a way that no one has in... actually, that no one ever has."

He read the submission again with tears in his eyes. "I was at a conference, feeling lonely and depressed. It was late. I had a couple of drinks and accidentally came across your ad as I was searching for a snowblower to pick up when I got home. I guess you could say I wrote it when I was sleepless in Seattle."

He wrapped his arm around her waist as they trudged through the mounting snow to his car. He got a carton of chicken nuggets from the back seat and told the girls to go in the house for lunch.

"One other thing," Fordham said. "When I was at your house, I had a dream that you kissed me. Did you?"

"Oh, honey, if I had kissed you, you would have remembered it."

With that, David took her in his arms in a way that assured her she would never be outside of them for very long and kissed her in a way she was certain she would never forget.

**Flowers from the Heart:
Love Online after Forty**

I Got You, Abe

It's funny. When you get older, you think the world can't surprise you anymore. You think you've pretty much cornered the market on what there is to experience. And then, one day, you happily discover you're wrong. Life is an ever-evolving, beautiful mystery.

After I lost my husband, I never expected to find love again. I was resigned to occupying my time running errands, volunteering, helping my daughter, and playing Scrabble online. I was pretty good and could beat any opponent except one man. He had more words at his fingertips than I had excuses for not dieting. It was unnerving, but it was fun.

Then one evening, my daughter, the editor of this book, threw a casual dinner party and invited her boss, a widower my age. As we spoke, I realized that he was, in fact, my unbeatable Scrabble opponent. The coincidence was unfathomable, and we realized very quickly that a power greater than ours had drawn us together. We began dating, and soon after, while we were online playing, he laid out a perplexing seven-letter word: *m-a-r-e-e-m-i*.

I challenged him and said, "What's *mareemi*? The hair of a sterile goat?" When he didn't answer I stared at the letters *m-a-r-e-e-m-i* until I figured out he had just proposed. Being a bride at my age has made me realize that the most important thing in life is to keep on playing because sooner or later, all the letters will fall into place.

Love-Lines

by Fordham Prince

WHEN I FIRST STARTED this book, I felt unqualified. What did I know about love? I had a failed marriage and more dates than I cared to count. Love was the last thing I expected to find in cyberspace or anywhere. But as I read your stories, I began to feel more optimistic. I learned that love is the one thing we all have in common. We all want it. We all fumble to find it, and we're all grateful when it finally finds us.

I received one story in particular that I read time and again. It was from a man who had lost his wife but not his heart. I dreamed of how it would feel to be in love like that, and in time, the warm, gentle words of this man made me realize it was possible. Life is mystical because sometimes we find the very thing we're looking for without really looking at all.

In my case, it was a chance friendship with the principal of my daughter's school. He and I had a lot in common and became close friends. But sometimes, we miss the obvious until it shows up right under our noses. One day, in my daughter's art project about what a real family looked like, the obvious appeared. There, drawn in colorful markers, were the principal and his daughter, completing the family I had always wanted. It turns out he was my special friend and the contributor of the story titled "Prince Charming" in this book. His inspiring tale led me to my very own happily ever after.

Not long after my mom got married, my Prince Charming proposed over a game of rock-paper-scissors. It may sound silly, but it's meaningful to us. Our wedding was soon after because our girls couldn't wait to be sisters. We're excited to see how they're going to react to the arrival of their new baby brother or sister...

Yes, I, too, found true love online moments before I closed my book, believing there were no love-lines left to be read.

Also by Sheri Langer

Love-Lines

Watch for more at screenluvr2.wixsite.com/sheri.

About the Author

Sheri Langer is a chocoholic writer and editor who routinely feasts on romantic comedies. She's been known to spontaneously reenact scenes from classic favorites like *When Harry Met Sally*.

A self-proclaimed, moderately talented home-cook, Sheri spends a fair amount of time concocting dishes that can never be repeated. A creative rebel at heart, she has always colored outside the lines and has an instinctive aversion to recipes. To keep the calories from getting too out of hand, Sheri does step and aerobic workouts in the privacy of her bedroom, where no one has to be subjected to her lack of rhythm.

An avid word fan, Sheri frequently plays Just Words, Boggle, and Scrabble, mostly against the computer so she has excellent odds of winning. With her four kids all grown up, three of whom live in various locations across the map, Sheri and her guy, Brad, spend much of their down time watching General Hospital and football, shopping, and pursuing the best ice cream on the planet. Much to the chagrin

of their waistbands, they can often be spotted sitting on a bench outside their favorite creamery, eating obscenely overstuffed giant waffle
cones.

Please feel free to connect with Sheri on social media. You can
help her procrastinate by engaging in spirited exchanges or viewing
pics of her great-looking family and ridiculously adorable cat, Zoe.

Read more at screenluvr2.wixsite.com/sheri.

About the Publisher

Dear Reader,

We hope you enjoyed this book. Please consider leaving a review on your favorite book site.

Visit https://RedAdeptPublishing.com to see our entire catalogue.

Check out our app for short stories, articles, and interviews. You'll also be notified of future releases and special sales.